IN PRAISE OF

THEN CAME HOPE

"***Then Came Hope,*** by Emerald Pointe Books, Awarded Second Place, 2007 Word Weavers of Central Florida Award for Fiction."

✦✦✧✦❀✦✧✦✦

"The many fans of historical fiction will be delighted with this story. A very fine read."

DAVIS BUNN
Best-selling Author

✦✦✧✦❀✦✧✦✦

"*Then Came Hope* shoves aside danger and prejudice to usher in forgotten dreams and a chance at love."

DIANN MILLS
Best-selling Author of *Lightning and Lace*

✦✦✧✦❀✦✧✦✦

"Louise M. Gouge skillfully breathes life into the written history about the plight of African-Americans during the post-Civil War era and takes you on an action-packed journey of freedom and love."

TONI V. LEE
Author of *Expectations*

✦✦✧✦❀✦✧✦✦

"I really enjoyed reading *Then Came Hope*. What an inspiring story of courage, forgiveness, and most of all, love. Delia's character shows us that only when we understand our value through God's unconditional love, can we accept love from others. I'm looking forward to the sequel!"

PROFESSOR THERA WOODARD
Coordinator of International Study and Exchange
Valencia Community College
Orlando, Florida

THEN CAME HOPE

A NOVEL

LOUISE M. GOUGE

Emerald
Pointe
BOOKS

10 09 08 07   10 9 8 7 6 5 4 3 2 1

Then Came Hope
A Novel
0-97851-373-8
Copyright © 2007 by Louise M. Gouge
Represented by:
Wendy Lawton
Books & Such Literary Agency
Central Valley Office
P.O. Box 1227
Hilmar, CA 95324
209-634-1913
wendy@booksandsuch.biz

Published by Emerald Pointe Books
P.O. Box 35327
Tulsa, OK 74153-0327

This story is dedicated to Mattie and Aunt Mary
and all of their sisters and brothers.

And to David, always.

If the Son therefore shall make you free, ye shall be free indeed.

John 8:36

CHAPTER ONE

pril 1865

Delia ran as hard as she could.

All the while, terror nipped at her heels.

Had Massuh set the hounds on her?

Ungrateful!

Lazy!

Worthless!

God will punish you!

Plantation voices screamed in her head, but she ran anyway.

Nothing in her hand. Nothing in her pockets. Nothing in her heart but fear. Nothing in her head but blind determination never to be beaten again. Never to be spit on. Never to have her hair torn out by a vicious young mistress.

Staggering, stumbling, falling, lungs bursting. Terrified.

Branches reached out to seize her but only managed to tear off her headscarf and scrape her cheeks, hands, and legs. She tripped over roots but got up and ran again.

She ran through the woods because of the gray-clad soldiers on the roads. She didn't know the roads anyway, not any more than she knew the woods. In all her seventeen years, she'd only been off the plantation maybe five, six times. Once the war started, plantation folk didn't go anywhere.

Rumors came. Some said President Lincoln freed the slaves. One by one, two by two, black folks slipped away in the night.

Delia would hear about it from Beulah, who'd whisper that Ol' Massuh had the dogs out looking for some other worthless fool who'd believed "all dat Yankee talk."

Her dark face smoldering, Beulah would glare at Delia. "Don't you be thinking of going nowhere. We belongst to Massuh and Missus. It be Gawd's will and Gawd's law." She'd turn away from Delia with a snort. "Who'd want ya anyhow?"

Maybe nobody would want Delia. Maybe she didn't know the roads or the woods. But Delia knew north, so north she ran. She ran hard, from just after midnight when the moon rode high to break of daylight when the sun burst over the distant horizon amid blazing red and purple clouds, like the bruises left on her light brown skin by Miz Suzanne.

Anytime Delia cried about the pain, old Beulah would scold. "Quit yo' fussin'. Just you wait. Men'll do you worse than any missus."

Delia knew what that meant. She knew she didn't want to be around when Massuh's sons came home from the war.

And so she ran.

Just after dawn, Delia came to a stream where she bent over to work out the stitch in her side. She splashed water on her face and legs to wash away the sweat and soothe the stinging scratches. Then she took off her shoes to wade barefoot for a while. She'd heard Ol' Sam tell how dogs couldn't follow a scent in water.

Ahead to her left, a water moccasin slithered off the bank, and Delia froze. The snake clamped its mouth around an unsuspecting frog. Certain he would not notice her, Delia hastened past the death scene. She came upon a fragrant blackberry patch blanketed with five-petaled white blossoms, but her search for fruit among the thorns proved futile. She'd have stolen one of Beulah's biscuits if the old woman hadn't guarded her kitchen like a hawk day and night, sleeping there on a cot, her rolling pin in hand.

Now back in the woods, Delia wondered if she could last much longer. Should she huddle down in a patch of brush to sleep?

Something splashed on her face, and she jumped. Then she laughed. Rain. She always liked rain. It had soothing powers. But the sprinkle soon became a downpour, and Delia felt her courage washing away. She must keep walking, but without the sun, she'd lost north. Which way to go?

She stumbled through dense undergrowth amid a stand of tall pines. Brambles tore at her wet skirt like hooks, but she yanked the skirt free and kept on going.

As the rain let up a bit, a building came into view—a barn at the edge of a field. No house nearby, just charred remains of a wall and a brick chimney. She edged nearer and listened for any sound that might signal danger. But what did she know of danger sounds outside of the plantation? A galloping horse? A growling dog? A screaming mistress?

A feeling of helplessness filled her, and she glanced upward. The misting rain blended with her tears. "Mama, help me." She didn't know if there was a heaven, but if there was, Mama was there. Maybe she could hear her, maybe she could help. Delia had been calling on her for eight years now, ever since Missus had her mama beat to death.

Delia shuddered away the memory. She'd think on that later.

The barn beckoned. She crept closer. Through a gap in the wall, she peered in. People! Delia jerked back and hunched down. Nobody inside stirred. She peered in again. They appeared to be asleep, some lying on the bare floor, others resting against walls or posts. An old woman leaned into the arms of a gray-haired man. A glimmer of hope lit Delia's soul. Perhaps she would find kindness here.

Because every face she saw was colored.

✦❖❀❖✦

Ezra jerked back into the thicket. Not ten feet away, ragtag soldiers wandered down the muddy road, remnants of a company whose gray wool uniforms now hung in tatters on their gaunt frames. Crouched low in the bushes, Ezra felt like a twice-painted target in his faded blue garb. In battle he had seen how the rebs treated black Union soldiers. While they might take a white Yankee prisoner, a Negro who had dared to raise a hand against the South would be viciously slaughtered and his body desecrated. Many in his regiment had died that way.

Why God had spared him, Ezra did not know. Yet, separated from his companions, he believed the Lord would see him safely home to Boston. That is, if he could stay hidden from the rebs now pouring back into South Carolina. What he needed was a change of clothes, but he was not likely to find one. Or maybe, after traveling all night, he just needed to rest so he could think more clearly.

The long line of soldiers dwindled to an occasional straggler. Enfield rifle in hand, Ezra moved from his hiding place, adjusted his knapsack on his back, and crept deeper into the woods. Hunger gnawed at his belly, but shooting a rabbit or squirrel—if he could find one—might bring unwanted attention. Best thing would be to find a place to sleep all day, then search for food before dark.

The rain had stopped, at least for a while, and the sun broke out between the churning clouds. Ezra had stayed fairly dry in the thick woods and had managed to add a little rainwater to his canteen.

He came to a field overgrown with weeds and bordered by a broken fence. On the far side stood the burned-out shell of a house and a rundown barn. He followed the perimeter of the field, staying close to the surrounding forest. In every joint and muscle, his body begged for mercy, and he longed to give in to his exhaustion. *Just a few more yards,* he promised his aching legs.

The hinges looked rusted. They might screech if Delia opened the door. She found a hole in the wall, crawled through, and sat just inside, where she could run away if she had to. Shivering in her wet clothes, knees drawn up to her chin, she watched and thought on the group as best she could in the dark barn. A shaft of light beamed down on the old couple and made their woolly silver hair shine. If she'd not seen the woman, she wouldn't have entered. Was she a fool for trusting her own kind like this when they mostly looked like field hands? Maybe, but she couldn't go on alone, not without sleep and food. She leaned her head back against the wall and wished for sleep.

"Chile, where ya come from?"

Delia jumped awake and stared at the old woman kneeling before her. She brushed her hand across her eyes. How long had she slept?

"I…I'm sorry. I'll go…." Delia started to move.

"No, no, chile. Don't be scared. You's all right."

At the kindness in the woman's smile, Delia's eyes burned, and she couldn't stop her tears.

"Shh, don't fret. We's all in the same fix. Have you had anything to eat?"

"No, ma'am."

The woman handed her a withered apple. "It ain't much, but it'll hep."

Delia could only mouth the words "thank you." The fruit's tangy flavor burst on her tongue like a promise. She devoured it in a few bites and wiped her wet lips with her sleeve. "Thank you." This time her voice held strong.

The woman chuckled. "You's welcome, chile. Now, I'm May Brewster, and that over there…." She tipped her head toward the others, all still asleep except the old man. "He be my man Willard."

Willard nodded at Delia. "Miz." His dark face conveyed the same kindness as May's.

"I…I'm Delia."

"You got a last name?"

Delia blinked. "No, ma'am."

"We just took our old massuh's last name. You could do dat."

Delia's stomach turned. Was it the apple or the idea of carrying her hated owner's name for the rest of her life?

May patted her hand. "You think on it. Up north, you need a last name. You's free to do what you wants now. You don' belong to nobody but yourself."

Delia stared at her, not sure she could believe it. Free? Was it possible? Wouldn't Massuh come pretty soon and drag her back to the plantation?

Again May chuckled. "It'll take some git'n used to, but we gots a whole new life ahead of us now. You got plans for what you gon' do? You got people?"

Delia shook her head. "No. No plans. No people." Fear pricked her soul. She hadn't thought that far ahead. "What'll I do?"

May threw her head back and laughed aloud, then hurried to shush herself. "Oh, chile, praise the Lawd, anything you wants to. You'll find work and git paid real money for doing it."

Delia's heart seemed to jump. "Paid? Money?"

May again smothered her own laughter. "Can ya believe it? I'm not sure I do. But that's what we hear from—"

The barn door whined open, and stark daylight poured in, silhouetting the dark figure of a soldier with his gun pointing toward Willard and the group of sleepers.

A few feet from the door, May and Delia gasped, and the soldier quickly pointed the gun toward them.

"Don't move. Don't move an inch." The man stepped into the barn and pulled the door closed behind him. He blinked several times and glanced from the women to the group and back again. He laughed a nervous laugh like he was relieved and lowered his weapon.

"Sorry. Didn't mean to scare you." He removed his cap and brushed his sleeve across his brow. "Mind if I join you?"

Once his eyes adjusted to the darkened barn, Ezra studied the people gathered there. The dank smell of wet, moldy hay assailed his nostrils, then came the odor of unwashed bodies. He struck a casual pose, but every nerve in his body prepared for attack. Early on in the war, he'd learned that southern Negroes often sided with their masters and might turn on their own kind when it came to a fight. How would these people act now that the war had ended?

The two women on his left seemed harmless. The young one's eyes were round with fear. Four or five others seemed to be just waking up, except the old man, who regarded Ezra calmly.

"Come on in, suh." The man beckoned. "We's glad to have ya."

As Ezra drew near, he could see them studying his uniform. A child stood up and broke from his mother's grasping hands.

"Is you a Yankee soldier?" The boy rubbed sleep from his eyes and approached Ezra.

"Yes, son, I am."

The boy ran to him and threw his arms around his legs. His mother jumped up and came to touch Ezra's arm. A man and a youth helped the old man stand, and they all surrounded Ezra, touching him, patting him, almost knocking him over in their eagerness to welcome him.

"I hear'd there was colored Yankee soldiers, but I never believed it."

"Did ya know the war's over?"

"Is there any mo' witcha?"

"Ya had anything to eat?"

Unable to answer all their questions at once, Ezra laughed. "Hold on. Hold on." He turned to the old woman. "No, ma'am, I haven't eaten in two days. Thought I'd shoot a rabbit if I can find one."

"A rabbit?" The little boy licked his lips and stared at Ezra's gun with wide eyes. "Wouldn't dat be sumpin'?"

"Sure would." Ezra patted the boy's head. He looked around the group again. The old woman handed him a shriveled apple, and he nodded his thanks. "Where are you folks from?"

One man, who looked a little older than Ezra, stepped nearer. "Don't much matter where we're from. It's where we're going, and that's north."

"Amen." The dark young mother stepped over and looped her arm through the man's. "It be a brand-new day for us."

"I'm Willard Brewster." The gray head nodded toward the old woman. "That's my wife, May." He stuck out his hand to Ezra. "What's yo' name?"

Ezra gave him a firm handshake. "Ezra Johns. I'm from Boston…and hoping to get back there soon."

"Why, dat's jes' where we's headed," the old man said. "Me and May gots chi'drun up there. Our boy bought his freedom twenty year ago and then come back down and freed our girl." He glanced at his wife. "He woulda bought ours, but the war come up afore he could git it done."

Ezra smiled at the delight on his face. "Then maybe we can travel together." He turned to the others. "Where up north do you plan to go?"

"Maybe you could help us figure that out." The youth wore trousers that were ragged and far too short for his gangly legs. "I'm Adam Monroe."

Ezra shook hands with him and then turned to meet the others. The man near his age was Leviticus Barton, and his wife was Alice. Her lighter-toned son asked to be called Frederick, after Frederick Douglass.

"That's a fine name." Ezra clapped his shoulder. "I met Mr. Douglass one time and heard him speak several times while I was growing up in Boston. His sons Lewis and Charles serve in the same regiment as I do."

To a person, the group sighed or spoke their admiration and friendly envy for his good fortune.

Ezra turned to the young girl who'd looked so frightened when he entered the barn. She hung back behind the old woman.

"And your name, miss?"

She glanced up and quickly looked back down. "Delia."

Ezra felt something pop in his chest. No, more than a pop. More like when he first shot a rifle and the kickback almost knocked him to the ground. "How do you do, Miss Delia?" His words breathed out in a whisper, and Ezra felt his face grow hot. He looked around the group, but no one seemed to notice his plight. He turned to May. "Is this young lady your granddaughter?"

"Oh, no, chile. She got here jes' afore you did. We ain't even got acquainted."

Everyone now turned to Delia, but she only stared back, her brown eyes exuding a mixture of fear and confusion.

"No need to talk, chile." May put her arm around the girl. "I done tol' you we's all here in the same fix. If we work together, we can all get safely up north. It's not as if the dogs is chasing us. We's *free*…"—she sang out the word like an anthem—"…and nobody can take us back again."

Ezra saw that Delia's posture did not relax in May's embrace. Poor girl. Poor lovely young woman. The rest of these folks seemed to understand, or at least hope, that they would be all right. Maybe Miss Delia just needed to be around them for a while. For his part, he would be very pleased to help her find a home and a happy new life— maybe in Boston.

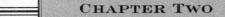

CHAPTER TWO

$\mathcal{D}$elia watched as the others settled back down to sleep through the day. A fresh April breeze blew the smell of wet grass through a small gap in the barn wall. Outside, birds chirped their spring love songs. She could almost let herself relax, almost give in to the bone-weariness throughout her body. But the soldier still made her a bit skittish, though she couldn't say why.

She could see these other folks had been nothing more than field hands, but they seemed like good people, 'specially Miz May. Delia nearly broke down and cried when the skinny old woman gave her a hug. Imagine Beulah giving that kind of comfort to anyone who wasn't white. Being a house slave and the family cook, she thought she was somebody. She even treated the other house slaves, including Delia, with the same disrespect. Well, Beulah had it all to herself now. She could just stay with Massuh and Missus.

Just before Delia dozed off, she wondered why she'd waited so long to leave.

Every instinct told Ezra to stay awake. Why had he been so quick to trust these people? Just being Negroes did not make them honest. A lot of desperate people roamed the land now that the war was over. Maybe they would slit his throat and take his gun. He lay facing them, with his back to the wall, watching as they resumed their rest.

What's wrong with you, man? Has the war destroyed your humanity? Lord, don't let it be so.

Ezra inhaled a deep breath and pulled in all the moldy stink of the ancient barn, including traces of a familiar odor—horse manure. He almost chuckled. Who would have thought that could be a welcomed smell? Since boyhood, he had worked in his father's stable on Boston's Beacon Hill. They kept horses and rigs for wealthy patrons whose townhouses had no place for outbuildings. The work was dirty and exhausting, but it had put Ezra through school. He'd had more than three years of college before enlisting in the army. Harvard had educated his mind, but the army had made him a man.

He prayed every day he would not become bitter, as some of his fellow soldiers had, over the monstrous things he'd seen—and done—in the war. As weariness claimed his senses, their faces came to him, hard, cold, cruel. Ezra shivered at the hatred in their eyes, for they seemed to revel in killing.

Now other faces appeared—kinder, wiser, even in the midst of battle. Brave George Heywood, cut down in their regiment's first real fight. Childhood friends Peter Blake and Randall Simpson. Colonel Shaw, who had died not ten feet from Ezra as they tried unsuccessfully to take Fort Wagner.

Grief ripped through his heart when he saw Shaw go down. At the order to retreat, he tried to pull him back to the beach. He kept reaching down the embankment for the torn body just beyond arm's length. One more yard, one more inch, and he could save him. Cannonballs roared past him and exploded in deafening thunder. Blinding flashes of fire burst just inches from his face. Smoke clogged his lungs. He could not breathe. He could not rise or run. The very air around him seemed to press him into the earth.

Lord, help me!

But even his voice failed him. A shell burst nearby with dazzling brilliance and electrified the air. Ezra's hair seemed to stand on end, and he could hear other soldiers cry out around him.

"Hush, child." A mellow, soothing voice crooned nearby. "It jus' be lightnin'. Don' be scared."

Ezra bolted up, trembling. Alice sat with young Frederick in her lap and hummed a tune. Ezra gave his head a quick shake, drew in a deep breath, and smiled to himself. It was just a nightmare, just lightning striking nearby.

⁕⊹⧚⊹⁕

Cold rain blew through the gap in the wall and chilled Delia. She'd woken up at the first crack of lightning and lay still, listening to the late-afternoon storm. Back at the plantation, Miz Suzanne was always afraid and clung to Delia like a baby in this kind of weather. After the storm, she'd shove Delia away and call her a rude name. Had it been just yesterday when that mean girl slapped her again for no reason at all? Well, that was the last time she'd slap Delia.

Giddy joy brought her up from her bed of musty old hay. She sat back against the wall and brushed dirt and straw off her white blouse. At the plantation house, she'd slept beside Miz Suzanne's bed on a trundle with a smooth, clean mattress. But she wouldn't trade all the cleanness in the world for this grand new life. *Free,* May said. *You don't belong to nobody but yourself.* Delia shivered with excitement. She longed to find out what all that meant. Even with her belly rumbling in time with the outside thunder, even with fear still nibbling at her soul like the barn mice nibbling straw in the corner, she'd never look back.

Lightning struck nearby in a blinding flash, making the air sizzle like a chicken in a fryin' pan. The boy cried, and his mother pulled him to her lap. The soldier jerked upright, his face filled with alarm.

Delia almost laughed at him. Big, strong soldier scared of a little lightning. She watched him shake off his sleep and grin to himself. Maybe he'd just been startled. She liked his smile, bright ivory in a dark brown face. His black eyes were lively, his gaze steady. She'd never seen a Negro with that kind of confidence. Would he change around white people like every other colored person she'd ever known?

One by one, the others were waking up. May had told her they all came from down in the southern part of South Carolina and had met on the road a few weeks before. May said lots of folks wandered the roads these days, both black and white, and not all could be trusted. If Delia wanted to stay with the group, she'd be welcomed. In those few words, the old woman said a lot of things. The notion Delia liked best was that maybe, for the first time in her life, she'd found friends.

May's dusky skin seemed all the darker for her gray hair. Willard was a little lighter, but not by much. Like most field hands, these folks carried the blacker strains of their race. Delia glanced at her own fair arm. No one could mistake her for white, but like her light-skinned mama, she had been favored for house duties. She'd always felt she was somehow better than those who toiled in the fields. She'd have to think on that now.

Delia watched Leviticus scoot over to Ezra and motion Willard to join them. "You s'pose once the rain lets up we can find somethin' to eat out there?" He eyed Ezra's rifle.

"We'll give it a try." The soldier rummaged in his pack and pulled out a little bag. "I don't have much ammunition left, and it's unlikely I can get more."

"Don' worry 'bout that," Willard said. "The Lord will provide when we need it, and not a minute sooner."

Ezra's eyes lit up, and he gave the old man a broad smile. "Yes, indeed, sir. He surely will."

Delia's heart seemed to jump into her throat. His smile made the whole barn brighter.

"Rain's letting up." Ezra stood and used a thin rod to stuff his rifle with powder, shot, and flint. With Leviticus and Adam, he left the barn, but not before tipping his cap to Delia. Again her heart stirred. No one had ever paid her that honor.

"Come on, chile." May waved her over. "You and me gotta git a fire goin'."

"Fire?"

May chuckled. "Why, sho'. How else we's gonna cook that rabbit?" She handed Delia some broken boards.

Delia followed the old woman outside. Her hands full of hay, May marched over to the burned-out chimney and set down her bundle. She found a wet branch and swept stones from the fireplace, then used some of the hay to soak up the moisture. After arranging the dry hay and boards with care, she drew a small jelly jar full of matches from her pocket and lit the fire.

Delia didn't know what to think. "Where'd you get them matches?"

May glanced over her shoulder. "We pick up things along the way." She pulled a few little sweet potatoes from her pocket and set them close to the flames.

"You mean you steal?"

May turned, hands on hips, and shook her head. "Lawd, no, chile. We trade. I sewed a man's buttons on his shirt, and he give me a handful of matches." She held up the little jar. "I put 'em in here to keep 'em dry. And Alice and me found dem sweet potatoes in dis garden. Most nobody'd want to eat 'em, but we's used to makin' do."

Delia's face burned. "I...I'm sorry."

"That's awright." May turned back to her fire. "You don' know me. I don' know you. But the good Lawd put us together for a reason, so you ask me anything, and I'll tell you right out."

A sharp crack sounded in the woods, followed by a happy whoop. A half-minute later, another softer sound echoed the first. Soon the three men returned carrying two wet, limp rabbits.

Leviticus found branches to make a spit for roasting while the rest of the band gathered to watch Ezra skin the animals with his pocketknife. Alice had found a rosemary bush in the ruins of the kitchen garden. She stuck several stalks into the thicker parts of the meat. Their mouths watered as their dinner hissed and crackled over the open flame.

"Just wish we had a bit of salt to sprinkle on it," May said. "That always brings out the flavor."

"I have some in my pack." Ezra hurried back to the barn, and Delia came near to giggling as she watched him acting like a happy boy with a new toy.

He hadn't been gone long when two scruffy-looking white men approached the group, almost like they appeared from nowhere.

Delia felt her heart quiver. What would these men do?

"You all can just scat now." The bearded man with scraggly red hair shoved Willard to the ground and called him a wicked name. "Go on. Git."

"What're you talking 'bout?" shouted Leviticus.

"Git your hands off him!" Adam cried.

Both looked about ready to jump the intruders. Delia shook with fear but moved to help May lift Willard up. Alice stepped in front of her son.

"We said git, an' we mean it." The second man, younger, taller, and just as scraggly, pulled a large knife from his belt and held it out, like he was ready to slice anybody who came near. "We gonna take them rabbits and have ourselves some supper, and you coloreds can just clear outa here. Go on, y'hear?"

"You're the ones who are leaving." Ezra came up, rifle in hand and ready to shoot. "Step back and leave right now."

The two men stared at him. The first man spat on the ground and threw a nasty curse at him. "You one of them colored Yankee soldiers, ain't you? Come down here where you don't belong to fight your betters."

"I believe that argument is without merit, considering the outcome of the recent conflict. Now if you gentlemen will kindly turn around and make your exit, we were about to have our supper."

Now everybody stared at him. Delia'd never heard a black man talk with such a strong, rich, *commanding* voice…or such pretty words.

"Uppity, that's what you are." The second man sneered. "When you're with your own, you can be mighty brave. Just don't go out alone, boy, 'cause there's plenty of real men who'll take care of you."

The two turned to leave, but May stepped up, her eyes filled with sadness. "Truth is, if you'da jes' asked, we'da shared."

Both men glared at her.

Ezra stood stiff and alert, staring at them as they crossed the field. "You folks go ahead and eat. Then I'll take my turn."

"Please, sir," said Adam. "Let me be the lookout." His eyes gleamed with respect.

Ezra looked at the young man for a bit. "All right. Just hold my gun, like so." He put the loaded weapon on the ground, barrel up, and showed Adam how to hold it away from his body, yet ready for use.

Willard knelt down. "We gots lots ta be thankful fo'. Let's pray."

Everybody but Adam knelt down. He lowered his chin reverently, but his eyes watched out for danger.

Delia thought Willard went on a bit too long in his prayer. He seemed to thank God for every good thing he'd ever received in all his long years. But she had to agree with his last words.

"Lawd, we thank You fo' dis fine young soldier You sent ta guard us. And we thank You fo' dese here vittles. May dey give us stren'th fo' da road ahead. Amen."

Delia glanced at Ezra. Tears shone in his eyes.

Right then, she thought she might just want to pick his last name for her own.

CHAPTER THREE

*O*nce again, Ezra felt like a target. Maybe staying with these good people was a bad idea. He didn't want to endanger them because of his uniform. Glancing down, he brushed the dirt off of the worn woolen fatigue jacket. Even though faded from two years of wear, its blue color could not be mistaken. If he cut off the two gold stripes on each sleeve and brass buttons down the front, people might not be so quick to assume he was a soldier, though the thought depressed him. One day he hoped to have a son to whom he could pass this uniform as a proud reminder of his service in the war. But future possibilities must not put these good people at risk today.

Lord, what should I do?

"Son?" Willard hobbled over to Ezra. "You look troubled. You thinkin' 'bout goin' on ahead? Nobody'd fault ya fo' it."

In the fading daylight, the old fellow reminded Ezra of his grandfather, a gentle, wise man who had been proud when his grandson enlisted in the army. Grandfather was an articulate, educated man, but the same aged wisdom shone in both men's eyes.

"No, sir. That never crossed my mind. I know the Lord brought us together." He brushed his hand along his jaw. "I'm just concerned about this uniform. Those men seemed to have a special hatred for my being a soldier."

Willard nodded his head. "Dat's so, dat's so. I saw it m'self." He stared off in the distance for a moment, then turned back to Ezra. "May's got some stuff in her bag. Let's see what we can figure out." He turned to where his wife was cleaning up the remains of their supper. "May, come on over here, honey."

Ezra could not help but notice the affectionate smile on the woman's face when she approached her husband. How long had they been married? Did they have children? Would he ever know that kind of devotion? Ezra shook his head. Where had these questions come from? Seemed like they started this very morning when a shy young lady named Delia smiled at him.

"Won' be no trouble, a-tall," May said once she heard of Ezra's concerns. She motioned everyone back to the barn and dug through her patchwork bag.

With several in the group offering suggestions, Ezra was outfitted with a faded brown shirt, which felt a little tight but bore no trace of his association with the military. His trousers would have to do for now, despite the stripe down each side. Over time, the satin had become frayed and torn, so May promised to snip the stripes off when they stopped for a rest in the morning.

"Nobody'll see dem at night." May adjusted the shirt on Ezra's shoulders and beamed at her handiwork. He bent down and placed a kiss on her cheek, and she laughed with delight.

He folded his blue fatigue jacket, shirt, and forage cap and placed them at the bottom of his knapsack where no one would be likely to find them.

At twilight, they moved out to the empty road and headed north. Ezra and Leviticus set the pace, taking into account the frailty of the old folks. Ezra checked often to be sure they did not fall behind. He noticed that Delia seemed to be watching out for the very same thing.

⁕

"You doin' awright?" Delia walked beside Miz May and Mr. Willard, matching her steps to theirs in the fading light.

"Sho' thing, honey." Mr. Willard had a spry step in spite of being bent a bit. He'd probably spent his whole long life leaning over, picking cotton.

"Jes' fine, sweet chile." Miz May was missing some teeth, but Delia felt good when the old woman smiled at her. "You doin' awright?"

"Yes, ma'am." Delia glanced ahead.

She could barely make out the soldier and the other man, who walked slow and careful, watching out for danger. The moon would be showing up shortly, so they'd have light again.

"Miz May," she said, "what'll we do in the nights when the moon's dark and we can't see where we're goin'?"

Miz May didn't answer right away. With each step, she pulled herself along with her walking stick, a carved branch of cedar with some little bells tied to the top. "I s'pose we'll wait and see. No tellin' what's ahead."

"Sho' would be nice to walk in the daylight," Frederick said, walking alongside his mama and holding her hand like he was scared to let go.

Delia might have said those words herself, but they sounded better coming from a child. Besides, she didn't have any real plans. These folks seemed to know where they were going, so she'd stick with them. Being with them was better than being alone.

The rising moon cast a dim light on the road, so they walked a little faster, though not too fast for the old folks.

Delia stared ahead at the broad back of the soldier. Ezra. She liked the way his name sounded. He'd been real nice that one time he tipped his hat to her.

Imagine a free black man from up north coming down here to fight so she could be free too. A whole regiment of them. Just thinking on it made her heart feel good. That was another reason to stay with these folks. She had a feeling Ezra would keep them all safe.

Toward morning, they stopped to rest among some trees alongside the road. Ezra shot two fat possums, and Miz May cooked them with a little rice and some wild onions. Delia watched to see which plants the old woman picked so she could get her own if she needed to.

"Miss May," Ezra said, "how do you manage to make everything taste so good when you have so little to work with?" He settled back against a tree and patted his belly like a satisfied man.

Delia hid a grin and looked away. Ezra was one fine-looking man.

Miz May chuckled. "Dat salt you give me hep a lot. But they's plenty o' seasonin's in the woods jes' 'bout ever'where." She chewed on a bite of possum. "Dat's the last o' the rice I brung with me, so's we's gonna have to eat roots 'less we can git mo' rice."

"This road must lead to a town, or else it wouldn't be here." Ezra looked off in the distance. "We might be able to find a store and buy more food."

"Buy?" Leviticus stared at him. "How you gonna *buy* somethin'?"

Ezra frowned, like he wished he hadn't said that about buying. Then he shrugged his shoulders. "I have a small amount of money, just a couple of dollars from my army pay."

Everybody stared at him with their mouths hanging open.

"You'd buy food to share?" Leviticus asked. "With people you jus' met?"

Ezra shook a pebble out of his shoe. "Of course I would."

Delia thought her heart would burst. She'd never known anybody like him.

"You's a real good man, Ezra Johns." Mr. Willard wiped his eyes and sniffed out loud.

The others told him the same thing, except Delia. She couldn't seem to get the words out. Anyway, why would he care what she thought?

"Will they sell to colored?" Adam sat by Ezra against the big oak tree. "I mean, can you jus' walk in a general sto' and ask to buy food?"

Everybody considered the question for a bit.

"We'll just have to try it," Ezra said.

"Well, we bes' git some rest." May pulled two little pillows from her bag and handed one to Willard. "Delia, honey, come on over here and lay down by me." She patted a grassy spot beside her under the branches of the oak tree, where the sun might not get too hot.

"Now, dis is how we gonna sleep." Miz May talked like she was somebody. To Delia's surprise, everybody else listened. "Alice, you come on over and lay down by Delia, then little Frederick, then

Leviticus." She looked over at Adam and Ezra. "You all jes' stay right where you is."

"Yes, ma'am." Ezra had a funny look on his face, like he was about to laugh. But he didn't.

Except for Delia, everybody had a bag or knapsack to use for a pillow. Miz May gave her a big square of brown cotton.

"Jes' gather up some leaves and set this over 'em." She showed Delia how. "You feel better if you don' git a crick in yo' neck."

"Yes, ma'am." Delia did what Miz May said. "Thank you, ma'am."

She lay down and tried to think about sleep, but too many thoughts came to mind. Had it only been the night before last that she'd run away? Just two mornings ago when Miz Suzanne had slapped her for the last time? She reached up to touch her jaw. The swelling had gone down considerably.

These folks seemed real nice, all except Alice. Not that she'd been mean or called Delia a name or anything like that. But more than once, Alice had looked at her like she wished Delia hadn't come along. Delia didn't mind too much. The field hands back at the plantation had acted about the same to her. Leviticus didn't pay her any mind, but Alice's little boy was nice, and Adam called her "Miz Delia." That made her feel good, the way Miz May's smile did.

She would stay with them for now so she could learn how to get along away from the plantation. Ezra said he had a little money to buy food, and Miz May said something about getting paid to work. Did Miz May and Mr. Willard and the others know how to go about doing that?

Back at the plantation, the only slaves who had money were the men Massuh had hired out to work at other plantations for a while. Then they'd have to give Massuh most of it. Still, they had something to keep for their work and could buy anything they wanted with it.

What kind of work could Delia do to get money? She'd have to remember to ask Miz May, 'cause she sure couldn't ask Ezra—not when her heart started to pound real hard every time he looked at her.

✦✦✧✦✦

A bright ray of sun burst through the waving oak branches and warmed Ezra's face. From the sun's position, he could see it was almost noontime. He rolled to his side and opened his eyes. The usual itching started right away, but he forbade himself to scratch. Few men in his regiment had been spared an infestation of lice. He wondered if his companions would be disgusted if they noticed the vermin on him. If only he could take a bath…but that would require more than the small stream they had found that morning in a nearby field.

Ezra sat up and studied the little stream. It seemed to flow from the tree-laden hills just to the northwest. Surely the thick forest must have a deep water source and perhaps more game. They'd be able to travel during the day if they walked through the woods.

At their meal of dandelion greens and possum meat they'd saved from the night before, Ezra proposed his idea.

"It won't be much harder to walk over the hills in the daytime than on the road at night. What do you think?"

He looked around the group, and his gaze stopped at Delia. What a pretty girl. But he must not stare at her this way. The blush on her fair cheeks suggested she had no idea how lovely she was. He wanted to ask her if she would help Miss May and Mr. Willard up and down the hills, but he could not get the words out. How foolish. Perhaps his hesitancy came from his long absence from the company of young ladies. He turned to hear what Leviticus had to say.

"I like dat idea. Me and Alice and the boy can manage. Adam and the girl can help the old folks. Walkin' in the daylight shor' will be easier."

With all in agreement, they gathered their belongings and trekked along the path beside the stream. A half-mile into their journey, they encountered a small group of Negroes camped on the other side of the stream. They appeared to be just waking up. Ezra gripped his rifle, wondering if he should load it.

"How do, ya'll?" One of the men lifted his hand in greeting.

Beside him, a woman stirred and sat up, a smile lighting her dark face. "How do? Come on over an' set a spell." She beckoned to the travelers.

Returning their wave, Ezra looked at Leviticus. "What do you think?"

"Don't rightly know. Can't hurt, I don' s'pose."

"Why, look. They's jes' a fam'ly." Miss May grinned. "See them chid'run?"

Ezra looked again and felt a little foolish as he took in three young people rubbing sleep from their eyes. Although one seemed about Adam's age and nearly a man, their harmlessness was evident in their wide-eyed stares and open smiles. The girl gave Delia a friendly smile as if inviting her friendship. The youngest was a boy of about ten years, but he grinned at little Frederick as if inviting his friendship.

"Where are you headed?" Ezra crossed the stream and turned to help Miss May step over the water, while the rest of their party followed and crowded around the campers.

"We's headed to Indiana. How 'bout you?" The man stood and reached out to Ezra.

"Boston." Ezra gave his hand a firm shake.

"Boston?" The woman put her hands on her hips. "I hear that's a mighty fine city."

"Yes, ma'am, it is." Ezra wished the words back. No use telling them that was his hometown, at least not until he knew if they could be trusted. "What takes you to Indiana?"

The man and woman started talking at the same time, then stopped. The man put his arm around the woman's waist. "You go ahead, honey. You the good talker."

"Hush, now." She gave him a little shove. "You do very well, Titus."

Their banter brought a chuckle to everyone. Ezra wondered if she had been a house slave, for her proper speech was spoken in well-modulated tones.

Titus nodded his appreciation to her. "Awright, then. Last week, jes' after our massuh give us leave to go, we met up with this Yankee soldier. Well, it was a whole bunch of Yankee soldiers from Indiana. But this man, he say he have a farm up there that need good workers. Well, suh, I been on the plantation all my life, an' I know farmin'. So I say I be right proud to come to work for him. He say come, so I'm a-comin'. Me and my wife an' chid'run."

"Tha's jes' real fine," Mr. Willard said. "You's a strong young fella, so you gonna do awright."

"What road you takin'?" Leviticus asked.

Ezra had thought of the same question. Maybe these folks would want to travel with them.

"We's headed west. We's gonna follow the Mississippi as best we can on up to the Ohio. This man's farm is jes' acrost from Louisville, Kentucky." Titus's eyes were bright with hope. "Jes' sayin' all those names give me a good feelin' 'bout the journey. The good Lawd bless us with good, strong bodies, so we gonna be awright." He peered around the group. "I s'pose ya'll is headed east."

"Northeast. We're goin' over them hills so we can walk in the daylight." Leviticus tilted his head toward the foothills.

"Um-hum. Sounds like a good idea." Titus nodded his approval.

"Ya'll had anythin' to eat?" Miss May spoke to the woman. "If you hungry, we got some greens and a few scraps o' possum lef' from las' night."

"Praise the Lord, that's so very kind of you." Titus's wife seemed about to cry.

The family's eager response settled the question of whether or not to move on. Like Ezra's own grandmother, Miss May wanted to take care of everyone. With Alice and Delia's help, she brought out the food and set it before Titus and his family. As they ate, the two groups sat in a circle and shared stories of their travels and warned each other about dangers from both man and beast.

"We'd better get back on the road," Ezra said at last. He stood and shook Titus's hand. "Godspeed on your journey."

"We gonna make sure to pray for ya'll." Titus clasped Ezra's hand in both of his. "God bless you, now."

With good-byes said, Ezra and his party resumed their trek toward the foothills, following the little stream until it cut too far to the northwest. Then they set a northeasterly course.

Just as Ezra had expected, the hike up the inclines and down into the little valleys proved strenuous. What he had not expected was the resiliency of the two elderly people. Perhaps the rest had helped them. That evening as they camped in the forest, he shook his head in wonder.

"You folks do amaze me." He studied Mr. Willard's face in particular, for the old man had seemed to have more difficulty breathing than his wife.

"Why, boy, I been workin' the fields since I was not much bigger'n a tadpole." Mr. Willard laughed at his own humor. "I ain't whipped yet."

"'Sides," Miz May added, "we gots to git to our chi'drun. Ain't givin' up till we gits to Boston." Her eyes twinkled with enthusiasm. "Don' you be thinkin' 'bout quittin' on our account."

Ezra grinned at her. "No, ma'am, I won't." But he would make sure to set a pace slow enough for them.

Few words were spoken on their second day in the forest because climbing took all their energy. Early that afternoon, they heard the unmistakable sound of rushing water as they came over the top of a hill. Their hopes were rewarded when they saw a creek flowing though the ravine, its width ranging from six to ten feet. Everyone hurried down the hill for a drink from the bright, clear stream.

"Let's stay here for a few days to rest." Ezra once again studied the old couple for signs of exhaustion.

"Fine idea." Mr. Willard sat down on a fallen tree trunk. "Won' do no harm to catch our breath, will it, May?"

She chuckled in a way that reminded Ezra of his Aunt Patience in Boston. "I's not too proud to admit I's ready fo' a rest," she said.

Ezra laughed. "Miss May, I was just about to say the same thing myself."

He gathered his courage and turned to ask Miss Delia how she'd made it through the day. But she was headed down to the stream.

Tonight. I'll find something to say to her tonight after supper.

With that thought, he went out looking for firewood.

earing a borrowed shirt, Delia knelt beside the cold creek and scrubbed her white blouse, thankful that Miz May had given her a bit of lye soap to remove the odor of three days' sweat. How stupid she'd been to run off without a thought for where she was going or what she'd need. Miz May and Alice had planned ahead and brought sewing kits and extra clothes. Willard had an old pocketknife. The others had tin cups, plates, forks, or other useful things. Delia could hardly believe some of their owners had supplied these items. Despite Mr. Lincoln's proclamation, she couldn't guess what Massuh and his family would have done to her just for *telling* them she was leaving. They surely never would have given her any help.

While her blouse soaked in a small eddy by the bank, she sat on a rock to dip her aching feet in the stream. That was another mistake. Miz Suzanne's castoff hightops made poor walking shoes. The others wore different kinds of old shoes, but none had two-inch heels. Delia already had swollen feet from that first night of running. Then she'd turned her ankle more than once walking on uneven roads and up and down those hills. Now every step hurt.

The sun would set in another hour, and she needed to hurry back uphill to the camp and help Miz May fix supper.

"My, what a pretty sight."

Delia jumped, and her heart began to pound. Across the creek, a tall young man stood fishing at the water's edge, a broad smile on his brown face. Was he making fun of her, calling her pretty? Everybody knew she was nothing to look at. She pulled her blouse from the stream, gave it a quick wringing, and turned to dash away.

"I...I'm sorry. I didn't mean to scare you, miss. Please don't go."

At his disappointed tone, Delia turned back. The man now slumped against a tree. He looked so sad, she pushed away her fear.

"I won't do you no harm." With his head tilted to the side and his full lips puckered in a pout, he eyed her like an old hound dog. "I swear."

She tried not to smile at his silly behavior, but a grin got the better of her. "No need to swear. I believe you."

His good-looking face lit up again. He started to cross the stream, but she took a step toward camp.

"I gotta get back to my...my folks." Inside, Delia excused her lie. *They're the nearest to folks I ever had.*

"Sure." He stopped and nodded. "Sure thing. You do that."

With hesitance Delia stared at him for a bit. "You hungry?"

He shrugged. "No more'n ever'body else these days."

What would May do right now? Just the other day, she'd been ready to feed those mean white men who tried to steal their rabbits.

"We might have an extra bite."

He swallowed. "I'd be mighty grateful, miz."

Again he started across the stream, and again she stepped back, this time holding her arm out with palm up.

"You can follow, but not too close."

He winced, and Delia felt ashamed. He was just another drifter, like all of them except Ezra. This one didn't look like a soldier. He wore a faded gray shirt and tattered black trousers and carried a knapsack on his back. A slouch hat hung from his belt. Had he been a slave?

"I'm Delia," she called over her shoulder as she walked up the hillside.

"Call me Jack."

"Pleased to meet you, Jack."

"Mighty pleased to meet you, Miss Delia."

She puckered her lips to keep from laughing. He sure liked that word "mighty."

The camp was in a small clearing not too far up the wooded slope. She was glad they'd decided to walk in daylight from now on.

Happy sounds came from the group. Miz May and Alice sang a spiritual while they cooked. Willard laughed. He was probably teasing Frederick, from the sounds of the boy's giggles. Delia's heart swelled. These *were* her folks, just as sure as if she'd been born to them.

"Hold it right there." Ezra stepped from the bushes, flanked by Leviticus and Adam. He held his gun at his side, and all three glared at the newcomer.

Delia glanced behind her to see Jack glower at the men.

"It's all right. It's all right." She stood between Jack and the others. "This is Jack. I asked him to have a bite with us."

Leviticus and Adam relaxed and stepped over to shake Jack's hand, but Ezra didn't move. Instead, he turned a questioning stare toward Delia.

"Do you know this man?"

She flinched at his sharp tone. "No, but...."

"How do you know we can trust him?"

"I...I...." Her knees grew weak. Would he hit her?

Ezra continued to frown. "You should have checked with me before inviting him." He brushed past her and walked over to the other man, his hand extended. "Jack, I'm Ezra Johns. I didn't mean to be rude, but you know how careful we all need to be these days. Come on over and meet the rest of the folks."

"Sure, sure, mighty glad to." Jack greeted the others and turned once to wink at Delia.

His gesture didn't help. Ezra's tone had cut into her heart like a knife, making clear his feelings about her. He might as well have kicked her, just like Miz Suzanne.

✦❈❈❈❈✦

With the campfire banked to a steady glow, the group gathered around it to let their squirrel and potato supper settle. Seated against a tree, Ezra kept his eye on Jack, who'd found a place close to Delia. Ezra worried that Jack intended to sleep beside her. Would he attempt something so improper? If so, should Ezra tell him to move? Would Delia want him to?

Leviticus refused to be convinced that the man needed to be watched, so Ezra would get no help in the matter. In fact, the whole group seemed to welcome him without question, which Ezra could not bring himself to do. Something about the man set Ezra's teeth on edge, but he could not figure out what it was. Was it the way the others had accepted him so quickly? That would be foolish. They were good people and had accepted Ezra with the same kindness. Yet it troubled him that the man did not seem hungry, as the other travelers were.

His heart had nearly stopped when he saw Delia coming back into camp with the man close behind her. With no time to load his gun, he was about to attach the bayonet when she defended the newcomer. Delia's apparent innocence might get her into a lot of trouble if she was not careful.

As for Jack—winking at an impressionable young woman was improper. Even now, he leaned toward her in a way that implied familiarity. Ezra took some comfort in the fact that she did not seem to know how to respond to Jack's smooth talk. He could see by the firelight that her fair complexion had turned pink. She chewed her bottom lip and stared at the ground.

"Well, as I said, Miz Delia, I'm mighty grateful to you for invitin' me to this fine supper." Jack drew figures in the dirt with a stick.

"Nothin' to it, Jack," she said. "These are good folks. I knew they'd welcome you."

Ezra noticed a slight smile flicker across her lips as she spoke, and a wave of displeasure swept through him. *Lord, forgive me for my lack of charity, but I just don't trust this fellow.* Maybe he'd grown hardhearted during the war, when he'd learned to trust only his fellow Negro soldiers. Or maybe it was just plain old jealousy. Here he thought he had all the time in the world to learn about Delia and see if the Lord wanted them to be more than friends. Then Jack came along and ruined everything with his flirting ways.

Ezra blew out a soft sigh and adjusted his knapsack behind him like a pillow, trying to get more comfortable against the tree. His efforts proved useless; he didn't expect to get much rest.

He suddenly remembered a worthless fellow who'd courted his sister before the war. He'd been all smooth talk, too, but he never got around to proposing. Father was just about to run him off when the man stopped coming to visit their Beacon Hill home. Maybe Jack was that same sort. Maybe he'd leave them in the morning.

At least Ezra hoped so.

❈

Delia didn't dare look at Jack. If he said "mighty" one more time, she'd laugh in his face. Why did he keep talking to her, anyway? And all those silly compliments saying she was pretty and sweet as honey—what was she supposed to say when he was lying through his teeth? Beulah had made it clear she wasn't much to look at and nobody would ever want her. Everything that had ever happened to her backed up that opinion—except for the way Massuh looked at her from time to time. He didn't seem as mad at her as Missus and Miz Suzanne always were. One time he gave her a new yellow scarf and told her it looked nice around her neck. But that evening Miz Suzanne ripped it off her, threw it in the fireplace, and used the poker to make sure it burned. Delia had run outside to escape being beat with that same hot poker. She sighed at the memory.

"You all right, Miz Delia?" Jack leaned toward her again, and she leaned away toward Alice, who sat on her other side.

"Yessuh, I'm fine. Jus' tired." Delia felt her face warm at her complaint. Sweet old Miz May never fussed about being tired.

"I know, I know." Jack's eyes filled with sympathy. "A sweet little gal like you shouldn't have to be on the road this way. Have you ever thought of settlin' down? I mean, now that we're free, we don't have to think about goin' up north. We was promised forty acres and a mule by the government. That's enough for any man…or woman."

He raised his eyebrows like he expected an answer, but Delia couldn't guess what she was supposed to say.

"Now you hush that talk," Miz May said. Seated on the other side of the fire, she used her carved staff to rise to her feet and then lumbered over to Jack and Delia. "This lil' gal is too young to settle down. She got her sights set on goin' north. If you ain't goin' north, don' try to slow her down." She tapped Jack's leg with her staff. "Now you scoot over. Me and Willard is sleepin' here."

Jack's dark eyebrows bent down in a frown, almost like he was mad. "Now, Miz May, I'm mighty comfortable right where I am. I'm all settled in." He glanced behind her, where Willard stood. "You and the old man can jus' go on back over yonder." He waved his hand toward the other side of the fire.

Miz May seemed to grow five inches. She lifted her staff and brought it down with a thud into the soft dirt, jangling the little bells tied to its top and raising a small cloud of dust.

"Boy, I said git, an' I mean git." Her voice held a powerful lot of authority, almost like a white mistress's.

Delia gasped and eyed Jack. Would he stand up and hit Miz May for talking to him that way? Where'd a field hand learn to talk like that?

But Jack lifted his hands in a plea. "Now, ma'am, I—"

"You, nothin'!" Miz May's eyes blazed. "Delia sleeps between Miz Alice and me, and that's all they is to it. You can sleep over by that tree with Adam and Ezra." She pointed toward Ezra, who was watching the whole thing.

It seemed to Delia Ezra was trying to keep from grinning. Why would he think this spat was funny? Where she come from, any plantation slaves who argued got whipped.

Delia glanced around the group. Everyone was staring at Jack. He looked around, too.

"Awright, awright, I'm goin'." He stood, brushed off his trousers and picked up his knapsack. He leaned down toward Delia and winked. "I'll see you in the mornin'."

"'Night." She gave him a little wave.

Miz May brought her patchwork bag over and sat down. She put her arms around Delia and rocked her for a while, humming softly. Then she sat back and brushed her rough hand along Delia's cheek.

"Honey chile, you gotta watch out. You gotta watch out."

Delia stared at her in the darkness and could barely make out the features of her dark, wrinkled face in the last glow of the fire. "Yes, ma'am." She had an idea of what Miz May meant, but right now her tender embrace and gentle humming brought a bittersweet ache to Delia's heart. Long ago, her mother used to rock her that way, and now it felt so good, she wanted to cry.

CHAPTER FIVE

$\mathscr{E}$zra inhaled a long, slow breath of fresh morning air. The rich scent of pine startled him, and his eyes popped open. They had camped the night before in the forest, but that did not protect them from danger. How could he have let down his guard that way, to sleep so soundly when he was supposed to be on watch?

A quick glance around the camp showed nothing amiss. The fire had long ago burned out, and the small pile of wood he'd collected last night lay near the charred remains. Everything was in readiness for breakfast. Now he just had to catch some game.

The others still slept, and he breathed out a sigh of relief. God had watched over them even if he had not. His gaze rested on Delia, as pretty sleeping as when she was awake. But watching her while she slept felt unseemly, so he quickly turned away. Whether she was awake or asleep, he would not stare at her the way Jack did.

Jack. Ezra looked toward the spot where Jack had slept. Empty, just as he'd hoped. A pang of guilt shot through him.

"Lord, I ask You again, please forgive my lack of charity. I came down here to fight for the freedom of men like Jack, not just for more like-able people." Yet he could not ignore how relieved he felt when he considered not having to watch out for Jack's foolishness.

He quietly stood and drew in another deep breath, giving himself permission to enjoy the scent of the pine trees and wildflowers blooming in the early spring. From their tree-sheltered campsite on the side of a low hill, he gazed out toward the east at the first rosy fingers of dawn breaking over the morning fog that had settled into the valley below. What a beautiful sight.

Rosy fingers of dawn? Hmm. Now what had made him recall Homer? Was it his longing to get back home to all his books? Maybe he'd have a chance to brush up on his Greek and read *The Iliad* and *The Odyssey* in their original language. Maybe he'd go back to college and finish his degree. Possibilities brightened before him like a promise, just like the dawn.

He glanced over toward Delia, who lay curled up by Miss May. Would she like to learn how to read? He might ask her today if the opportunity presented itself. Now that Jack was gone, he'd make a point to talk to her. He should have been talking to her all along, but not the way Jack did. No fancy sweet talk, just friendly conversation. He made up his mind long ago never to sweet-talk young ladies or at least not to flatter them. If he could not be truthful, he would not say anything at all.

He chuckled silently at the memory of the little scene the night before. Just when he'd thought he was alone in not trusting Jack, dear old Miss May made it clear she was watching the newcomer, too. Delia was safe in her care and could learn a lot from her if she wanted to.

Ezra had been taught to respect the wisdom of older people, and he had a strong feeling the Brewsters were a storehouse of wisdom.

Their earthy insights and spiritual understanding had been evident ever since he'd met them three days earlier. The incident with Jack had just confirmed it.

Pulling his shaving gear from his haversack, Ezra grabbed a bucket, and made his way to the nearby spring. Kneeling several yards below the rocky spot where the pristine spring spouted from the dark earth, he splashed handfuls of frigid water on his face. The icy shock drove away the last of his sleepiness. He quickly stropped his razor, shaved, and freshened himself. Last evening's icy bath in the stream had been refreshing, and he did not itch quite as much as before. He'd been sweaty and dirty for most of the past two years, but somehow being clean seemed especially important now.

Laughter and chatter drew his attention back to the camp. The others must be waking up in fine spirits, as he had. He filled the bucket at the mouth of the spring, drank deeply, and filled it again. The coffee would be good this morning, even if it was made from pine nuts or whatever Miss May found to brew it with.

He walked along the side of the hill, not minding the water sloshing from the bucket onto his trouser leg. On a bright, sunny day, as this promised to be, the fabric would dry quickly. Coming through the maze of giant willow oaks, loblolly pines, and countless varieties of bushes, he stopped short.

Ahead stood Jack in the middle of the admiring travelers. In his hands he held up a line full of fat, shimmering, wiggling mountain trout.

"Fish!" Frederick hopped up and down. "That'll sure be some nice change from all them rabbits and possums."

"I'll git my fryin' pan to cook 'em up." Alice hurried to her knapsack.

"Mmm-hm." Adam rubbed his hands together. "Fine catch, Jack."

"Gonna taste real good with a little o' dat rosemary on 'em." Miss May looked up at Jack with open admiration, just as if last night had never happened at all. Just as if he were her favorite grandson.

Stifling his disappointment over the man's return, Ezra stepped forward and set the bucket down by the cold remnants of last night's fire. "Good catch, Jack. You'll have to teach me how to do that."

Was that a smirk he saw on the man's face? If so, it quickly vanished. "I'll be mighty glad to teach you all I know, friend." There was no mistaking the subtle mockery in his voice.

Ezra felt an unpleasant twist in his belly. Then it hit him—Jack reminded him of a fellow soldier he'd trained and fought with, one who knew everything in the world until the bullets started flying in battle. He had been the first to hide from the conflict until shame drove him out to fight alongside his brothers-in-arms.

All right, Lord. You brought Jack among us, so You'll have to show me how to treat him as You would.

But Ezra could not help thinking that a rattlesnake had just crawled into camp, with no intention of leaving. And there he was, shaking his rattles at Ezra like a challenge.

Ezra gave Jack a pleasant smile. "I'll appreciate that, *friend.*"

✦✛╬╢❋╟╬✛✦

Delia had hated fish ever since she'd choked on a fishbone and Beulah had laughed at her.

"Serves you right for eatin' leftovers off the Missus' plate." Beulah had pounded her back and then given her a piece of buttered bread.

The bone soon went down, but no matter how hungry she got, Delia still couldn't think about fish with any pleasure.

After Alice and Miz May fried the trout, they passed around a tin plate with a piece of fish, along with some greens they'd found and boiled.

"Now, honey," Alice said to Frederick. "Be careful 'cause they's bones in it. Feel it with yo' fingers like this, and then pop it in yo' mouth." She showed her son how to eat the fish.

The boy's eyes sparkled as he downed his first bite. "Um-um. This sho' is good."

Delia sat down beside Frederick and followed Alice's instructions, too. She nervously worked the fish with her tongue and was surprised at the pleasant, mouth-watering flavor. And no bones! She tried for a second bite, felt a bone in her mouth, and easily removed it. Her stomach demanded more, so she copied Alice in mixing the fish with the greens and ate her fill. Washing it down with some tasty red tea Miz May had made from tender sassafras roots, Delia figured she'd never had such a fine breakfast in her life.

While they ate, the men talked about their plan to rest a day or two. Mr. Willard said he and Miz May hated to hold everyone back, but Leviticus promised him that Frederick and Alice could use a rest, too.

"We been on the road for longer than you, sir." Leviticus clapped Mr. Willard on the shoulder. "It's about time for us to sit a spell."

"Awright, awright, then." Mr. Willard laughed his funny, cackling laugh that reminded Delia of a quacking duck. "Jes' recollect that anytime you young'uns need to go on, you can. We won't bear any hard feelin's."

"Mr. Willard," Ezra said in a gentle voice, "I wouldn't think of leaving you behind. I believe the Lord brought us together so I could help you find your children in Boston."

Delia looked over toward him, trying not to stare. Last night he'd seemed distant, but now he spoke so kindly to Mr. Willard that she could hardly believe it was the same man. She thought about his coolness the night before and the way he talked to her and to the old folks. She breathed out a soft sigh so no one would notice, her heart full of self-doubt. Just like Beulah said, nobody would ever truly care about her. Well, maybe Miz May did, but that was because the old dear was such a good woman. For now, that would have to be enough for Delia.

She hurried to help Alice and Miz May gather up the plates and pans to be washed down at the stream. She knew she had to do her part so they wouldn't ask her to leave.

***

"Since we'll be here for a couple of days, let's try to get some venison." Ezra held up his gun to indicate his confidence that they could get another variety of meat to strengthen them for the journey ahead. "I saw deer scat all over the place when I went to the spring."

"Sounds good to me." Leviticus stood up from the large flat stone he'd been sitting on. "What can I do to help?"

"Can I help?" Frederick clapped his hands and grinned. "Can I?"

Ezra smiled at the boy even as he shook his head. "Sorry, son. The fewer we have out in the woods, the less likely anybody gets shot by accident."

"Yessuh, awright then." Frederick's eagerness disappeared, and he stood still. But he did not pout, as many boys of Ezra's acquaintance might have done. These former slaves had probably always had to watch their behavior, even as children.

"Leviticus," Ezra said, "you and Jack can make your way down to the creek, then head upstream. It's still early, so there might be some deer taking their morning drink. I'll go up to that little rise over there." He pointed to a small, rocky bluff with enough bushes for him to hide in. "Then you can drive the deer my way."

"I was plannin' on makin' a shelter." Jack remained seated against a tree and pared his fingernails with a large hunting knife. "If we're stayin' in these woods for a while, we're gonna get rained on every afternoon. Might as well make ourselves at home."

Ezra considered his words. A shelter would be a good idea, but he didn't want Jack to be in camp when Mr. Willard and the women-folk returned from the stream.

"I'll go with you." Adam appeared almost as eager as Frederick. The youth stood about five feet four inches, probably as tall as he'd ever grow, but his steady gaze proved he was near manhood.

"All right, Adam." Ezra turned to Leviticus. "Shall we wait until Miss Alice comes back so she can watch Frederick?"

Leviticus scratched his chin. "Well...."

"He can stay with me," Jack said. "I'll need some help cutting saplings."

"Thank you, sir." Leviticus gave Jack a brief nod, then turned to his son. "Now, boy, you mind him, y'hear?"

Frederick's eyes widened with renewed eagerness, and once again he danced happily about the campsite. "Yessuh. Yessuh!"

Ezra would have laughed at the boy's swift change of mood if he hadn't doubted the wisdom of leaving him with Jack. How did

Leviticus know he could trust the newcomer? But as they left the camp, Ezra chided himself for being so suspicious. Even though Jack had sweet-talked Delia last night, that did not mean he could not be trusted to watch Frederick.

"Lord, watch over that boy. I know he's not Leviticus's natural son, but he loves him as if he were. Please don't let him have cause to grieve his decision."

Ezra himself had become fond of the boy in the past few days. His uncomplaining nature encouraged everyone in the group, even Delia. This morning at breakfast, she'd watched Frederick as closely as his mother did to be sure he didn't eat any fish bones.

Ezra chided himself again. He must not start thinking about Delia when he needed to be tracking deer. But he couldn't help it. Just as Frederick had been trained not to complain, Delia must have been forced to hide her feelings, too. She rarely spoke and seemed a bit like a frightened rabbit.

How could he help her know it was all right to say how she felt? Even before his thoughts formed a prayer, he knew the answer. Tonight he would take out his Bible and read to the whole group. He would find just the right passages, those that compared their new freedom from the bondage of slavery to the Christian's freedom from the bondage of sin.

He stifled a laugh as he crept through the forest's dense undergrowth. His grandfather had once declared that Ezra would make a fine preacher, yet Ezra had never felt that calling. Maybe now he'd get a chance to try preaching and find out if Grandfather had been right all along. For the first time in his life, it did not seem like such a bad idea.

All right, then, Lord. Just show me the way, and I'll follow.

CHAPTER SIX

*D*elia watched the hindquarter of the white-tailed buck sizzle above the campfire flames, and her mouth watered in anticipation. She'd never tasted deer, but the smell stirred up her appetite something fierce. Venison, rabbit, mountain trout, and especially the sassafras tea Miz May had made—all were delights she was surprised to find out here in the woods.

The rest of the deer meat hung high in a tree a short ways downwind of the camp. Ezra and Leviticus had skinned the animal right away, then buried the innards way out in the woods so panthers and wild hogs wouldn't come into camp looking for them. Along with the meat, the men had brought back the heart, liver, and hide. Mr. Willard was telling Frederick how they'd make that hide into something useful.

"When I was a boy about young Adam's age, I run off down to the swamps of Florida and lived with some Injuns. Afore I was caught and brung back, I learned a powerful lot about livin' off the land, most o' which I done forgot over the years." Mr. Willard quacked his duck-laugh. "But I do recall how the women stretched out them deer hides on a wood frame and scraped 'em clean."

"How we gonna scrape it if we ain't got no knife?" Frederick asked his question with polite curiosity and then eyed Jack's large blade.

"Why, boy, I got a knife, but that ain't what we use." Mr. Willard laughed again, and his eyes sparkled with affection. "We go down to the creek and find jes' the right rocks and chip 'em on another rock until they's sharp. Then we goes to scrapin' till the job is done."

Frederick's eyes got big. "Ain't nothin' you don' know, is they, Mr. Willard?"

The old man shook his head and grinned. "Lawd, boy. I got lots mo' to learn. Da man who thinks he knows it all, he's the one who don' know nothin'."

Delia drank in his wisdom and savored it, just like the dark red tea that seemed to fill her with "git up and go," as Beulah used to say. Delia would work hard to remember everything she learned from these folks.

Their laundry lay spread over the tops of nearby bushes, and as the day wore on, most of it quickly dried in the sunshine and breeze. A few clouds crept up over the horizon and promised another strong afternoon rain. Delia glanced a short ways up the hill toward the shelter Jack had built where several slender pines grew next to a rocky embankment. He'd used thin strips of new bark to tie branches of the long-needled loblolly into a layered covering and then cleared the floor of the little refuge. It looked like all nine people would fit inside, but it would be a tight fit. Seemed like a lot of trouble to go to for just a couple of days, but maybe she'd think different when the rains came.

With everybody busy at some task or other, Delia thought she should put her hands to work, too. She looked over toward Miz May, who sat mending some dried laundry. Ezra was hunkered down beside her, and the two talked and laughed. Maybe Delia could help Miz May sew. She wandered in their direction. Just as she came within earshot, Ezra stood up and hurried away toward the creek. She held back her disappointment. The man couldn't stand to be near her.

"Come on over, Delia." Miz May beckoned to her and patted a spot on the log where she sat. "You lookin' for somethin' to do?"

"Yessum." Delia gathered her skirt to keep it out of the dirt before she sat down.

"You doin' awright, chile?"

"Yessum, I'm fine. I jus' want to make myself useful. If I ain't doin' enough, will you tell me?"

Miz May sat back and gave her a long look like she was about to scold. "Why, gal, we all done had enough o' slave massuhs, ain't we? You pitch in right fine when they's work to do. Jes' sit fo' a spell and enjoy this nice afternoon. See dem squirrels?" She pointed to two chattering tree rats that scampered about the branches overhead. "They's havin' a good time, ain't they? And listen to dem birds." She cocked her head and smiled at the birds twittering nearby. "Hear dat knockin'? Dat's a redheaded wood-pecker diggin' his dinner out o' some pine tree. You hear dat water down at the creek, flowin' on and on over all dem rocks? You hear all dat, chile?"

"Yessum." Delia tried not to smile. Miz May sure took a lot of pleasure from such everyday sounds.

"Dat's the music o' the forest, and it's playin' jes' for us." Her face beamed with pure joy.

A funny feeling, nice and warm, eased through Delia's insides. Music of the forest just for her, and nobody could take it away from her.

"I never thought of it that way."

Miz May chuckled in her deep, throaty way. "Honey, dat's what freedom is all about. We all gots ta work to git food and shelter, and sometimes it's harder than others. But da good Lawd wants us to set back and take a breath from time to time."

He did? Delia wondered what an ignorant field hand would know about the Lord. The preacher at Massuh's church had said slaves was born to their lot, and the only way to avoid perdition was to work hard and mind their betters. Seated beside Delia in the balcony of that country church, Beulah would always say "Amen" when he said that. Maybe Miz May hadn't ever been to church.

"Now, here, honey." Miz May handed Delia a wool stocking. "You git busy darnin' this'n, and I'll do da other'n."

The "music of the forest" hummed around them quietly as they worked. Far to the east, thunder growled a soft threat. Soon they'd finished the stack of mending and folded the clean clothing in neat piles.

For the first time in her life, Delia felt satisfied with her work, especially since Miz May praised her tight, even stitches. She'd done her best, not because she feared a beating but because she took pride in doing a good job, a task she'd *wanted* to do. That old preacher would have called her pride a sin and said she was bound for perdition. Maybe she was, but she didn't care. She was just pleased she didn't have to listen to him ever again. In fact, she never had to listen to another preacher as long as she lived.

That thought made her want to get up and dance.

<hr>

Ezra grinned to himself. If all went well, Frederick would soon have a ball to play with. Miss May had given him the idea. He hurried back down to the creek where he'd buried the insides of the deer. He dug up the stomach and bladder, washed them thoroughly in the creek, and rubbed a little of his precious store of salt into them.

He'd never done anything like this before. Back home in Boston, though, he'd spent many afternoons playing baseball with his friends. If he could figure out how to make balls from these deer organs and maybe cover them with some of the skin Willard was working on, he could teach Frederick how to play. It was sure worth trying. Every boy needed to know how to play baseball.

Would he be able to draw Delia into the game, too? She probably had not had much fun in her life, either. The thought encouraged him.

Lord, help me teach these dear people about some of the things they'll face in the city, even the games, so they'll be prepared for their new life.

After using his knife to remove the last of the veins and blood, he swished the two organs in the water one last time and then headed back up the hill. Miss May sat with Delia, and between them lay a stack of clothes.

He hesitated at the edge of the camp. He wanted the balls to be a surprise, so he'd have to wait until Miss May was alone. Delia looked up at that moment, so he quickly hid his treasures behind his back. She frowned, stood up, and walked away. Had he somehow made her angry? Then another thought occurred to him. Maybe she didn't like him. Maybe that was why she never said much around him. Oddly, the idea did not discourage him. Instead, he felt challenged to win her over. For a moment, he could understand Jack's sweet-talking ways, but he'd never resort to that. He would just have to pray and seek the Lord's guidance on how to befriend her.

Delia wandered up toward the top of the hill, where she sat on a low, flat rock and thought about Ezra. She didn't care what he hid behind his back, but why had he frowned when he saw her? To think she'd sat there darning his socks. In fact, she'd washed them too. She let out a weary sigh. He was just like Miz Suzanne, mad at her no matter what she did.

She tried to let the music of the forest soothe her, but for some reason no birds were singing. The squirrels had disappeared, too, and she was a bit too far away from the creek to hear its rushing waters. Everything was quiet nearby. But the sound of thunder moved closer and closer; the clouds looked like black balls tumbling around in the sky.

At the first big splash of rain, Delia jumped up and ran down the hill. Everyone scurried to Jack's shelter and crowded in, nervously laughing as they made room for each other and their most important possessions, 'specially those that might be ruined by getting wet. Adam and Leviticus held some firewood to keep it dry for cooking the evening's supper. While the rain poured down harder and harder, just a few drops made it through the loblolly thatching.

The shelter was tall enough for everyone but Jack and Ezra, and the two men had to hunch over—one on each side of Delia. She couldn't decide which way to turn; both men smelled of a hard day's work in the sunshine. Stuck between them, Delia wondered if they all wouldn't do well to have a good wash-down instead of hiding from the rain.

"You awright, Miz Delia?" Jack smiled. It seemed he moved just a little bit closer to her.

"I'm awright." She stared down at the ground. His big smile made her feel good.

"You did a fine job on this shelter, Jack." Ezra spoke right near her ear, and she jumped. "Sorry, Miss Delia." He moved back as far as the rocky wall of the refuge would let him, like being close to her made him nervous.

Lightning cracked bright and loud, and everybody jumped, then laughed. After a spell, the shower let up and finally dripped to a stop. They all went back to their tasks. Miz May and Alice went off down toward the creek to collect dandelion greens and roots for the venison stew they'd be fixing for supper. Delia hoped they found some wild onions, too. She really loved onions.

Just as Adam and Ezra were getting the fire lit, a doe and her fawn broke through the wet bushes nearby.

"Quick, shoot it," cried Frederick.

"No, son," Ezra said. "We have enough meat, and you never kill a nursing doe." He seemed troubled by the animals' unexpected appearance.

"Look!" Leviticus pointed to several snakes slithering up the hill.

Delia made up her mind not to scream, but she did hurry over to the fire.

The forest suddenly came alive with animals of every sort moving rapidly for higher ground. Alice came running back to camp, her face twisted with terror.

"Flood!" she cried. "The water's risin' fast! We gotta git to the hilltop."

"Where's May?" Mr. Willard grabbed Alice, his eyes filled with fear.

"She tol' me to git up here and tell y'all. She's comin', I swear." Alice pulled away from the old man and grabbed Frederick. "We got to go. It's coming this way!"

Leviticus, Adam, and Jack grabbed what they could of their possessions and moved toward the rocks above. Below, the thunderous roar sounded closer, like a giant rolling down the creek bed. Ground squirrels skittered past, carrying young in their mouths. A wild hog dashed past among the pines.

Delia stared down the hill. She couldn't swim, but she couldn't let Miz May drown. Gathering up her skirt so she could run fast, she started down toward the creek. Mr. Willard stood wringing his hands.

"No!" Ezra caught up with her and gripped her arm. "You take Mr. Willard uphill."

"No!" she shouted. "I'm goin'!"

"I said no." Ezra's eyes blazed, and he shoved her toward the old man. "You do what I say. I'll get Miss May." He turned to run down the hill, calling over his shoulder, "Don't you worry, sir. I *will* get her."

"Lawd, hep him." Mr. Willard lifted his eyes upward, the worry on his face evident and tears streamed down his cheeks. "Hep him!"

Delia grabbed Mr. Willard's arm. "Come on! We gotta get up there!" She tugged at him.

"You go on, chile. I gots ta wait for my May."

In the distance, Delia saw the water rising fast, pushing brush and tearing out small trees. "You come on, now, sir!" She could barely hear her own voice above the roar of the flood. "I got a job to do. You don' want that Ezra mad at me, do you?"

His eyes seemed to clear, and he saw her now. Just as the waters entered the campsite, he hobbled uphill beside her faster than she thought possible. They reached the bluff. Jack and the other men pulled them to safety.

Below them, the flood crested as the raging waters swept by, drowning everything in sight and roaring so loud that it was all they could hear. But as evening approached, the waters slowly began to lower, leaving the hillside scraped almost clean, with only the oldest, hardiest trees still standing.

Ezra and Miz May were nowhere to be seen.

CHAPTER SEVEN

*E*zra plunged into the rising stream and scooped up Miss May just seconds before a wall of water slammed into them. It knocked him to his knees and pulled both of them under the turbulent waves. He held onto her frail form as tightly as he could and fought with his legs and his free arm to bring them to the surface. His eyes stung. He spat out water and desperately gasped for air. Broken trees and other debris slammed into them, and the flood washed them down the gorge.

"Help, Lord!" Ezra cried.

"Mercy, Lawd!" Miss May screamed.

Ahead, Ezra saw the shuddering branches of a tree that seemed to be holding its own against the deluge. He kicked his legs violently to direct the two of them toward it. With one arm grasping Miss May, he shouted out another "Help us, Lord!" as he used his other hand to grab on to a branch. Pain ripped his arms, but he held on tight, making sure Miss May wasn't torn from his grip. Miraculously, he was able to pull them both into the refuge of the great oak, where he held them fast for what seemed like forever.

Ezra didn't know whether the old woman was dead or alive. When the deluge slowed and the roar began to diminish, he found footing in a crotch in the larger branches and held her against the trunk of the tree. After some time, she groaned and stirred in his arms. He almost sobbed out his relief, even though she had not fully awakened.

"Lord, please don't let her be badly injured," he whispered.

Soon darkness crept over the landscape, and the waters began to subside, leaving them drenched and shivering. Still he held on, praying the strength of his arms would not surrender to the pain shooting through his muscles.

"Willard?"

"No, ma'am. It's me, Ezra."

"Where's Willard?"

"He's all right, Miss May." *Lord, forgive me if that's not true.*

She emitted a shaky laugh. "Praise be."

"Yes, ma'am. Praise be." He shook away the memory of the dazed, frightened old man and the hurt look on Delia's face when Ezra had shoved her. But what else could he have done to make her get out of harm's way? It was the only way he could save her and the Brewsters.

In the dark, moonless night, he could barely see Miss May's form or the tree that harbored them, much less the landscape below. What was left of their clothing clung to them, tearing at their scraped skin as the fabric dried.

"We can't get down from here until morning," he said, "so let's ease down to sit where these branches spread out."

"Oh, I don' know if my legs'll bend. They feel froze stiff."

"Let's give it a try, ma'am. We don't want to fall out of the tree while we're sleeping." He urged her with a little pressure of his knee against the back of hers.

"Now, boy, don' you be gittin' fresh." She chuckled in a shaky but warm tone.

Right then he knew she would be all right. "No, ma'am, I won't."

With some difficulty, they worked their way down to straddle the large branch. Ezra leaned back against the main tree trunk, and Miss May leaned against him. He held on to her, grateful that his arms could be in a different position. Throughout the night, he fought sleep, dozing off from time to time, then shaking himself awake to keep watch over Miss May.

Dawn revealed a damaged creek bed and a hillside landscape with broken trees and animal carcasses strewn about. It also showed them how high up in the tree they were.

"Oh, Lawdy, why don' You jes' take me home now." Miss May shook her head in dismay. "Ezra, honey, you jes' gonna have ta leave me. Ain't no way I can git down from here."

Ezra peered down at the distance to the rocky ground—fifteen feet or more. There wasn't a single branch below them that might help them get down. He expelled a long, whistling sigh, but then regretted showing his lack of faith.

"Now, Miss May, you know the Lord didn't keep us alive through the flood and all through the night without having a plan for us." Brave words for her benefit, yet he could not imagine how he would get this fragile little lady out of the tree without running the risk of hurting her. He would have enough trouble getting himself down.

Miss May took a turn at sighing. "Dat's so right, son. Now, Lawd, I'm sorry for my unbelief. But if You please, can You git us down soon? I gots ta git to my Willard afo' he thinks I'm dead."

"Amen," Ezra said in a cheerful tone. But deep inside, he could not help but wonder how God planned to rescue them without angels flying down from heaven to carry them to the ground.

In the early morning, just as the sun broke over the far plains, Delia sat on the hilltop and held on to Mr. Willard, rocking him gently. "Don't worry, don't worry," she hummed, despite her own despair. Miz May had been the best thing ever to come into her life. Why'd she have to drown?

"Lawdy, Lawdy, have mercy on an old man." Mr. Willard wept with choking sobs. "Let me die and be with my May."

Frederick hovered nearby and dug his toe into the dirt. "Mr. Willard, if you die, who's gonna help me make somethin' of that deer skin?"

Delia had seen the skin wash away in the flood, but she didn't tell the boy.

Alice joined him. "Yo' chi'drun'll be lookin' for you up in Boston. Don' make them lose both o' you."

Mr. Willard rubbed his shirtsleeve across his eyes and nodded. "Can somebody write? Can somebody take 'em a letter from me?"

"No suh," Alice said. "The only one who knew how ta write was that soldier fella, and he's gone, too. You gotta tell 'em yourself." She eyed Delia and raised her eyebrows.

Delia couldn't guess what she was supposed to say.

"Look what I found hangin' in a tree." Adam came running up to the group. "It's Miz May's bag." He held up the wet patchwork bundle.

Mr. Willard held out his arms and grabbed the bag, paying no mind to how it drenched his shirt. "May, May, honey. It's all I got left o' you."

"Let's take a look, old man." Jack reached out his hand for the bag. "There'll be some things we all can use in that."

Mr. Willard leaned against Delia. "No suh. This is all I have left of my May."

"Let him alone." Delia glared at Jack, wondering where she'd found the courage to talk like that to the man standing above her.

"Yeah, leave him alone." Adam, small as he was, stood with his chest puffed out in defiance.

Without a word, Leviticus and Alice stepped up on either side of Adam.

"'Sides that," Adam said, "you got Ezra's knapsack and gun. What mo' you want?"

Jack eyed them all and worked his jaw for a bit. Then he lifted his hands, palms toward them in a peaceable manner. "Now, now, listen, folks. Every group needs a leader, and a leader needs to take stock for the good of everybody."

"We did fine afore you came," Adam muttered.

"Who caught them fish, boy?" Jack glared at him. "Who built that shelter? You know how to do all that?"

Adam seemed to get littler. "No suh."

Leviticus scratched his chin. "Well, suh, I s'pose we do need a leader, like you say. I don' rightly know what we ought to do next."

Jack lifted his head and stared around the group. Delia wasn't too sure she liked the way he was smiling.

"I know a place just a little ways south of here on the Pacolet River, down near Spartanburg," Jack said. "It's a place where we all can get work. We'll have a place to sleep and food to eat. All we have to do is help the folks get their crops planted and take care of livestock."

Everybody looked at him and then at each other.

"Come on, now. Y'all ain't scared of a little work, are you?"

Delia felt a chill that went clear down to her stomach. Did he mean to drag them all back to being slaves? She looked around at the group. The others seemed to like his idea.

"Did Spartanburg git burned to the ground by the Yankees, like Columbia?" Leviticus asked.

"Not that I know of. I ain't been down there since before the war." Jack shrugged and grinned. "White folks is a little desperate to get workers nowadays. They'll treat you right. You can leave if you don't like it. What do you say?"

"Well," Leviticus said, "we can get our stren'th back...and maybe earn a little money. At least git some mo' food fo' the road."

The others voiced their approval of the idea. All except Mr. Willard. He just sat there beside Delia on the ground and stared off in the distance.

"Mr. Willard, sir." Delia hugged him close, just like Miz May had done to comfort her. "You want to go to this place he's talkin' about? You could rest your bones there for a spell."

He looked at her through watery eyes and sniffed deeply. "I reckon if ever'body else is goin', I'll go, too. Can't go to Boston by myself."

Something inside Delia kicked like a horse, and she got mad. "Mr. Willard, we can go do plantin' for those folks, work for them long enough to get some decent vittles to get our stren'th back. But I promise you one thing. You and me is goin' to Boston come hell or high water. High water already came our way, so I guess we just got hell to deal with."

Mr. Willard's eyes let off a sad, sweet feeling. "Honey, no use ta talk that way. I see what the Lawd wants o' me...and you, too. He wants us ta take care of each other. You awright wid dat?"

Delia didn't quite catch all his meaning, but she nodded anyway. "Yessuh. I'm awright with that." But as far as she was concerned, the Lord had nothing to do with it.

CHAPTER EIGHT

"*I* guess I should have jumped down this morning when I still had some strength." Ezra's words scraped through his parched throat. He felt so tired, he thought he might fall out of the tree and take Miss May with him. He would not tell her he feared she might fall without him to steady her. "Then I could have gone for help."

"I wouldn't want you to break yo' legs on my account." Her voice sounded weak, and she leaned against him lethargically.

The sun shone through the broken tree branches. Ezra could not see a single cloud on the horizon. No afternoon rain would come to slake their thirst. It seemed as though nature had decided to stay calm for a while.

As the day had worn on, he'd begun to feel every bump and scrape he'd received in the flood. Although Miss May did not complain, he thought surely she must feel her own wounds. Their clothes had dried in the warm spring breeze, but they themselves were grimy, and both he and Miss May had lost their shoes in the flood. In the nearby field, where mud lay over the grass like a torn blanket, buzzards dined on animal carcasses. Ezra thought that more than one of the disgusting creatures were eyeing the two of them as tomorrow's breakfast. What more could go wrong?

"A little mercy here, please, Lord," he mumbled.

Miss May jumped. "What's that?"

"I'm sorry. I didn't mean to wake you."

"You didn't, boy. What's that sound? Way off thataway?" She pointed toward the unflooded woods to the south, where a road led through the trees and into a meadow.

Ezra strained to listen and then chuckled. "Your hearing certainly is excellent. Sounds like horses and wagons and…marching men." He knew the sounds of soldiers moving forward in formation.

"You s'pose we can git dem over here to hep us?" A note of hope graced her weak voice.

He gently patted her shoulder. "We'll give it our best try."

She pulled in a quick breath. "You don' s'pose they's Southerners?"

He swallowed the fear her question evoked. "All we can do is wait to find out." Most of the Southerners he'd encountered were not coming home in formation but rather straggled home the best they could. Furthermore, these troops were headed north, not south.

"Now, don' holler too soon, less'n yo' voice give out." Miss May wriggled where she sat, though, betraying her desire to cry for help right away.

Ezra fought his own inclination to cry out as soon as the troops tramped out of the forest and into the meadow. Through the broken branches of their treetop refuge, they could see blue-uniformed men marching in fairly even lines over the rough terrain. A colonel on a bay stallion rode in front, and several other officers followed him. At the back of several hundred or so foot soldiers—perhaps up to a regiment—

various types of wagons rattled noisily along, undoubtedly filled with provisions for the troops.

"Glory be," Miss May cried. "Thank You, Lawd."

"Glory be," Ezra echoed, but with some reservation. He and his fellow black soldiers of the 54th Massachusetts Regiment had endured many indignities from white Union troops. Would these men treat them any better? *Lord, please let them be good men.* Then he realized they would not know he was a soldier. He could hold back that bit of information.

No, it was his duty to report to the colonel, just as any man separated from his unit must do upon finding another company. But if they insisted he join them, where would that leave Miss May? He lifted another silent prayer right before he began to yell.

"Help!" He pulled his once-white handkerchief from his pants pocket and waved it through the branches. "Help us."

"Hep!" Miss May cried. "Hep, hep!"

The men gave no indication they heard the frantic calls or saw the waving. It appeared that they would pass by only fifty yards away and never even know of the two unfortunate souls they might have saved.

"Help!" Gripping the tree branch to keep from tumbling over, Ezra leaned toward them as far as he could without knocking Miss May to the ground. The bellowing came from so deep inside him that Ezra thought he'd torn the insides of his throat.

Two of the men on horseback turned their heads. Heartened, Ezra and Miss May yelled as loud as they could, although their voices had nearly given out.

The two men seemed to confer with their colonel. He nodded, and they spurred their horses across the meadow to the tree.

"Now, what kind of mess have you two darkies got yourself into?" The young, brown-haired lieutenant grinned up into the tree, his tone condescending and perhaps a little cruel, like the sneer on his beardless face.

Ezra felt a flicker of fear. Maybe it would be better to die stranded in a tree rather than hanging from its branches.

"Shut up, George." The red-haired major looked up with a kinder expression on his well-lined face. "Did the flood wash you up there?"

"Yes *sir*," Ezra said.

"That must have been horrifying. You're lucky to be alive. Don't worry. We'll get you down." The major turned to the other man. "Lieutenant, go tell Colonel Rule we need one of those sutlers' wagons over here."

"Yes sir." The sneering man rode away.

"Thank you, sir." Ezra could not entirely give in to relief.

"Bless you, boy." Miss May seemed to have no trouble trusting the soldier.

"My name's Hutchins." The major pulled out a canteen from the supply bundle behind him. Urging his horse close to the tree, he climbed to his feet in the saddle, leaned against the trunk, and tried to hand the canteen to Ezra. But he was not tall enough, and Ezra could not lean very far down, so the effort proved fruitless.

"I'm sorry. We'll get you water as soon as we can." The disappointment clouding his eyes told Ezra this was a good man. But what about the others?

The sutler's tall, hard-topped wagon proved to be the answer to their prayers. The two soldiers stood on the roof and reached up as Ezra helped the woman down, doing his best to help her maintain a certain dignity. When his turn came, he was shocked at how weak his arms were, but with the other men's assistance, he did not fall. Surrounded by helpful soldiers, equally weary Ezra and Miss May made their way to the grassy meadow. There they sat on the ground and shook from relief, even as they drank deeply of stale canteen water.

Ezra wiped his mouth on his shirtsleeve before realizing how dirty it was. He brushed the soil from his face and exhaled in relief that the worst of their ordeal was over. Maybe he could repay the soldiers' kindness by showing them the springs where they could get fresh water. They'd have to dig out the flood damage, but it would be worth it to have that excellent water to drink. But a glance up into the hills revealed how far from the camp they had been swept.

The soldiers had broken ranks and sat on the grass. They watched Ezra and Miss May with curiosity—and perhaps, gratitude—for this rest from their march. Some smoked pipes or rolled cigarettes. Others played baseball in the clearing. The officers had dismounted from their horses and now conferred in the shade of nearby trees. From their gestures and the way they surveyed the landscape, they seemed to be considering whether or not to set up camp.

"How about something to eat?" The sutler knelt beside them. "I got stew and biscuits left from last night's supper or cold provisions from today's dinner."

Officers' food. The foot soldiers usually fixed their own mess. Ezra could feel his stomach cry out to be filled.

"Miss May, what will you have?" he asked.

She laughed. "It'll be manna from heaven, no matter which'n we have. But I sure could savor a bite o' that stew."

"And you, boy?" The bearded, well-fed sutler looked at Ezra.

He cleared his throat. "Uh, if it's not too much trouble, may I see the colonel before I eat?" An enlisted man did not dare eat officers' food unless he was granted special permission.

The sutler pawed at his scraggly beard. "Well, I s'pose so. Henry...." He beckoned to his Negro helper, who hurried over.

"Yessuh."

"Would you get this old granny some stew and biscuits? I'm taking this boy to the colonel."

Assured that Miss May was in good hands, Ezra followed the sutler. As they approached the group of officers, he felt his heart in his throat. Strange how fear could give him energy in spite of his hunger and weakness.

As Ezra passed the soldiers, their stares burned into him, but he would behave properly, no matter what. "Be a gentleman," his father had often advised him. "That's the only way to earn respect."

The sutler caught the colonel's attention. "Colonel Rule, 'scuse the interruption, but this boy asked to speak with you, sir."

"Yes, what is it, boy?" The colonel twirled his waxed mustache and stared down his nose at Ezra.

Ezra pulled himself up to his full height and held his right hand to his forehead in a salute. "Corporal Ezra Johns, 54th Massachusetts Regiment, reporting for duty, sir."

✦❖❁❖✦

Delia walked beside Mr. Willard at the back of the group. Jack seemed to know right where he was going, and she didn't like that one bit. It had taken her a long time to get up the courage to run away from the plantation. Would a Negro man lead his own people right back into slavery? Maybe she should run again. But every time she thought about it, she looked at brave old Mr. Willard hobbling along on his swollen ankles, and she couldn't leave him. She would keep her promise to help him get to Boston. Besides, she was the only one he trusted to carry Miz May's patchwork bag, so she had to stay with him. It felt good to be trusted instead of scolded for every little thing she did or didn't do.

When the sun reached its highest, they stopped under some trees to forage for food. Dandelion greens and roots were the only thing they could find. Jack tried to shoot a rabbit, but when he missed on the first shot, rabbits and quail and all sorts of critters ran or flew for safer places. Ezra would never have missed that shot.

During their walk, Delia had spent most of her time thinking about how to help Mr. Willard. Now that they sat around a campfire boiling greens in the only pot they'd been able to save from the flood, she kept thinking about the handsome soldier who'd led them for those few days. He was a quiet sort. Though it seemed he hadn't liked her much, he'd been a good man, of that she felt sure. He'd been kind to the old folks and played with little Frederick. It cut into her heart to think of him dying in the flood.

Enjoying the pleasant smell of the burning wood, Delia broke off bits of a twig and tossed them into the flames. That helped her think. She didn't like Jack, and she couldn't understand why he liked her. Or pretended to like her. She knew enough about men and women to know she couldn't trust those big smiles, 'specially after what Miz May said about watching out. Beulah had told her the same thing, and now she figured it must be true.

Delia was the only female around who didn't have a husband. Jack'd say all kinds of nice things to her, but she knew better than to like him back. She recalled seeing boys talk real nice like that to some of the older girls on the plantation. Once they got what they wanted, they'd go off after a different girl. Delia wondered if Ezra would do that sort of thing.

But no use wondering. Ezra was dead. And all the sadness in the world wouldn't bring him or Miz May back. To give it all an end, she flung the last of her stick into the fire and watched it burn down to nothing.

Once the food was done, they all sat in a circle around the campfire, and each person took a turn dipping into the greens, with Jack being first and poor ol' Mr. Willard being last. Delia sat beside him and made sure he had several good bites left in the pan. But he had no heart to eat, so she saved it to give him later.

Halfway through their afternoon walk toward the promised work, she slipped into a daze, wondering if it had all been a dream— running away, meeting Miz May, and meeting the handsome soldier she'd been drawn to from the moment she first saw him.

What difference did it make? What was the use of hoping for anything when she knew deep in her heart that things would never change for her? She'd always be a slave to what other people told her to do. If not for Mr. Willard needing her, she'd wonder what use there was in living.

As the sun started setting, Jack fell back from the front of the group and slowed his pace to hers.

"Go on, old man." He tapped Mr. Willard on the shoulder, none too softly.

Mr. Willard frowned at Jack and then at Delia. "Awright." He limped ahead to catch up with Frederick.

"Ol' fool." Jack jerked his head toward Mr. Willard.

"No, he ain't." Delia couldn't believe her own courage. "He's a good man."

"Shor' he is. I didn't mean nothin' by it." Jack grinned at her and blinked his big black eyes. "Ain't nobody ever tol' you what a pretty little thing you are?"

Delia felt her stomach turn. Miz May's words haunted her. *Watch out.* But what girl wouldn't want a man to tell her she was pretty? Even a girl who knew it wasn't true would still want to hear it.

"My ol' mistress used to tell her daughter 'pretty is as pretty does.'" Delia always wondered if Missus really knew how ugly Miz Suzanne's doings were.

Jack threw back his head and laughed. "Ol' wives' tale, gal. Ol' wives tale. Nobody cares about that stuff anymore. We're free, and we do what we want."

Delia felt a chill—one that was not at all pleasant—sweep down her back.

Watch out. Miz May might as well be walking beside her, warning her not to let this man get on her good side.

"What I want to do is walk with Mr. Willard." Again she wondered where she'd found courage to talk to him like that.

Jack laughed again. "Awright. You jus' take your time, 'cause I got all the time in the world."

He moved up to the head of the small procession, and Mr. Willard fell back in step with her. After they'd walked a few hundred yards, he reached into his pocket and pulled out his folding knife.

"Miz May would want me to give this to you, chile." He gave her a stern look. "You watch out, now. An' if'n you need to, you use it."

Reluctantly, but with a different kind of shiver running down her spine, she took the knife and slipped it into her skirt pocket.

CHAPTER NINE

*E*zra determined to hold his salute until Colonel Rule returned one. But the tall, brown-haired man simply stared at him, his mouth slightly open as if he could not quite grasp what Ezra had said. Maybe he was shocked by Ezra's clothing or offended by his smell. Maybe the man despised Negroes.

After several uncomfortable moments, the red-haired major cleared his throat, and the colonel shook off his momentary stupor to offer an indifferent salute in return. Ezra dropped his arm to his side and sent up a prayer of thanks. He could not have held it up much longer. In addition to hunger and exhaustion, he now felt every bruise and scrape from the flood.

"Fifty-fourth, you say?" The colonel frowned, and he gave Ezra a sidelong glare. "Why aren't you with your regiment, boy?" He studied Ezra up and down. His eyes rested on the frayed trousers. "Where's the rest of your uniform?"

"Sir, I became separated from my unit several weeks ago during a skirmish near Abbeville and...."

"Why didn't you try to find them?"

"I did, sir, but they'd moved out. Then I heard the war was over, and I'm assuming they're headed back to Boston. As for the rest of my uniform, sir, it was lost in the flood."

Again the colonel frowned and twirled his mustache. "Who's your commanding officer? Where'd you fight?"

"Colonel Hallowell, sir. Florida, sir, then down in Honey Hill and Boykin's Mill, Charleston and Savannah." Ezra knew if he did not eat soon, he'd collapse at the colonel's feet.

"Where in Florida?" barked the colonel.

"Olustee, sir."

The officer straightened just a little. "Well, you pronounced it right. What was your position at Olustee?"

Ezra swallowed hard. "Rear guard, sir."

Colonel Rule drew himself up to attention. "Soldier, I was at Olustee. As our rear guard, the 54th saved our hides. You have my gratitude." He gave Ezra a crisp salute. "Where's that sutler? Get this soldier something to eat. Get him some clean clothes to wear and some boots."

"Thank you, sir." Ezra saluted weakly, hoping his legs did not give out from weariness and relief.

"Begging your pardon, sir." The ill-mannered lieutenant stepped forward. "Are you going to believe this…this *Negro*, just on his word?" His voice resonated with contempt.

Ezra did not have the energy to be offended by the man's rudeness, but he did feel certain the lieutenant had another word in mind for him.

The colonel stared at the younger man for a moment. "Lieutenant, you know as well as I do that soldiers often get separated from their units. In a time when mayhem and speculation rule and the truth about any particular battle is hard to find, this man knows his commanding officer and the exact positions and order of his regiment's engagements. That's enough for me." He glanced at the other officers. "Furthermore, he sounds more educated than any of you. Yes, I believe him."

The lieutenant scowled at Ezra but said no more. One or two of the other officers chuckled.

Colonel Rule turned back to Ezra. "Soldier, I don't know where your regiment is right now, but I give you my permission to continue on home to Boston. I'll write orders for you so you won't be charged with desertion."

"Thank you, sir." *Thank You, Lord.* He had not once considered the possibility of being thought a deserter.

"I said get this man some clothes," the colonel shouted toward the sutler's wagon.

The rotund, bearded supply man lumbered over to Ezra. "Come on, boy. After you eat, I'll get you somethin' to wear."

"Sutler!" The colonel strode over to the man and hovered above him. "This isn't a boy. This is a man and a soldier. See to it that you treat him with respect."

"Yes sir." Even though he was a civilian, the sutler offered a clumsy salute. He motioned to Ezra to follow him. "This way, sir."

In the shade of his tall wagon, Miss May sat dozing against the back wheel. Ezra sat beside her and quickly devoured a plate of stew and two hard biscuits. He breathed in the fresh spring air and eased into a little nap.

When the two of them awoke, they did so to the sight of a fully bivouacked company of soldiers. White tents had been set up in tidy rows, and soldiers went about their various duties. Ezra wondered if he and Miss May should be on their way before the colonel changed his mind and conscripted him. But he decided that having another filling meal and a good night's sleep would be a better plan.

After much discussion, he and Grady, the sutler, agreed that civilian clothes would be the best choice for traveling through the South. Among his used goods, Grady found some garments large enough for Ezra and others small enough for Miss May. He also offered a little lye soap and some salve for their wounds.

Ezra and Miss May returned to the now-quiet creek where each found a private place to bathe and don their new clothing.

"Won't my Willard be surprised to see me in men's clothes?" Miss May laughed with delight and stared down at her trousers and half-boots. "How do I look, son?"

"Fine and dandy, Miss May." Ezra was relieved at her quick recovery and not a little amazed at her endurance. He would surely never complain about being tired around her. Nor would he complain that his brown trousers were a little too big around the waist and his gray shirt a little snug across the chest. At least his new boots fit.

Late in the afternoon, he stood watching the soldiers resume their baseball game. The ball came flying his way, and instinctively he thrust out his hand and grabbed it. Despite his sore arms, he flung the ball toward first base. The baseman caught it, and the runner was out. Hearty protests and several rude insults bellowed forth from the team at bat, but the team in the field shouted hurrahs.

"You can play with us anytime, fella," the pitcher said.

To avoid a brawl, the sergeant acting as umpire allowed the batter another chance at home base. No one protested when Ezra took a place in the outfield or when his team came to bat and he took a turn. He knocked the ball almost into the woods and made it to third base before the fielder threw the ball to home. It seemed to him that the other team now played with more than just friendly competitiveness.

But at the end of the inning, just as he was about to quit to avoid conflict, Corporal Ballinger, his team's pitcher, offered him the ball.

"Let's see what you can do with this." Ballinger's pale blue eyes sent out a challenge.

Ezra could not refuse. He'd watched the man deliver his underhand pitches in New York style. *Didn't this fellow know that baseball began in Massachusetts and that Boston players thought underhand pitching was unmanly?* Ezra would not be the one to tell him.

Standing in the pitcher's position, he wound up and threw the ball overhand directly into the catcher's hands. The batter swung high and late, then cursed at Ezra.

"Throw it the right way, darkie." His scowl showed he meant business.

"Sorry. That's Massachusetts style. It's all I know."

"Hey, will you show me how to do that?" Ballinger called from the sidelines.

"Be glad to." Ezra grinned. "Sergeant, do I have to pitch underhanded—the New York way?"

The umpire scratched his head. "I don't reckon so. Do whatever's legal to win. I hear tell this overhand throwing is what everybody's doin' these days anyway."

Having that affirmation, Ezra continued to throw until he had three men up, three men out. With each effort, his aching arms seemed to loosen up and reclaim an old habit. Maybe this exercise was just what he needed after holding on to that tree and Miss May for so many long hours.

Mess was called shortly thereafter, but several men crowded around Ezra and asked for tips on how to throw overhand. In exchange, one private gave him a baseball.

"Thank you, soldier." Ezra turned the hard ball in his hands. This was much better for teaching Frederick than the ball he'd planned to make from deer insides.

"Aw, don't mention it." The private seemed embarrassed. "I got an extra one."

After he wandered off, Ballinger approached Ezra again. In his hands, he held something wrapped in a woolen blanket and seemed as embarrassed as the private.

"Look here, I need to see some more of that overhand throwing. We're campin' here for a couple of days waitin' for the rest of the regiment to meet up with us. You stick around and show me how you hold the ball, and I'll give you what I got in this." He held out the bundle.

"You don't have to give me anything." Ezra grinned at him. "I'm always happy to show a fellow soldier something about baseball."

Ballinger looked off in the distance and took in a deep breath. "Look here, a man's gotta have something to trade for what he gets."

Ezra studied him for a moment. Maybe he was being foolish to turn down the trade. The blanket would keep Miss May warm at night, and whatever was inside might also help on their journey. If nothing else, Ballinger seemed to need to give it to him.

"I understand." He reached out and took the bundle. "Thank you. I'll see you after supper."

Ballinger cleared his throat. "Umm, that *thing* inside there...."

"Yes?" A nervous flutter swept through Ezra's stomach.

"Umm, I took it off a rebel corpse after Antietam. I planned to keep it for my son, if I ever have one. But I think you might need it now."

Ezra remembered his lost uniform jacket and his hopes of passing it on to a son. "I understand," he repeated. "Maybe after I get home, I could return it. Where're you from?"

"Massachusetts. New Bedford."

Ezra laughed. "I'm from Boston. I'll look for you when your regiment returns."

Ballinger gave him a crooked grin. "Sure thing. See you after supper."

"Sure thing," Ezra echoed.

He hurried back to the sutler's wagon, where Miss May bustled about helping Grady and Henry fix their evening meal.

"Now, son, you jes' set down by the wagon," she said, "and I'll bring you somethin' to eat."

"Miss May, I'm not going to let you wait on me." He gave her a peck on the cheek. "*You* sit down, and I'll serve you."

She chuckled. "Chile, you done saved my life. Let me do somethin' fo' you."

He saw the earnestness in her eyes. Like Ballinger, for her own self-respect, she needed to do something for him. "Yes, ma'am."

As he eased himself down by the wagon wheel, every muscle in his body seemed to cry out, but he would not complain. It had been a rough two days, but the Lord had seen them through. With a contented sigh, he studied his new acquisition. The woolen blanket had seen some wear and more than a few washings. It had shrunk to a good, tight weave but still felt soft enough to wrap around Miss May at night. He untied the leather string around it and slowly unwrapped the blanket to see what was inside. When he saw it, he laughed to himself. Never had he seen such a large, well cared-for Bowie knife. This would be an excellent aid to their survival in the days to come. Even its tan leather sheath had been oiled to a shine.

"*Thank You, Lord.*"

CHAPTER TEN

Delia, Alice, and Frederick gathered more dandelion greens for supper while Mr. Willard started the fire. He'd refused to turn over Miz May's matches to Jack, making Jack hopping mad at him. Then Jack settled down a bit and took off hunting with Adam and Leviticus. Delia sure hoped he got something, because she was awful tired of greens.

A single gunshot sounded in the distance, followed by a whoop. Soon the three men came back to camp with two rabbits.

"How'd you git two?" Frederick danced with excitement. "I jus' heard one shot."

"Jack missed 'em both," Adam said, "but Leviticus and I caught 'em as they was runnin' away and wrung their necks."

Jack scowled. "That was my plan all along. Why'd you think I had you stand out in the field that way?"

Delia bit her lips to keep from laughing. She felt a bit sorry for Jack and his bad aim.

"I'll be skinnin' these now." Grabbing the rabbits from the other men, Jack walked past Delia and brushed his arm against her. "I'll be talkin' to you this evenin', pretty girl."

She shuddered at his touch and wondered what he wanted to talk to her about. Whatever it was, she didn't want to hear it.

Jack had no trouble skinning the rabbits with that big knife of his. Soon they were sizzling above the flames next to the greens boiling in the pan. Jack scooped up the innards in the skins and carried them away from the campsite.

Mr. Willard came over to where Delia sat. "I got a plan." He huffed as he lowered himself to the ground beside her.

"Yessuh? What's that?" She looked into his aged face with interest.

"Come nightfall, before we all git ready to lay down fo' the night, you wait till Jack's off in the woods—you know what I mean? Then you scoot off and find you a place to sleep where he can't find you."

The solemn look in his eyes sent a chill through Delia. "Where would I go?"

He frowned and stared off for a bit. "Whilst you was out gittin' the greens, did you see any little spot that you might hide in?"

"I wasn't lookin' for a spot like that." She thought for a bit. "Well, I did see a skunk burrowed in under some bushes over yonder." She pointed toward the woods. "Didn't get too close, o'course, or you'd already know it."

Mr. Willard laughed, then quickly got quiet. "Tst." He jerked his head toward Jack, who'd just returned to camp.

"You do what I tol' you, chile, then come back in the mornin'." Mr. Willard clambered to his feet and went to check on the rabbits.

All through supper, Delia's stomach churned with fear. Did she dare run off that way? Would Jack be mad and take it out on Mr. Willard? But why would he? He'd already said they were free and could do what they wanted. One thing she didn't want was Jack all over her.

After they'd finished eating, Jack pulled Ezra's knapsack in front of him. "Time to see what we got in here besides powder and shot." He untied the straps, threw back the flap, and looked inside.

Delia's stomach had a new reason to be unsettled. It seemed like violating the dead for Jack to dig into Ezra's things. She saw Mr. Willard frown, but everyone else just seemed curious.

"Hmph. Here's somethin' we don't need." Jack lifted out a black book and tossed it into the smoldering fire.

Mr. Willard gasped and lunged for it, but Adam beat him to it. He pulled the book out just as flames started to lick its leather cover.

"Don't you know this is a Bible?" Adam smacked the book to stop its burning. "I recollect seein' one of these when the massuh took us all to the church meetin'."

Jack snorted in his rude way. "What you gonna do with that? Can you read?"

"No, but we might be able to sell it to somebody who can read." Adam held it close. "I'll keep it if'n you don't want to carry it."

"That's the Word o' God." Mr. Willard whispered, his eyes watering. "You treat it with respect, boy."

"Yessuh, I will." Adam ran his hand over the cover. "It's awright now. Just a little scorched." He placed it in his own cloth bag.

Jack laughed. "Who'd buy that anyways?" He continued to dig in Ezra's bag. "Now here's somethin' more useful." He pulled out the soldier's faded blue jacket and stood to shake it and put it on. "Just fits. How do I look?" He strutted around the campfire for a bit.

"Looks mighty fine, sir," Leviticus said. "Only trouble is, some white Southerner might shoot you fo' fightin' against 'em."

Jack looked like he was considering that idea. He pulled off the jacket and started to throw it in the fire. Then he turned to Adam. "You want this, too?"

Adam laughed. "No suh. I don' want no trouble with nobody."

Jack held it over the fire. "Here goes, then."

"I'll take it." Delia said the words without thinking.

Jack shot her a look. "Wearin' his coat ain't gonna bring him back." He stared at her with a mean grin.

"Jus' give it to me." She tried to sound firm, like Miz May, but her voice trembled.

"Awright, awright." He walked over and knelt down to put the coat around her. His hands stayed on her shoulders, and his hot breath sent a shiver down her back. "Why didn't you tell me you was cold? I can keep you warm."

She tried to shrink down and disappear, like she'd always tried to do when Miz Suzanne beat her. But he held on, just like her former mistress.

"Let her be." Mr. Willard got up and gripped Jack's arm.

Jack shook him off. "Mind yo' own business, old man." He got back up but bent down again and brushed her cheek.

She turned away, and he chuckled as he went back to dig in Ezra's pack.

Leviticus stood up and stretched. "Think I'll get some rest. C'mon, Alice, Frederick. Let's figger out where we're gonna sleep."

The others in the group went about getting ready for the night.

Like always, they had a men's side and a women's side where everybody could go do their business. The sun had gone down behind the hills, and just a little daylight lit the area. Jack took a turn going to the men's side. Mr. Willard looked at Delia and lowered his chin. She lifted her eyebrows just a little so as not to give away their plan, then she wandered toward the women's side.

Walking quiet-like, she found the big bushes where the skunks lived. Sure enough, they were burrowed in right where she'd seen them before. A mother skunk and several babies peeked out at her with tiny bright eyes that reminded her of little embers from the fire. The faint, musky smell of the animals tickled her nose. She circled wide to keep from disturbing them and found a good spot about ten feet away behind the same row of bushes.

The skunks didn't seem to mind her being there, so she made her own little burrow. She scooped last year's brush and moldy leaves into a small pile and sent bugs and ground spiders skittering away in all directions.

The mother skunk lumbered out of the burrow and began to eat the bugs. As she came close to Delia, she stopped and stared a minute, almost as if she was thanking her for the feast. Then she went back to eating.

"Glad to help," Delia whispered. "Now if you can jus' do for me, I'll be grateful, too." She covered the pile of leaves with the square of brown cloth Miz May had given her. Then she snuggled into Ezra's large jacket and lay down. His scent still lingered on the wool. It was an earthy, working-man smell, but it was also a whole lot better than the skunk. Delia almost chuckled.

Would Jack be able to see her? In the deepening shadows, she couldn't make out the lines of her brown skirt, but her paler face might catch a bit of light. How could she hide it?

"Delia, honey."

She jumped. Fear shot through her at the sound of Jack's voice. He was about twenty feet away. He sounded friendly enough, but she did not answer. Could he see her? Could he hear her teeth chatter? She clamped her mouth and held it shut real tight.

"Delia?"

His large body was a big, dark shape against the last bits of light in the sky.

"Come on out, girl. It's dangerous for you to be off by yo'self."

Delia curled up and covered her face with her arms. She could hear the leaves and brush beneath her rustling from her uncontrollable shaking. Surely Jack could hear them, too.

"Delia!"

She jumped again. Jack sounded mad now, almost like a snarling dog. The thud of his footsteps sounded closer.

Help me, Mama. Help me.

"Now, Delia, you git over here—hey, hey, hey! Git away, git away!" Jack's voice rose to high pitch, sounding almost like a creaky wheel.

Delia uncovered her eyes and saw him backing away, his hands stretched out in front of him. Between them, the mother skunk stamped her little feet and growled a low warning. Delia could see the broad white stripe down her back and tail; it was all fluffed out. Delia squeezed her jaw hard to keep from laughing despite her fear. Jack wasn't the only one who was mad.

Don' be a fool, Jack. Don' rile her anymore than she already is.

He stopped about thirty feet away. "Awright, girl, I done seen you, and you can just stay there. If that skunk gits you, don' be thinkin' you comin' back to my camp."

She thought he turned away, but he spoke again. "You'll be sorry, girl. You'll be sorry. You don' know what you missin'."

Delia tried to still her trembling body as relief swept through her. Jack was wrong. She knew exactly what she was missing, and it was something she wanted no part of.

Snuggling deep into Ezra's warm jacket, she saw the skunk's white stripe as she waddled back to her babies. Delia whispered, "Thank you, little mama." Then she rolled over and stared up toward the bright star rising in the east.

Thank you, Mama.

CHAPTER ELEVEN

The sound of rustling leaves crept into Delia's dreams. She woke up suddenly but kept her eyes shut. Close by, something—or somebody—was making a scratching sound. She took a quiet breath. Staying still, she slowly opened her eyelids. In the misty morning fog, she could barely make out a form in the bushes. About ten feet away, a chicken, brown and plump, was scratching some undergrowth into a pile. Delia watched with interest as the hen settled into the nest and wiggled and shuddered and pretty soon clucked out her pride at what she'd done. Then the critter got up without so much as looking at the brown egg she'd laid and started pecking around on the ground for her breakfast.

Delia eyed the egg. That'd be *her* breakfast once the hen got a little farther off.

Just when she started to get up, another kind of rustling started behind her. She slowly turned over and saw the mama skunk headed for the egg. Delia sat up, and the skunk stopped, fluffed herself up a bit, and let out a little growl. Delia swallowed hard. The skunk's musky smell was light right now, so she'd better not rile her.

"Awright, little mama, it's yours. I owe you for last night, and I sure ain't gonna fight you for it."

The skunk waddled over to the egg, cracked it open with her sharp teeth, and ate it all up before heading back to her babies.

Delia sighed. Now what? Her belly rumbled, and if she didn't get something to eat, she wouldn't go far this day.

The hen was still scratching for bugs, so she slowly got up and crept toward it with her brown cloth in hand. She guessed it was tame because it didn't run away. As quick as she could, she snatched up the bird, covered its head to keep from getting pecked, and wrung its neck in two seconds. Delia chuckled. She'd done this all her life back at the plantation. The hen didn't even have a chance to squawk.

"Now what?" This time she wondered out loud but in a soft whisper. Without matches, she couldn't cook the chicken. As much as she hated to do it, she'd have to go back to the camp. But that way she could share the chicken with Mr. Willard and the others. She'd give the old man a nice, juicy thigh and Frederick a drumstick. She picked up Ezra's jacket and headed back to the group, laughing at the thought of giving Jack the backbone.

The others were just getting up when she walked into the small clearing.

"Go on." Jack scowled at her. "Git. We don' want you and your skunk smell."

Delia glanced around with a smile and held up the chicken by its legs. "Y'all don't want me? Awright, then. Me and Mr. Willard'll just go over yonder and fix our breakfast."

Everybody but Jack hurried over to admire her catch.

"I don' smell no skunk," said Adam. "That's some fine chicken you got there, Miz Delia."

Mr. Willard winced as he walked, but a big smile lit up his dark face. "Chile, chile, look at you. Look at that fine fat chicken. You know how to git them feathers off?"

"Sure do. Been doin' it since I was six years old." She walked toward the small stream on the other side of the camp with Mr. Willard close behind.

"Awright, now." Jack caught up with her. "Old man, you git back there and start the fire. Girl, you give me that chicken, and I'll cut off its head." He reached out, but Delia turned so he couldn't take her prize.

"No. Git away." She felt pleased with her own braveness. She'd fight him hard for that chicken. "I got a knife, and I can fix it up jus' fine." She jerked her head back toward the camp. "*You* go start the fire." She turned away without waiting to see if he'd do what she said. The sound of his heavy footsteps began to fade behind her like he was going back to the camp.

"You done told him." Mr. Willard laughed, and his duck-quack voice sounded like music to her. "He jes' needs to know he can't bully folks."

"I s'pose." Delia knelt by the water and took Mr. Willard's knife from her pocket. She held the chicken down on a rock and with several quick strokes cut off the head. Then she held the body up to let the blood run out before washing the chicken in the stream. "You have a good night?" She eyed Mr. Willard as she started plucking feathers, a job she could do in her sleep.

He seemed to wilt a bit and let out a weary sigh. "I miss my May. She was a good, wise woman. Don' rightly know what I'll do without her." A big tear slipped down his cheek. He brushed it away. "I know the good Lawd has a reason for all He do, so I jes' have to go on with the work He give me. But my heart won' never stop achin'."

Delia nodded and swallowed a lump in her throat. "I still cry over my mama sometimes. She died when I was nine."

He shook his head. "Dat's awful, chile, jes' awful. Was it the fever dat took her?"

As she plucked, Delia laid the feathers in a pile so she could make a pillow. "No suh. She got on the bad side of the missus, and the missus had her beat. She died from it."

Mr. Willard made a funny sound in his throat, part cough and part swallow. He wiped his eyes and looked at her. "Lawdy, Lawdy, those folks is gonna have lots to answer fo'."

Delia plucked faster, wishing she hadn't said anything about Mama. "Yessuh," she said, silently wondering who those folks would answer to. She wouldn't ask Mr. Willard, because he'd just say they would answer to the Lord. She didn't want to hurt his feelings by saying she didn't believe in the Lord. If there was a God, why did He let all the bad stuff happen? But she wouldn't ask the old man that. Kind as he was, he'd just been a field hand. What did he know?

⋆╫┼╢⊛╟┼╫⋆

Ezra spent the morning teaching several of the soldiers how to throw overhand. Ballinger seemed to have a natural talent for it.

"With the war being over, they'll be hiring men for professional teams up north." The corporal spoke to Ezra as if they were old friends. "That'd be some job, wouldn't it?"

"Yes, it would." Ezra glanced toward the sutler's wagon where Miss May stood watching. "Well, it's time for me to go."

"What's your hurry?" Ballinger raised his eyebrows in a friendly way. "You could stay with us till we meet up with the rest of the regiment. Even travel up north with us."

Ezra shook his head. "As much as I appreciate your invitation, I need to get back on the road. Mrs. Brewster is depending on me to help her find her husband." He tilted his head toward Miss May.

Ballinger looked her way and then nodded. "I have a lot of respect for you, Ezra. I hope to meet up with you again some day." He reached out and grasped Ezra's hand firmly.

"Let's be sure we do that." Ezra met his grip with equal firmness.

Perhaps influenced by the well-liked, athletic Ballinger, other men approached Ezra to shake his hand farewell. Several pressed coins into his hands, and others gave him tins of food or a canteen or a compass. Even Colonel Rule donated a parting gift—a razor, strop, and lathering cup. Ezra gratefully accepted everything and went to collect Miss May.

"Son, look at what Henry done give me." She held open a knapsack with cooking supplies and some potatoes. "We's all ready to go find my Willard."

Ezra scratched his head in amazement. "These men certainly have been openhanded, haven't they? Who would think they'd treat...." He glanced around to be sure no one was listening. "I understand Henry's helping us out, but I'm just not used to such kind treatment from white people, not since I left home. Maybe they're so pleased that the war is over that they feel generous." He chuckled. "Maybe they just don't want to carry everything with them on the long trip home."

Miss May patted his arm and gave him a motherly smile. "Now, chile, don' go thinkin' such things. It's da Lawd who done spoke to their hearts. He give us favor in their sight like da Lawd done with

Moses. And like the chi'drun of Israel, we's goin' out laden with plenty so's we can git to the promised land."

"I believe you're right, Miss May. Here, let me carry that."

He took the canvas bag from her and put his treasures inside. Although not as well-made as his army-issued leather knapsack, it should be sufficient for their journey. He pulled its two straps over his shoulders and looped an arm in hers. They started northward across the meadow.

Just beyond the encampment, they found a road and decided to follow it.

"If we run into any trouble, we can take to the hills again." Ezra glanced at Miss May. "Is that all right with you?"

"Dat's awright with me. I jes' hope I can git me another walking stick. Willard carved that cedar stick fo' me more'n twenty years ago fo' Christmas. I sho' do miss it."

She limped along at her usual slow pace—and with her usual cheer.

"I'll keep an eye out for a good stick for you."

"Bless you, son."

Several wagons passed them, as well as other wanderers who traveled the roads on foot—farmers hauling hay, weary soldiers in faded gray uniforms, men of no particular description. In each case, Ezra guided Miss May to a safe place at the side of the road where they both bowed their heads respectfully. Some travelers cursed them but most ignored the two plainly dressed Negroes.

"I reckon they's hankering to git home," Miss May chuckled after four Confederate soldiers walked past without a word. "Ain't got no time to bother with coloreds headed north."

"Yes, ma'am, I suppose so." Ezra nodded his agreement. But he could not dismiss a nagging feeling that sooner or later they would run into a bitter, angry Southerner who might take his rage out on them.

CHAPTER TWELVE

The morning breeze was pleasant enough, and the trees lining the wide road protected the travelers from the heat of the sun. But Delia's heart seemed to sink lower in her chest with each mile they walked. They should be going north, not southeast.

"You sure you want to go to this place?" She glanced over at Mr. Willard. "Seems awful far to go for somethin' we're not sure about."

He pulled off his slouch hat and wiped his forehead with his sleeve. "Ain't nothin' sure, chile,'cept the Lawd." He plopped the hat back on and lifted his chin toward Jack, who walked ahead of the group. "He's a mite bossy, but I believe he'll git us some work, jes' like he said. Cain't go far without workin'. I been thinkin' we might earn enough money fo' us to take a train all the way to Boston."

"A train?" Delia's heart lifted off her stomach. "Wouldn't that be somethin'?" She'd never even seen a train.

"Sho' would." He chuckled but then wiped away a tear. "May woulda loved to ride a train."

Delia couldn't stand to see the old man in such grief. "You think we can git enough money for that?" She tried to make her voice sound hopeful, though she felt some tears trying to come out, too.

"Shh." Jack lifted his hand to halt the group. "Listen. Up ahead. We gotta git off the road and into the trees." He herded Leviticus and his family and Adam toward the bushy undergrowth beside the way.

Delia stopped and set her hand on Mr. Willard's arm. "What *is* that sound? It sure is all rattle and clatter."

He cocked his head to listen. "Mm, sounds to me like men and horses and all sorts of things. Must be soldiers comin' this way."

"Soldiers?" Delia stared up the winding road. "Yankee soldiers?"

"Come on, you two." Jack waved his hand and looked worried. He stepped over to Mr. Willard and took his arm to draw him into the bushes. "We gotta hide."

Standing in the middle of the road, Delia put her hands on her hips the way Beulah did when she was cross. "If it's Yankee soldiers, we don't got nothin' to be scared of." She tried to copy Beulah's sassy ways.

"Well, that's jus' it, gal." Jack rolled his eyes like he thought she was stupid. "You don' know if they's Yankees or southern. Now git over here."

Delia felt of a mind to give him a little more trouble, but she thought on what he said. Southern soldiers were a constant worry, so she hurried to take Mr. Willard's other arm. Then she and Jack helped him over the ditch beside the road.

Kneeling down behind a large bush, she listened with the others. "If they're Yankees," she whispered, "I'm gonna step out and say 'thank you' to them."

"If they's Yankees," Leviticus said, "I'm gonna ask 'em if they have anything we can eat."

Seated beside him, Adam patted his knapsack. "If they's Yankees, I'm gonna see if anybody wants to buy Ezra's Bible."

"Don' be fools." Jack scowled at each of them in turn. "Yankees don' give a lick about coloreds."

Delia felt her mean streak getting wider. Didn't Jack know it was the Yankees who'd set them free? "We'll see."

Sure enough, it was a long line of white soldiers wearing blue uniforms who marched up the road five men across. Every one of them carried a bulging knapsack on his back with all sorts of things hanging from it. The stomping, clattering noises got louder and louder, and dust flew up all over the place, 'specially from the horses ridden by two fancy-dressed men in front.

"They's the officers." Mr. Willard's eyes sparkled with respect.

"Here I go." Adam hopped up and pulled Ezra's Bible from his pack.

Delia wanted to reach out and grab the book, but she held back. No sense in cheating Adam out of a little money just because she still missed the man who'd owned it.

Adam jumped the ditch and ran to the roadside. He lifted up the Bible to one of the officers.

"You want to buy a Bible, sir?"

The officer glanced at him. "No, boy. Already have a Bible."

The other officer waved Adam away and kept on going. Adam's shoulders slumped a little, and Delia hurried out of the bushes to join him beside the road.

"Don' give up." She waved her hand at the passing men. "Hey, somebody please buy this Bible. We ain't got no money for food."

All of the passing soldiers looked her way. Some of them whistled as they went by.

"Hey, pretty girl, come with me," called one man. Others laughed or said rude words.

Delia thought the whole lot of them smelled like they needed a bath.

One soldier left his place in the line and ran up to another like he was asking him a question. Then he turned back and came over to Adam and Delia. To Delia's surprise, he was smiling.

"How much you asking?" The young blond soldier stared at the book and then looked Adam square in the eye like they were friends.

Adam swallowed. "Um, I don't rightly know how much to ask."

Jack came up beside Adam. "Five dollars." His upper lip curled in a sneer, and he looked down his nose at the soldier. Delia never saw a black man look at a white one like that without getting hit.

The soldier didn't seem bothered by Jack's rudeness. "Aw, shucks, I don't have that much." He started to turn away.

Delia nudged Adam. "Ask him how much can he pay," she whispered.

"How much can you pay?" Adam sent her a quick, grateful look and stepped toward the other man.

The soldier turned back. "I got two dollars left from last month's pay. I got an extra tin cup and some beef jerky."

Adam glanced at Delia, and she gave him a nod.

"That sounds good." He handed the book to the soldier and took what he offered.

"Where're you folks headed?" The soldier held the Bible close to his chest like it was a baby. He didn't seem in a hurry to get back to the others.

"We's goin' south of here to work on a farm." Adam pointed the way the soldiers had come from.

The man laughed. "Why, that's the wrong way, fella. You're free now. Why don't you go up north?" He glanced at Delia and touched the bill of his stubby little blue hat. "How do, miss?"

She stared at the ground. No white man had ever been so polite to her. "Fine, thank you, sir."

He cleared his throat. "Well, you folks think about going north." He took off his knapsack and tucked the Bible into it. "May the Lord watch over you on your journey."

As he ran back to his place in the line, Delia stared after him. Jack was wrong. Some whites did care about coloreds. Why, if that was how white folks treated Negroes up north, she didn't want to waste any time getting there.

❋

"Are you all right?" Ezra must have asked Miss May that question a hundred times since they'd set out from the army encampment that morning.

"I'm fine. I'm jes' fine." She smiled up at him, but her expression looked more like a grimace. Leaning on the oak stick he'd found for her, she stopped and took a deep breath. "Jes' smell them flowers." She bent her head toward a small field of spring wildflowers waving in the late afternoon breeze. "Thank You, Lawd, for the beauty of Yo' world."

"Amen." Ezra smiled, but he also watched her with concern. How much farther could she travel in one day? They should probably stop for the night fairly soon.

"Awright, then, let's git goin'."

"Yes, ma'am."

The wide road stretched past the field and into a wooded area. Despite the thick growth of trees that muffled most sounds, familiar noises wafted toward them on the breeze.

"Sounds like another army encampment up there." Ezra wished he could hurry ahead to see if they were friend or foe. But he would not leave her.

"Praise be." Miss May started to walk a little faster. "Let's git up there and see what the Lawd have planned fo' us with these folks."

Once again Miss May's faith had gently rebuked Ezra. He caught up with her and with each step felt his enthusiasm grow.

They emerged from the wooded area into a narrow meadow where a small company of Union soldiers had bivouacked.

"The officers should be over there." Ezra pointed to a large white tent. "I think I should report to the officer in charge." The thought worried him because this man might require him to stay with his fellow soldiers.

Miss May shook her head. "You got that paper from Colonel Rule sayin' you free to go?"

"Yes, ma'am." Ezra chuckled. He could guess what she was thinking.

"Den you don' need to be reportin' to nobody. You free to go."
She nodded her head decisively, as if that settled the matter.

"You're right, of course, Miss May. But I'll feel better if I speak
to the officer."

"Awright, den, but I's goin' with you."

Again he laughed. "Yes, ma'am." He shifted his knapsack
higher on his shoulders so he could more easily stand at attention
before the officer.

They drew the usual stares and comments as they tramped
across the uneven ground, but they'd learned to ignore such nonsense.
They approached the tent where a captain and a lieutenant conferred
at a table outside.

Ezra hesitated. Should he ask a sergeant or corporal to introduce
him? Before he could decide, the captain looked up and saw him. He
pulled a cigar from his mouth.

"Now what do you want?" The bearded, middle-aged man
scowled. "I'm so sick and tired of you begging darkies. Go on. Get
outa here. We can't feed every ex-slave in the South."

"Sir—" Ezra began.

"I said get out, and I mean get out." The man's bushy brown
eyebrows furrowed above his blazing blue eyes, and his jaw jutted out
like a mean bulldog's.

Ezra gulped back his fear. It had been some time since he'd
been yelled at by an officer. "Yessir." He flung up his right hand in
an instinctive salute and then realized how foolish he must look.
"Yes, boss." He gripped Miss May's elbow and wheeled her around.
"Let's go."

She glanced up at him with an unmistakable twinkle in her eye. "I tol' you, son." Then she laughed.

He heard the man cursing as they started away, walking back toward the road as fast as Miss May was able. Just before they reached it, a private with curly blond hair ran up to them. Ezra tensed and wondered if he should step in front of Miss May to protect her. But the young man gave them a big smile. Ezra glanced at Miss May. She did not look the least bit worried.

"Say, I'm sorry the captain was rude to you." His blue eyes exuded kindness. "He's got a lot on his mind. Are you folks hungry?"

Again Ezra looked at Miss May. She seemed to be taking all of this in stride.

"Bless you, son." She tottered a bit and leaned on her staff. "Yes, we's a mite hungry. Can I do some sewin' fo' you in exchange for a bite to eat?"

The soldier drew back a little, as if surprised by her offer. "Why, no, ma'am. The Lord commands us to feed the hungry. I count it a privilege to obey Him."

"That's very kind of you, sir." Ezra started to reach out his hand to him but could not bring himself to do so for fear he would be misunderstood.

"Come on over to my tent. I got some stew cooking." He led them toward the edge of the camp. "I got me a new Bible today. Bought it from some folks alongside the road. Would you like to stay around for Bible reading? I feel the call to be a preacher when I get home, and I figured I'd practice on these fellas." He waved his hand to take in the whole camp. "Some of them sure do need it more than others."

"Oh, chile." Miss May almost wept. "It's been so long since I hear'd the Word o' God. I'd be so blessed. Will you read to me about Moses and the chi'drun of Israel?"

The man gently patted her shoulder. "Yes, ma'am, if that's what you'd like to hear. But first, we got to get you fed." He stopped in front of a small tent where a cast-iron pot of stew simmered over a fire. Ezra thought he smelled a hint of boiled horse, but he decided not to ask what was cooking.

She eyed the pot with interest. "Feed da body, den feed da soul. I like dat."

The soldier laughed. "Yes, ma'am. That's just what I was thinking."

He knelt down to stir the stew, which, despite its smell, appeared to be mostly potatoes and greens, and not much of either. Yet he was willing to share it with the two weary wanderers.

Once again, Ezra felt rebuked for his lack of faith in God's care. But how could a Negro expect such kindness from a white man he did not know? Even now, some of the other soldiers who camped nearby sent angry looks their way. Ignoring them all, the young preacher-to-be whistled "A Mighty Fortress Is Our God" while he dished up the humble fare for Ezra and Miss May.

Ezra would do his best to never forget this man. And perhaps some day he'd find a way to return his kindness.

CHAPTER THIRTEEN

"*L*et my people go. Let my people go. Oh, how we cried out to the Lawd. And the Lawd done brought His chi'drun out of Egypt." Miss May's dark eyes glistened in the firelight, and she wiped a hand across her cheek.

"Yes, ma'am, He did." Jimmy, the blond, freckle-faced soldier, sat near her with the Bible open in his lap.

"That was some mighty fine readin', son. I jes' love dat story."

"I can understand why." Jimmy thumbed the pages reverently. "Ezra, do you have a favorite story you'd like for me to read?"

Ezra cleared his throat. He could not do it. He could not claim his Bible back from this good-hearted young man. But his grandfather had given it to him when he graduated from school. When he arrived back home, what would he tell the old man? And how could Ezra find out how Jimmy had obtained it without Jimmy finding out it had been his? *Lord, help me.*

"I've always been partial to John 8:36." Ezra reached over and squeezed Miss May's hand. "If the Son therefore shall make you free, ye shall be free indeed."

"Oh, dat's a good 'un. It sho' is." She squeezed his hand in response. "Free, indeed. Free, indeed. Thank You, Lawd."

Jimmy stared at Ezra. "Say, I just noticed you sure talk good. Do you know how to read, too?"

Ezra picked up a stick and drew in the dirt to avoid Jimmy's probing gaze. "Yes."

"How'd you learn?" Jimmy bent toward him, his brow furrowed. "I thought it was against the law to teach slaves how to read."

Ezra looked up. "It was. But I wasn't a slave. I grew up in Boston."

"Boston?" Jimmy burst out. "Why, what are you doing way down here?"

"Shh." Ezra glanced around, but no one watched them. "I was with the 54th Massachusetts Regiment." He spoke softly, but pride edged his voice. "I got separated from my unit earlier this month. Then I found out the war was over, so I'm headed home."

"Whooee." Jimmy whistled. "Aren't you scared of being called a deserter?"

Ezra shook his head. "We met up with a Colonel Rule two days ago. He wrote some orders that keep me in the clear."

"Colonel Rule!" Again Jimmy's volume alarmed Ezra.

"Shh. Yes. Why?"

"Why, we're supposed to meet up with Colonel Rule, but the captain can't find him." Jimmy snickered. "Now, if he'd just been a little more polite to you, you could have told him right off where the old man is." He wrinkled his forehead. "Guess I'll have to tell my sergeant what you said." He stood up and brushed off the seat of his pants.

Ezra felt a twinge of panic. "Wait." He stood and touched Jimmy's arm. "May I ask you a question first?"

"Sure." Jimmy stopped. "Go ahead."

"You said you bought this Bible from some folks alongside of the road."

"That's right."

Ezra chose his words carefully. "It looks familiar. Can you tell me about the person who sold it to you?"

Jimmy raised an eyebrow and glanced away thoughtfully. "I was so glad to see the Bible, I didn't pay much attention. I been wanting one for a long time."

"Anything would help. Was he white or—"

"He was a Negro boy, maybe sixteen or so and about this high to me." He held his hand against his ear lobe.

Adam!

"Was he dark or light?" Ezra prayed he'd remember.

"He was a little lighter than you. Now, his sister—"

"His sister?"

"Yes. She was a pretty girl, real pretty, but lots lighter than the boy."

Miss May clambered to her feet and tottered over to join them. "Did you see a ol' man, a ol' Negro man with 'em?" Her face lit up with hope.

Jimmy shook his head. "No, ma'am. But there was a big fellow, a dark one about your size, Ezra."

"Dat's Jack." Miss May looked up at Ezra. "What you s'pose happened to my Willard?" Her eyes filled with tears. "My po' Willard."

Ezra put an arm around her. "I'm sure he's all right, Miss May. Delia looked after him. I know she did."

Miss May sniffed and pulled a handkerchief from her pocket to wipe her nose. "Lawd, I hope so. I hope so."

Jimmy scratched his head and eyed the two of them. "You know those folks?"

"I think they're the right ones." Ezra nodded. "We were all traveling north until we became separated by a sudden flood up in the hills three days ago."

"My land, that must have been something. I'm glad you're all right." Now he scratched his chin. "Hm. That's strange. These folks were headed south toward Spartanburg. I told them they were going the wrong way." He shook his head. "No sense in going south if they're wanting to go north. Well, I'm off to see the captain. Don't go anywhere, you hear?"

Miss May hung onto Ezra's arm and tottered anxiously from one foot to the other. "Oh, we gots to go find 'em. Can we go right now?"

He pulled her into a gentle embrace. "Miss May, where's your faith? It's going to be all right. We'll go in the morning."

She pulled away, laughing softly. "Shame, shame on me. Look at how da Lawd done work all dis out, yet I'm still not believin' His goodness."

Ezra thought for a moment. Here he'd meant to comfort her, but her words summed up the whole truth of the situation and ended up comforting him. Not only had the young soldier been exceedingly kind to Miss May and him, but he had also become the link that would send them back to Mr. Willard and their other friends. Only God could have arranged these circumstances. Ezra would willingly relinquish ownership of his Bible as a small token of his gratitude to the Lord…and the future preacher.

+IHI(※(HI+

"How you 'spect me to cook a decent meal when you don't git the cookin' pot clean? Look here." Alice held out the pan to Delia, and her dark eyes narrowed. "You jes' a lazy gal use ta livin' up in the big house. Don' know nothin' 'bout real work." She scratched at a bit of dried on greens with her fingernail.

Seated on a log, Delia cringed, remembering Beulah's scoldings. "I done my best. It was dark down at the stream last night." And she'd been scared Jack would come after her again.

"'I done my best'," Alice mocked with a hateful sneer. "Don' know what yo' mama teach you, but it sho' ain't how to clean no pot." She turned away and started to shake dirt off the greens they'd picked for supper.

Delia jumped up, hands on her hips. "Don't you talk about my mama, you...you field darkie." She'd once heard Missus say she was so mad, she saw red. Now Delia knew what that meant.

Alice spun back around. "You think you somethin' fo' yo' light skin, don't you? I'm gonna tell you what all us *field darkies* know 'bout you and yo' kind. While we was out sweatin' in the fields, yo' mama was up at the big house havin' a fine time with the massuh. That's where you come from."

Delia swayed a bit. In the corner of her eye, she saw Jack leaning against a tree with his arms crossed and a big grin on his face. Frederick watched his mama with his mouth wide open till Leviticus pulled him away toward the woods. Adam was busy making sure the campfire took. And Delia started to shake.

"Hush, gal." Mr. Willard spoke to Alice, but he came and put his arm around Delia's shoulder. "Jes' *hush,* I tell ya." His words came out strong and deep for such a weak old man, and everybody stopped to listen. "You think her mama was havin' a fine time with the massuh? Maybe so. But did she have any say-so in it? No. Not any mo' than the rest of us had a say-so in nothin'." His voice got softer, and everybody seemed to lean closer to hear him. "Then the missus had her mama beat to death fo' all dat *fine time.*"

Alice gasped. Her eyes grew bigger. She bit her lip and turned back to sorting the greens. "I saw plenty o' beatin's where I was," she muttered. "I saw field hands bleedin' bad and near to dyin'." But she didn't sound hateful this time.

Delia shook, and Mr. Willard held her tighter. "It's awright, chile. It's awright."

She looked around. Jack wasn't grinning anymore. He just stood there frowning, like the others, like they all wished they hadn't heard what Mr. Willard said.

Of a sudden, Delia pulled loose from him and ran into the woods, past trees and bushes and rocks until she fell down in a heap, not caring a bit about the pebbles that bruised her hands and knees or the tears that stung her eyes and burned her cheeks.

"Mama, Mama."

All these years since Mama died, Delia'd wondered why Missus had her beat so bad. Deep down, she knew the truth. She'd heard the whispers from the other slaves, 'specially the children of the field hands when they wanted to be mean to her. But Beulah always said not to pay them no mind.

"You may be nothin'," Beulah told her time after time, "but you's better than a field hand."

Delia had always believed her. But what difference did it make? What difference had it made for her beautiful, sweet mama to be Massuh's favorite when Missus could have her beat to death?

Massuh? Why, that meant he was her father. The thought made her feel sick.

"Delia?" Alice called out. She sounded worried. "Delia, honey, where is you?"

Sitting back against a big rock, Delia bunched up her knees to her forehead. She didn't want to talk to anybody, 'specially Alice.

"Delia." Alice tramped over the underbrush and came over to sit by her.

"What do you want?" Delia sniffed hard and wiped her cheeks with her skirt.

"I'm so sorry 'bout yo' mama, Delia. I'm so sorry fo' bein' mean to you." She stared out into the woods like she was thinking. "It come to me jus' now how we's all been under a black cloud of evil, even house slaves." She eyed Delia. "Here you is, alone in the world, but I got a fam'ly." She bit her lip like she was thinking some more. "You know Frederick ain't Leviticus's son, don' you?"

Delia shook her head. She hadn't thought about it.

"Why, jus' look at him." Alice raised an eyebrow in surprise. "He awful much lighter than me or Leviticus. You can see that, cain't you?"

Delia nodded.

"I love my son, but his pappy was a real mean white overseer. I didn't have no say-so in the matter, jus' like yo' mama didn't, God bless her."

Delia pulled some twigs from her wool stockings. "Don't look like Leviticus minds at all. It's plain as anything he loves Frederick like his own."

Alice grinned just a little. "Yep. I's one blessed woman to have a man like him." She lifted her eyebrows and grinned a little wider. "Can I tell you a secret?"

Delia thought it was funny the way she asked, like a little child asking for sweets.

"I don't mind."

Alice put her hand on her belly. "We's gonna have our own chile come August."

Delia drew back. "Your own chile?" She'd thought Alice was just nice and round. To think a baby was growing in that fat belly.

Alice laughed. Then Delia did, too.

"I'm real glad for you." Delia got up and put out her hand to help Alice stand. They walked back toward camp arm in arm. "Alice?"

"Yeah, honey?"

Delia sent her a sidelong glance. "I'll clean the pot better after breakfast."

"Awright." Alice sent a sidelong glance back to Delia. "You's a good girl, Delia. You coulda took up with Jack, but you didn't. I'm glad, 'cause he ain't the kind of man who jus' has one girl."

"Yessum. I kinda figured that." Delia grinned. "I think he wanted to see us fightin'."

Alice snorted. "I'll show that man what fightin's all about."

They talked and laughed all the way back to camp.

Delia was able to laugh, but her heart ached for her mama worse than it had in a long time.

✯ ✯ ✯ ✯

CHAPTER FOURTEEN

"Hurry up, son." Miss May picked up her walking stick and started toward the road. "I gots to catch up with my Willard."

"I'm coming." Ezra lifted his canvas knapsack and slipped his arms through the straps. It seemed heavier this morning, undoubtedly due to his fatigue. He turned to Jimmy with a smile. "She sure keeps me going."

The private laughed. "She's a spunky little lady, isn't she?"

"She sure is." Ezra reached out to him. "Thank you again for your kindness. Neither one of us will ever forget you. We'll be praying about your plans to become a preacher. That's a worthy calling, and I know you'll do well."

"Thanks." Jimmy gripped his hand and shook it. "I'm sorry the sergeant didn't believe you'd met up with Colonel Rule. He really hates Ne...." His face grew red. "I mean...."

Ezra clapped him on the shoulder. "Never mind. I understand. I only hope they don't keep you men marching all over the place when you could join your regiment by late this afternoon."

Jimmy glanced across the field toward the officers' tent. "I might tell the captain what you said myself. I don't like the idea of being on a wild goose chase. Sure wears a fellow out when he's carrying all he owns in his knapsack."

"Well, good luck." Ezra turned to follow Miss May.

"Hey, you." A sergeant ran toward Ezra, his bearded face glowering. "Where do you think you're going?"

Ezra could only stare at him. What now?

"Sir, this man was just leaving with his granny." Jimmy stepped between Ezra and the other man. "He's a free man, sir." Worry and a hint of fear wrinkled his freckled face, yet he braved his superior nonetheless. Ezra's respect for him doubled.

"Never mind that, private." The sergeant moved past him and faced Ezra. "The captain wants to see you. Come with me."

In an instant, several thoughts darted across Ezra's mind.

I'm a free man, and I'm leaving.

I saw the captain yesterday, and that was enough.

It will serve you right to wander all over South Carolina looking for your regiment.

But that would only add to Jimmy's misery.

Lord, forgive me.

"Will you please see to Miss May?" Ezra asked Jimmy. "All right, sergeant, I'll come with you."

Once at the officers' tent, Ezra waited while the sergeant went inside. Soon the captain flung open the tent flap and stepped out.

"All right, boy, what's this all about?" He snatched the cigar from his mouth and flung ashes about as he gestured toward the sergeant.

"Talbot here tells me you saw Colonel Rule. How do I know you're not lying?"

Ezra resisted the temptation to act the fool. He stared evenly into the officer's eyes. "The gentleman in question has a small scar on the right side of his forehead that grows pale when he's angry."

The captain stared back for a moment. Then he blinked. "Very well. Where is he?"

"Do you have a map?"

"Lieutenant!" He flung back the tent flap and stepped inside. "Get me that map."

"Yes, sir." The junior officer quickly unfolded a large square of drafting linen and laid it on the table at the center of the tent.

"Now, show me what you know." The captain curtly motioned Ezra inside.

Ezra studied the dark ink lines on the map. It contained a few topographical errors, but since they did not affect the captain's objective, he decided not to risk the man's ire by pointing them out.

"You're right here." He tapped a spot, ignoring the officer's snort. "We left Colonel Rule and the rest of your regiment day before yesterday morning." He moved his finger along the road line past several intersections. "Right here." He touched the regiment's location. Shifting his knapsack higher on his shoulders, he started to leave the tent. "Now, if you'll excuse me...."

"Wait!"

Ezra refused to cringe at the officer's barking tone. This was getting tiresome.

"Sergeant, get this man some food, blankets, whatever he wants."

Surprised, Ezra stifled a grin. "Thank you, sir."

The captain snorted again. "Never let it be said I don't return favors."

Ezra followed the sergeant to the company's small supply wagon where a soldier gave him the items he requested, placing them all in a cotton flour sack. Then he joined Miss May, said good-bye to Jimmy again, and started down the road.

"What all'd you git?" Miss May set a brisk pace beside him.

"Some biscuits, a little honey, some salt, a few slices of beef or horse. I can never tell which it is." In spite of the heavier weight he now carried, his steps matched hers in lightness. "We'll have a fine dinner this noon."

"Oh, it's a wonder how the Lawd do take care of His chi'drun." She kept her eyes focused on the road as if she saw Mr. Willard Brewster coming their way.

When the sun stood overhead, they found a shady spot beside the way. While Miss May spread out the food, Ezra opened his knapsack to adjust the lumpy load. To his surprise, his Bible lay among the contents.

"What on earth?" He pulled it out and caressed the cover where a burn mark marred the leather, then opened it. Inside, where his name had been inscribed long ago by his grandfather, was a small slip of brown paper bearing penciled words.

"Thanks for the loan of your Bible. Your friend, Jimmy Shipley."

Ezra swallowed hard. "Thank You, Lord."

Just as Miss May had said, it was a wonder how the Lord did take care of His children.

✦ ▪▰▪ ❋ ▪▰▪ ✦

Toward the middle of the afternoon, Jack started to walk faster, just about the time Frederick and Mr. Willard had almost gone their limit for the day.

"Why's he in such a hurry all of a sudden?" Delia raised her hand to shield her eyes as she watched him disappear over a small rise.

"Can't never tell with that one." Mr. Willard huffed out his words like he always did when he was tired. "How do?" He stopped and lifted his hand to wave at a man walking toward them. "Fine day for a walk."

Delia loved the way Mr. Willard paused to give a friendly word to every colored person he saw. Of course they all moved off the road for white folks. Either way, they got a minute's rest from their walking. She wondered if that was his plan or if he just liked to talk to people.

This fellow had a cotton bag slung over his shoulder and a skinny brown dog at his heel. "How do." The man waved back at Mr. Willard, then paused to tip his hat to Delia and Alice and nod to Adam and Leviticus. "Where y'all headed?"

Frederick knelt down to pet the dog, and it licked his face. The man grinned and patted the boy's bare head.

"Don't rightly know." Leviticus wiped sweat from his upper lip. "We're following that fella yonder." He pointed up the road.

"Didn't see no fella 'cept a white man on horseback goin' that way." The man looked back to where he'd come from.

"Oh, my," said Adam, "Jack done gone off and left us."

Delia'd been thinking the same thing for the past half hour.

"'Course, they's a side road over that rise." The man pointed. "Could be your man took off down that road. They's a farm over there. Y'all have a good day, now, y'hear? C'mon, Runt." He walked off whistling, and his dog trotted behind him.

"Glory be." Leviticus pulled off his hat and slapped his leg with it. Dust flew everywhere. "I bet that's the farm he's takin' us to."

"May be." Mr. Willard limped a step or two, then started to pick up his pace. "Only one way to find out." He pulled himself along fast with his walking stick like somebody'd lit a fire under him.

Frederick gave out a little whimper that made Delia's heart ache. That boy never complained, no matter how hard things got. She wished she could carry him—that somebody could carry him. But they all had enough to tote without adding more to their burdens. For the child's sake—and Mr. Willard's—she hoped they reached the farm soon.

On the other side of the rise, they found the side road, just like the man said. They would have missed it if they hadn't known where to look, 'cause weeds had overgrown the two wagon-wheel tracks. Leviticus and Adam led the way, watching for snakes, like they always did.

About fifty yards from the main road, the side road dipped and narrowed into a wooded spot. Delia helped Mr. Willard down the slope.

The woods weren't too thick or deep, and soon they reached a clearing. About another fifty yards ahead stood a ramshackle old house. Its unpainted gray boards had seen a lot of weather, for they bowed in and out and had lots of gaps, like the walls of shacks in the slave quarters back on the plantation.

"Where's the big house?" Alice asked.

"Must be further on. Let's go." Leviticus walked ahead.

As they came near the house, they started to see signs of life. A thin goat tied to a stake grazed at the edge of a grassy area. A mother dog nursed two puppies under the wide front porch. Chickens wandered around the dirt yard, clucking and pecking for their dinner. Three cats fought over something in the high grass. The group stopped in front of the house.

"Should we go up and knock?" Adam started toward the front steps.

Before anyone could answer him, a white woman came out the door, followed by Jack. She was tall, about up to Jack's ears, and looked strong for a woman. Her tanned face was lined, probably more from the weather than from age. Her bushy brown hair was tied back in a gray bandanna. She wore a simple brown cotton dress with a few patches on it. The skirt hung limp, like she had no petticoats to plump it out like real ladies always did.

She stepped off the porch, walked toward the group, and then started circling, staring, studying them one at a time. Delia could see everybody else was as surprised as she was. And nobody seemed able to say a word.

The woman stopped at Delia, and her stare traveled up and down, stopping at her breast and then her face. She glanced up at Jack, her angry gaze questioning him with blue-white iron pokers where her eyes should have been.

Delia felt her skin crawl, and she shook against her will. She'd never been on the auction block, but somehow she now knew what it felt like, at least a little bit. Would the woman hit her, like Miz Suzanne had?

The woman moved on, a sneer on her thin lips as she studied Mr. Willard, showing him none of the respect his age was due. Again, she looked up at Jack, who leaned against one of the square porch pillars, his eyebrows bent down like he was worried.

"This is all you brought me?" The woman's voice sounded deep and strong, almost like a man's. "This is all you think I need to work this farm?"

CHAPTER FIFTEEN

"No, no, no." Jack bounded down from the porch. "You don' see what you got here. Look at this." He grabbed Leviticus's shoulders. "This un's real strong. He can work like two men."

Leviticus stared at Jack, his mouth and eyes wide open like he was too surprised to talk.

"And this un…." Jack grabbed Adam and made him stand beside Leviticus. "This un's young, but he can go all day in the hot sun."

Adam jerked himself free from Jack's grip and scowled at him.

Jack pointed to Alice. "She's a hard worker, too. She can work right alongside the men."

Alice's eyes narrowed, and Delia thought she was about to speak her mind. But Jack went on.

"Now, the boy and the old man, they'll earn their keep, just a bit slower." He didn't look at Delia, but jerked his thumb in her direction. "She ain't no good in the field, but she can cook and clean house."

Delia looked at the others. They stood staring at Jack like they couldn't believe what they were hearing. She didn't know what to think. Just when she'd made friends with Alice, Jack was about to spoil it.

The woman kept on staring, too, first at one of them, then at another. "Well, if this is the best you can do, I s'pose we'll have to make it work out." She ran her finger under her nose and sniffed real loud. "Take 'em out back and show 'em where they'll be sleeping." She moved toward the front steps of the house.

"Hold on a minute." Alice put her hands on her hips. "I ain't no slave no mo'. You want me to work for you, you tell me how much you gonna pay me."

Delia gasped. That'd get Alice hit for sure.

The woman whipped around and drew herself up tall, standing over Alice. "You show me what you're worth, and then we'll talk about pay."

Alice wet her lips and glanced at the others. For a minute, she seemed about to wilt like a thirsty plant. She set her eyes on Leviticus, then on Frederick. She lifted her chin up at the big woman, and her black eyes blazed. "You want us to work for you, you tell us how much you gonna pay us. Now."

Delia thought she'd burst with pure pride over Alice's braveness. She could never be that brave to a white person.

The woman glared at her for a bit. Then she stepped back. "Awright, awright, we can talk about pay. I don't have money right now, but I got a place for you to live and food for you to eat while we grow a cash crop to sell. Then they'll be a little money for ever'body." She turned to Jack, who still looked worried. "You didn't tell them all this, did you?"

"No, I didn't tell them."

Delia wondered if anyone else noticed he didn't say "ma'am."

The woman gave out a little snort. "It figures." She sniffed again. "Up front, just so y'all know, I never owned a slave. Not many white folk in these parts did. Me and my pa farmed this place with a few hired men. Pa's dead, and the hired men all went off to war. Now it's just me, and I can't farm it by myself. Jack came along, and I told him if he found some workers to help us, I'd pay him good when the crops came in." She looked around at the group. "You want work? Stick around. If you don't, get off my land." She climbed the front steps and went into the house.

"Now, don't that beat all?" Mr. Willard walked around shaking his head. "What y'all think 'bout this?"

"It's good work, folks, jus' like I promised." Jack slapped Leviticus on the back and grinned at everybody. "Now, come on out back, and I'll show you where you'll sleep."

"Can we git somethin' to eat first?" Frederick looked drawn and weak, like he was about to faint.

Alice pulled him close to her and brushed his cheek with her hand. The pain in her eyes ate into Delia. How hard for a mama not to be able to feed her child.

Alice looked up at Jack. "My boy's gotta eat. Can you see if she's got a bite of bread or somethin'?" She nodded toward the house.

Jack frowned and bit his lip. He glanced up toward the front door and then back at the boy. Was he afraid of the woman? Delia sure was.

"Awright." He went up the four steps in two strides and into the front door without so much as knocking or calling out.

"I hope I didn't make her too mad." Alice held on to Frederick and turned to Leviticus. "He can't go on. We gotta stay."

Leviticus shrugged. "I ain't never been scared of hard work. This'll do as good as any other place." He looked around the group. "What do y'all think?"

"It's awright with me." Adam eyed the chickens. "Y'all s'pose she'd give us one of them to eat? Wouldn't that be somethin'?"

Mr. Willard chuckled. "Long as Delia cooks it." He looked at her. "Honey, you look awful worried. What you thinkin' 'bout?"

Delia shook her head. "I'm awright." Her belly fluttered with hunger and fear. "But I made up my mind. If she don' give the boy somethin' to eat, I'm not stayin'."

Alice looked close to tears. "That's good of you, Delia."

The door slammed open, and Jack came out carrying a plate of biscuits. "See, what'd I tell you? You stay here and work, and you won't go hungry."

Everybody was too busy grabbing the biscuits to answer him. All except Delia. Taking this food obliged them to the woman, and she'd surely make them pay off the debt.

"They's butter on 'em!" Adam talked around his mouthful.

Butter!

Delia's dry mouth began to water. She grabbed one from the plate and bit off almost half. It felt awful good going down. But the same food that fed her hunger also fed her fear.

Had she just sold herself back into slavery for a buttered biscuit?

"Have you seen a ol' Negro man travelin' this way?" Miss May held on to Ezra's arm for balance and called out to every person who passed by. "He's travelin' with three younger men, two women, and a little boy." Her hope never seemed to wane.

Some travelers, especially whites, ignored her. But several people mentioned seeing a group that fit the description she gave.

"Saw an old gentleman goin' that way early this mornin'." A colored man pointed down the road. "Friendly old fellow wearin' a brown jacket and gray trousers and a black hat with a big brim. Those other folks was with him, too, one of 'em a real pretty young lady."

"Thank ya, thank ya." Miss May nodded to him and then lifted her gaze. "Praise the Lawd, we's almost caught 'em, son." She walked faster for a few dozen paces before she had to slow down and catch her breath.

"Yes, ma'am. Seems like it." Ezra studied her drooping posture and heavy breathing. Clearly, this was becoming too much for her. "Miss May, I'm thinking maybe I should try to find some work I can do in trade for food. It won't be long before our food is gone, and there's not much game so close to the road."

"Oh, my, and jes' when we's so close." She shaded her eyes and stared far ahead. "But I am powerful hungry." Her shoulders drooped a little. "No sense in goin' on without food."

"Well, then, let's see what we can do about that." He put an arm around her and helped her along at a slower pace.

By mid-afternoon, he'd offered his services to three different white men on horseback who appeared to be farmers or businessmen. One rode past muttering a curse. The other two had said they had no work. As the sun dipped lower, Ezra thought Miss May would give out completely, and he was not too sure about his own strength.

Hearing the rattle of a wagon behind them, they moved to the side of the road.

"Whoa." The white man driving the battered old conveyance called to his skinny mule. "Say, you the man looking for work?"

Ezra felt a sudden infusion of energy. "Yes, sir. What can I do for you?"

The deeply tanned man wiped sweat from his face with a stained handkerchief. "I got a farm about a half mile past that rise in the road.

I could use some help fixing up my barn and tending my crops. I'll pay you five dollars a month along with food and a place to sleep."

"I'm your man." Ezra glanced at the back of the wagon.

"Yes, yes, you can ride. Hop in, you and your granny." The bearded man waved his hand toward the back. "I'm Owen Burns. Granny, can you cook and sew?"

"Why, yessuh, Mr. Burns, I surely can." Miss May seemed energized by this new situation, too, for she climbed into the wagon without any help from Ezra.

"Good," Mr. Burns said. "You can help my mother. She's been…uh, doing poorly."

Once Ezra took his place beside Miss May, the man slapped the reins, and the mule moved forward. As they drove over the rise in the road, Ezra noticed a thin column of white smoke just beyond a small wooded area.

"Are there many farms around here?" he called out to Mr. Burns.

"Oh, yes," he responded over his shoulder. "Mostly small ones like mine." He gestured toward the smoke. "That's Kate Saunders's place. It borders my land. She runs it by herself, though I can't see how with all the work there is to do on a farm."

Ezra thought he detected a note of sadness in the man's voice. He'd said Miss May could help his mother. Did that mean he did not have a wife? And did he want the Saunders woman's land, or did he want the woman? Ezra chuckled to himself. That was foolish speculation and certainly none of his business.

The wagon turned down a deeply rutted side road and now rattled even more loudly than before. Ezra decided he would wait until they reached the farm to ask Mr. Burns if he knew anything about Mr. Willard and the others. Surely it was to one of these small farms that Jack had led them. At least, that was what Ezra prayed.

$\mathcal{E}$verybody followed Jack through knee-high grass around to the back. Delia circled wide when they passed two large lilac bushes. The fragrance of lilacs brought up bad memories of the plantation. They grew all over the place down there. Sometimes Miz Suzanne would grab a lilac branch and beat Delia with it. Lilac branches could raise an awful welt that stung for days.

Behind the house, a variety of vegetables had been planted in a large garden, but the weeds were crowding them out. Delia hoped she'd get to tend the garden. She'd always liked to weed because it got her out of the house and away from Miz Suzanne. There in the garden she could think and dream. And there, less than two weeks ago, she'd decided to run away. Now she couldn't escape the feeling that she'd been caught and brought back to the plantation, even though the big house wasn't so big and was a rundown mess. As she came around to the back of the house, she caught the stink of pigs and heard their grunts.

"Out yonder's the fields." Jack pointed beyond a row of bushes to maybe thirty or forty acres of cotton just starting to come up.

"Beyond that, you can see the Pacolet River that runs down to Spartanburg." He waved his hand off to the right. "That woods is full of snakes and wild hogs, so don't go there."

"Um-um." Mr. Willard stared out at the fields. "I thought my days of pickin' cotton was over." He looked down at his hands and rubbed the calluses and scars.

Leviticus sighed. "Well, we know how to do it. Won't need no trainin'."

"Is that the quarters?" Alice nodded toward a rundown building.

"No, that's the barn." Jack's right eye twitched a little, like he was nervous. "Ain't no quarters here." He pointed to the right of the barn. "That's the house where y'all will sleep."

"That's just a lean-to." Alice glared at Jack. "A shack all grown over with weeds. You gonna chase out the rats and snakes afore we go to bed tonight?"

He lifted his chin. "You got time afore the sun goes down. I got important stuff to do."

"Where you sleeping?" Adam gave him a sidelong look.

Jack folded his arms across his chest. "It ain't none of yo' business, but I'll tell you anyways. I'll sleep in the big house to guard Miz Saunders."

"Uh-huh." Alice snickered. "I bet you gonna guard Miz Saunders."

"You hush. You lucky to be here." He started toward the house but turned back. "Don't git sassy jus' 'cause you been fed afore you did any work."

"Jack." Leviticus let his knapsack slide off his back to the ground. "We're here to work, and we ain't scared of workin' hard. But you gots to respect my woman, or we're leavin' right now." His back straightened, and he seemed to get a little taller, though not near as tall as Jack.

Her heart pounding hard, Delia sidled up to Mr. Willard and held his arm. "I sure hope they don' fight," she whispered.

"Shh." Mr. Willard patted her hand. "Jes' watch."

Jack relaxed real quick. "Say, now, let's not git all riled at each other. Things are bound to be a mite tense till we all find our place here." He clapped Leviticus on the shoulder like they were old friends. "I'm puttin' you in charge of fixin' up that little house. It's got two rooms, and you can decide where ever'body sleeps."

"See," Mr. Willard whispered. "A bully always backs down if you stand up to him."

Delia nodded, but she didn't agree. She'd seen her mistress get meaner when anybody stood up to her.

Jack stepped over to Adam. "I got jus' the job for you. See that swing blade over against the barn wall? You git this grass cut back so we can walk a bit easier here in the backyard. Take what you cut over to the barn to feed the milk cow."

"Awright, I'll do it." Adam took off for the barn.

Jack grinned real big at Alice. "How long's it been since yo' boy had milk? Bessie puts out three gallons a day. Why'd you think you got butter on those biscuits?"

Alice's mouth dropped open. "Milk. You hear that, Frederick?" A shine came to her eyes, and she set a hand on her belly. "Leviticus, you know that'll be good for the boy and...." She gave him a little nod.

Delia wondered if anybody else knew about Alice's baby.

Leviticus studied Jack for just a bit. "Awright, then. But you respect my wife."

"Sure thing." Jack was bareheaded, but he made like he was tipping a hat and gave a silly bow. "Miz Barton, would you be so good as to help your husband clean out the little house?"

Alice rolled her eyes. "House? Some house. Come on, Leviticus, Frederick. We got a shack to clean out."

Jack turned his big grin on Mr. Willard.

"Old man, you know how to prime a pump?" He pointed toward the water pump about fifteen feet from the back door of the big house. "I reckon Miz Saunders needs a bucket of water right 'bout now for fixin' supper. Can you do that?"

"I can." Mr. Willard limped toward the pump like his feet hurt, but he kept on going.

Delia started to follow him, but Jack held out his hand, not quite touching her arm. She stopped, and her heart raced.

"Did you see what I done for you?" His dark eyes stared right into hers.

She shook her head, not wanting to answer.

"Why, gal, don't you pay attention? I tol' Miz Saunders not to make you work in the fields. You can do the housework and keep that pretty light skin of yours out of the sun. I done that for you." He frowned and pouted like his feelings were hurt.

It was a hot day, but Delia shivered. "You didn't have to do that. I can work in the fields." She sidled past him through the weeds and followed Mr. Willard.

"Ain't you gonna say 'much obliged'?" Jack called after her.

"I said I can work in the fields. I didn't ask you for no favors." Saying "obliged" would be way too dangerous, almost like she was his woman. She'd never be his woman, no matter what he said or did.

Anyways, it seemed to Delia—and to the others, from what she could tell—that Jack already had a woman.

⋆✦✧❋✧✦⋆

"You brought home darkies?" Mrs. Burns sat in a rocking chair on the front porch with a rifle across the lap of her worn but well-made dress. The gray-haired woman had the weathered, wiry look of a hard-working farm woman. "Why, boy, they'll steal us blind and kill us in our sleep." At her feet lay an old hound dog fast asleep, obviously not bothered by the newcomers.

Mr. Burns shook his head. "Now, Mama, don't go spouting all that ignorance." He climbed the front steps and gently took the gun from her. "This fella and his granny are nice folks just trying to get by like everybody else."

"I hate darkies. Always did." Mrs. Burns stood up and paced the porch. "I never let your pa own a slave 'cause I didn't want them sons of Ham on our land." She shook a fist at her son, and the wrinkles on her face deepened to an ugly scowl. "Now you done bought these two and brung 'em here to kill us for sure."

"Mr. Burns, sir." Ezra jumped from the back of the wagon and helped Miss May down. "Maybe this isn't a good idea."

He glanced at Miss May. Her forehead crinkled, and she looked as doubtful as he felt.

"Hang on a bit." Mr. Burns took his mother's arm. "We're going into the house to have a talk. Y'all wait right there." He steered his mother through the front door, an attractive if worn entrance with a large oval cut-glass window.

"Let's git our stuff and head up the road." Miss May lifted her small bag from the back of the wagon. She swayed slightly, and Ezra reached out to steady her.

"You need food, and so do I." He glanced toward the house. It appeared to be well built, but it could use a fresh coat of white paint and some repairs to its green shutters. "There's plenty to do here, so let's see if we can work something out."

"I ain't had much to do with white folks 'cause I was always out in the fields." Miss May shook her head. "But I can see dat woman's loaded down with more hate than most I seen. If I gits ta choose, don' rightly know if I wants ta deal with dat."

"It won't be for long." Ezra tried to sound more confident than he felt.

He looked beyond the house at the rest of the farm. Out back, the barn had collapsed on one side, and the other side did not look too steady. Cats skittered about among the other outbuildings, which also appeared to need repairs. A garden flourished beside the house, and a variety of flower bushes needed pruning. Ezra wondered how Mr. Burns could manage it by himself. Perhaps his mother took care of the house chores. She looked strong enough. But why had Mr. Burns said she needed help?

Mr. Burns came back outdoors with two bowls and handed them to Miss May and Ezra. "Here's a little leftover grits." He shrugged, as if he were embarrassed. "This ought to hold you till supper."

"Thank you, sir." Ezra accepted the bowl.

"Thank ya kindly." Miss May eyed the grits hungrily, then looked up at the man. "I'd be glad to hep ya fix dat supper."

"Well, I think we'd better give Mama a little more time to get used to you being here." He pointed behind him. "Sit on the steps while you eat. Then you can take the wagon out back and unload the grain, then unhitch the mule and turn him out into the field. Right by the barn, there's a little shack where you can put your things. I gotta go back in and see to Mama."

Ezra and Miss May waited until he went inside before eating the well-congealed grits. A hint of honey enhanced the bland taste, and the last drops of water in Ezra's canteen washed the meal down.

After tending to the wagon and mule, they inspected the little shack, which was in better condition than they had expected. Its unpainted walls were sound, and shuttered windows on two sides could bring through a cooling breeze. Four cots with dusty bedding sat in a line, suggesting that Mr. Burns had employed other farmhands at some time or other. The barn cats seemed to be keeping the rat population down.

Ezra insisted that Miss May sit down while he took the bedding outside. As he shook the dust from the tattered blankets, he could hear Mrs. Burns's angry, curse-filled tirade carrying on the evening breeze. But he was too exhausted to take Miss May away from this place, at least right away.

Old Mrs. Burns thought they would kill her in her sleep. Maybe she was the sort who would kill *them* while they slept. She was fairly tall and appeared to be the scrappy sort of woman who undoubtedly was very strong from years of hard farm work. Was she crazy or just hateful and mean? And was he crazy for staying?

"Oh, Lord, Lord, what have You brought us to this time?"

CHAPTER SEVENTEEN

"Come in here, girl." Miz Saunders sounded cross as she motioned impatiently for Delia to come up the back stoop. She pushed a strand of hair back under her gray bandanna, and her thick eyebrows bent downward.

Delia gulped. Real hard. She could obey, or she could run. She glanced at Mr. Willard, who was pumping water into a wooden bucket. He was breathing hard, like the effort was wearing him out. She couldn't bother him for advice now.

"Yes, ma'am." The words came out like an old, bad habit, contrite and fearful—and Delia hated herself for it.

"Bring that bucket of water." Miz Saunders waved her hand toward the pump and then went in the house, letting the door slam behind her.

"Here you go, chile." Mr. Willard lifted the full bucket and eased its weight over to Delia before heaving out a weary sigh.

"I got it." She gave him a trembling smile.

He looked up at the door and back at Delia. "Don' be scared, honey. She's all bark and no bite. Prob'ly not a happy woman, by my guess."

Delia gave out a dry little laugh. "Then you take her the water."

He chuckled in his duck-quack way. "You gotta deal with it, chile. Now, if'n she hits you, dat's another thing. Then we'll go some-place else, 'cause we ain't gonna stand fo' dat no mo'. But if'n she's jes' cross, let it roll off ya. Can ya do dat?"

Delia nodded. If he was brave, she could be brave. "Yessuh, I guess I can."

She carried the heavy bucket up the five back steps and set it down on the stoop to catch her breath. Miz Saunders pushed the door open.

"Get in here before every fly in Spartanburg County comes for supper." Her voice didn't sound quite so cross, just impatient. "Set it here." She pointed to a small table by the dry sink.

"Yes, ma'am." Delia inched her way across the bare, splintery floorboards and lifted the bucket to the spot. She couldn't keep from letting out a sigh of relief.

Miz Saunders snorted out a laugh. "You're stronger than you look. Why'd Jack say you weren't any good at working in the fields?" She put her hands on her hips.

Delia shrugged. "Jack say a lot of things that don't make no sense. I can work where you want me to work."

"Ah, so that's it, eh?" Miz Saunders dropped her hands to her sides and relaxed a bit. "Can you cook?"

"Yessum." Delia's heart lifted. She'd helped Beulah in the kitchen all her life. If Miz Saunders let her cook, she could make sure Mr. Willard and the others got enough to eat.

"Well, I hate to cook. That's your job now." Miz Saunders started to go out the back door.

"Ma'am?" Delia's heart pounded now, but she had to do what Mr. Willard said. She had to deal with it.

Miz Saunders turned back. "Yes?"

"We ain't stayin' here for good. Me and Mr. Willard are going to Boston soon as we can."

Miz Saunders gave her a long look. "Boston? Why Boston?"

"'Cause he has children up there, and I promised to take him to them." Delia felt a warm blush creep up her face.

Now Miz Saunders cocked her head like she was surprised. "You're taking that old man all the way up there?"

"Yes, ma'am."

The longer the woman stared at her, the more Delia's face burned.

"Hmm." Miz Saunders nodded. "All right, then." Her tone got softer. "Will you work through the summer? Until harvest?"

The nice, kinda tired way she asked made Delia braver. "I think so. I'll ask Mr. Willard." She forced herself to keep going. "We'd like to earn enough to ride the train. It'll be hard for him to walk that far, bein' so old."

Miz Saunders seemed to think about that for a bit. "I can't promise that much because I don't know how the cotton crop will turn out. But I can promise this. If you work hard, I'll be fair with you."

Delia grinned and nodded. "Thank you, ma'am."

"What's your name, girl?"

"Delia."

"Well, Delia, I'm Kate. And you can sleep here in the house, up in the loft, so you can get up early and cook breakfast for everybody."

Delia took a breath. Did she dare to ask? But she had to.

"Miz Kate, is Jack sleepin' in here, too?"

"Ha!" Miz Kate burst out laughing. "What makes you ask that?"

Delia gulped. "He said he needs to guard you at night."

"Ha!" Miz Kate laughed again. "I been guarding myself for over two years ever since my pa died. I sure don't need no Jack to guard me. Ha!" She shoved open the door, and as she went out, she muttered something about putting Jack in his place.

A slow smile spread over Delia's lips. She sure wished she could be there to see that.

She looked around the kitchen—her kitchen now. A table sat in the middle of the room with four chairs around it. The dry sink sat against the once-white walls. In a kettle at the back of the food-encrusted cast-iron stove, a chicken simmered in a plain broth. In a bin to the side, she found potatoes, carrots, onions, and some dried herbs to add to the pot. As she peeled the vegetables, she found herself humming, like Beulah always did. This was going to be a good job.

Delia was so glad she'd listened to Mr. Willard and dealt with her fear of Miz Kate. She was so glad she hadn't run.

✦✦✧❀✧✦✦

"Black-eyed peas with real ham, not just fat, and thick, sweet cornbread." Miss May reminisced about their previous night's supper. "Dat'll keep us goin' all day. C'mon, Ezra, finish up dat shaving so we can git on the road." She bundled up her few possessions and slung them on her back.

"I promised Mr. Burns I'd help him rebuild his barn." Ezra wiped the extra lather from his face. "I can't break that promise, now can I?" He cleaned his razor, folded it, and placed it in his knapsack.

Miss May let out a long sigh. "No, I s'pose not." Her usually cheerful expression drooped into a look of resignation.

Ezra hugged her. "It shouldn't take too long. A week. Maybe two. Most of the boards are still good, and I can straighten many of the nails and use them again." His mind was filled with plans for the structure. He'd helped his father build a new stable just before enlisting in the army. "And I'll be sure to ask Mr. Burns about Mr. Willard this morning."

"But what 'bout dat ol' woman up at da house?" Miss May jerked her thumb toward the house. "What we gonna do 'bout her?"

Ezra scratched his head. "I don't know. Avoid her as much as possible, I suppose."

"Chick, chick, chickee." Mrs. Burns called to her chickens not far from the shack. "Here, chickee, here, chickee."

Ezra and Miss May traded a look of concern. Had she heard their conversation? Ezra prayed she had not.

He could hear the *swisshh* of the feed being scattered. "I wish this place had a back door," he whispered. "I promised Mr. Burns I'd start work before breakfast, but she's right outside."

"Don' you go out dere." Miss May peered out the window, then quickly ducked back.

"I have to, Miss May. I promised. Now you just lie low." Ezra squared his shoulders and opened the door.

Standing in the middle of the barnyard, Mrs. Burns took a quick breath. And then she smiled.

"Why, there you are. Owen told me he'd hired a man. I'm Mrs. Burns, his mother. You must be Ezra."

Ezra stared at her, unable to answer. Was this the same woman they'd seen last evening? The wild blue eyes had softened, and her smile now offered a warm welcome. And she was not carrying a rifle, just a small cotton feed bag. She looked like a feisty but friendly farm woman, able to keep up with whatever work the farm required.

Behind him, Miss May said, "Tst."

"Yes, ma'am, I'm Ezra." He knew his face must be a study in confusion. He forced himself to remember his manners. "How do you do, Mrs. Burns?"

"Well, I'm just fine." Mrs. Burns continued to scatter feed to the chickens, which now clucked and pecked around the yard. "Where's your granny? I'd surely be obliged if she'd help me cook breakfast while you men work on the barn."

"Oh, my," Miss May whispered. Then she came out. "How do, Miz Burns. I'd be pleased to hep ya." With eyes wide, she looked up at Ezra and shook her head. "Lawd, have mercy."

Ezra patted her shoulder. "I think He already has."

"Come along, then, dearie. Now, what's your name?" Mrs. Burns beckoned to Miss May, who quickly followed her toward the house.

Ezra continued to stare at the woman for a moment. Then he shrugged. "Lord, please keep Miss May safe."

Mr. Burns emerged from the half of the barn that still stood. He carried a bucket of milk and walked toward the house.

"Getting hot already." He nodded to Ezra. "You ready to start work?"

"Yessir."

By the time Mr. Burns returned from taking the milk to the house, Ezra had his recommendations ready. Yet he longed to ask about the change in Mrs. Burns.

As if he guessed Ezra's dilemma, Mr. Burns said, "Mama's feeling better this morning."

Ezra decided not to question him further. From the look of things, the woman's infirmity was mental.

After Mr. Burns led the cow out to pasture, they made their plans and began tearing down the walls with crowbars and hammers. In no time at all, the clang of a hand bell announced breakfast, so they hurried to the back door.

Ezra and Miss May ate in the clean, well-stocked kitchen, while Mr. Burns and his mother ate in the formal dining room. The grits were hot this time and smothered with red gravy. Fried eggs, ham slices, buttered biscuits, and hot coffee rounded out the meal. Ezra and Miss May agreed that they'd never eaten a finer meal but also agreed that their weeks of hunger probably affected that opinion.

As they finished the meal with blackberry preserves on a biscuit, Mrs. Burns walked into the kitchen. She dropped her china dishes to the polished hardwood floor, where they shattered in countless pieces.

"Owen!" she shrieked. "What are these darkies doing in my kitchen?"

CHAPTER EIGHTEEN

"Now, Mama." Mr. Burns set his dishes down on a side table and put his hands on her shoulders. "We talked about this, remember?"

Ezra and Miss May quickly stood. Miss May's eyes grew round with fear. If Mrs. Burns tried to attack one of them, could Ezra get them both out of the house safely?

"It's that Saunders woman." Mrs. Burns's eyes narrowed, and she trembled with anger. "She sent 'em over here to kill us in our sleep so she can have our land."

"Mama, nobody's going to kill us." Mr. Burns turned his mother so she faced him. "It's time to take your medicine. Come on, now. Let's go to your room."

He took a small, dark bottle from a cabinet and a spoon from a drawer, then led—or rather, pushed—his mother from the room. Glancing over his shoulder, he cast an apologetic grimace toward Ezra and Miss May.

"Let's git."

Miss May put words to Ezra's sentiments. It was time to leave.

They started toward the back door, but at the crackle of china shards beneath their thin-soled shoes, Miss May stopped and heaved out a sigh.

"Lawd, I can't do it. I can't leave dis mess. Somebody'll git cut." She looked around the kitchen. "Gimme dat broom." She pointed toward the corner by the door.

"You don't have to do this." Ezra handed her the broom. "Don't you want to go?"

Miss May stared up at him. Her furrowed forehead suggested she felt as confused as he did about the situation.

"Dat po' woman ain't right in da head, chile." She began sweeping. "Maybe da Lawd sent us here to pray fo' her...to hep her in some way."

"Hmm." Ezra picked up the larger shards and placed them in the metal kindling bucket beside the stove. "I don't know if we can help her, but I do know we can help Mr. Burns. I'm willing if you are."

She chuckled. "Remember what happen to Jonah when he say no to what da Lawd tol' him to do? I don' want to be no Jonah."

Ezra grunted. "I don't want that, either."

"Well, if that don't beat all." Mr. Burns stood in the kitchen doorway. "I expected y'all to be hightailing it out of here by this time. This is right decent of you."

Miss May stopped sweeping. "Yo' mama awright?"

Mr. Burns nodded. "Her medicine settles her down pretty quick. She'll sleep for a couple of hours now."

Ezra held the dustpan while Miss May swept in the last fragments. "Sir, I'm ready whenever you are to go back out and work on that barn."

"Sure thing." Mr. Burns grabbed his broad-brimmed hat from a peg on the wall. "Granny, I can't expect you to take care of Mama, but...."

"Don' you worry, son." Miss May brushed dust from her shirtsleeves. Hands on her hips, she glanced about the room. "I'll clean up dis kitchen and mop up da last bits o' glass. I can cook dinner if'n you want."

Mr. Burns's eyes reddened. "I'd be much obliged." He walked toward the door. "Her room is right down the hallway. If she wakes up...." He stopped and stared out the back door for a moment. "Just ring the dinner bell if you need help."

Ezra followed Mr. Burns out to the barn, where they silently resumed taking apart boards. Mr. Burns seemed deep in thought, so Ezra hesitated to ask any of the dozen or so questions that swirled through his mind. Instead, he asked the Lord to direct their conversation, if they were to have one.

Sweat poured from both men, and more than once they stopped to drink cool water from the barnyard pump and to splash some on their heads. Mr. Burns stopped now and then to pet his hound, which had settled itself nearby.

After his second dousing in about three hours, Ezra shook the water from his hair and gazed around the land. In the distance, he could see a river. Thick woods bordered the western boundary of the farm. Out in the cotton field, he saw seven men tending the plants. Even from a distance, he could see that a couple of them were white.

This was not what he was used to seeing in the South, at least what little he'd seen of land being worked during the war.

"Mr. Burns, sir?" Busy once again, Ezra wedged his crowbar under a board and pried it upward. "I see you have men out in the field. Why'd you hire me if you already had them?"

Mr. Burns glanced toward the men, squinting as sunlight reached under his hat brim. "They're day laborers." He wiped away sweat from his eyes. "Truth be told, they won't come near the house." He tilted his head in that direction. "Mama."

Ezra stared at him for a moment before remembering his manners. "I'm sorry to hear that." He looked toward the house. *Lord, please keep Miss May safe. It will be my fault if anything happens to her.*

"Say...." Ezra thought he'd try one more question. "By any chance, have you heard about a small group of black folks hiring out to a farm in this area? Four men, two women, and a boy?"

"Nope." Mr. Burns motioned to Ezra to help him carry several boards to the pile that would be reused. "'Course, there's lots of comings and goings these days. Men coming back from the war, former slaves wandering all over creation with nothing to do." As they moved the wood, he paused and blinked. "Sorry. No offense intended."

"None taken." He would not mention that he'd never been a slave unless it became necessary.

Mr. Burns seemed open to talking, so Ezra decided to press on. "Did you go to war?"

Mr. Burns shook his head. "Nope. Nobody here to take care of Mama or the farm." He snickered. "Least ways, that's what I told 'em."

Ezra questioned him with a look.

Mr. Burns shrugged. "Just like my pa, I didn't believe in slavery. I didn't believe in the Southern cause."

The dinner bell's clanging startled them both. When they looked toward the house, however, they saw Miss May on the back stoop beckoning to them. Both men washed themselves at the pump and dried off before entering the house for the noon meal.

In the kitchen, Miss May had set four places at the table and spooned out egg salad onto each plate. Mrs. Burns stood at the dry sink chopping radishes with a large butcher knife. As the men entered, she lifted the knife and touched the point to her index finger. A queasy feeling churned in Ezra's belly when she gave them a too-sweet smile.

"Why, Owen, have you brought a guest for dinner?"

✦┉┣┫❀┣┫┉✦

"You done that, didn't you?" Jack stood at the edge of the garden where Delia knelt to thin the turnips.

"Done what?" She refused to look at him.

"Don't you be playin' that game, gal." Jack stepped over one row of foot-high pea plants. "You done spoke to Miz Saunders and got me kicked out of the house last night."

Delia carefully tugged at every other spindly baby turnip, sacrificing more than half so that the rest could grow big. Next time she thinned them, the ones she pulled would be big enough to eat, along with their green tops.

"You listenin' to me, gal?" Jack stepped into Delia's row and kept her from moving to the next bunch of tiny plants.

With the back of her hand, Delia brushed her bushy hair off her forehead, wishing she'd worn a bandanna to hold it back. Scooting back in the dirt, she got up and turned away from him.

"Where you goin'?" He grabbed her arm and twisted her back around.

"Ow." Delia froze. She'd learned long ago it would hurt more if she tried to get away. "I didn't tell Miz Kate to kick you out. I swear."

"Miz Kate, is it? That shows you're lyin'. Me and her had a deal." He jerked her arm to pull her close to his chest. "We was gonna run this place together, the two of us. Now you done stepped in and ruined it."

Delia stared up into his blazing eyes. *If looks could kill.* She'd heard Beulah say that oftentimes about the mean way Miz Suzanne looked at her. Would Jack do more than just look at her that way? Would he kill her?

"I didn't do nothin', Jack." Her voice squeaked out, and she hated how it showed him her fear. She swallowed hard. *Help me, Mama.*

"Miz Delia! Miz Delia!" Frederick came running around the corner of the house with a fuzzy brown bundle in his arms.

Jack shoved her away a bit but held her wrist.

Frederick reached the garden and stopped so fast he almost fell over. "See what I got?" With both hands, he held out a puppy. "Miz Kate says I can keep it if'n I gather the eggs and sweep the steps." He pulled the puppy back to his chest, and it licked his face, making him giggle. "You want to see her?" He lifted a foot to cross the ridge of dirt around the garden.

"Now don't you come in here, baby." Delia kept her voice even. "That's an awful sweet puppy. Can you run tell your mama I need her?"

"What'd you do that for?" Jack twisted his hand on her wrist, and she bit back a cry.

"Yessum." Frederick ran toward the back field.

"Watch out for snakes," she called after him.

Jack shoved her down on a summer squash plant, and its spines bit into her palms.

"Me and you ain't finished yet, gal." He walked down the row and out of the garden.

Delia let out a sob. Frederick wasn't the only one who needed to watch out for snakes. Jack was just like a big ol' water moccasin, and sooner or later, he was bound to bite.

But feeling sorry for herself had never got the work done. She wiped tears and sweat on her sleeve, brushed her hands on her skirt, and tried to fix the squash. It was broken down to the root. Six more of the plants were doing fine, so Delia pulled out the ruined one to make room for the others to grow big.

Then she went back to the turnips, inching her way along the row. It felt good to have her hands in the rich brown dirt where the vegetables grew so well. She hovered over them like she was their mama.

Mama. Right when she'd called on Mama for help, Frederick had come along, and Jack had to let her go. Was Mama really up in heaven giving help when she needed it?

She'd have to think long and hard on that.

CHAPTER NINETEEN

"Delia, this place ain't looked this good since my ma died more'n eight years ago." Miz Kate waved her hand to take in the main room of the house—the kitchen, the parlor, and the dining room all in one. "Just over a week, and you got the whole place in order."

Delia glanced around the large living area. She'd washed down the walls to uncover some faded wallpaper and cleaned up the floors. She'd polished the dining table and other wood furniture. The hardest job had been taking the big parlor rug outside to beat on the clothesline.

"Thank you, Miz Kate." Delia curtsied out of habit, but she didn't mind showing respect to Miz Kate.

"Your friends are doing a fine job out in the fields, too. To think five people could weed that much in such a short time." Miz Kate set her hands on her hips and stared out the open back door. Her usual frown had softened considerably.

"Yessum." Delia traced the toe of her shoe along a seam in the freshly scrubbed, rough wood floor. "Miz Kate, I got a surprise for you." Her pulse pounded rapidly in her ears.

Miz Kate turned and gave her a quizzing look. "A surprise? What on earth?"

"I found that old tin bathtub out in the storage shed. I cleaned it up real good and brought extra water up to the house to fill it. The water's heatin' on the stove right now, and if I bring the tub inside, you can have a nice bath." *And I can have one after you.* "I can even do up your hair. I used to do Miz Suzanne's hair, and she got lots of compliments on it." Delia was almost breathless when she finished.

Miz Kate stared at her until Delia thought her heart would stop beating. Was she offended?

"I can't recall when I had my last bath." Miz Kate scratched her neck. "Ain't never had nobody do my hair since ma." She pulled off her scarf and ran a hand through the tangled brown curls, sending a cloud of dust into the air. "It sure could use some doin'."

She leveled a cross look at Delia. "You trying to turn me into a lady or something?"

Delia's stomach quivered. "No, ma'am. I jus'—" Oh, that sounded bad!

Miz Kate laughed out loud. "Never mind, girl. I'm just funning with you. A bath sounds downright good. I'll take it right after I eat." She rolled her shoulders and stretched out her arms. "You go on now and carry supper out to the folks."

"Yessum." Delia placed a pot of stew and a pan of biscuits on a wooden tray and headed out the door. She liked cooking, but she could hardly wait to get her hands on Miz Kate's hair. The woman wouldn't know her own self in the mirror when Delia finished.

That evening in the kitchen, Miz Kate dug out a soap bar her mama once used. "Might as well do it up proper." She breathed in the bar's gardenia fragrance. "Oh, my, that sure reminds me of Ma." Her eyes sparkled, like she was happy and sad at the same time.

After brushing Miz Kate's hair to loosen up the dirt, Delia helped her get a good scrubbing all over. Then she took little strips of cotton and tied curls all over her head.

"We'll get up early in the morning, and I'll comb it out proper." Delia stood back and surveyed her work. "That's gonna be real pretty, Miz Kate."

Miz Kate stared into the mirror of her plain dressing table. Just as Delia had thought, she didn't seem to know herself.

"Miz Kate, would you mind if I use the bath water?"

Miz Kate blinked and looked up at Delia in the mirror like she didn't really see her. "Sure. Go right ahead."

After Miz Kate went to bed, Delia warmed the bath with another kettle full of water from the stove, working quietly so as not to wake her mistress. Delia hadn't had a bath in a long while, other than a splash or two in the creek, not since using Miz Suzanne's bath-water on the plantation.

As she soaked in the lukewarm water and lathered up the lye soap she used to wash dishes, she thought about when she had run away. She didn't regret it for a minute. Miz Kate'd said she'd pay Delia for the work she was doing, so this was a good place to be for now. Boston would be even better. Maybe she could make some money cooking and cleaning for some ladies up there. Mr. Willard's children might be able to help her find a job. Maybe, just maybe, she could do ladies' hair. But would somebody pay her to do something she loved so much?

In the dim light of the kerosene lamp, she dried off and slipped into an old nightgown that had belonged to Miz Kate's mama. It would feel so good to go right to bed, but she decided to dip most of the water from the bathtub and toss it out the kitchen window. She'd always hated to leave a job like that till morning.

She dipped out the first bucketful and flung it through the open window.

"Hey!" Jack's voice squawked right in front of her. He sounded just like a mad rooster. "Hey, what you think you're doin'?"

For just a blink of an eye, Delia was startled. Then she was scared. Had Jack been watching her take a bath? And Miz Kate, too?

She peeked out into the darkness and heard Jack cussing something fierce. His voice grew softer like he was walking away. She had to take several deep breaths to keep from falling on the floor laughing out loud, for fear she would wake Miz Kate. It served Jack right to get doused by dirty bathwater. Too bad it couldn't clean out his wicked insides.

Delia put the window down low enough to keep a man out and still let in a cooling breeze. She braced it with a piece of an old broomstick so it wouldn't go further up. Then she took sticks from the stack beside the kitchen stove and did the same with the other windows and barred the front and back doors. In her cozy loft above the main room, she rested her head on Ezra's wool jacket. Inside the jacket was the small bundle of chicken feathers sewed into her brown square of cotton. Maybe she could collect more feathers for her pillow from Miz Kate's chickens. She thought about the scraps in the sewing bag she found and decided that pretty patchwork curtains would look nice in Miz Kate's kitchen...and her bedroom window, too.

"Granny, I don't know how you figured it out." Mr. Burns leaned back in his chair at the kitchen table and cleaned his teeth with a toothpick. "Mama ain't had one of her spells in over a week. All I have to do is tell her she's about to see you, and she thinks you're company."

Miss May glanced at Ezra before answering. "Well, suh, I noticed she jes' got skittish when she come on us all the sudden."

Mr. Burns nodded. "I shoulda seen that myself. It ain't like her spells started when I brought you home. She's acted that way around Negroes all my life. All her life, too, from what my pa used to tell me." His face grew red. "No offense, mind you."

Ezra cleared his throat. He had felt hatred from many whites in his life, but Mrs. Burns's behavior seemed extreme. "No offense taken, sir. But I wonder why she reacts as she does. As a southern lady, hasn't she seen us often enough?"

Mr. Burns swirled his coffee around in his cup and took a long drink. "You're a mighty smart man, Ezra, and a hard worker. I respect you, so I don't mind telling you what my pa once told me. Mama was born in 1805 out in Louisiana while it was still a territory. When she was six years old, her folks were killed right in front of her." He frowned and stared into his coffee cup as if he did not want to continue.

"Why, the po' chile." Miss May's eyes grew moist. "Never knew that could happen to white folks."

Ezra calculated the year. "That was 1811. Was that during the Charles Deslonde revolt?"

Mr. Burns nodded. "Yep. Biggest slave revolt in U.S. history." His eyes shifted from Ezra to Miss May and back again. "You know about that?"

"Yes sir." Ezra would not tell him that he had learned about the violent incident in high school. Flaunting his education was a bad idea, maybe even dangerous. "Word gets around."

"Yep, yep, I suppose it does," Mr. Burns said. "Well, after my grandparents' deaths, Mama's uncle packed her up and moved back here to be close to family. He'd never own a slave after that." He scratched his chin. "I think that's why he favored my pa when he came courtin' Mama."

"Hmm." Ezra sent up a silent prayer of thanks for that unknown gentleman.

"Mama was a belle around these parts." Mr. Burns seemed in no hurry to get back outside to work on the barn. "Lots of suitors. But my pa won her hand."

Ezra wondered at the sorrow in Mr. Burns's eyes. Most people expressed a measure of happiness over their parents' union. No doubt his mother's illness of the mind had made the family's life difficult.

Mr. Burns's face brightened. "Granny, that was a fine dinner. Mama said so too when I took her upstairs for her nap."

Miss May smiled with shy pleasure. "I jes' hope you don' mind us all eatin' together. I ain't never ate with no white folks."

Mr. Burns shrugged. "Don't bother me if it don't bother you. I got so much work to do that I'm just glad you're doing the cooking. And it keeps Mama from having one of her spells."

Ezra drank the last of his coffee and set down the cup. Miss May's scrapple and greens had indeed been delicious. "The barn will be finished in another week. Then Miss May and I will have to move on and try to find her husband."

"I hate to hear that." Mr. Burns scratched his head. "I'm getting used to having you two around. Tell you what—when we're done with the barn, I'll take you into town, and we'll ask around. Shouldn't be too hard to find out if your old man came this way."

"Oh, I'd be real obliged, suh." Miss May beamed at Mr. Burns.

Her gratitude stirred up conflicting feelings in Ezra. He longed to see her reunited with her husband, just as he longed to see his own family back in Boston. He also hoped to see Delia again. But would she still be with Mr. Willard? And would she have believed any of that scoundrel Jack's smooth talk?

Just as he had for the past couple of weeks, he prayed for each of the people he and Miss May had traveled with. Try though he might, he could not help pleading the Lord's extra protection for Delia.

CHAPTER TWENTY

✯ ✯ ✯ ✯

*D*elia untied the cotton strips and worked her hands all over Miz Kate's scalp to smooth out the parts between the curls. She swept the hair up real fancy on the crown of her head. Just like she'd expected, her brushing and washing had tamed the dull brown tangles into silky, shiny hair that was easy to work with. And, just like she'd expected, Miz Kate again stared into the mirror like she didn't know herself.

"Gracious, Delia, where'd you learn to do that?" Miz Kate reached up to touch the curls held in place by hidden hairpins.

Delia gave her a shy smile in the mirror but didn't answer right away. Miz Kate knew she'd been a slave, but it pained Delia to talk about it.

"Come on, girl, tell me. Did you do it for your old mistress?" Miz Kate's tone was soft, and her face was lit with kindness.

"Yessum." Delia breathed in the sweet smell of the gardenia soap on Miz Kate's hair. "I done all the ladies' hair at the plantation. Even Missus liked my way of doin' it better than her girl's." She wouldn't mention Miz Suzanne, who often slapped Delia if even one curl didn't please her.

"I can see why." Miz Kate looked at Delia in the mirror and back at herself. "I ain't looked this good since I was a girl."

"'Scuse me, Miz Kate, but you ain't much more'n a girl now." Delia's heart fluttered. She'd always said nice things like that to Miz Suzanne because she had to. Now she really meant it. Would Miz Kate mind?

Miz Kate grimaced. "I'm twenty-eight, but I look forty." She ran a hand alongside one eye like she was trying to smooth out the lines in her skin. "Well, I did look forty until now. My land, how just taking a bath and having my hair fixed changes things." She stared at both hands, scrubbed clean of most of the dirt ground into them by hard work on the farm.

Delia had never seen a lady with callused hands and broken nails. Where could she get some of that balm the ladies on the plantation used to soften their hands? Miz Kate needed to take better care of herself.

"Well, I s'pose we'd best get busy." Miz Kate stood up and walked to the wardrobe. "Can't run a farm by staring in a mirror." She pulled out her work clothes and then stopped, reaching back into the wardrobe. "Well, look here." She pulled out a blue calico dress with white ribbons and lace at the collar and cuffs and stared at it like it was something special. "Um-mm. What a day that was. Ma and I had spent many an evening making this dress, and I wore it only once." She held it up in front of her and looked in the mirror like she was checking the fit. "I guess I could wear it again if I had someplace to go."

"Why, Miz Kate, you could wear it to town." Maybe she'd take Delia with her. "Or visiting, or—"

Miz Kate took a quick breath. "A visit. That's it. A visit. Just a short one, mind you, but I could do it." Her eyes sparkled with excitement. "Delia, hurry and fix breakfast. I gotta do this before I get scared and back out."

"Yessum." Caught up in Miz Kate's happiness, Delia hurried to the kitchen. She'd already started cooking the grits, so she added a small log to the woodstove, shoved the biscuits in the oven, and slapped some ham slices into the cast-iron skillet. They sizzled and popped, sending up a mouth-watering smell. Delia broke the eggs Frederick had brought in the day before and beat them into a creamy yellow liquid. Miz Kate liked her scrambled eggs just a tad bit wet, and so did Delia.

What was her mistress planning? From the look on Miz Kate's face, Delia thought it must be something special. Out from under all that dirt and messy hair, she was a pretty woman. Maybe she wanted to show off that fact to somebody. Whatever it was, Delia wanted to help her.

Still in her nightgown, Miz Kate could hardly eat her breakfast. "It's good, Delia, but my belly's all a-jitter." She downed the last of her coffee and jumped up from the table. "Go tell Jack to saddle my mare, then hurry back to help me get dressed." She started toward her bedroom. "And tell Adam to bring me the fattest piglet. Tell him to wash it up good." She giggled like a little girl. "I'm gonna find a piece of ribbon to tie around its neck."

Delia laughed, too, as she ran to obey. Whatever Miz Kate had planned, she hoped to hear all the details when it was over. Miz Suzanne used to tell Delia all about everything she did and every place she ever went. Delia couldn't say many nice things about Miz Suzanne, but she sure had liked her stories.

The other folks were finishing their breakfast when Delia rushed into their shack with the orders. Adam ran to fetch the piglet right away, but Jack just scowled.

"Where's Miz Kate goin'?" He lounged back in his chair like he had all day and no work to do.

"I don't know." Delia glared at him. "I do know she's in a hurry. If you don't want to saddle her horse, maybe Leviticus will. And I'll tell Miz Kate you didn't have time for doin' what she said."

Alice and Mr. Willard chuckled.

Jack stood up and stretched. "Don't go mouthin' off to me, gal. I'll have that mare saddled before you're back to the kitchen."

Delia didn't bother to see if he would do it. She ran back to the house and found Miz Kate struggling to fasten the buttons down the back of her dress.

"I guess this is why I haven't worn it." Miz Kate laughed nervous-like. "Can't reach all the buttons."

"Never you mind, ma'am." Delia quickly fastened them and then fixed Miz Kate's hair again. "You look pretty as a spring day."

In just a few minutes, everybody had gathered in the yard behind the house. Astride the old mare, Miz Kate reached down to Adam for the squirming piglet but then shook her head. "Oh, Lordy, he'll jump right outa my hands for sure. Adam, run get me a burlap poke from the barn. Shake it good for dirt and spiders and put the little rascal in it."

Adam handed the fat, pink piglet to Delia, who'd never held one in her life. It nearly wiggled right out of her arms while Alice tied Miz Kate's red ribbon around its neck.

"Where you goin', Miz Kate?" Frederick asked what they all wanted to know. "Whatchu need that pig fo'?"

"Hush, boy." Alice tried to shove her son behind her, but he peeked around her, his black eyes large and round with curiosity.

Miz Kate laughed. "I'm going to repay a debt, boy, at the farm beyond them east woods and 'bout a mile down the road." She glanced around the group. "Y'all know what you're s'posed to do, so don't let me down."

Adam hurried back and held open the burlap poke so Delia could drop the squealing piglet into it. He gathered the opening, tied it with a leather strap, and handed it up to Miz Kate. "Here you go, ma'am."

"Thank you all." Miz Kate hung it on the saddle and reined her horse away from them toward the road. "Getup, Ginger." She dug her heels into the mare's flanks and trotted away, her curls bouncing all over her head and her blue calico dress flapping in the breeze. She looked like a pretty bird flying away.

Delia and the others watched until she disappeared around the corner of the house and the sound of Ginger's hooves on the hard road could no longer be heard.

"Awright, ever'body get busy." Jack waved his hand toward the cotton field. "Don't you let her down, now, y'hear?"

"Don't need you to tell us what to do," Leviticus mumbled as he and the others walked that direction.

"You get on back to that kitchen, gal." Jack stood with his fists on his hips like he thought he was somebody.

Delia had a bad feeling skitter down her back. With Miz Kate gone, would Jack come into the house?

"I got water to fetch and bread to make and dinner to start fixin'." She glared at him and copied his posture, fists on her own hips. "I know what I'm s'posed to do. What're you s'posed to be doin' now?"

"Don't you worry. I'll take care of myself." He stalked off toward the barn.

But when Delia came back out to the water pump after fetching her bucket, she saw Jack heading into the woods, right in the direction of the farm where Miz Kate had gone.

Ezra stood outside the half-built barn and straightened nails on an anvil while Mr. Burns used a crowbar to pull more nails from old boards. From time to time, both men needed to mop sweat from their foreheads.

Only 8 A.M., and this June day was already hot. They had been up since 5 A.M., and Ezra kept looking toward the house with the hope that Miss May would ring the breakfast bell soon. Now, instead of the bell, he heard the clopping of an approaching horse's hooves.

"Well, I'll be ding-busted." Mr. Burns stared beyond Ezra to the path beside the house. "My, my, what a pretty sight. Wonder what she wants."

The old hound, Tick Bait, looked up and said "woof," then flopped his head back down on the grass.

Ezra turned to see what had drawn their attention. A large-boned white woman rode a big, reddish-brown mare into the farm-yard. Despite the woman's size, she was indeed a pretty sight. Her blue dress flounced around her, making for a lovely picture of femininity. Her elegant hairdo looked more appropriate for a ball than for a day in the country. Ezra glanced at Mr. Burns, whose expression bespoke far more than mere admiration.

"Howdy do, Miss Kate." Mr. Burns dropped his crowbar and hurried over to her. "Mighty good to see you." He tipped his hat.

The lady's expression mirrored Mr. Burns's. "Howdy, Owen. You doing all right?"

"Can't complain."

Miss Kate bent her head toward the house. "How's...?"

Mr. Burns shrugged. "Not too bad. I hired a little old colored granny to help out, and Mama's taken to her."

"A colored woman? That's a surprise." Miss Kate looked over at Ezra and back at Mr. Burns. "More new help?"

"Yup. Granny's boy. He happened along just when I needed help with this barn."

Miss Kate surveyed the building. "Hm. I might try to hire him away from you. He does good work."

Ezra smiled. "Thank you, ma'am."

But Owen Burns and Kate Saunders weren't paying attention to him, only to each other.

After several quiet moments, Mr. Burns shuffled his feet. "Um, can I help you down? You had breakfast?" His voice, usually so steady, wavered.

Miss Kate's laugh also wavered a little. "I can't stay. I got new folks, too. They work pretty well, but I gotta keep on top of one of them. Funny thing is, he's the biggest and strongest of the lot, but likes to boss the others around."

Jack! She had to be talking about Jack. That meant Mr. Willard was right beyond those woods—and Delia, too! Ezra started to speak up and ask about them, but just at that moment, the bag on the side of Miss Kate's saddle came to life, wiggling and squealing.

"What on earth?" Mr. Burns cocked his head and chuckled. "What do you have there?"

Miss Kate laughed. "Go on. Take it. It's yours."

"Mine?" Mr. Burns lifted down the bag and untied the strap. Out jumped a baby pig. It fell to the ground and dashed first one way, then the other, still squealing its lungs out.

"Catch him, Ezra." Mr. Burns started after the pig.

"Wait." Miss Kate reached down to touch Mr. Burns's shoulder. "He'll be fine. He won't go far." She drew back her hand and appeared to be embarrassed at touching him.

Ezra tried to return to his work as discreetly as possible, but the sound of straightening the nails on the anvil would be too intrusive. He sat down on a log and counted the straightened nails, a completely useless exercise. When would he get a chance to ask about Mr. Willard? He had to ask.

Mr. Burns's laughter came a bit more easily now. "Kate, you look so pretty. I remember that dress from the fall barn dance back in '59." He stared down at his boots for a moment. "I've seen it in my dreams more times than I could count." He looked back up at her. "Blue's a nice color on you."

Her sun-browned face took on a tinge of pink. "Thank you."

Mr. Burns cleared his throat. "Uh, do you plan on telling me about that pig? Or are you gonna keep me guessing?"

Miss Kate's laughter was light now and even a bit saucy. "Why, Owen Burns, are you gonna tell me you don't recall me shooting your prize pig back when we were kids?"

He looked astounded. "Well, I'll be ding-busted. Now that you mention it, I do recall that. But you didn't mean to do it. Pa said not to fret over it."

She lifted her head. "And *my* pa said never let a debt go unpaid."

Mr. Burns took another long look at his boots and scratched his head. "Too bad they never saw eye to eye on much of anything."

Ezra went through the motions of counting more nails. *Lord, please give me a chance to ask her....*

"You hussy!" Mrs. Burns came running across the barnyard, brandishing a rolling pin.

"Now, Mrs. Burns, honey, calm down." Miss May hurried after her as fast as her arthritic legs permitted.

"Get off my land, you brazen girl." Mrs. Burns's voice did not contain a hint of mania or hysteria, just raging anger. "Get away from my boy before I beat you silly." She flung the rolling pin toward Miss Kate.

Miss Kate pulled back on the mare's reins barely in time to dodge Mrs. Burns's weapon. The rolling pin struck the ground nearby, causing the mare to rear up and whinny. While Mrs. Burns bent over to catch her breath, Miss Kate regained control of her mount and rode a safe distance away before turning back.

"Thank you, Mrs. Burns." Miss Kate's expression, no longer pleasant, was twisted into a snarl. "Thank you for reminding me...."

"Kate, don't go. Don't go!" Mr. Burns cried out. "Will you marry me?"

She shook her head, and her mass of curls came tumbling loose around her shoulders. "Like I told you last time you asked five years ago, I'll marry you when she's locked up or six feet under, and no sooner."

She spun the mare around, slapped her haunches, and took off in a gallop.

Mr. Burns stared at her retreating form, his shoulders slumped. Miss May questioned Ezra with a look, but he could only shrug. Mrs. Burns walked over and picked up her former weapon.

"Granny, how careless of you to leave my rolling pin out here in the yard."

CHAPTER TWENTY-ONE

*O*wen, please pass the grits."

Mrs. Burns sat at the end of the kitchen table, appearing as sane and proper as anyone. Mr. Burns was another story. His pale eyes bulged, his jaw rippled as he ground his teeth, and his hands trembled.

"Don't talk to me, Mama."

Ezra looked across the table at Miss May, whose worried frown reflected his own feelings. He hadn't had a chance to tell her that the people working on Miss Kate's farm might be Mr. Willard and their other friends. But he was not about to bring up the subject now.

"Don't be rude, Owen. I'm your mother and—"

"*Don't* talk to me." Mr. Burns slammed his fist down hard.

All the dishes and silverware bounced with a jangle. Milk sloshed from the pitcher. Eggs and ham slid around their platter.

He shoved back and glared at Mrs. Burns. Ezra feared the man might strike her and prayed he would not have to interfere. But even though Mr. Burns trembled from rage, he merely turned and stomped out the back door.

"I must speak to his pa about that boy's temper." Mrs. Burns dipped her spoon into the bowl of grits Miss May had set before her. "Granny, you make the best grits."

Miss May gulped down some coffee. "Thank you, ma'am." Her hand shook as she set down the cup.

Hungry though he was, Ezra had difficulty eating. Maybe the Burnses would settle down by lunch.

"I guess I'll get back to work." Ezra forced a smile. "Would you please excuse me, Mrs. Burns?"

She smiled back serenely. "Of course, young man. You run along. Granny and I will have a nice visit."

Miss May gave him a reassuring nod. "Dat's right, we will."

Praying as always for Miss May's safety, Ezra went out to the barnyard to find Mr. Burns separating old weathered boards with a particular vengeance. Nails and splinters flew about the yard. Usable lengths of wood had crowbar-shaped chunks torn out of them.

Ezra's question nagged at him, but he wouldn't risk Mr. Burns's ire until he had paid them. He resumed his job of straightening the nails, beating a rhythm on the anvil much like the pace of troops marching to war. His former sergeant's cadence call echoed in his mind. Although this was not his battle, he felt an urging from the Lord to see it to the end, if only through prayer.

They continued their work in silence for some time. Mr. Burns seemed oblivious to the sweat pouring down his face. Usually, by this time of day, he had moved into the shade to protect himself from a painful sunburn.

Mr. Burns stopped at last to gulp down a dipper of water from the drinking pail. He poured another dipperful over his head. "Well now, Ezra, you sure have seen all our family dirt, haven't you?"

Ezra studied him for a moment to see if he should answer…and decided to listen.

"I learned from my pa that Ben Saunders was the only man in these parts who wouldn't court my mama. Unfortunately, he was the only man she wanted." Mr. Burns looked toward the house. "I guess we always want what we can't have." He shot a brief glance in the direction of Miss Kate's farm and sighed wearily. "My poor pa had to live with that for over twenty years before death gave him a rest from it.

"Now it's Kate's turn to bear the brunt of Mama's anger even though Kate never gave her a reason for such hate. Mama always said what a pretty little girl she was. Then Kate turned sixteen, and Mama was all done with nice things to say about her."

He brought over a handful of bent nails and dropped them in one of the small wooden boxes at Ezra's feet. "I've loved that gal since we were kids, but I don't blame her for refusing to marry me. I guess we're both just too stubborn, 'cause I refuse to lock Mama up in the asylum."

While Mr. Burns talked, Ezra kept on pounding nails, nodding or shrugging at the appropriate times. When he became a minister, he would need to listen to stories like this all the time. Even if he could not help Owen Burns, at least the man's monologues gave him a better understanding of difficult situations. His own childhood had been unencumbered by such woes.

"You're a good man, Ezra." Mr. Burns clapped him on the shoulder and left his hand there, claiming Ezra's full attention. "And you weren't no slave, neither."

Ezra started. "Uh, well, sir...."

"If anybody else comes around here, just keep your fancy talk to yourself. And don't stand there so much like a soldier, understand?" Mr. Burns's stare bored into Ezra until he was forced to return a crooked grin and a chuckle.

"Yessuh, boss."

"Ha!" Mr. Burns threw back his head and laughed. He patted Ezra's shoulder and threw down his crowbar. "There's your granny about to ring the dinner bell. Let's go eat."

As usual, Mrs. Burns gave no indication that anything amiss had happened earlier in the day. Mr. Burns appeared to have resolved his anger. And Granny had fixed a fine mess of black-eyed peas, turnip greens, and corn bread. Ezra plunged his fork into the greens with the eagerness of a hard-working man, as did his boss.

Halfway through the meal, Mrs. Burns daintily wiped her mouth with her napkin and then shook a finger at Ezra.

"Young man, I'm on to your games. Don't you come looking in my bedroom window again like you did a while ago, you hear? I'll have my son sic his dogs on you."

Ezra nearly choked. "Ma'am, I didn't...I wasn't...."

"Now, don't go adding lies to your wickedness." Mrs. Burns turned to Mr. Burns. "Owen, you see to it."

Mr. Burns slumped in his chair and shook his head. "Mama, Ezra's been with me all morning."

A look of genuine confusion swept across her face. "Well, who on earth was that Negro man staring at me while I took my nap?"

At the sound of pounding hooves in the backyard, Delia grabbed a tea towel to dry her hands and hurried from the kitchen. Her heart raced with expectation.

Miz Kate jumped down from old Ginger before the mare came to a halt and didn't even get her legs all tangled in her billowing skirt. She slapped the horse's haunches, sending her toward the barn. Disappointment cut into Delia when she saw Miz Kate's pretty hairdo all undone.

"Jack!" Miz Kate yelled out in an unladylike way. "Delia, where's Jack?"

"Uh…I think he's down at the river or someplace over that-away." She waved her hand in the direction of the woods. She wanted to tell on Jack, but she couldn't bring herself to do it. She'd always hated the way Beulah told on the other slaves and got them in trouble.

Miz Kate let out a string of cuss words like Delia had never heard from a lady. "Guess I'll have to unsaddle her myself," she muttered as she strode after Ginger.

"Oh, my." Delia twisted the tea towel into a bunch. She remembered all the times when Miz Suzanne got angry with somebody else and took it out on her. Should she run away? Should she go out to the fields? No, dinner would be ruined if she did. She hurried up the back steps and into the kitchen just in time to keep the potatoes from boiling over. That would've been an awful mess to clean off the stove.

Soon Miz Kate stomped in the back door and cussed all the way to her bedroom. Delia couldn't keep herself from following. Her mistress was tearing at the buttons on the back of her dress, and Delia hurried to help her.

"Miz Kate, what happened?"

"Crazy, crazy. That woman's plumb crazy, and she's ruined just about ever'body's life in these parts." Miz Kate yanked the dress over her head. "If he was half a man, he'd lock her up and...." A sob broke up her words. "Here, take this." She shoved the dress at Delia. "Use it for rags. No. Burn it. Get it out of my sight."

"Yessum." Delia shook, yet somehow she knew Miz Kate wouldn't hit her. "Please let me help you. Please tell me what happened."

Miz Kate stared at her like she was a stranger. Then she flung herself down on the bed and cried.

Delia bent to touch her shoulder but pulled back. Best to leave the poor woman alone. Maybe when she finished her crying, she'd tell Delia what had happened.

She held up the dress. In spite of a few tears in the back, it was still pretty, and the cotton, though faded, was still strong. It would be a shame for it to go to waste. With Miz Kate being such a big woman, there'd be plenty of material for Delia to make herself a dress after she left here. With that thought in mind, she hurried up to the loft and tucked the dress under her mattress.

Guilt nibbled at her conscience like a mouse on a corn cob, but she quickly dismissed it. This was *not* stealing. Miz Kate had thrown the dress away as surely as if she'd flung it on the trash heap herself. Everybody knew it wasn't stealing to make use of somebody else's trash.

At least she hoped it wasn't.

Chapter Twenty-Two

*E*zra held a weathered plank across the sawhorses while Mr. Burns sawed off the rotten end. They had made progress that afternoon toward redeeming usable wood from the old barn to finish the new one. Mr. Burns's mood had improved as the boards stacked up. Ezra hated to remind him of that morning's unhappy events, but he had no choice.

"Mr. Burns, sir, I wonder if you would mind if I walked over to Miss Saunders's farm this evening? I'd like to see if Miss May's husband is one of her new helpers." He looked for a hint of displeasure, but his boss's expression remained placid. "She sure misses him. They've been married over forty years."

"Forty years? Lawsy mercy, that's something." Mr. Burns shook his head. "To think some slave owner let a couple stay together like that instead of selling one of them off."

"Hmm. Imagine that." All his life Ezra had heard how slave owners often broke up families. He lifted up a silent prayer of thanks that the Lord had protected the Brewsters from such a cruel practice.

"Don't know about you, Ezra, but I can't abide thinking of keeping them apart any longer. You take my mule and ride on over there right after supper and check."

Ezra grinned. "Why, thank you, sir. That's very generous. But I could just walk through those woods." He pointed toward the thick growth of trees to the west.

"No, I wouldn't let you risk goin' through those woods, least ways not alone and not at night." Mr. Burns cocked his head knowingly. "Panthers. They stalk their prey, circle around, and attack from behind. No, you never want to be out there alone."

Ezra shuddered. "Ah, I see."

"You can hear them scream sometimes in the night." Now Mr. Burns shuddered, as if copying Ezra. "Once you hear that sound, you ain't never gonna forget it. It's almost human. So go ahead and ride Long Ears over there. He's awright for ridin'."

"I will, sir. Thank you very much."

Mr. Burns gave him a quick nod. "I owe it to Granny for the way she's helped with Mama. Never saw nobody who could manage her that way."

They worked in silence for several moments, but Ezra's mind raced. Would Delia be there? What would he say to her? Would he even be able to say anything? What a simpleton he had been not to talk to her before. She was shy, so he should have made more of an effort to befriend her. Was it too late now? Had Jack already won her heart?

"What now?" Mr. Burns set down his saw and brushed sawdust off his hands as he looked past Ezra. "Don't need another visitor today, 'specially not the parson and that gabby wife of his."

Ezra turned to see a one-horse phaeton coming down the road.

"How do? How do?" The driver, a white man, wore a tall black hat and black suit. Beside him sat a lady in the severe dark clothing of a minister's wife. Both waved and smiled as they drove into the barnyard.

"Afternoon, Reverend." Mr. Burns lifted his broad-brimmed hat. "Afternoon, Mrs. Hardy." He nudged Ezra and tersely muttered, "Get the horse."

Ezra caught his meaning right away. Mr. Burns could treat him as an equal when they were alone, but when other white people came around, Ezra's place was that of a servant. Momentary disappointment gave way to expediency. He would cause nothing but trouble for himself and perhaps never get back to Boston if he resisted southern ways. He hurried to grasp the horse's bridle while the minister helped his wife down from the carriage.

"That's a fine barn you're building there." The minister studied the structure and nodded his approval. Then he looked at Ezra as if he were an inanimate object. "What's this?"

An unpleasant feeling arose in Ezra, but he pasted on a bland smile.

"Why, Owen." The minister chuckled. "A man who refused to own slaves when it was legal, and here you have...." He tilted his head toward Ezra.

Ezra forced his smile to remain in place.

"He's *hired* help, Reverend." Owen again tipped his hat to the lady. "Mrs. Hardy, you're looking mighty fine on this hot day. Have you come to see Mama?"

"Why, yes, we have, Mr. Burns." The smile on Mrs. Hardy's face looked so strained that Ezra almost laughed. She was playing a part, just as he was. "We've even brought some lemonade made by my Mary. She's stayed with us, you know, just like all our other servants.

They love us so much that all this emancipation nonsense just goes right past them." She cast a brief glance at Ezra.

He focused on a bird flying across the cotton field. So this was what Mr. Burns had to contend with from his neighbors. No wonder he needed Ezra to act servile.

"Lemonade?" Mr. Burns beamed. "Why, Mrs. Hardy, your kindness lifts a man's soul clear to heaven with gratitude. How good of you to remember how much Mama likes to drink lemonade." He brushed more sawdust from his hands. "Can I carry it inside for you?" He walked to the back of the phaeton and threw back a canvas covering to lift out a large green crock. "Here we go. Let's go see Mama."

As he started away, he shot a quick look back at Ezra. "Boy, tie that horse up in the shade and come on over to the house. You been working hard all day in the hot sun. I'll pour you a glass of this lemonade myself, one for you and one for Granny."

Mrs. Hardy gasped.

"Yessuh, boss." Ezra swallowed a laugh.

The reverend blustered a bit, but he and his wife followed Mr. Burns to the house.

Ezra soon sat on the back stoop enjoying a refreshing glass of lemonade almost as good as his mother's. With some little effort, he put aside thoughts of the white people inside the house and their foolish ways. Instead, he began to plan what he would say to a certain young lady if he saw her that evening. He wished he had his volumes of Shakespeare or Browning. Then he chuckled.

Guess I'll have to make up my own poetry this time.

Delia dried the last pot and carried the dishpan outside to dump the dishwater on the kitchen garden. She hung the tea towel on the line to dry and then gazed around the barnyard.

Miz Kate had gone out to check the fields with Jack and Leviticus, and the others were in their shack. Or maybe Mr. Willard had taken Frederick down to the river to fish. Sure as anything, Alice was doing something to make that shack a nice home for all of them, like she did every night no matter how tired she was.

Delia started to go see how everybody was doing but went out front instead. There was something about the way the breeze blew across the covered front porch that not only cooled her off but also set her mind to dreaming about going to Boston with Mr. Willard. Back on the plantation, she'd never had a minute to herself for that kind of dreaming. Here, Miz Kate didn't seem to mind if she sat for a spell after chores were done. 'Course, she always did more than Miz Kate expected.

Sitting out here in the old rocking chair, she didn't have to smell the stink of the pigs or listen to their ugly grunts, and she couldn't hear the cow or chickens calling for their supper. Nothing to hear but crickets and songbirds. Nothing to smell but sweet lilacs. In just over a week, she'd come to love that lilac smell, 'cause nobody here made a switch from its branches to beat her with.

This summer evening, with the sun still hanging above the horizon, she gazed off in the distance beyond the woods. There she saw a little cloud of dust rising right about where the main road was. A bunch of blackbirds flew up sudden like from the trees on either side of the farm road just as Delia heard hoofbeats coming her way.

She stood up quickly and watched as a long-eared mule loped along the road toward the house. The man on the mule wore a big brown slouch hat, but she could see right away he was colored.

The man drew up to the house, whipped off his hat, and gave her a low bow and big smile.

"Good evening, Miss Delia. You certainly are a welcome sight."

Delia felt herself sway. She grabbed the arm of the rocker, which only made her dizzier, so she dropped back into the chair.

"Ezra Johns." Her words came out all soft and breathy, but her heart pounded so loud, she could hear it.

"Yes, ma'am." He grinned real big and jumped down from the mule, then tied it to the hitching post. "It certainly is good to see you."

"B-but…you…you're dead." No, he wasn't. She could smell the mule, and it didn't smell nothing like lilacs.

Ezra laughed, and his smile got so big, it even lit his fine, dark eyes. "Oh, no, I'm not. I'm alive and well. Here." He reached out to her. "Shake my hand, and you'll see I'm real."

"Oh, my." Delia stood up on trembling legs and reached out. As she touched the callused, well-formed hand, she felt a jolt so powerful, she thought she'd been struck by lightning. With a gasp, she pulled her hand back. Then she laughed out loud. Then she could hardly keep from throwing her arms around his tall, handsome self. But—

"Ezra Johns, if you're standin' there alive and you don't have Miz May with you, then get on that mule and ride off now. 'Cause I ain't goin' through grief over her dyin' with dear ol' Mr. Willard again, y'hear?" Where had those words come from? Delia knew she didn't have that kind of courage.

But Ezra just stood there grinning. And leaning toward her like he was just as glad to see her as she was to see him.

"Miss May is alive and better than ever. She's over at the next farm, where we found work. When your, uh, the lady who lives here came over this morning, she mentioned hiring a group of people to work for her. I just knew it had to be you and the others. How's Mr. Willard? Are all the others here, too?"

Delia nodded. Her heart had begun to settle down, except now it just seemed to hum with joy. The evening breeze was still blowing, but Delia's face felt as hot as when she stood over the stove cooking.

"Oh, I do long to see Miz May. When can we see her?" Tears filled her eyes when she thought about Mr. Willard finding out she was alive.

"Tomorrow's Sunday, so we'll have most of the day off. I'll bring her over then. Is that all right?"

He was asking her opinion. Her heart raced again. "Yes, that'll be real fine." She thought for a moment. "Ezra, my heart's pounding like crazy to know she…and you, too, are alive. I'm scared Mr. Willard's heart might give out if we surprise him too sudden. What should we do?"

Ezra frowned and nodded like he was thinking on it. "Hmm. Maybe you could tell him first thing in the morning before we come over. Can you keep it a secret until then?"

"Hmph. Ain't no man or woman alive can keep a secret like me." She gave him a smug look, and he laughed again.

It seemed that they looked at each other for a long while. Delia thought she'd never felt such happiness, though she couldn't tell why.

"You looking for work?" Miz Kate came out the door, with her dog Sheba at her side.

Delia jumped. Ezra blinked, and his jaw fell open like he didn't know what to say. Sheba jumped off the porch and smelled him. Ezra let her lick the palm of his hand. He bent down to pet her, and she licked his cheek, so he scratched her behind the ears.

"You're that fella who works for Owen." She got a funny expression on her face. "Did he send you over?"

"No, ma'am." Ezra stood back up. "My granny and I were traveling with Miz Delia and the others when we got separated by a flood up in the hills."

Delia stared at him. He was trying to sound southern colored, but he wasn't doing a very good job of it.

Miz Kate scowled at him. "You ain't gonna take my workers, are you?"

"No, ma'am. But Mr. Willard is my granny's, um, Miss May's husband, and—"

"And he thinks she died in that flood," Delia broke in. "Can you just think how happy he'll be to know she's alive?" She slumped her shoulders and bent toward Miz Kate as humbly as she could. They didn't need no trouble with her.

Miz Kate looked off in the distance, and her eyes got red. "Yep. I can think that." She turned back toward the house. "You be careful how you tell the old man, y'hear?"

"Yessum." Delia waited until Miz Kate got inside, and then she stepped closer to Ezra. His working-man smell tickled her nose, but she didn't mind. "What went on over there? She come home crying."

Ezra scratched his chin and took his time before he spoke. "I must ask the Lord to forgive me if this is gossip. Apparently, your Miss Kate and my Mr. Burns would like to get married, but his mother is, um, well, she's a problem."

"Oh." Delia stared into his eyes. *What was wrong with gossip? How else did folks find out about anything interesting?* "Well, that's just real sad."

"It's a little bit like Romeo and Juliet."

"Who?"

Ezra laughed. "They were sweethearts whose families kept them apart." He glanced toward the house and then back at Delia. "Someday, I'll tell you the whole story."

A pleasant shiver swept all through her. "I'd like that."

He chucked her chin, then seemed surprised by his own action. "How about on the way to Boston? Are you still planning to go?"

"Un-huh. Are you?" Stupid question. Delia wanted to kick herself.

But he laughed. "Yes. And I have every intention of seeing that you and the Brewsters get there safely. And the others, if they still want to go." He walked over to the hitching post and untied the reins. "Well, I'd better go before anyone else sees me." He jumped on the mule. "Good-bye, Delia. See you in the morning."

She gave him a little wave and then sank back down in the rocker.

What a fine day this had turned out to be. Dear ol' Miz May was alive.

But she was most happy that Ezra was, too.

CHAPTER TWENTY-THREE

*J*ust before he rode out of sight, Ezra turned back and waved to Delia one more time. As he hoped, she still sat on the porch watching him. At fifty yards, he could still see her pretty smile, and the happiness that filled his chest was like nothing he had ever felt in his life.

He should not have chucked her on the chin. That was what grown-ups did to children. She certainly was not a child. But she had looked so beguiling when he had mentioned Romeo and Juliet, the gesture had seemed natural. He must not do that sort of playful thing again, at least not until they knew each other better.

He longed to tell her stories, to teach her how to read them for herself. To teach her how to live in the city and to be the fine lady she was meant to be.

"Lord, please guide my friendship with Delia. Help me not to be in a hurry." He glanced up through the trees and spotted the evening star in the fading daylight. Delia was like that star, just starting to shine.

A twinge of guilt crept into his mind for thinking only of his own concerns. "And, Lord, thank You that the Brewsters will be reunited tomorrow morning."

Back on the main road, he continued to smile to himself until some white men approached from the other way on horseback. He pulled the mule over to the side and took off his hat, avoiding their stares.

Lord, make them pass on by.

But the men stopped right in front of him.

"What're you doing with that mule, boy?"

The better dressed, middle-aged man sported white streaks through his black beard. His younger companion resembled him except for the well-worn Confederate uniform on his gaunt form and a cavalry officer's broad-brimmed hat on his head. A hint of whiskey wafted on the breeze toward Ezra, but he could see they were not entirely drunk.

"I work for Mr. Owen Burns, suh. I'm headed back over there now." He despised his feeble attempts to sound southern. He despised the way he trembled. But he could not help it. Did the men believe him? What would they do if they thought he was lying or had stolen the animal?

"Maybe we ought to follow you," the younger man said. "Pa, what do you think?"

The older man shifted in his saddle and looked back over his shoulder toward the Burns farm. "Might be a good idea. Go on, boy. We'll be right behind you."

"Yessuh." Ezra put his hat on and reined the mule toward the Burns' farm road. It was just over a mile from the Saunders road—a short distance in the country. But for Ezra, it seemed like a hundred miles. His back tingled with frightening expectation, for he had seen the guns the men wore in their waist holsters. Would they shoot him for sport?

How long had it been since he had felt this same fear? Not in battle. That was a raw terror of a different sort, and he had been with his fellow soldiers. No, it had been back on the streets of Boston after he had played baseball with a group of other boys, some of them white. Five men, who most likely were slave-catchers, had followed him home as it grew dark, just as now. Only by ducking through alleys near the African Meeting House had he avoided being kidnapped and probably carried down south to be sold into slavery. The practice of kidnapping Negroes and selling them into slavery had gone on for years.

The desperate aloneness he had felt then had marked him in a cruel way. If he had been taken south, no one ever would have known what had happened to him. And if these men murdered him, his friends would never know. His family would assume he had been killed in battle. The memory filled him with a sense of desolation.

Mercy, Lord. Mercy.

At the road to Mr. Burns's farm, he guided the mule off to the left and continued his journey.

"Boy," the older man called out.

Ezra pulled back on the reins and turned around. Dread brought a bitter taste up into his throat.

"Go on, now." The older man waved his hand. "You're all right."

"But, Pa...." The son glared at Ezra. "How do you know you can trust him?"

"Easy, son. This boy may ride with a little too much confidence for a Negro, but he's not scared of heading down this road either. It's evident he belongs here." The man spat a wad of tobacco on the ground and then turned his horse. "You got to watch for things like that now that darkies don't need papers to be on the road."

His son followed him, and the two chuckled as they rode away. Had their harassment been some sort of cruel game? Ezra tried to shudder away the sick feeling in his stomach.

Remembering how Delia had changed her posture when Miss Saunders came out of the house, he shook his head. At first, the pert, almost sassy way she had spoken to him offered evidence of a budding confidence, and he had been delighted. Yet she had crumbled in the presence of her mistress. He must get her away from here. He must take her where she could hold her head up high and know her worth before God and man.

His fear of these southern whites felt like shackles on his soul, making a lie of both his lifelong physical freedom and his spiritual freedom in Christ. The parson and his wife, these two men, the entire South—none of them would change anytime soon.

Ezra knew he must leave this place as quickly as possible—and take Delia and the Brewsters with him.

※

Delia set the breakfast tray in the center of the rough plank table. She and Alice ladled gravy over biscuits as the others said how good the food smelled. The two women served the food on tin plates and poured coffee into tin cups.

Delia's stomach fluttered. The news she was about to give them had kept her up most of the night. First she'd think about how to tell

Mr. Willard. Then she'd think about Ezra's fine dark eyes and friendly smile. Then she'd be excited about seeing Miz May again. Then she'd start all over again with Mr. Willard. She never could decide what to say to him.

"What'd you put in this gravy to make it so good?" Adam always said something nice about her cooking.

"Oh, jus' some ham drippin's and a little salt." She'd keep that dash of hot sauce a secret.

"Mr. Willard's gonna take me fishin' down at the river." Frederick had gravy all over his chin 'cause he ate his biscuits with his hands instead of using a fork. "Will you cook up the fish we catch?"

Delia grinned at him. "I sure will." She looked around the group while they ate. Even Jack gave her an agreeable nod when he bit into his second biscuit.

"Mr. Willard," she said, "I heard some good news last night."

"That so?" He raised his eyebrows, and his eyes twinkled like he'd like to hear more.

"Yessuh." She sat beside him on his cot and put her arm around his shoulders. Then she swallowed hard when tears she hadn't planned on kept her from talking.

"Why, honey, what is it?" He gave her a hug.

"Mr. Willard, I done found out our Miz May is alive."

"What?" His eyes got big, and he sat back. "What you talkin' 'bout, chile?"

"I cain't believe it." Leviticus moved closer.

"Why, how in the world—?" Alice said.

Oh, she hadn't meant to blurt it out that way. "Ezra Johns come over last night. He's workin' right down the road on the next farm on the other side of the woods. He and Miz May didn't drown in that flood. He's bringin' her over this mornin'.'"

Everybody got real quiet. Her tears made it hard to see, but she noticed one thing. While everybody else looked at each other all startled, Jack's smart-aleck grin showed he wasn't the least bit surprised by what she said. He must have seen Ezra and Miz May when he followed Miz Kate, but he never said a word. Delia thought it was the best thing he'd ever done—and maybe the worst all at the same time.

"Well, if that don't beat all." Leviticus hugged Alice and messed with Frederick's curly hair. They all laughed.

Adam grinned and patted Mr. Willard's shoulder. "That's good news, ain't it?"

Mr. Willard just sat there nodding, and a smile lit up his whole face. "Thank You, Lawd. Thank You." He pulled out his handkerchief and wiped away tears with his trembling hands. "Glory be, when's they comin'?"

Delia laughed and cried at the same time. "He jus' said this mornin'."

"Oh, Lawd, thank You. Thank You." Mr. Willard lifted his hands up like he was praying and stared at the ceiling while more tears came down his cheeks. After a bit, he pulled himself together and looked at Delia.

"Is she awright? Is she well?"

"Ezra says she's better than ever. Can you believe it?"

"Glory be." Mr. Willard clapped his hands. "Lawd, You done looked down on this ol' man and brought him joy in old age."

After breakfast, everybody except Jack hurried around cleaning up the shack like they were having company. Jack just sat in a corner and frowned.

"Miz May always made us clean up the camp." Alice brushed crumbs off the table into her hand. "I want her to be proud of us."

"Here's that knife and fork you give me out of her bag." Adam handed them to Mr. Willard. "She'll need them now."

The others returned small items Mr. Willard had given out when he thought she was gone for good. He sat there grinning from ear to ear.

Delia took the dirty dishes back to the kitchen and cleaned them up. Miz Kate sat by the front window mending clothes. She looked lonely, so Delia went and sat by her to help.

"You like that boy, don't you?" Miz Kate gave Delia a little smile.

Delia shrugged a bit, but she couldn't keep from smiling back. "Yessum."

"I could tell he likes you a whole heap." Her smile got bigger. "I hope y'all will be happy."

Delia felt her face getting hot. "Oh, it ain't got to more'n likin'. We only knew each other for a few days afore the flood sent them one way and us the other."

Miz Kate laughed. "Maybe not for you, Delia. But like I said, I can see he likes you a whole heap."

Her words made Delia feel good. Better than the words, her care, her interest made Delia feel like she had a friend. She could stay right here and look after Miz Kate the rest of her life and be happy. Miz Kate sure needed somebody to look after her. 'Cept Delia was headed for Boston at the end of summer, her and the Brewsters and Ezra Johns.

Those thoughts ended when hoofbeats sounded outside the front door.

"He's here. They're here." Delia set aside her mending and dashed outside.

Ezra was helping Miz May down from the mule, and Delia hurried over to give her a big hug.

"Oh, Miz May, it's so good to see you. Mr. Willard's out back jus' waitin' for you."

"Chile, you's prettier than ever." Miz May patted Delia's cheek. She peeked around her. "How do, ma'am."

Miz Kate stood on the front porch with Sheba. "Welcome, Miss May. You go on around to the back and make that old man happy."

As Delia, Ezra, and Miz May rounded the corner of the house, Mr. Willard came hobbling across the barnyard. Miz May met him by the water pump, and they cried and held on to each other for the longest time. Watching them made Delia's heart ache, but in a good way.

"He looks well." Ezra bent toward Delia. "I can see you took good care of him."

She glanced up at him. "Well, what'd you 'spect? That's the last thing you tol' me to do afore you and Miz May went swimmin' in that creek. I always do what I'm tol'." She wrinkled her nose just a bit like Miz Suzanne did at one of her beaux.

Ezra seemed to like it, because he chucked her chin again, just like the night before. And again, he looked surprised by what he'd done. Delia laughed, and so did Ezra. But she noticed Jack standing on the other side of the group, and he wasn't smiling at all.

✫ ✫ ✫

CHAPTER TWENTY-FOUR

Delia sat beside Miz May and held her hand as they all rested under the shady branches of a live oak. Her mind was on the fried chicken keeping warm in the oven and the biscuits ready to bake as soon as Ezra's little church meeting was over. She noticed that everybody 'cept Jack leaned toward Ezra waiting for him to start.

"The angel of the Lord encampeth round about them that fear Him and delivereth them." His Bible on his lap, Ezra looked around the group. "Today, we can all testify to God's deliverance, can't we?"

"Amen." Miz May leaned against her husband, who sat next to her.

"Amen." Mr. Willard squeezed Miz May's hand.

"Seems to me He coulda done a whole lot better job." Jack stood off a bit from the others and waved one of the stinky cigars he'd made from old tobacco leaves he'd found in the barn. At least the smell kept some of the pesky flies away.

"Why'd He have to wash this poor little old lady down that gully?" Jack pointed at Miz May, and his jaw stuck out like it did when he got mad. "If God's so almighty powerful and good, why was we born slaves?"

Delia didn't believe for a minute Jack cared about Miz May, but for once, she agreed with him. If God took care of them that feared Him, why'd her Christian mama have to be beat to death? She shifted around on the smooth grass to pull a pebble from under her leg. Ezra'd never been a slave, so what did he know? She'd never say that, but she had to wonder.

"Why, son." Mr. Willard turned to look over at Jack. "They's always gonna be wicked people in dis here world, people who don' care who they hurt, long as they git what they want."

"That's true," Leviticus said. "I knowed free coloreds who owned slaves and was jus' as mean to 'em as any white man."

"Well, we're all free now." Adam moved over to where he could see the pages while Ezra read, though Delia knew he couldn't read any more than she could. "And I'm sittin' here thinkin' it had to be God who brought this Bible back to Ezra after I sold it to that soldier."

"Amen, amen." Mr. Willard chuckled. "And it be God who brought my May back to me."

Everybody 'cept Jack hummed or amened their agreement to that. Long as Delia lived, she just knew she'd always get a happy feeling when she remembered the sweet tears of joy the old couple had shed this morning over by the water pump. What a happy sight that had been.

"Awright, now." Leviticus got to his feet. "Since we're havin' a church meetin', I'd like to testify 'bout somethin' God done, like Ezra done said."

"Go on, brotha'." Jack sounded to Delia like he was making fun of Leviticus.

But Leviticus just went right on. "God worked it so's we could be workin' here for a lady who treats us good, lets us have fried chicken for Sunday dinner, and says she'll pay us when the crops get sold. Thank You, Lawd." He gave a quick nod of his head for good measure, then sat down.

Jack stepped over closer to the group and pointed to himself with his thumb. "*I'm* the one who went out lookin' for you all so's you could be workin' here, and don't you forget it. And *I'm* still awaitin' for my forty acres and a mule."

"Forty acres and a mule?" Ezra shook his head. "Jack, that's not a law yet. General Sherman issued a field order about it, but neither the president nor Congress made that promise. You can't count on it happening."

Delia looked around 'cause everybody had got real quiet.

Mr. Willard cleared his throat and slapped his knee. "Well, I don' want no mule or no forty acres no how. I done worked in the fields long as this ol' body can take. No suh, I's goin' north to Boston to see my chi'drun, and that's where I'll spend the rest o' my days."

Him and Miz May looked at each other and smiled.

"I'm thinkin' I'd like to stay right here and work for Miz Kate." Leviticus turned to Alice. "How 'bout you, honey?"

"I do like her, and I think she's fair. Besides, we're free to go any time we want to, if'n we change our minds." Alice held Frederick close with one hand and put her other hand on her round belly. "And my boy and my baby won't never be tooken away from me and sold to somebody else. I'm glorifyin' God for that all by itself."

Adam nudged Ezra with his elbow. "Go on. Read some more."

Waving away a gnat, Ezra picked up his Bible and turned some pages. "Speaking of freedom, John 8:36 says 'If the Son therefore shall make you free, ye shall be free indeed.'" He closed the book.

"Many men fought and died so you could be free from the evil institution of slavery. But Jesus Christ is the only one who can make you free from sin."

"Delia." Miz Kate stood by the back door hollering and waving. "You gonna cook them biscuits?"

Delia jumped to her feet, but not before she saw Ezra's disappointed look.

"We gotta eat." She shrugged her regret at leaving and then ran across the yard to the house.

She and Miz Kate went inside.

"How'd your church meeting go?" Miz Kate got the potato masher out of the cupboard and started working over the pan of cooked potatoes.

"Jus' fine, ma'am. Jus' fine." Delia wouldn't tell her she'd interrupted right when Ezra was getting to the good part.

"Well, that's nice." Miz Kate poured a little cream into the potatoes and mashed some more. "Why don't you take that old tablecloth in the buffet drawer and spread it out under that tree for a picnic?"

"Thank you, ma'am." Delia worked up some courage, then said, "Would you like to join us?"

Miz Kate smiled but shook her head. "Naw. I'm gonna take a nice long nap after dinner. My pa always made us observe the Sabbath, and I think it's a good practice."

Delia thought a nap sounded good, but she'd much rather spend the afternoon finding out more about what Miz May had been doing for the last few weeks. And Ezra, too, of course.

Especially Ezra.

Disappointment filled Ezra as he watched Delia dash across the yard toward the house. Even though she had frowned when he spoke of God's deliverance, she seemed interested in what he read from the Bible. He sent up a quick prayer that he would have another chance to talk to her about Jesus. Before he gave his heart away completely, he must find out if she was a Christian.

"Go on. Read some more o' that stuff." Jack glared at Ezra and sent a rude glance in Delia's direction.

Ezra cleared his throat to keep from rebuking Jack. The man clearly had no respect for God's Word, and the look in his eyes revealed something far less than respect for Delia. After another prayer for Jack's salvation, he continued.

"You folks might think I don't know what you've been through, and I'll admit I don't. But there are others who have known cruel bondage and even death at the hands of their persecutors." He turned to the book of Hebrews, chapter eleven. "'Now faith is the substance of things hoped for, the evidence of things not seen.'" He continued to read the chapter, which first told of the strong faith in God that the Old Testament believers had and then described the terrible torture and deaths of others who had dared to stand up for their faith.

"Just as Mr. Willard says, there are wicked people in this world. The only way to overcome that wickedness is through faith in God. Not faith that things will go our way or that we'll receive forty acres and a mule. But faith that God is who He says He is— almighty and powerful—and that He cares about each one of us, whatever our circumstances."

"Amen," chorused Mr. Willard and Miss May.

"That's right." Leviticus said at the same time.

"Mama, what's circus stances?" Frederick gazed up at his mother with such a pure innocence that Ezra felt a lump in his throat.

Alice licked her lips and turned an entreating look toward Ezra.

"Circumstances are the things that are happening in our lives." Ezra decided that he must use simpler words when addressing these dear people.

"Well, I'm plannin' on makin' good stuff happen in my life." Jack puffed on his cigar for a moment. "I ain't waitin' 'round for any more bad stuff to happen. If the president and Congress don't give me my forty acres and a mule, though I worked all my life for no pay 'cept bein' beat by the massuh, then I might just have to find a way to git them myself."

"How much you been beat?" Adam looked at Jack with disgust. "I seen your back. Ain't got one mark on it. Not like this." He pulled up his shirt to reveal several raised, crisscrossed scars that had been on his dark brown back long enough to heal to a dull gray.

Alice gasped, and the men groaned.

"Lawd, have mercy." Miss May's fresh tears revealed her horror. "An' you jes' a boy."

Ezra swallowed hard. Adam *was* just a boy, not more than fifteen. How could anyone be so cruel as to beat him that way?

Jack stepped toward Adam and leaned over him. "You callin' me a liar, boy?"

Ezra closed his Bible and stood. "Well, Jack, we all agree that slavery is evil. We can thank God that it's all over now, can't we?" He started to give Jack a friendly pat on the shoulder. But Jack's eyes blazed with anger bordering on hatred, so Ezra simply smiled.

"Thank God for *nothin'*." Jack stormed off toward the barn, and his vile curses caused Alice to quickly cover Frederick's ears.

"Lawd, Lawd, hep that boy." Miss May swayed back and forth where she sat. "He was bad when we met him, and I see he got even badder."

"It was all we could do to keep him off Miz Delia." Mr. Willard shook his head. "If'n we hadn't all watched out for her...."

Ezra shuddered away the rage those words incited. He sat back down beside the Brewsters.

"Tell me, sir, did you have a chance to talk to Miss Delia about, um, about her faith?"

Mr. Willard shook his head sadly. "Oh, son, that chile's got a bitter root. Not like Jack, but maybe jes' as deep."

"Tell him." Alice moved closer and nudged Mr. Willard. "He should know."

"What is it, honey?" Miss May asked.

Mr. Willard sighed. "That sweet chile's mother was the massuh's mistress. Delia's the massuh's chile, and she hates that so bad. When she was jes' a little gal, the missus had her mama beat so bad, she died."

"Lawd, have mercy." Miss May began to weep. "Oh, *Lawd*, have mercy."

Ezra felt as if he had been slammed in the chest by a baseball bat. Poor Delia. Poor, sweet Delia. How could he help her get beyond such horror? The answer came to mind as quickly as the question had. Only God could help her...if she would let Him.

CHAPTER TWENTY-FIVE

Miz Kate had already eaten and gone to her bedroom to take a nap, so Delia packed all the food in a basket and covered it with the faded yellow tablecloth, then closed the lid. She stuck her head out the back door and hollered at Alice.

"I can't carry all this by myself. Would you help me?"

Alice came running, followed by Frederick and his puppy. Seeing Miz May nudge Ezra and point her way, Delia grinned to herself. Her helpers arrived real quick and came into the house.

"May I carry the basket, Miss Delia?" Ezra gave her one of his fine smiles. It lit up the whole kitchen.

"I'd be obliged." She had to turn away 'cause of the way he looked at her. Not ugly or rude like Jack did, but kindly, like Delia was somebody who deserved respect. She didn't know what to do with that look, so she shoved the heavy, covered basket into his hands.

"They's a tablecloth inside. Spread it out first and then set out the food. Alice, can you carry the plates? I'll bring the lemonade.

Frederick, here's some napkins. Now you keep that dog of yours away from the food, y'hear?"

Ezra chuckled as he did what he was told, and so did Alice.

"Yessum." Frederick grinned, eyeing the basket.

Outside, everybody said how good the food smelled, and that made Delia happy. She sat like a fine lady at the head of the table to dish it out, just like Beulah used to sit at the head of the kitchen table and do for the house slaves. 'Cept Delia would serve out generous portions of potatoes and greens and biscuits instead of being stingy like Beulah.

Before she could start, Jack reached toward the meat platter, so she slapped his hand with the meat fork. "Just hold on there." Beulah's voice echoed in her mind, saying those same words.

"Hey!" He scowled at her but did what she said.

"We got to feed children and old folks and ladies first. Frederick, what piece do you want?" Delia liked being the boss, if only about the food.

The boy's dark eyes got big and round. "Can I have a drumstick?"

"You sure can." She put one on his plate with the other food, then served Miz May and Mr. Willard. After them came Alice.

As she spooned gravy over Alice's potatoes and passed her the plate, Delia felt a nervous twitter in her belly. If she served Jack next, he'd think she favored him. If she served Ezra next—

"I like white meat." Jack sat cross-legged on one side of the tablecloth and gave her a sly grin. "Gimme some o' that white meat."

Delia had cut the white meat off the bone to make it seem like there was more. "Awright. Here's your white meat." She filled his plate, but gave it to him without looking up. His grin said something she didn't understand.

When she gave Ezra his food, he gave her another one of those nice smiles.

"Thank you, Miss Delia."

She felt pure pleasure clear down to her toes.

After everyone was served and Mr. Willard blessed the food, they all dug in. Delia thought Miz Kate had put a bit too much salt in the potatoes. And maybe Delia could have added a little more hot sauce to the gravy. The chicken was falling off the bone from having sat in the oven all that time, and its crisp crust had softened to mush. The gravy had lumps as big as dumplings, and the greens were tough and tasted gritty, like she hadn't washed all the garden dirt out of them.

Delia wanted to cry so bad she almost couldn't swallow. Her first chance to cook for Ezra, and she'd failed. Only the biscuits were perfect. She'd made two for each person, one for butter and one for gravy.

"My, oh, my, Miz Delia." Leviticus licked his fingers and tossed a thigh bone to Sheba, who'd been sitting close by waiting for that very thing. "You done outdid yourself." He glanced at Alice. "Why, you cook almost as good as my Alice."

"This is excellent." Ezra nodded his agreement as he wiped his hands on his napkin. The look in his eyes was honest. He really did like her cooking.

Everybody else gave her compliments, too.

Delia felt her face heat up with a happy blush. "I got pie."

"With cream?" Adam grinned.

"Well…." Delia puckered her lips to keep from grinning back. "I s'pose we could have a little cream."

While the others clucked their eagerness like a bunch of hungry chickens instead of a bunch of people who'd just been fed, Delia stood to go get her pie.

"I'll help." Jack got up, too.

She hesitated until she noticed that the look in Jack's eyes was all about pie, not her. With a shrug, she went toward the house.

The two apple pies needed more sugar, but no one else seemed to notice. Maybe the cream helped.

After they'd all eaten their fill, Delia wanted that nap. Miz May must have seen it, 'cause she said she and Alice would clean up. Delia shook crumbs off the tablecloth and stretched out on it—in clear sight of everybody else where Jack wouldn't bother her. She loved being down close to the ground where she could smell the grass and clover.

She saw Ezra go off to the woods for a bit. Soon he came back with a stick. He pulled a ball from his pocket and gathered Frederick and the menfolk together. Delia heard Ezra tell them all about a game called baseball. They all seemed happy, even Jack, once they got busy figuring out how to play the game in the backyard.

Just before she dozed off, Delia wondered where they found the energy to play anything on such a hot day.

◆╫╪╣❋╠╫╪◆

Ezra never felt quite so invigorated as when he was playing baseball. Even having to use the short stick he had found for a bat, even having to temper his activity to accommodate Frederick, he still felt the thrill of competition.

"Easy, now." Ezra stood behind the boy and guided his hands while Leviticus gently tossed the ball. "Swing."

The stick made contact, and the ball flew several yards. Frederick jumped up and down with excitement.

"Run, boy, run." Leviticus reached out as if to grab the ball, but it rolled past him. He turned the other way. "Where'd it go?"

"Run, Frederick!" Ezra gave him a little shove.

Frederick giggled and squealed as he ran toward the rock they had placed for first base.

"Now, where'd that ball go?" Mr. Willard stood with one hand on his hip and the other shielding his eyes as he looked up at the sky.

Adam caught on to their ruse and pretended to look toward the woods. "He done knocked it clear out of the county."

Jack ran to center field, snatched up the ball, and headed for Frederick, who had just rounded second base and was scurrying toward third.

Leviticus stumbled toward Jack, knocking the ball from his hand. "Hey, sorry, man." He clapped Jack's shoulder. "Lost my balance."

Jack snorted out his disgust with a curse. "You ain't gonna teach that boy nothin' if you let him get by all the time. When did you get by with anything when you was a kid?"

"It's just a game, man." Leviticus offered the taller man an apologetic frown. "And we ain't slaves no more. Our kids won't be raised like we was, havin' to work hard from the time they can walk. We can give 'em a little slack in the reins."

Ezra watched Jack's smoldering face, surprised at the anger Leviticus's words ignited. Jack responded by stomping away and disappearing around the corner of the house.

In a short time, Frederick grew tired and lay down near Delia in the shade of the oak tree. Miss May collected Mr. Willard for a stroll down by the river. After a few more turns of batting the ball to each other, the men dispersed for their afternoon rest.

Even though his family took an occasional Sunday nap in Ezra's boyhood home, he had built up his stamina in the army. Now he had no patience for resting in the daytime, for it only served to keep him from sleep that night and make him sluggish the next day. Clearly, the others had no such difficulty. Yet he could not fault them. All were hard workers who deserved a break from their routine.

If Jack had not gone too far, perhaps Ezra could use this time to talk to him and find the cause of his deep bitterness.

Lord, guide my words. Please help me to minister to Jack.

As he walked toward the corner of the house, he heard a dog growling.

"Git off me. Git. Git." Jack's voice was hushed and urgent.

Ezra came around the corner to see Miss Kate's dog, Sheba, gripping Jack's trouser leg as if she were trying to pull him away from the house. Ezra hurried to help.

"There, girl, it's all right." He knelt by the dog and stroked her head. "Easy, girl, easy."

Sheba loosened her hold and turned to lick Ezra's face. Her breath blasted his nostrils with the smell of digesting chicken bones.

"Whoa, girl, that's enough." He chuckled as he moved her head away. He stared up at Jack, who had pulled up his trouser leg. "Did she bite you?"

"What do you care?" Jack ran his fingers over his calf.

Ezra could see no injury. At least the skin did not appear broken. "She seems like a good dog. Wonder why she grabbed you that way."

"Hey." Miss Kate's voice sounded just inside the window closest to them. "I'm trying to sleep in here."

Ezra caught the look of guilt that flashed across Jack's eyes. A sick feeling filled his stomach. Had Jack been watching Miss Kate sleep? Something nagged at the back of his mind, but he could not bring the thought forward.

Oh, Lord, give me strength. And wisdom. And opportunity.

He tilted his head toward the front of the house and mouthed, "Let's go up there."

Jack shrugged and walked ahead of him. Sheba stuck close to Ezra's side.

"Jack, we never had much of a chance to get acquainted." Ezra leaned against the porch railing. "I'd like to amend that now." Why had he said "amend" when "fix" would have worked just as well? He must not cause Jack to stumble by sounding too educated.

Jack spat into the lilac bushes by the corner of the house. "I don't need no Yankee colored man comin' down here to be my friend. You Yankees done caused enough trouble for me already."

"What?" Ezra almost laughed. Was this man crazy? "What trouble did we cause?"

Jack spat again. "All this emancipation stuff. You come down here meddlin' where you don't belong tellin' black folk they's equal and ought to be free."

Ezra could form no words to respond. Was Jack crazy? He sounded like a southern white man, not a Negro. But with that ebony complexion and those strong African features, there was no mistaking his race.

"I worked my way up from the fields." Jack picked up a stick and whacked it against the edge of the porch. "I never caused no trouble. Always 'yes, boss, whatever you say, boss, let me do that, boss,' to the overseer until I got to work as the plantation carpenter. I watched house darkies and learned how to act around white folks." A sardonic smile crept over his face. "The missus took a likin' to me. When Massuh died, she move me into the house to be her *bodyguard*." The arrogant curl of his lips, the sly narrowing of his eyes, the sordid oiliness to his tone, all shouted that Jack had been far more than a bodyguard to his mistress.

"You Yankees." He snapped the stick in half to emphasize his anger. "Yo' General Sherman comes marchin' along and burns my plantation. The missus up and died of apoplexy. And them Yankees had the gall to tell us we was free." Again he snapped the twig pieces before throwing them at Sheba.

The dog growled but slunk under the porch.

"Free?" Jack spat out a curse. "That plantation and every slave on it woulda been mine. Now where would I go?" He stared at Miss Kate's house and snorted. "This rundown shack ain't nothin' but kindlin'. Too bad it didn't burn instead of Miz Jones's place."

As heartless as Jack sounded, Ezra understood why: Jack had worked hard to rise above his background. Yet his later actions had been terribly misguided. Then a thought occurred to Ezra.

"Jack, I can see your point. But you're a smart, ambitious fellow. Why don't you use your new situation to start a business? If you were a carpenter, you'll have all the work you could ever want rebuilding homes that were lost in the war."

"I ain't takin' a step back like that." Jack stared at the house again. "It ain't much, but it's more than forty acres, and they's more than just a mule in the barn. And that Kate's a lot more woman than my ol' missus."

Ezra again could only stare at him. It was clear that Jack knew nothing of Miss Kate's affection for Mr. Burns. At last, Ezra put words to his concerns. "Surely you don't expect—"

"Just shut your mouth, boy." Jack placed his fists at his waist. "I'll have her, and I'll have Delia, too. A little white meat, a little dark meat. And there ain't nothin' you can do to stop me." He jutted out his chin with a clear challenge.

A door slammed shut in Ezra's soul and locked out every former charitable feeling toward Jack. He slowly stood to his full height to lock stares with this evil adversary. Against his faith, against his upbringing, he felt a strange new thrill in this dangerous competition, one far stronger than his feelings for baseball.

"I believe the two ladies can make their own decisions about whose attentions they wish to accept."

Jack snorted and hurled a curse at him. "What're you gonna do if I *help* them make up their minds?"

Lord, give me grace not to hit this man. Ezra counted to ten, just as his father had taught him to do when dealing with playground bullies. But his stare into Jack's dark, soulless eyes never wavered.

"I'd say you'll have me to deal with, Jack, and I assure you, you won't like that. Not one bit."

"What's goin' on out here?" Miss Kate came out the front door rubbing sleep from her eyes. "Ezra, don't you be comin' 'round here threatenin' my workers, you hear?"

Jack smirked. "Afternoon, Miz Kate. You have a nice rest?"

Ezra cleared his throat. "I'm terribly sorry, Miss Saunders. I'll watch my words."

Jack grabbed Ezra around the shoulders as if in a vise grip. "It's just man-talk you heard, Miz Kate. It don't mean nothin'."

Her brow wrinkled with perplexity and a measure of disbelief, but then she relaxed. "All right." She turned and reentered the house.

Ezra shrugged free. "You lie well, Jack."

Jack threw back his head and laughed. "I do, don't I?" Then he leveled an arrogant stare on Ezra. "And don't you forget it."

CHAPTER TWENTY-SIX

Delia ran her hand over the blue wool jacket again, but this time she felt different. Instead of being sad like when they all thought Ezra was dead, she thought her heart might float right out of her body with happiness. Would he be surprised to see it? Would he be pleased that she'd kept it for him? If she hadn't seen Alice give Miz May back her bag, Delia might have forgot to return the jacket.

She climbed down from the loft and hurried outside to the backyard where the others were gathered to say good-bye to Ezra and Miz May and Mr. Willard.

"Ezra." She held the jacket behind her back. Her face felt hot, not from the late afternoon sun or from rushing downstairs, but because she'd never called him by his first name before.

He turned that fine smile on her and looked right into her eyes. "Yes, Miss Delia?"

Delia couldn't breathe. She thought she might fall over right then. All she could do was shove the jacket at him. "Here."

He didn't take it right off. He just stared at it like he'd found an old friend. When he finally reached out, Delia could see his eyes had got red as he looked it over. She felt her own eyes start to burn.

"I—I never expected to see this again." He ran his hands over the two yellow stripes on the arm and touched the brass buttons. Then he looked back at her.

"Miss Delia, I don't know how to thank you for taking care of this for me. I never expected...." He cleared his throat. "I had hoped to pass it down to...to someone in my family. Now I can do that."

He stared into her eyes with such a gentle look that she had to look down and dig her bare toes into the grass to keep from passing out. "It wasn't nothin'."

He laughed real soft. "No, it wasn't 'nothing.'" He sort of winced a little. "I mean, it's truly *something* to me."

She smiled and shrugged. "Well, I'm glad."

"Say, Jack." Adam waved to Jack, who was standing a ways off. "You got Ezra's knapsack. Why don't you give it back now?"

Jack didn't answer, but he did go into the shack and come out with the bag.

"I ain't gonna need it no more 'cause I ain't gonna be travelin' nowhere." He shoved it at Ezra and gave him a grinning look that Delia didn't understand.

"Thank you, Jack." Ezra's smile was a whole lot nicer, and he took the bag without looking inside.

Delia thought he should've checked to see that everything was still in it.

Miz Kate came out the back door and walked over to where they were all standing. Delia wondered if she felt strange being with all these colored folks. But Miz Kate didn't seem to mind it at all. Delia had always hated being the only slave in a room full of whites.

"Willard," Miz Kate said, "I think it right fine of Ezra to get you a job over at Mr. Burns's place, but I don't want to let you go. For an old fella, you sure do work hard, and good, too." She shaded her eyes from the sun and frowned at him. "I won't be able to replace you."

Mr. Willard's shoulders slumped. "Miz Kate, please let me go. May done promised she'd go back over there and see to that lady, that Miz Burns. I jes' can't be away from my May no mo'."

The unhappiness in his voice made Delia want to cry. She looked from one person to another. Surely Miz Kate couldn't make Mr. Willard stay. The others seemed as worried as Delia was.

Miz Kate shook her head. "Old man, you don't have to ask me. You ain't a slave anymore, and I ain't never owned one. I'm just saying I could use your help. What if May stays here with you?"

Miz May didn't wait for Mr. Willard to answer. "No, ma'am. I's made a promise to Mr. Burns that I'd see to his mama, jes' like Willard said. I'd be ashamed to face the Lawd if'n I broke that promise. I gots to go back. Now you can understand that, cain't ya, ma'am?"

Miz Kate sighed. "Yes, I understand." She gave an impatient wave of her hand. "Go on. Lord knows Burns needs you worse than I do." She turned toward the house, then back to Mr. Willard again. "Take care." She gave him a little smile before going back inside.

Delia could hear everybody breathe out a soft sigh. Even Jack seemed pleased that the couple got to be together again. Miz Kate might not have been able to make Mr. Willard stay, but she could have made trouble over him going.

While the others were saying their good-byes, Ezra came over to Delia. He was holding that jacket like he thought it might get lost again.

"I asked Miss Kate if we could come back next Sunday." He shot a quick look toward the house. "She said we could, but she can't afford a chicken every week. If I caught some rabbits, would you mind cooking them for us?" He seemed a little out of breath when he finished.

Delia tilted her head in a saucy way and looked up at him, like Miz Suzanne used to do with her beaux. "We ate lots of rabbit after the war started. If *you* can catch 'em, *I* can cook 'em."

"That's wonderful. I knew you could." He glanced over his shoulder. "Well, I guess we should go. Miss May will be cooking supper over at the Burnses' house tonight, so we mustn't be too late."

Delia shrugged. "Go on, then." She gave him a little smile.

His black eyes sparkled in the sunshine, and he didn't seem to want to go. After a minute or two, he went to help Miz May and Mr. Willard mount the mule. With his jacket and bag slung over his shoulder, he led the mule toward the road while everybody waved and shouted good-bye.

Delia let out a big, happy sigh. She'd keep busy this week so Sunday would come around soon.

Just as she started back toward the house, she saw Jack looking at her. Like other times, the hot day didn't keep that cold chill from her back. Though she was glad Mr. Willard had gone to be with Miz May over at the Burns place, who was going to look out for Delia when Jack looked at her that way?

On the road back to the Burns' place, Ezra whistled in tune with the melody humming in his heart. Astride the mule, the Brewsters were making their own music with soft, loving conversation born of their forty-year marriage. Would Ezra ever know that kind of love, the kind his parents and grandparents had? He sent up a silent prayer that he would find a woman who wanted the same thing. Would that woman be Delia? Just the thought of it made him happy, yet he still prayed for caution.

She had promised to stay with Miss Saunders until harvest and, like Miss May, would not break her promise. That showed character. He himself must keep his promise to Mr. Burns to finish the barn, and Miss May would stay to help with Mrs. Burns as long as he worked there.

Ezra liked the idea Delia had mentioned to him about earning enough money for train fare to Boston. Smart girl, and caring, too. She loved the Brewsters and wanted their trip to be as easy as possible. Her plan probably was the best, even though it would keep them here for most of the summer. But where else could they have food, shelter, and a salary?

When they came down the last hundred yards of the farm road, Ezra whistled a louder, more piercing sound. Now Mr. Burns would know to talk to his mother about their arrival so she would not be alarmed.

As planned, Mr. Burns brought her out on the front porch and waved his welcome. Although she appeared a little confused at first, she seemed to relax and gave a little wave of her own.

Near the front porch, Ezra helped the Brewsters dismount. Miss May took Mr. Willard's hand and led him to the steps.

"Ma'am, this here's my man Willard."

Miss May smiled, but Ezra could see the concern in her eyes.

Mrs. Burns turned to her son. "Owen, I don't like all these darkies coming here, but you say they have to stay. All right, then. No more, though, you hear me? And not that one who keeps looking in my window. You keep him away."

"All right, Mama. I will." Mr. Burns stepped off the porch. "Miss May, will you see to Mama?"

"Yessuh." Miss May squeezed her husband's hand and moved toward the porch.

Ezra could see the tension in Mr. Burns's rigid posture and tightened jaw and prayed that all would go well.

"Let's go fix supper, ma'am." Miss May opened the front door.

"All right, dear." Her head held high, Mrs. Burns entered without another word.

"I was hoping our day with the minister's family would help." Mr. Burns's posture relaxed. "Seems like it did."

That evening, Ezra knelt under the stars and poured out his concerns to the Lord. His silent prayers had become the mainstay in his life, but it always felt better to give voice to his petitions.

"Father, I thank You that our friends all are safe and well. Thank You that they have paying jobs and can hold their heads up with self-respect in their new freedom. Lord, please smite Jack in the heart and show him that he needs Your salvation. May this summer hurry by...." He stopped and chuckled. "May this *week* hurry by so I can see Delia again. Lord, keep her from harm."

A twinge of concern tickled his mind. Thinking on it, he felt it unwise to leave her with Miss Saunders. *Would Jack do something rash? No. He talked big, but he was not a fool. He would never jeopardize his life for one reckless, evil act against either of the women.*

Would he?

CHAPTER TWENTY-SEVEN

*D*elia's hands shook as she hurried to clean up the dinner dishes. After five weeks of coming over every Sunday, Ezra had asked her to take a walk with him down to the river. What would they talk about? Would she even be able to say a word? She tried to remember what Miz Suzanne had said to her beaux to keep them coming back to see her all the time.

"Now, chile." Miz May peeked in the kitchen door, with Alice right behind her. "You jes' go on out for yo' walk. Me and Alice'll clean up."

Grabbing a tea towel to dry her hands, Delia looked at their big grins and felt her face get hot. "You don't mind?"

"Girl, go on. Git out there." Alice laughed. "Don't you keep that boy waitin'."

Delia grabbed a couple of fresh mint leaves from the cupboard and popped them in her mouth. Beulah always made her chew them after she ate so her breath wouldn't stink when she tended to Miz Suzanne.

"Does my hair look awright?" She'd got up early to fix it up on top of her head, but she'd sweat a lot cooking dinner, and strands kept coming down. She'd never fixed her own hair too good.

"You's as purty as them wildflowers out in the field." Miz May reached up to tuck in a loose strand.

"Aw, Miz May—" Again, Delia felt heat in her face that was not from cooking. Miz Suzanne and Beulah had always told her she was unsightly and unwanted.

"Hush, girl. I say you's purty, and I ain't lyin'."

Miz May's steady stare said she meant what she said. But Delia didn't rightly know what to do with that idea. Nobody had ever told her such a thing.

"Now you git, like we said." Alice took Delia's arm and pulled her toward the door and shoved her out. "Go on."

Alone on the narrow porch, Delia looked to the backyard, where Ezra and the other men played baseball.

Adam stood at the home spot with the hitting stick—the bat, Ezra called it. Ezra was just about to throw the ball, but he looked her way and stopped, then tossed the ball to Leviticus.

"See you later." Ezra half-ran toward Delia like he couldn't wait to be with her.

Her heart felt near to busting, even more than when she saw him and Miz May and Mr. Willard ride up every Sunday morning. She couldn't stop shaking.

"Shall we go, Miss Delia?" Ezra reached up his hand to her like she was a lady who needed help walking down the steps, even with her being barefoot.

Well, if that was the way he saw her, she'd act that way. She put her hand in his, gathered her skirt, and held her head high as she stepped down to join him. When she reached the ground, he tucked her arm in his, and they took off walking.

They didn't say much on their way down the path to the river 'cept what a nice day it was and didn't the cotton look good and didn't the woods smell fresh and clean after last night's rain. By the time they could hear the water shushing on by, Delia's heart had slowed down, and she didn't shake so much.

"I want you to know I asked Miss May if I should invite you for this walk." Ezra let her hand go and leaned back against a tall pine tree. "She said I'd have to answer to her if I did anything improper." He chuckled real soft and looked out on the river.

Delia leaned against another pine tree and watched the bugs that flew over the water, just asking to be eaten by some fish. Sure enough, a big ol' bass jumped up, caught a June bug, and made a loud splash in the process.

"Hm, looks like good fishing down here." Ezra kept on staring at the water. "Maybe we should have bass for dinner next Sunday." He looked at her. "What do you think?"

Delia ached to say some smart thing like Miz Suzanne would. But all she could say was, "Do you like hush puppies? I know how to make 'em, and they go real good with fish."

His smile almost made her toes curl. "If you make them, I'll like them." He laughed out loud. "Whatever they are."

That made her laugh, too, and even feel a little bit saucy. "You don't know what hush puppies are? Why, how on earth can you be in the South and not know about hush puppies?"

He shrugged. "Well, army food isn't exactly fancy cooking. And not many folks invited us in for dinner as we marched through their land."

Delia laughed. "I wish I coulda seen that. A whole line of colored soldiers marchin' up to some fancy plantation and settin' all the slaves free. I can jus' see those white folks gettin' real scared and runnin' off."

Ezra suddenly looked sad. Had she said something wrong?

"Oh, Delia, I wish it had been that simple." He shook his head. "War's an awful thing, but I'd fight all over again if I had to." He picked up a stone and skipped it across the water's flowing ripples. Then he smiled. "The Lord gave us the victory so that...well, for one thing, so you and I could meet."

Delia's face felt warm again, and that made her mad. She knew her face had taken on a pink shade. If she was dark like Alice or Miz May, her feelings wouldn't show up on her face that way for everybody to see. "I'm glad we met." She chewed her lip for a minute. "Did you know I'm half white?" Now she stared at him, daring him, testing him.

He looked surprised at the question. "Uh, well, I suppose." A little frown crossed his forehead. "Why do you ask?"

"You don't mind?"

His face crinkled up like Frederick's did when he got confused, making Ezra look like a little boy. "Why would I?"

Delia's heart seemed to flutter like the butterflies dancing over the blackberry bushes nearby. "Don't know. Never knew a Yankee colored man before you."

Ezra stepped over to her and rested his hand on the tree just above her head. He leaned close, but not too close. "Well, Miss Delia, I am very pleased to know you. I'm so pleased that..."—he looked away thoughtful like, then turned to her again—"...that I'd like to take you home to meet my parents." He gave a quick nod of his head and stood back with his arms crossed and a grin on his face. "What do you think of that?"

Delia made herself smile. She even nodded back at him. What he said seemed important to him, but why?

Then she knew. Late at night, she often stared up at the dry, gray beams of her loft and whispered her thoughts about Ezra to Mama just as if she was there. She did it because she had no one else to talk to. But mostly, she did it because she wished her mama could meet this fine-looking man who was brave and good and seemed to like her.

If he'd told her he thought she was pretty, that would've been nice. But if he wanted her to meet his parents, it meant a powerful lot more. It meant he *respected* her. A happy feeling flowed through her, just like the river flowed through the land, soft and peaceful.

"That'd be real nice, Ezra."

Overhead, blue jays called out "tra-ay, tra-ay," and bees buzzed through the nearby clover, sipping at sweet-smelling flowers so they could go home and make honey. Delia could be here with Ezra all day without saying a word and still be happy.

"Miss Delia, I'd like to discuss, um, talk with you about something important." He'd gone back to lean against his tree.

"Awright."

"When I was reading the Bible to everyone this morning, you seemed distracted. Maybe even bored." He nudged a pebble with his boot. "Don't you like to hear God's Word being read?"

Delia wandered over to the nearby blackberry patch and plucked a small, withered blossom. Its sweet fragrance lingered, but no fruit had formed on the stem. She glanced upward, wishing this God of Ezra's would just appear and help her figure things out. Would Ezra stop liking her if she told him the truth, that she was having trouble believing in this God of his and wouldn't trust Him even if He was real? But Bible reading seemed so important to Ezra, that it was becoming important to her too.

"I do like the Bible." Who would punish her for that lie? "It's jus' that I got to thinkin' 'bout dinner cookin' in the oven. You all depend on me to cook it right. That's why I seemed—what was that word?—distracted. But I ain't...I'm not bored." She'd noticed Ezra never said "ain't."

A big smile spread across his face. "Ah, I see. Yes, I think my mother has that same problem. She's always concerned about Sunday dinner while we're in church. I guess every woman feels that way."

"Well, isn't that somethin'." Delia wondered if Beulah had ever felt that way. She just knew Beulah got up early and worked extra hard on Sunday mornings so she could go to church and have a good meal on the table for Sunday dinner, too. If she hadn't given Massuh a good meal, Missus wouldn't have let her go to church.

"So, what's your favorite Bible story?"

Delia tried to think of a story, but nothing would come to mind. "I like all of 'em."

"That's even better than having a favorite." He looked at her for a minute, like another question was on the tip of his tongue. "It's no longer against the law for you to learn how to read. Would you like to learn?"

She shrugged. "Never thought much about it."

"Ah, knowing how to read is a wonderful thing." His eyes lit up again. "If you'd like, I'll teach you."

If she needed to read to make him keep liking her, she would learn to read. Besides, that would give them more time together.

"I wouldn't mind," she said.

The nice smile on his face told her she'd said the right thing.

✷ ✷ ✷ ✷

CHAPTER TWENTY-EIGHT

"Adam, tell us what you think of what Delia just wrote." Ezra sat under the oak tree with his friends, who were now also his students.

"Now, Miss Delia, Ezra's done showed you the difference between a *p* and a *q,* but you got 'em backwards again." Adam's tone was polite, but his eyes danced merrily. "And when you write it in words, a *q* always takes a *u* after it."

"Well, at least I don't say 'done showed' no more. It's '*already* showed.'" Delia wrinkled her nose at the young man. "You got to listen to Ezra and talk proper like he does."

Ezra bit back the temptation to correct her errors. When they had begun their reading and writing lessons the previous month, Adam had provoked Delia into a friendly rivalry. When Ezra noticed how she began to assert herself, he decided not to interfere.

"That's awright, Delia." Jack frowned at the smooth board where she had written her words with charcoal. "I don't see no difference 'tween them two letters either."

"I do! I do!" Frederick waved his hand, just as Ezra had taught him. "Can I write my letters next?"

"Now, honey—" Alice began.

"Oh, let the boy," Leviticus said. "He gonna be a good writer, ain't you, Frederick? Ezra, is it awright for him to write next?"

"Of course. It's never too early for a child to begin learning to write." Ezra beckoned to the boy. "Your turn."

"Yessuh." Frederick jumped up and took the slender piece of charcoal from Delia.

While he labored over his letters on the board, Ezra watched Delia out of the corner of his eye. She had not been embarrassed by her error, as she had been at the beginning. In fact, these Sunday lessons revealed a different side to each person. Leviticus and Alice had joined his class, but they clearly did it for Frederick's benefit.

Even Jack had changed. After their confrontation earlier in the summer, Jack had backed off, just what Ezra had prayed he would do. Although he watched Delia far too often to suit Ezra, she made no complaints about his behavior toward her during the week.

"Jack, why don't you write your letters on this board?" Ezra had spent a long time sanding down the surface of several old boards and finding just the right consistency of charcoal to write with. He offered one to Jack.

Jack hesitated but then grasped the board. He looked at Ezra's example, a length of wood carefully carved with the alphabet and propped against the oak tree. Leviticus kept it hidden during the week in case Miss Saunders decided to forgo her weekly nap and find out what her workers were doing on Sunday afternoons.

With furrowed brow, Jack made a mark. Doubt filled his face. He wiped the soft charcoal off the makeshift slate with his sleeve, leaving a broad smear. Sweat beaded on his forehead. He tilted his head to study the letters and tried again. His *A* looked fairly good, but his *a* was backward and just as tall as the capital letter.

Frederick peered over his shoulder. "No, Jack. That ain't how you do it."

"Git away, boy." Jack growled at him.

"Hey." Leviticus pulled his son into his lap. "He jus' tryin' to hep."

"I don't need no baby helpin' me." Jack stood and threw down the board and charcoal. "I don't need nobody helpin' me for nothin'." He stalked away with his back hunched up like an angry bear.

"Jack." Ezra called out.

But Jack ignored him and headed toward the thick woods between the Saunders and Burns' farms.

The group sat quietly for a moment.

"Say, Miss Delia." Adam had a teasing gleam in his eye again. "I bet I can write my letters faster and better than you."

Delia tossed her head and sent a grin Ezra's way. "No, you can't." She grabbed the board Jack had dropped, wiped it with a damp cloth, and began to write. Adam hurried to start, too. With all the others cheering, in the end, he finished first, but she formed her letters more accurately, even her *p*'s and *q*'s.

When it became clear that everyone had studied enough, Ezra dismissed the class. This was his favorite time, the time he could spend alone with Delia.

"I felt bad about Jack." Ezra longed to reach out and take Delia's hand as they walked toward the river, but he did not wish to rush their friendship. "He's strong and could be a good leader."

"Jack don't, uh, doesn't care about anybody but himself."

In one way, Ezra was glad she held that opinion, because it meant she did not harbor romantic feelings for the other man. Still, he felt obliged to care about Jack's soul despite their earlier confrontation.

"Perhaps his pride is wounded because you younger folks are doing better than he is with his lessons."

Delia shrugged. "I suppose." She glanced over her shoulder. "Just between you and me, I'm guessin' he's a mite put off 'cause Miz Kate done sent him out to work in the fields."

"Wasn't he working there before?"

"Oh, no. He set hisself, I mean, himself up like some overseer, but Miz Kate wouldn't have none of that." Delia giggled, but then frowned. "I don't mean no harm, Ezra. But you know how Jack is."

"Hmm. I see." Ezra was not bothered by her attitude. He'd learned from Mr. Willard that Jack had pestered her during the long days after the flood had separated the travelers. Ezra wished he had been there to protect her, but God had seen to the matter. Perhaps recent events had humbled Jack.

"Who knows? Maybe Jack could be a fine leader if he could learn some temperance and to think of others before himself." Ezra pushed away the temptation to find any satisfaction in Jack's come-uppance. "We must pray that Jack will turn his heart toward God."

Delia gave him a sweet smile and nodded. "That's awful good of you, Ezra."

On the way back to the Burns' farm, Ezra chuckled to himself as he thought about the way Adam had provoked Delia into their little competition. Yet he found his thoughts more on Jack than the woman he cared about. *Lord, please save Jack and raise him up to be a leader. And please help him to be able to read.* It seemed strange that after all this time, a grown man could not form a simple letter.

Lead rein in his hand, Ezra walked toward the Burns' farm, glancing back from time to time to be certain Miss May and Mr. Willard were comfortable astride Long Ears. The ancient mule was an unusually docile animal, which always set Ezra's mind at ease. The old couple need never fear being thrown.

Ahead Ezra saw two white men approaching on horseback. One looked familiar. He led Long Ears to the side of the road and held his bridle while the mule shifted restlessly.

"Hang on, honey," Mr. Willard said to Miss May.

"Easy, boy." Ezra patted Long Ears. "I know you want to get home. So do I."

"I hope they jes' pass on by." Miss May pressed back against her husband.

"Amen to that." Mr. Willard held her close.

The young men stopped in the middle of the road. Ezra had seen one of them several times on his trips to the Saunders' farm. The former Confederate soldier had filled out in the past couple of months, improving his appearance. That is, all but the arrogance in his face.

"You darkies goin' back over to the Burns' place?"

"Yessuh, boss." Ezra's southern pronunciation had improved with practice. He smiled and bobbed his head agreeably, but inside, his stomach churned. What could he do if they tried to hurt the Brewsters? His Bowie knife, hidden in his knapsack, would be no match for their rifles and sidearms.

"Y'all need to know I'm deputy sheriff now. Name's Massey, and this here's Case. He's a deputy, too." Massey spat a wad of tobacco near Ezra's foot. "Now, if Burns lets you go over to the Saunders place every Sunday on his mule, that's awright. But you need to know we don't like darkies wandering all over gettin' into trouble, so y'all stay on the farm the rest of the time, y'hear?"

"Yessuh," Ezra and the Brewsters chorused.

"Afore the war, darkies needed to have papers to walk out in public with decent white folks." Case leaned out of the saddle toward Ezra. "Them Yankee soldiers in town might let you all go where you want, but they ain't always gonna be here." He shot a sly look at Massey. "All this *reconstruction*...." He stared back at Ezra and curled his lips into a sneer. "It ain't gonna work, so don't you bother gettin' uppity, you hear?"

"Yessuh, boss."

Ezra could only guess why these men felt it was necessary to talk to him this way. Perhaps they threatened all young, strong Negro men. Without a doubt, their remarks were directed only at him.

They both glared at Ezra with clear distrust. As much as he would like to stare back at them, he gave them another agreeable nod, slumped his shoulders a little, and looked down at his own boots.

For several moments, they sniffed rudely, spat out more tobacco, and shifted in their saddles. Ezra wondered if they hoped he would do something to incite reprisal. *"Please help us, Lord."* He knew the Brewsters were praying, too.

"Well, let's go, Case." Massey reined his horse away. "I think this boy's got the message."

Case laughed. "If he don't, we'll make sure he does."

The two men galloped away.

Ezra looked up at the Brewsters. The resignation on their faces reflected generations of slavery. Anger welled up inside him. They were free. They should no longer have to endure such debasement of their dignity, their very humanity.

"Now, Ezra." Miss May reached out to touch his shoulder. "Don't git all riled. They can't take away what matters most. The Lawd knows His own."

"Dat's right," Mr. Willard said.

"Yes, ma'am. Yes, sir."

Ezra swallowed the bitter words he longed to say. He had not fought for two long years to see things get worse for Negroes in the South. He must get these dear people safely to Boston, and soon.

He had promised Mr. Burns he would stay until the barn was finished. But even with Mr. Willard's help, the project had gone on for well over two months. Sometimes it seemed to Ezra that Mr. Burns deliberately failed to buy the right supplies in town or found too many excuses to check on the workers in his cotton field. Yet he could not be faulted for the summer rains that slowed their progress or the times Mrs. Burns demanded that her son take her to visit the preacher and his wife.

As they continued their short journey back to the Burns' farm, Miss May started to hum, and the hairs on Ezra's neck began to tingle.

Soon she would start to sing either a spiritual song or one she made up for the occasion. A man would have to be soulless not to be moved by her rich, warm voice, echoed in fine, deep tones by Mr. Willard.

"Lawd, I'm comin' home to glory. Sinner, don't git in my way." Her meter was brisk, and Ezra suspected she was trying to cheer him.

"Sinner, don't git in my way," Mr. Willard echoed.

"I can see the light of dat heavenly city."

"Sinner, don't get in my way." Ezra added his tenor voice in harmony with Mr. Willard's bass.

"No need to bother sendin' that chariot."

"Sinner, don't git in my way."

"'Cause I'm gonna fly on the wings of freedom."

"Sinner, don't git in my way."

By the time they had reached the strip of woods that cut across the farm road, Ezra's spirits had been lifted by the song more than ever before. They would have to stop singing now because Mrs. Burns did not care for their music. But it had already done its work. Those sinners they had met on the road would not be able to get in their way much longer. Just as Miss May had sung, very soon, they would fly on the wings of freedom…all the way to Boston.

CHAPTER TWENTY-NINE

"Miz Kate, do you want turnips and greens or okra for dinner?" Delia lifted the tin kettle from the stove and poured hot water into the dishpan. "Or maybe some squash?"

Wearing a pair of her pa's trousers and an old shirt, Miz Kate stood across the room by her gun rack loading shot into her rifle. "Well, if I can get me a rabbit or two, we ought to have turnips to go with 'em. Save the okra to go with the chicken tomorrow. Bring in some of your fine tomatoes and some corn and onions, and I'll show you a recipe my mama got down in New Orleans. Oh, and a couple of them little peppers, too."

"Yes, ma'am."

Her gun under her arm, Miz Kate walked through the kitchen area to the back door and stared out at the fields. "That cotton's looking good. Ought to be ready for harvest by early September, if the rain holds off just before it's picked. Leviticus knows what he's doing. I sure do hope he's gonna stay in these parts." She seemed to be talking to herself as she put on her big slouch hat and went outside.

Delia watched as Miz Kate called to Sheba and headed for the woods. Rabbits would taste real good for dinner, and Delia had figured out just how to cook them up nice and tender. A little vinegar would get rid of the wild taste.

She hummed to herself while she washed the breakfast dishes and cast-iron skillet. After she finished, she'd tend to her sewing. Today, she would let out her skirt waist just a mite due to all the good food she'd been eating this summer. Back on the plantation, Beulah was always so stingy with the food for the house slaves that Delia had been skinny all her life. It felt good to have a little roundness on her bones. From the look in Ezra's eyes, he seemed to think she looked all right.

She fetched water to refill the tank on the stove, set another log into the fire, and made sure the flue was open just enough to draw up air and keep the fire going. Then she dug out the sewing box.

The first piece she worked on was the blue gingham dress Miz Kate had told her to burn back at the first of summer. She'd have to hurry in case Miz Kate shot her rabbits and came back soon. She'd already mended the torn buttonholes and now finished stitching the side seams. She'd have to try it on some other time, but one day she'd be proud to wear this dress in Boston.

After taking it back to its hiding place up in the loft, she took off her skirt and blouse and sat by Miz Kate's bedroom window in her camisole and petticoat. The August heat wore a body down, so she stood and moved aside the patchwork curtain to let in the breeze. Then she hung her sweat-dampened blouse on one side of the curtain rod. The skirt waistband was wet, too, making it hard to push the needle through. Delia carefully rubbed the needle against her scalp to oil it up a bit. It then slid into the skirt with ease.

"My, my, ain't that a pretty sight?" Jack stood at the window, his arms resting on the sill and a sly look on his face.

Delia gasped and jumped up, holding her skirt in front of her chest. "Git away. Go on. Git. I throwed water on you last time you stared in a window. I might just throw something a whole lot worse." She glanced toward her sewing scissors.

"Now what kind of thing is that for a pretty girl to say? All I want is to watch you sittin' there sewin'." His eyes took on a look that made Delia's stomach churn.

"Jack, you been real good all summer. Ever'body's startin' to like you." Delia bit through the cotton thread, then slipped the skirt over her head. She wanted to shut the curtain but was scared to go near to the window. "Don't go messin' that up, you hear?"

Jack snorted. "You think I care what those field darkies think? I ain't gonna be out there with them much longer. I tol' you before, Miz Kate favors me." He grinned. "And I favor you."

Delia's mind spun. Jack was a fool for thinking Miz Kate favored him. Just this morning, it was Leviticus she said she hoped would stay around.

"Well, I don't favor you, so go on. Git." Trying not to step too close to the window, she stretched out her hand to take her blouse from the curtain rod.

Jack reached in and grabbed her wrist and pulled her down to her knees.

"Ahh." Delia tried to twist away. "Don't do that."

Jack pulled her close to the window. "I ain't no dog that you can say 'git' to, so don't you be talkin' to me that way no more. You hear me, girl?" He shook her arm.

"Ow. I'm sorry, Jack. Don't." Delia's eyes filled with scalding tears.

"Don't tell me 'don't.'" Jack put his head and arms through the window and grabbed her around the waist. His mouth was close to her ears, and he talked in a low, mean voice. "You been treatin' me like dirt ever since we met."

"Help!" Delia screamed from the top of her lungs. "Help me."

"Shut up." Jack's hand covered her mouth. With his other arm he grabbed her roughly and dragged her through the window. "Ain't nobody 'round to hear you."

Fear choked Delia, but she forced herself to bite down hard on Jack's hand and kick him with all her strength. Even without shoes, she hit her target.

"Ow!" He dropped her to the ground. "You little—"

As she tried to struggle to her feet, he slammed his open hand against the side of her face. For a second, all she saw was blackness. When her eyes cleared, she lay on her back with Jack on top of her and his hand back over her mouth. Delia could hardly breathe, and the rough ground bit into her back. *Somebody, help me! Mama, help me! God, help me!*

Jack's face was right by hers. "You ain't nothin' but a piece of trash. I showed you respect and got Kate to bring you in to work in the house. Then how do you treat me?" He moved his hand and pressed his mouth against hers while his weight pressed her into the dirt.

For just a second, Delia felt like she was somebody else standing to the side watching. He was kissing her. She'd never been kissed before, and her heart was busting with fear.

She gathered all her strength and twisted violently, but that only hurt worse. Stunned, she could not move. Jack seemed to touch her all over at the same time. She could not breathe. Her head felt like it would explode.

Suddenly, loud noises sounded somewhere close by. A growl. A voice hollering. Barking. Snarling. A man hollering in pain, cursing.

Air. At last. Delia filled her lungs with a deep, desperate gasp. She sat up.

"Git off me! Git off me!" Jack yelled.

Sheba clung to Jack's ankle. He tried to run away, dragging the dog as she held on. Jack reached down and grasped the fur behind her head and yanked and yanked. He slammed his hand down on her head. She yelped and let loose. Jack kicked her hard in the side. She yelped again and shied away.

"Git!" Jack stamped his foot at her.

Sheba ran under the side of the front porch and growled at him.

Jack turned back to Delia.

Run, you fool! But she could not move.

"You ain't nothin' but trash." Jack spat on her right in her face. "You make me sick." He stomped away and disappeared around the corner of the house.

Hardly feeling anything, not even the spit that ran down her cheek, she started to get up. But Sheba limped over, nestled against her, and put her head in Delia's lap.

"You're a good girl, Sheba." Delia rubbed the dog behind her ears. Sheba's tail slapped the ground.

Delia didn't know how long they sat there that way. She should get up. Go inside. Get dinner ready. But she felt like she'd been beat halfway to death. Her camisole was torn. Her bare arms were scraped and starting to sting.

"Delia, what're you doin' out here?" Miz Kate came around the house, her trousers and shirt showing some blood stains.

"You shoot some rabbits, Miz Kate?"

Sheba limped over to Miz Kate and whined.

"What is it, girl?" Miz Kate knelt to touch a bloody spot on Sheba's side.

Delia hadn't noticed it before.

"What happened here?" Miz Kate got up. Her face got pale around the freckles. "Delia, what happened?"

Delia started to shake. Then dry sobs came out. Then tears. Choking tears. She struggled to stand but only made it to her knees.

"Oh, Miz Kate." She covered her face and sobbed.

Miz Kate knelt down again and put her arms around Delia and stood her up. "What happened? What happened?" Her voice trembled. "Delia, you've gotta talk to me."

Delia forced herself to draw in a breath. She shuddered as air filled her lungs. "I'm sorry. I'm sorry, Miz Kate."

Miz Kate pulled Delia's head to her shoulder, then pushed Delia back a little to stare in her eyes. "What happened?"

Delia sucked in more air while her whole body shook from the effort.

"J-Jack."

Miz Kate's eyes got big, and her mouth dropped open. "Jack? Oh, dear God. Did he...?" She glanced down the length of Delia's body and back up again. "Did that low-down snake—?"

"No, ma'am. No. B-but he tried to. Sheba bit him." Delia looked over at the dog, who lay on the ground still wagging her tail. "Bless you, Sheba. Thank you, girl." She'd make sure Sheba got lots of good scraps and bones from now on.

"That dirty, no good—" Miz Kate set her hands on Delia's bare upper arms and bent down to stare in her eyes. "Listen to me. I'm gonna get rid of him right now. You go out to the field and get Leviticus and Adam. Can you do that?"

"Yes, ma'am."

"Awright. Go on, then." She let loose of Delia and turned away.

"Miz Kate, you gotta know somethin'."

She turned back. "What's that?"

"Jack...he said...."

Miz Kate faced her, hands on hips. "What did that snake say?"

Delia bit her lower lip and looked down. "He said you favored him."

"I *what?*" Her deep-toned voice made it all the way up to a shriek.

Delia jumped but laughed, a nervous sort of laugh. "Like I told you way back when we came here, he said he'd be stayin' in the house...with you."

"I remember. You meant as a guard, right?" Miz Kate's eyes showed she knew that wasn't so.

"No, ma'am. He always meant to be in...in your bedroom."

Miz Kate just stared at Delia for a minute.

"Go put some clothes on and then get the men. I'm gonna get my gun."

"Yes, ma'am." Delia hurried to obey. Her whole body ached, but she went on with fear clutching at her heart, a thousand thoughts running through her head. She hated Jack. She wanted him to go away. But she didn't want him shot. She didn't want him dead.

Or did she?

CHAPTER THIRTY

*M*iz Kate, you got it all wrong." Jack stood outside the barn looking innocent with his round eyes and the big ol' grin he saved for white folks. "This girl been after me ever since we met. I had to fight her off."

"Shut up. Just shut up." Miz Kate stood ten feet away from Jack and held her rifle pointed right at his chest. "You're callin' me a fool to think I'd believe that kind of junk."

Leviticus and Adam stood at Miz Kate's shoulders. A few feet away, Delia stood arm in arm with Alice, while Alice clutched Frederick close to her other side.

His eyes now wide and wild, Jack looked at everybody like he was trying to figure some way out of this. Delia had never seen him look scared that way.

"You owe me. You all owe me." Jack put his fists on his waist. He stared at Miz Kate. "I brought you workers jus' like you ask. I worked for you out in that field and all over this dirty little farm." He shot a mean look at Leviticus. "You gonna stay and work for this white woman? You think she plannin' to pay you fair? You a fool, Leviticus. Adam, you ain't no better."

"Shut up, Jack." Miz Kate shook, but Delia could see it was anger that caused it, not fear.

"You gonna shoot me?" Jack sneered at Miz Kate. "You can't kill me. It's against the law."

Miz Kate coughed out an ugly laugh. "If you're dead, the law ain't gonna help you. I got a right to defend my place, 'specially against a colored man who hurt my huntin' dog and beat up on my housekeeper." She shot a quick look at Delia, then moved her body a little more sideways, like she was fixing to shoot. "I'll give you about five minutes to git your stuff and git off my property. Leviticus, Adam, make sure he don't take anything that don't belong to him."

Jack looked around at everybody. For just the tiniest second, he looked like a little boy who'd been whipped. If Delia didn't hate him so much, she might have felt sorry for him.

"Boy, I said 'git'." Miz Kate growled out the words in her deep voice while she pulled back on the rifle lock. "I got one shot here, and I never miss."

Jack jumped. Raw fear filled his eyes. He ran into the shack by the barn with Leviticus and Adam right behind him.

Delia moved closer to Alice. Alice hugged Frederick real tight. Miz Kate took in a deep breath and blew it out.

Jack came outside toting a canvas bag. Delia and Alice gave each other a quick look. The bag was the one Leviticus had carried from the plantation where they'd been slaves. But when Leviticus came out, he didn't seem to mind that Jack had it.

"He done give that bag to Jack," Alice whispered.

Delia nodded. Jack ought to be grateful for that kindness. He'd need a bag on the road. He'd had Ezra's knapsack, then nothing. But Jack just spat on the ground.

"I never did like this place. Never did like any of you fools." He threw the bag over his shoulder. "I know a place down the road where they know how to treat a man. I'll git good money there. She ain't even paid you all yet. You think she gonna pay you?"

"Boy." Miz Kate's voice was tight, like she was holding in some powerful anger. "You git now, and don't you ever set foot on my land again. You hear?"

Jack held still for just a second. He pulled back one foot and scuffed dirt toward Delia. Then he stomped past them all toward the road, limping every few steps on the leg that Sheba bit.

Once he had rounded the corner of the house, Miz Kate released the rifle lock and looked around at everybody. "I don't trust him. Adam, you follow and make sure he gets all the way to the main road. Stay far enough behind so he don't decide to turn on you."

"Yessum." Adam lit out running.

She huffed out a big breath, like she was glad it all was over. "I don't know if he was just talkin' big or if he really does know another place to work." She looked worried. "Leviticus, saddle my horse. I'm gonna ride over to Burns's place and tell him what happened and to be on the lookout. Burns can get the word out so nobody'll hire him." She started toward the house, then turned back to Leviticus. "I'm gonna give you a handgun in case he comes back while I'm gone."

He shook his head. "Miz Kate, I don't mean no disrespect, but I ain't never used no gun. I might hurt somebody."

"I'll do it." Delia gasped. Had she said those words?

Miz Kate gave her a long look. "Awright, then. C'mon. I'll show you how to use it."

⋆⊶⫶⊛⫶⊷⋆

Ezra sat on the chopping log in the barnyard and drew his Bowie knife across the whetstone to make it razor sharp. He and Mr. Willard had butchered the pig the day before, and Ezra's knife had proved better for the job than any of Mr. Burns's. Its handle fit into his large hands as if it were made for him, and the long, wide blade was thick enough to slice through any animal hide. Ezra had cut up the pig with no trouble. He was grateful to Corporal Ballinger for giving him the knife.

He also was grateful to Mr. Burns for giving him a job that had provided sustenance and a place to sleep for the Brewsters and him. But after last Sunday's encounter with the deputies on the road, Ezra had come to a decision. Whether or not the barn was finished, whether or not Mr. Burns paid them, they would leave next week for Boston. This coming Sunday, he would ask Delia and the others if they wanted to go, too.

"It's gettin' close to dinner, Ezra." Mr. Burns came out of the barn dusting off his shirt and trousers. As usual after a morning of hard work in the late August heat, his face was covered with sweat-streaked dirt, and his smell preceded him. "You 'bout got that knife sharp again?"

"Yes, sir." Ezra slipped it into the sheath. He didn't smell any better than his boss. "I'll put it away and go find Mr. Willard."

"You do that." Mr. Burns started toward the house. "Well, if that don't beat all. Here comes Kate, ridin' like a swarn of mad bees was chasin' her."

Miss Saunders galloped into the backyard and reined her horse to a stop just a few yards short of Mr. Burns. For a moment, she sat in the saddle breathing hard and staring at him. Her eyes held an expression Ezra almost found humorous. It seemed as if she had arrived with a matter of great concern, yet forgot it the moment she saw Mr. Burns. Mr. Burns stared back at the lady as if she were the most beautiful being he had ever seen, despite her flyaway hair, rumpled clothing, and flushed, freckled face.

Ezra wondered if he should quietly retreat into the barn so they could discuss whatever matter had brought her here in such haste. Seeing they had eyes only for each other, he began to edge away.

"Kate." Mr. Burns took the horse's bridle. "You're lookin' real fine today, as always. What brings you over here in such a dither? Will you stay for dinner?"

She brushed hair back from her face with the back of her hand. "Now, Owen, you know your mama won't let me stay to talk, much less have dinner. No, I came over to warn you about that colored fella who was workin' for me, that Jack."

Ezra stopped. Fear gripped him. He stepped toward them. "Is everything all right? Is everyone all right?"

Miss Saunders stared at him with surprise. Perhaps Ezra was not supposed to enter this conversation, but she would simply have to endure it.

"Excuse me, ma'am, but is everyone all right?"

"Yes, now that I got rid of Jack." Miss Saunders wiped her sleeve across her sweaty upper lip. She now looked at Ezra with a frown. "Delia's all right, Ezra. I promise. He did rough her up a bit, but Sheba bit him and drew him off her."

"Off of her?" Ezra thought he would choke on the words. He snatched up his knife from the chopping block and secured the sheath to his belt. "Excuse me, Mr. Burns. I have some business to attend to." Ezra strode toward the woods between the two farms. He wouldn't risk running into those deputies on the highway.

"Wait." Miss Saunders called. "He's not there."

Mr. Burns caught up with Ezra and grabbed his arm. "Ezra, don't be a fool. She said he's not there."

"Where is he then?" Ezra shook with rage. His eyes refused to focus. All he could see was his hands around Jack's neck, squeezing the life out of him. Never in battle had he felt such a personal hatred for the enemy. Southern troops had fought to defend their cause, but Jack was a slimy, self-centered barbarian with no respect for anyone. And he had hurt Delia. "I will kill him." Had he said those words or only thought them?

"Simmer down, Ezra." Mr. Burns grasped Ezra's shoulders and shook him. "Kate says he's gone. Don't go causing trouble."

Still trembling with rage, Ezra focused on him. "What would you do if someone harmed Miss Saunders? How is this any different?"

"Listen to me." Mr. Burns gripped Ezra's shoulders harder and seized his gaze. "There's a lot of people around here just lookin' for a chance to string up a colored man. If you go lookin'—"

"So you're telling me I can't take care of my…"—Ezra hardly knew what to call his band of friends, much less what to call Delia— "…my people? Not even against another Negro man?" He spat out the words, hating himself for all that they implied.

"I'm tellin' you we got to work together in this, man." Mr. Burns looked at Miss Saunders. "Ain't that right, Kate?"

She nodded. "I swear to you, Ezra, I won't let nothin' happen to her. To them." The pain in her eyes told him she meant every word. But how could a woman, even one as strong as Miss Saunders, fend off a monster like Jack? Did she even know that Jack had planned to pursue her, too?

Peace begged entry to his thoughts. He resisted. He must get to Delia and be sure she was not harmed. *Peace.* The feeling nudged him again. He swallowed hard and drew in a shuddering breath.

"All right, then." He relaxed his posture for their benefit. *All right, Lord.*

Both Mr. Burns and Miss Saunders exhaled their relief. But Ezra felt no relief at all. Somehow he must go to Delia.

"Just keep Jack off your property." Miss Saunders glanced toward the house. "Uh-oh. Here comes Mama."

Mrs. Burns had emerged from the house, a butcher knife in hand, and was descending the back steps.

Miss Saunders turned her horse. "'Bye, Owen."

"Marry me, Kate."

"Ha!" She kicked the horse and galloped away.

Mrs. Burns flung the knife across the yard just as Miss May came running out to apprehend her.

"Now, Miz Burns." Miss May retrieved the knife and looped her arm in Mrs. Burns's. "We almost got dinner ready, Mr. Burns. Time to wash up."

"Awright, Granny."

Mrs. Burns bent toward Miss May as they walked away. "Did I tell you that colored man was looking in my window again just a while ago?"

"Yessum, you did." Miss May nodded. "Le's us go in an' git dinner on the table."

"Not Ezra, mind you. He's all right. It was that other one."

"Yessum. I still gots to mash dem taters. Will you fix dat fine gravy o' yours?"

After they were out of earshot, Mr. Burns shook his head. "Granny sure has made a difference around here, but I swear, I'm gonna have to put Mama in the asylum." He walked over to the water pump and primed it. "I'm thirty years old, and Kate's twenty-eight. We shoulda had six kids by now." He pumped water, catching some in his hands and splashing it on his face and head. "It's gonna kill me and Mama both, but I just don't want to waste any more time."

Still fighting his restlessness, Ezra waited for his turn to clean up. "Then you'll understand that I think it's time for me to take the Brewsters to Boston. You'll have to find other help to finish the barn." With the words being spoken, he felt his pulse slowing. This evening after supper, he would go to Miss Saunders's farm and tell the others.

Mr. Burns regarded him for a moment, then reached down to scratch Tick Bait behind the ears. "Hmph. Guess I deserve that. I put off finishing the barn just like I put off building a life with Kate. Guess I'd better get busy with both of 'em."

"That's an excellent analogy, sir." Ezra wished back the words as soon as he said them.

"A what?" Mr. Burns crinkled his face in confusion. Then he laughed. "Ezra, you got no business workin' on a farm. Go home. Teach school. Get out of the South before they kill you for bein' uppity."

Ezra breathed out his relief. Mr. Burns had not been offended. "Yes, sir. I think I'll do just that."

CHAPTER THIRTY-ONE

While daylight faded, Ezra wended his way through the thick woods, leaving small notches on every fifth pine tree. To keep his bearings and avoid walking in circles, he checked for lichen on the rocks and moss on the north side of the trees. Walking to Miss Saunders's farm on the roads would have taken him less time than this direct but too-dense route. But he could not risk another encounter with those deputies.

In the thick of the forest, he crossed a small stream. Its eastward flow indicated the direction of the river and confirmed he was still traveling the right way. Under the protective canopy of pine and oak, he soon cooled from the heat of the day, but the deepening darkness made the trek more difficult. Nocturnal animals began to skitter about searching for food. A distant owl hooted its warning to field mice. A harmless sound, but Ezra shivered, recalling Mr. Burns's warning about the panthers. He almost wished he had told his employer about this little trip to Miss Saunders's farm.

Finally Ezra emerged from the forest to see familiar buildings. Smoke curled up from the chimney above the shack where the Bartons and Adam lived. Where Jack had lived until today. If Ezra were not in a hurry to see Delia, if he had not already eaten supper, he would sample whatever aromatic food Alice was cooking in that humble home. As it was, he decided to tell Leviticus that he was here before the dogs announced his presence. This evening, no breeze blew up from the river, or they would have caught his scent before this.

As he approached the open door, Frederick's pup sidled up to him and licked his hand. A poor guard dog but a good companion for the boy.

Inside Frederick was practicing his letters at the small table while Adam and Leviticus looked on. Alice bent over the low iron stove tasting a spoonful of string beans from a boiling pot.

"Evening, folks." Ezra wanted to hurry on to the house. He longed to tell Delia about leaving first. But these people had journeyed with him for a long time. He must also give them a chance to come with him.

"Ezra."

Leviticus stood and came to the door to shake his hand, followed by Adam. Frederick threw himself at Ezra, who caught him, as always, and swung him into the air.

"What you doin' here? Come on in for a spell." Leviticus retrieved his son, set him on the dirt floor, and clapped Ezra on the shoulder. "You hear 'bout Jack?"

"Yes." Ezra sat with the men at the table. "It was just enough to make me realize it's time to leave. I came to ask if any of you want to go with me."

"Oh, Leviticus...." Alice wiped her hands on her apron and waddled over to join the men with her hands cupped under her round belly.

"Now, honey, it's awright. We done talked 'bout this." Leviticus gave her a fond smile. "Ezra, we gonna stay. Miz Kate is a decent lady. She tol' me this afternoon she wants me runnin' this place for her. Says we can git more workers, and I'll be in charge. All this summer long, she ain't never give us no cause to doubt her. Ain't that right, Alice?"

"That's right." Alice's face bore more age lines, and she seemed very near to bearing her child. No wonder she wanted to stay.

Ezra glanced around the plain dwelling. Not even a house. Just a shack.

Leviticus frowned. "Now don't you go lookin' 'round like that. I know'd it ain't much. Not even as good as the quarters back on the plantation. But Miz Kate say we can build on to it this winter after cotton harvest. It don't git too cold here for that."

"I understand." Ezra ran an affectionate hand over Frederick's coarse, tight curls. "Just make sure she lets this fine young man go to the school the Freedman's Bureau's going to build for Negro children."

"I will." Leviticus beamed. "It's a new day for the South. Both my children will learn how to read and write and do numbers. Why, they'll be able to write to you up in Boston."

"I'm counting on that." Ezra swiped at a mosquito that had landed on his arm. "Adam, what about you? You never really said what you wanted to do. Has this summer of working in the fields given you any direction?" He felt a little guilty for putting it that way, but Adam was a smart young man who would do well at a trade.

"No, sir. I like Miz Kate, too. I been thinkin' on it long and hard."

Ezra stood. "Well, I'm leaving tomorrow or the next day. You come over to the Burns' place and let me know." He said his good-byes to them and walked out into the dark.

The breeze had calmed somewhat. The dogs must have caught his scent because they came running from the front of the house howling at the top of their lungs. As they approached Ezra, their vigilance dissolved into playful familiarity. The large male pup nearly knocked him over with all his usual wiggling and licking, and Sheba sniffed his hand and then sat back on her haunches.

"Down, boy." Ezra scratched the male behind the ears. "Say, girl." He knelt down to Sheba, who always had better manners. "How're you doing? Good dog. Good dog." He accepted her wet lick on his cheek and gave her ears a thorough scratching, too. She deserved all the attention he could give her for protecting Delia.

In the dim light from the open shack door, he could see the clipped fur around the wound on her side and the slick salve someone had applied. It would heal, but Ezra wondered if Jack had broken her ribs. Had he hurt Delia this badly?

Rage rose in Ezra's chest. If Jack had been standing before him now, he would surely kill him.

No, he must not think this way. He *must* not feel this way.

"God, help me," he whispered. The struggle brought physical pain to his chest.

"Ezra, that you?" Miss Saunders stood silhouetted in the kitchen doorway.

"Yes, ma'am." He patted the two dogs again and stood up. "I came to see Delia."

"O'course you did. I shoulda made a nickel bet with ol' Burns, 'cause I knowed you'd come. I'd be a nickel richer, and I sure could use a nickel." She turned back into the house. "Delia, Ezra's come courtin'. Git on out here."

The humor in her voice encouraged Ezra but also brought heat to his face. Despite her earlier assurances that Delia was all right, Miss Saunders was not angry that he had come.

"Ezra?" Delia appeared in the doorway. The kitchen lantern cast her face into shadows, but her light step as she descended the stairs told him all he needed to know. She was, indeed, all right.

A wave of joy swept through him, and relief nearly buckled his knees. "Oh, Delia." He met her at the bottom of the steps and pulled her into his arms. He shook so hard he could barely stand as he fought to keep his emotions subdued. It was no use. "Oh, Delia. My Delia. You're all right." He laughed to hide choking sobs. "Delia, Delia."

She put her face in his chest, weeping and trembling as hard as he was. "Oh, Ezra."

He had no idea how long they stood there in each other's arms. As the height of their emotions subsided, they both laughed softly.

"I wanted to come right away."

"Miz Kate said you'd come." Delia hung her head in her shy way. "I didn't know if you would or not."

He took her face in his hands, barely able to make out her lovely smile. "I will come whenever you need me, no matter where you are. All you need to do is call me." A bit of light sparkled in her eyes. How he wished he could see her face more clearly.

He pulled her over to the back steps to sit down, then draped his arm around her shoulders. That felt so good, especially when she nestled close to him in response. He longed to kiss her on the lips, but he would not do so without permission.

"Did Jack hurt you?" Those were not the words he wished to say.

Staring off toward the river, she nodded.

"Do you want to tell me about it?"

She shook her head and shrugged. "Ain't no worse than Miz Suzanne ever done to me."

Ezra's heart ached. This sweet girl…woman…had suffered far too much in her short life. He must protect her, whatever it took.

"Delia, I'm leaving for Boston tomorrow or Thursday. The Brewsters are going with me. Will you go?"

She gasped. "Oh, Ezra, I don't know. Miz Kate needs me. What'll she do without me?"

Ezra glanced up toward the kitchen door, praying Miss Saunders wasn't within earshot.

"She's a strong, smart lady. She'll be fine, just like she was before."

Delia moved her skirt to the side and drew in the dirt with her bare toe. Ezra had noticed early in the summer that her shoes had worn out. Once they reached Boston, he would buy her a dozen pairs of shoes. And dresses and hats and—

"What'll I do up there?" Her voice held a tremor of fear.

He scratched his cheek, feeling the stubble of his fast-growing beard. It was a good thing he hadn't kissed her and scraped her tender skin.

"Why, you can do anything you like."

"I guess I could be a lady's maid. I hear you can git paid for that. You know any white ladies needin' a maid?"

Ezra puckered his lips to keep from answering crossly. "No, but I do know some Negro businesswomen who can help you discover what you want to do." *Or we could get married...*a thought he nearly spoke.

"My, my." She tilted her head back.

Ezra followed her gaze upward to where a thousand stars sparkled like jewels against the black velvet sky. A ruby necklace would look nice on her smooth throat.

"So you'll go with me?"

"It sure would be nice, but Miz Kate—"

Ezra scooted down a step and looked up at her so light would shine on his face. "Are you going to serve needy white women all your life, or are you going to make a life for yourself?"

"Ezra, are you out here tryin' to steal my housekeeper?" Miss Saunders stood in the doorway, blocking the light just as she seemed about to block Delia's future.

He stood up. "Yes, ma'am. That's exactly what I'm trying to do."

Delia jumped up beside him. A slender shaft of light revealed her furrowed forehead and dropped jaw. Ezra could feel her trembling.

She looked up at Ezra.

He took her hand. "I want you to go with me."

She looked up at Miss Saunders.

Miss Saunders put her hands on her hips. "Girl, don't you make the same mistake I did. You go with this boy, you hear?"

Delia sighed. She looked back up at Ezra.

"I'll go."

★ ★ ★ ★

CHAPTER THIRTY-TWO

As the sky lightened shortly before sunup, Ezra stood outside the shack, where he had spent the night, and said good-bye to Leviticus and his family.

"You been a good friend, Ezra." Alice handed him some cold corn bread wrapped in a square of cotton. She wiped dampness from her dark brown cheeks with her apron.

"Thank you, ma'am." Ezra put her gift in his pocket to eat along the way.

Tears filled Frederick's eyes as he grasped Ezra around the legs. "Who's gonna teach me how to read and write?"

Ezra knelt down eye to eye with him. "There's going to be a school for Negro children soon. Miss Saunders said she'd make sure you get to go. You're doing fine. Keep up the good work."

"But who's gonna play baseball with me?"

Ezra ran his hands over Frederick's coarse, beaded-up hair. "Your pa's a good ball player." He picked the boy up for a bear hug. "He'll be able to help you."

"That was real nice of you to give him that ball." Leviticus cleared his throat, as if he were trying to cover his emotions.

"Every boy should have a baseball." Ezra also tried to suppress his emotions. He loved this family dearly, yet he understood why they wanted to stay here. They would be happier working the land rather than trying to find a way to survive in a northern city.

After a final squeeze, he set Frederick down and turned to Adam. "Have you made up your mind?"

Adam swiped his hand across his jaw and stared off toward the river. "I think so." He walked a few yards away, then returned, scratching his head. "It ain't easy to decide. It just ain't easy." At last he nodded with conviction. "I think I'll go." He exhaled a laugh. "Well, don't that beat all? Just sayin' it makes me feel better. I'll go. Yes, I'll go. Don't it feel good just to say it?"

Ezra and the others laughed, too.

"I know what you mean." Ezra clapped him on the shoulder. "I woke up this morning with a light heart knowing that we'll be on the road this very day. You come on over to the Burns' place with Delia this morning."

"Yes, *sir*." Adam's smile radiated joy.

"You tell Mr. and Miz Brewster 'bye for us," Alice said. "We gonna miss 'em."

"I will. And I promise to write to Miss Saunders and tell her when we reach Boston. She'll give you all our news. Well, I'd better be on my way. I need to do morning chores one last time. It's the least I could do for Mr. Burns."

Ezra glanced toward the house. A thin stream of smoke arose from the stovepipe above the kitchen. That meant Delia was awake. Before he left, he must confirm the plans they had made last night.

As if she heard his thoughts, Delia came out of the back door and stood on the stoop waving to him in the dim morning light.

With a final good-bye to his friends, Ezra ran across the backyard to the house. He could feel the wide, foolish grin on his face but made no attempt to soften it. When he reached the bottom of the steps, he felt the smile fade as anger rose in his chest.

Her right cheek bore a dark bruise that extended from her temple to her jawline. Jack had done that. Yet last night she had dismissed her injuries as no worse than her mistress had done. Why was she so accepting of such cruelty?

"Delia." He choked out her name as he ran up the steps and pulled her into his arms.

Her eyes widened, and her smile disappeared. "Ezra, what's the matter?"

He gently touched the swollen cheek, and she winced. He pulled back his hand.

"Oh, Delia, look at what he did to you." Ezra's eyes burned as hot as the fire in his chest. "I couldn't see it in the dark last night, but now it's plain as day."

"It's awright." Delia shook her head. "It don't hurt too bad."

"No. It's not all right." Ezra trembled. *If he were here right now, I would surely kill him for doing this to you.*

"Ezra, ain't you gone yet?" Miss Saunders appeared in the door. Her welcoming smile faded, too. "What's goin' on here?" She looked at Delia. "Good gracious, child, that's a terrible bruise." She eyed Ezra.

"I don't blame you for bein' mad, but you watch out, you hear me? Jack's nothin' but trouble, and somebody oughta stop him. But he ain't worth goin' to jail for. He sure ain't worth hangin' for." She glanced down at the knife on his belt and then leveled a solemn stare into his eyes. "You hear me, Ezra?"

He took a deep breath, as he had before every battle during the war. A steadying breath that helped him regain control of himself. But, God forgive him, he could murder Jack for what he had done to Delia.

"I hear you, Miss Saunders." He loosened his hold on Delia. "Adam's coming with us. I told him to bring you to Mr. Burns's, but instead I'll come back over about noon to get you. Don't leave Miss Saunders's side."

"I'll be ready." Her voice quivered. Was she excited or afraid?

"I'll bring 'em over." Miss Saunders touched Delia's shoulder. "The road you want is down by Spartanburg. No sense in you backtracking. I'll bring my gun." She gave Ezra a nod and a wink.

The implication behind her gestures made his stomach turn. She could shoot Jack, and no one would care. Ezra couldn't even hit the man without being jailed as a public nuisance. Praise God they were leaving the South for good.

"Go on, now." Miss Saunders tilted her head toward the woods. "I'll take care of her."

"Yes, ma'am." Ezra gave Delia a gentle squeeze. "I'll see you soon."

Her eyes sparkled with tears, but they seemed to be from happiness, and she gave him a sweet smile. "I'll see you soon."

He set a quick kiss on her unbruised cheek and dashed away, picking up speed as he drew closer to the woods. A good, hard run would cool his temper, help him forget his rage toward Jack. It also would take him back to the Burns' farm more quickly. The sooner his chores were done, the sooner he could pack up everything and go home.

Home. How long had it been since he had even thought of home? Father, Mother, Aunt Patience, his sister Luella, and his many good friends. The first thing he must do in Boston was to report to his army unit and give his commanding officer Colonel Rule's letter as proof he had not deserted. Then school, helping Delia find her place, marriage.

Ezra stopped and leaned against a tree, laughing and catching his breath at the same time. Oh, yes, marriage. If the young lady would have him. To think he had kissed her cheek. That was not the way he had planned to kiss her the first time.

Just as expected, his running had improved his thoughts. He inhaled deeply, taking in the fresh, clean smell of pine trees in the morning air. Looking down, he saw that the tree he leaned against bore one of the notches he had cut for a guide back to the farm. Good. And there a few yards ahead was another cut. Bolstering himself with another quick breath, he walked as fast as the trees and undergrowth would permit him.

He reached the small stream at the center of the woods and bent down for a drink. As he lifted a handful of water to his mouth, a long, piercing shriek reverberated through the forest. A violent shiver darted down Ezra's back.

Panther!

He flung away the water, jumped up, and snatched his knife from the sheath.

Another shriek split the air. A scream—almost human, just as Mr. Burns had said—echoed after it.

Two panthers? If only he had a gun.

"Steady." He pulled in a breath. It did not calm him. "Help me, Lord."

What had Mr. Burns said about panthers? They stalked their prey. They might circle around to attack from the rear. Ezra moved with his back against one tree, then another. But that was no protection. A panther could be in any of these trees. He looked up. Could they see through the thick leaves? Did they hunt in packs?

A fourth shriek. Long. Plaintive. Dying out. Which direction did it come from? The thick forest might divert the sounds.

Ezra ran. Barely seeing the marked trees. Barely hearing yet another shriek, this time off to his left toward the river.

No more sounds. Was this good or bad?

Within minutes, he reached the forest edge. Running and fear had stolen the very air from his lungs. Where was the panther? He spun in a circle. Nothing visible in the woods. Nothing in the field below the house.

A moan, soft and desperate, came from the tall grass to the right. Odd, gurgling sound followed.

Ezra froze. Was the panther eating its prey? Mr. Burns's crippled old hound?

"Help."

The voice was so soft, so breathy, Ezra feared he had imagined it.

"Help."

He would run to the house, get Mr. Burns's gun.

"Ezra." Barely a whisper.

Light burst above the distant hills beyond the river and shot across the field. Ezra's eyes focused on a dark form covered with deep red that glistened in the morning sun.

Jack.

On quivering legs, Ezra hurried to kneel beside him. Dark blood oozed from Jack's chest. The wound resembled a savage bayonet wound. How could a panther do that? Even the cuts on Jack's arms did not look like claw marks.

Could Ezra stop the bleeding? With his knife, he slashed open Jack's shirt, pulled it off and rolled it up, then pressed it against the gaping hole.

"Lord, have mercy." What was he saying? Hadn't he wished to kill this man? Yet now he prayed for him.

"Jack, listen to me." Ezra longed for a canteen. How could he get Jack to the house without killing him? Should he leave him and run for help?

"Ezra." Jack's voice was weak, his eyes glazed.

"Listen, Jack. God loves you. Call on Him for mercy. Jack, do you hear me?"

"S-she…she…" Jack lifted his hand, then dropped it to the ground.

"Jack, Jesus Christ died for your sins. Put your trust in Him, and He will save you." *Please save him, Lord.*

"She got jewels." Jack coughed, and blood oozed from his mouth and around the balled-up shirt. "She got—" His eyes rolled back, and he went limp.

"What is this?" Mr. Burns stood above him, his rifle in hand. "Dear God in heaven, Ezra, what have you done?"

CHAPTER THIRTY-THREE

"Think you got enough food?"

Miz Kate helped Delia pack bread, meat, and root vegetables into an old satchel. They'd need to eat the meat and bread in the first day or so, but the sweet potatoes, carrots, radishes, and boiled peanuts would feed them for days.

"All we can carry." Delia hoped Miz Kate wouldn't look too deep in the bag. "Thank you kindly for all you give us. I like this little sewing box. That'll really help."

"Don't mention it. You been a real help around here. You know, I think I'll just take my wagon on down to Spartanburg and get some supplies. That way I can give you all a ride and get you on down the road a mite sooner."

"Oh, Miz Kate, you been so good." Guilt swept through Delia. "I...I wish...."

Miz Kate gave her one of her sideways looks, like she knew Delia's secret. "What is it, girl? You changin' your mind?"

"No, ma'am. But...." Delia just couldn't do this. She lifted all the food from the satchel, pulled out the blue gingham dress, and shoved it at Miz Kate. "Here."

"What in the world?" Miz Kate took the dress but kept looking at Delia. "I thought I told you to burn this."

Delia hung her head. "Yessum. You did. But I ain't never had a blue gingham dress." Her eyes burned, and she sniffed back tears. "I ain't a thief, Miz Kate. I swear I ain't. You said burn it, but I just couldn't let a good dress go to waste. I took it up to fit me."

Miz Kate looked at the dress like it was an old friend. When she set it against her bosom and lowered her head over it like it was a baby kitten, Delia let go of her tears.

"I'm so sorry, Miz Kate." She could barely whisper the words.

Miz Kate reached out one arm and pulled Delia close. "Don't feel bad. I shoulda give it to you in the first place. But I was so wrought up over Owen that I never wanted to see this dress again." She shook it out full length, then draped it over the table to fold it up all neat. "Sure is a lot smaller." She chuckled. "Here. Let's put it in here." Miz Kate gently laid the dress back in the satchel. "You wear it someplace special, you hear?"

Delia wiped her cheeks with the back of her hand. "Yessum."

Then they both laughed.

"Oh, Delia, I'll miss you. Whoever woulda thought my best lady friend ever would be a colored girl?"

Delia felt her cheeks heat up. Could she get by with a little sassiness? "Well, I never thought a white lady could talk to me without hittin' me."

Miz Kate gasped. She stared at Delia with such a dark frown that Delia felt ashamed.

"I'm sorry—"

"No. Don't you ever say you're sorry when you been hit." Miz Kate shook her head. Then she shrugged real hard like she was trying to shake off her bad feelings. "If that Ezra don't treat you right, you come on back down here, you hear?" She gave Delia a little grin.

Delia smiled back. "Yessum. I'll do that."

"Now, you'll need a pot or two to cook in. You can have this and this." She lifted a tin pan and a cast-iron pot from their hooks above the stove. "Here's a cookin' spoon."

By the time they finished loading up Miz Kate's wagon for the trip, there was more than Delia and Adam could carry.

"I ain't been able to pay you wages yet, so this is the least I can do. I can get by till the cotton sells."

Delia and Adam said their good-byes to Alice, Leviticus, and Frederick.

"You been a family to me." Delia held on to Alice for a long while, hugging her sideways on account of the baby.

"You goin' to a good place." Alice hugged back just as hard. "Be happy, girl. Be happy."

Delia nodded. "I will. You, too."

"Come on, Sheba." Miz Kate motioned to her dog, who jumped up beside her on the driver's bench. She slapped the reins against the horse's haunches, and the wagon began to roll.

With heavy heart, Delia sat beside Adam and hung her feet over the back, waving to her friends until the trees got in the way. Up on the main road, she scrambled up to the wagon front by Miz Kate to watch for the road to the Burns' farm. Now her heart began thumping. She was going to Boston, wherever that was. Best of all, she was going with Ezra.

"I'm telling you, I didn't kill Jack." Ezra helped Mr. Burns load the bloody body onto a wheelbarrow. "You have to believe me."

"You think I'm a fool? More'n once, I heard you say you were gonna kill him. I heard the screams and came runnin'. You were kneeling beside him, blood all over you *and* your knife." Mr. Burns picked up Ezra's Bowie knife and slipped it alongside of Jack in the wheelbarrow. Then he retrieved his rifle from where he had laid it a few yards away. "Now take him up to the house. I gotta figure out what to do. Damn, Ezra, why'd you put me in this spot? You're a good man, a good worker. You had your whole future ahead of you. How could somebody so smart be so stupid as to do somethin' like this?"

Ezra strained to push the dead weight up the hill through grass and rocks. "But I didn't kill him. Umph." As hard as it was to push and talk at the same time, he must defend himself. "He was lying there—"

"Shut up. I gotta think." Mr. Burns was sweating in the cool morning air just as much as Ezra. "We could bury him, and nobody would ever miss him." He shook his head. "I don't want to turn you over to the sheriff. But if somebody finds the body after you leave, I'll have to answer for lettin' you go."

Halfway up the hill, Ezra stopped to rest. His mind raced in a hundred directions. Who could have killed Jack? Why had he been near these woods? Ezra closed his eyes and wiped sweat from his forehead.

Run. A sudden burst of energy infused him. He would run. He would take off running right now. Mr. Burns had only one shot. If he missed, indeed, if he even shot at all, he would not be able to reload before Ezra was out of range.

Delia's face came to mind. She would be here soon, she and Adam. How could he desert them? But if he was jailed or—he could hardly grasp the thought—*hanged,* what would become of her?

"Come on, now. Move." Mr. Burns seemed to have trouble sounding stern.

Ezra had to admit that if he had come across such a scene, he would have believed the worst, too. Mr. Burns had trusted him as few southern men would have. Ezra could not run. He could not leave until he had this man's good opinion again. He grasped the wheelbarrow handles, lifted, and shoved his weight into the task.

With only one more stop to rest, they reached the backyard just as the field hands arrived for work.

"Lem," Mr. Burns called out to one of the white men in the mixed-race group. "Come over here. I need your help."

Ezra's heart sank. What did Mr. Burns plan to do now?

All seven of the hands crowded around the wheelbarrow, exclaiming over the gory sight.

"Lawsy, what happened here?" Lem was the man who supervised the others as they worked the fields. Other than that, Ezra knew nothing about any of them.

Mr. Burns glanced at Ezra, then back at Lem. "This man's been killed. I need you to go into town and fetch the sheriff. You can take my mule."

"Yessir." Lem ran toward the corral beside the nearly completed barn.

"What happened, boss?" one of the Negroes asked. The four black men looked far more concerned than the two remaining white men.

Mr. Burns did not answer, but he did glance at Ezra again. The other men all took a step backward.

"Boy, what you done?" the Negro asked.

"He done made trouble for all of us," another black man said.

The other two Negroes hummed and amened their agreement.

Ezra could only shake his head. Protests would just waste energy.

"Lawdy, Lawdy, Mr. Burns." Miss May came running from the house. "Oh, Lawdy, Mr. Burns."

Mr. Burns stepped in front of Jack's body, as if to shield her from the sight. "Now, Granny, you just go on back in the house and—"

"Mr. Burns, yo' mama ain't in her bed. She ain't in the house. I went to wake her up, an' she was gone."

"What're you talking about?" Mr. Burns's face grew pale. "Where is she?"

"That's what I'm sayin', suh." Panting, Miss May pressed her hand to her heart. "She ain't in her room."

Mr. Burns swore as he ran toward the house and up the back steps. At the door, he turned back. "Ezra, don't you go nowhere, you hear?"

"We'll keep him here, boss." One of the white men gave Ezra a warning look.

If Ezra hoped for more sympathy from his own race, the scowls on the other men's faces removed all such expectation. And these were the people for whose freedom he had fought in the war. Wounded pride welled up in his bosom.

"I didn't plan to run."

"Good thing," one man muttered. Ezra did not turn to see whether he was white or black.

"Oh, Lawd!" Miss May saw Jack. "Mercy, mercy, what happened, Ezra?"

He had never seen Miss May so upset. Her shrill voice carried across the barnyard, and soon Mr. Willard came running.

"May, May, what's the matter?" He approached the group, his eyes wide with concern. "Oh, Lawd, what happened?" He pulled his wife into his arms.

"Jack's dead, and Miz Burns done disappeared."

At Miss May's brief report, a strange shudder swept through Ezra. Perhaps the screams he had heard in the forest had not been a panther after all. But had Mrs. Burns killed Jack? She might be wiry and strong, but surely she was no match for such a big man as Jack. And where had she gone? Instead of holding him here as if he were a prisoner, Ezra and the others should be looking for her.

The last scream he had heard came from near the river. What would happen if she drowned? Would they blame him for that, too?

Lem galloped past the group, riding the mule bareback. "Tell Mr. Burns I'll be back soon."

Mr. Burns emerged from the house, pale and clearly shaken. "Mama's gone. Granny, did you see her at all this morning?"

"No suh. I ain't seen her since last night when I put her to bed."

Mr. Burns ran his hands through his hair and stared around at the others, who seemed to watch him for direction. His gaze landed on Ezra, as if he somehow suspected him of Mrs. Burns's disappearance, too. But then he gave a decisive shake of his head and broke eye contact.

"You want us to tie him up, boss?" One of the white men asked the question.

Mr. Burns looked at him as if he had not understood. Ezra prayed he would say no.

"I won't go anywhere. We should be looking for Mrs. Burns, sir." Ezra eyed his Bowie knife, still tucked beside Jack's body. If he picked it up, they would surely jump him.

Before Mr. Burns could answer, the rattle and clatter of an approaching wagon drew everyone's attention. Miss Saunders drove her weathered box wagon into the barnyard. Beside her sat Delia, and Adam peered around them from the back.

Mr. Burns hurried over to grab the horse's bridle and greet Miss Saunders.

"Kate, somethin' real bad's happened." He reached up and helped her down. "Mama's gone. I don't know where, but she's not in her room."

If the situation were not so tragic, Ezra might have laughed. Mrs. Burns's disappearance was clearly more important to Mr. Burns than Jack's demise. And the quickly covered grin on Miss Saunders's face betrayed her disdain for the old woman.

"What's that over there?" Miss Saunders approached the wheelbarrow. "Good Lord, what happened?" She looked around the group. "What happened?"

Ezra felt a glimmer of hope. "When I came through the woods after leaving your place, I heard screams. I found Jack—"

"Ezra's knife was all bloody when I found 'em." Mr. Burns did not look at Ezra.

A gasp came from nearby. Delia stared at him, horror written across her face. "Oh, Ezra, what did you do?"

CHAPTER THIRTY-FOUR

Delia pumped fresh water into the drinking bucket and carried a dipperful to Ezra. Sitting there tied to an oak tree, he looked like a whipped dog. On the plantation, Massuh had sometimes tied up troublemakers, but never a good man like Ezra. She felt 'specially bad for thinking he could have killed Jack. When she saw how his eyes had filled with pain and hurt from her question, she knew he hadn't done it.

"It's fresh and cold." She knelt beside him and lifted the dipper to his lips.

He gulped down the water as fast as she could tip it. He tried to wipe the wetness from his chin onto his sleeve, but he couldn't reach it. Delia used her own sleeve to help him.

"Thank you." His voice was hushed, and his face was pinched with shame.

Her heart seemed to twist inside her. "You want me to cut you loose?" She glanced over her shoulder. "We're goin' out lookin' for Miz Burns. You could run after we get to the woods."

Ezra peered around her. "Is everyone going?"

"No. Mr. Burns said his mama would be scared of the colored men, all except Mr. Willard. He's takin' Miz May and Mr. Willard and Miz Kate and me."

"Miss Saunders is going?" Ezra shifted around like he couldn't get comfortable. Delia noticed that the oak tree had lots of roots sticking out of the ground where he was sitting.

"Yes, her and Sheba. Sheba's a good trackin' dog." Delia sent another glance toward the group. "Now are you gonna let me cut you loose before I go?"

Ezra looked like he was thinking about it, but then he shook his head. "No." The misery in his voice nearly broke Delia's heart. "Those men haven't taken their eyes off of me. They'd just catch me again, and they might tie me to one of those branches." He shot a quick look up in the tree and gave her a resigned smile. "Watch out for panthers and snakes while you're in the woods."

Delia's eyes filled with tears. "I think the baddest snake's already dead."

Ezra grunted. "I think you might be right. Oh, Delia, I assure you I didn't kill him."

She touched his cheek. "I know."

"Delia!" Miz Kate held her rifle under her arm. "Come on, girl. Can't waste any more time. Sheba's got the old lady's scent."

"Yessum." Delia bent near Ezra and kissed his cheek. His look of surprise made her laugh. "Well, you kissed me. Now we're even."

He laughed, too, but his laugh was a bit tight and strained. "Pray, Delia. Pray for God's mercy for both of us."

She stood up to go. Now was not the time to talk about God and praying.

"I will." She ran back to the others. "Yes, ma'am, Miz Kate."

As the group set out, she straggled behind waving to Ezra. The other men, who should have been in the cotton fields instead of watching Ezra, eyed her in an ugly way.

"Hey, pretty girl, you gonna give me a kiss, too?" One of the white field hands grinned at her in a way that made her feel sick to her stomach.

"My, my, ain't she fine?" a colored man said. "Hurry back, sweet thing."

Delia's cheeks felt like they were on fire. Even her own kind showed her no respect. Just Ezra. And they might hang him for no good reason. She bit her cheeks to keep from saying something ugly back to those men.

Awright, then, Ezra. I'll pray. God, have mercy on Ezra. And on me, 'cause I ain't never gonna find a good man like him again. But mostly for Ezra, 'cause he ain't done nothin' wrong.

"Come on, Delia." Miz Kate walked real fast down the hill toward the woods.

Delia ran to catch up. Behind them, Mr. Willard helped Miz May through the rocky field.

Mr. Burns walked far ahead, toting his rifle and hollering, "Mama! Where are you, Mama?"

Delia felt a pang of pity for him. Ezra liked him, so he must be a pretty good man. Ezra didn't even blame him for thinking he'd killed Jack. But that scared Delia. On the plantation she'd seen what white men did to coloreds who did something wrong...or when somebody said they did something wrong. The war being over hadn't made much of a difference as far as she could tell.

"God, if You're up there, You gotta help Ezra," Delia whispered. "I'll give up goin' to Boston and work for Miz Kate the rest of my life if You'll set him free."

Yet the idea of spending her life without Ezra made her heart ache.

"Miz Burns!" She took up the call, adding her voice to the small chorus whose voices echoed through the woods.

And while I'm at it, God, help us to find the old lady.

"Ezra."

"Hm?" Ezra shook himself awake. How long had he dozed here under the tree? He took a deep breath and tried to rub his eyes, but ropes held his hands fast.

"Ezra." The whispered call came from behind the tree. "It's me. Adam. I'm gonna untie you."

Ezra's heart raced. He glanced across the yard where the field workers watched him from beneath another tree. "No. Don't." The boy must not get in trouble for him.

"I can't let them hang you." Adam's tone grew more insistent. "It ain't right."

Ezra felt the ropes move. "No, Adam. I could never get away." He struggled to think. Only one idea came to mind. "There is something you can do. Get my knapsack. There's a letter in it from a Union colonel. Take that and my uniform to the Union headquarters in

Spartanburg. Tell the commanding officer the rebels are about to hang an innocent Union soldier."

"That's seven miles. They'll have you hunged before I get back." Adam's voice wavered as though he was choking back tears.

Peace settled in Ezra's heart. If he died, a small handful of honest people would grieve, but they also would know he was not a murderer.

"Maybe not." He had to cling to that hope.

Adam was quiet for a moment. "Awright. I'll go." A scuffing sound behind the tree told Ezra he had left.

Alone again, Ezra laid his head back against the tree and tried not to fall into despair. But he could not help himself. Just like the times in his youth when he had fought with street boys over some imagined insult, this was his fault. If he had displayed temperance regarding Jack's wicked behavior, Mr. Burns would not have been so quick to believe he had killed him. Ezra had been so blinded by jealousy and protectiveness that he had not used good sense.

"Lord, I don't deserve it, but please have mercy on me." Ezra swallowed the emotions that tried to choke him. "Please rule my temper from now on, even in the face of injustice. Let Your Spirit guide my words and actions and, most of all, my thoughts."

One stray thought, however, gave him further evidence of his dead adversary's wickedness. Mrs. Burns had seen Jack watching her through the bedroom window. Yet because of her other delusions and ravings, no one had believed her story. Jack had spoken of jewels. Perhaps he had planned to rob her. But why was he found dying at the edge of the woods? Mr. Burns had not mentioned anything about blood in the house. Had Mrs. Burns followed Jack there? Ezra's head reeled with the confusing details, not the least of which was how a woman, even a strong farm woman, could savagely stab a big man to death. And if she had killed Jack, had she come after him with that butcher knife she had once flung at Miss Saunders?

He must put these thoughts aside. If he only had hours to live, he should be praying for those he was leaving behind, just as he had before every battle during the war. He certainly needed to pray for Adam's success in reaching the Union headquarters.

He could not see the farm road from his position. Had Adam traveled that way? Had he reached the main road yet? Would he run into trouble with those deputies?

Ezra scanned the peaceful farm setting. Something was missing. The distant sound of a single horse galloping away drew his attention to the wagon that stood several yards beyond where the group of men sat.

"Oh, no." Ezra rolled his head back against the tree again. He did not know whether to laugh or cry.

That little rascal Adam had taken Miss Saunders's horse—stolen it! His trip to the Union headquarters would take a fraction of the time, but would they hang him for being a horse thief? Yet Ezra could not dismiss the surge of hope rising in his chest. Maybe the soldiers would come. And maybe they would be here in time to save him.

✯ ✯ ✯

CHAPTER THIRTY-FIVE

A dozen yards away from Delia, Miz Kate followed Sheba through the river birches and palmettos. The dog sniffed all over the place like she was on a trail, and Miz Kate followed with her rifle ready to shoot.

As they came closer to the river, Delia saw something white in the thick undergrowth of viburnum and wild hydrangea. She glanced toward Miz Kate, then sidled over to it. These people might use anything to condemn Ezra. If she could save him by hiding whatever that was, she'd do it, no matter what it cost her.

A long white cotton nightgown was snagged down low in a hydrangea bush. It was torn and covered with blood. Delia looked around for a stick so she could push it farther under and maybe even bury it.

Before she could find the right tool, Sheba came running and went straight to the nightgown. She sniffed and pawed at it and barked and ran back to Miz Kate.

"What is it, girl?" Miz Kate followed Sheba and bent down to look. She lifted the bloodstained gown and shot a glance at Delia. "You find this?"

"Yessum. I was tryin' to figure out what it was." Delia dug her toe in the wet riverbank. What would Ezra think of her lie?

"Hooo-eee!" Miz Kate stood up holding the shredded garment. "Looks like a panther done tore into this."

A panther? Delia gasped and glanced about the trees. "You think he's still around?" If a panther got the old lady, they couldn't blame Ezra for whatever happened to her.

"Naw. They're night hunters." She shook her head. "Poor ol' Burns. He'll be broke up bad if his mama fell to a panther." She searched around for a minute. "Sheba, where's the trail?"

She bent down to give Sheba a sniff of the gown. The dog took off running alongside the riverbank.

"Come on, Delia." Miz Kate ran after Sheba, her long legs covering the distance almost as fast as her dog.

Delia followed, her heart pounding.

Sheba splashed around a big rock that touched the riverbank, with Miz Kate close behind. Miz Kate stopped all of a sudden and just stared, her mouth wide open. Delia froze ten feet away.

"Delia, come help me." She untucked her shirt and took it off, leaving only her chemise to cover above her waist.

Delia couldn't move. She couldn't obey. She didn't want to see a dead old white lady all torn up by a panther.

✦╍╫╳╢✹╟╫╍✦

Ezra's stomach rumbled with hunger. It was past noon, and he had not eaten anything since Alice gave him corn bread early that morning.

Another rumble sounded from beyond the house, like a thundering herd of horses. Ezra exhaled a long breath. It was too soon for

Adam to be back. This had to be the local deputies. From the sound, Ezra could tell they had brought others with them.

"Lord, help me to have a good testimony. Whether I live or die, let some good come out of this." During the two years he had fought in the war, he had faced fear and death every day, yet never once had he run from the heat of battle. Today he would not permit himself to be any less courageous. Yet he could not still the anxious pounding of his heart.

A half-dozen armed riders rounded the house and came into the barnyard, followed moments later by Lem on the mule. Mr. Burns's workers quickly stood and grouped themselves, as if they wanted the authorities to know they were not the troublemakers. Indeed, several of them pointed to Ezra. He laughed ironically. If his hands were free, he would wave to them and say, "Greetings, gentlemen, I'm your man."

"Oh, Lord, help me, please. That kind of sarcasm will get me hanged for certain. And please help me with my southern dialect."

At the head of the group, Deputies Massey and Case dismounted and assessed the situation. After studying Jack's body, Massey strode over to the oak tree, crouched down at eye level with Ezra, and tipped back his broad-brimmed Confederate cavalry hat.

"I'm disappointed in you, boy." Massey's tone sounded sincere, and his grave expression revealed no animosity. "After all our warnings, I never thought you'd be the type to cause trouble." He shook his head. "Ain't nothin' I can do for you if it turns out you killed that man."

"Yessuh, I understand." Ezra gave him a solemn nod. "I didn't kill him."

Massey studied Ezra long and hard. "Well, I hope not. I'd hate to make an example of you." He rose and returned to the others. It appeared to Ezra that he was questioning them, but he could not hear their words.

All he comprehended from their gestures was that the other Negroes seemed to be making it clear to the deputies that Ezra was not one of them.

"Now, what's that?" Mr. Massey looked across the field toward the river. All eyes followed his stare.

Miss Saunders walked along a path toward them carrying a body as one would carry a sleeping child. Without a doubt, it was Mrs. Burns. Behind them, Delia hurried to keep pace with the larger woman. In one hand, she carried something white…and red. Ezra could not see what she carried in her other hand.

His heart sank. Was the poor old woman dead, too?

"Lord, have mercy." His prayer was not only for himself but also for Mrs. Burns.

As Miss Saunders strode into the barnyard, the deputy confronted her.

"What you got there, Miz Kate?"

"Out of my way, Massey." She brushed past him and continued toward the house with Delia at her heel.

"Now, you just hold on a minute, you hear?" Massey touched Miss Saunders's arm, not quite grabbing it.

Miss Saunders turned around, taking obvious care to keep her burden covered as much as possible. Mrs. Burns was wrapped in the younger woman's shirt with her bare legs hanging down for all to see. Ezra looked away. Even if the old lady was dead, they should not be seeing her this way. They certainly should not be staring at Miss Saunders in her chemise.

"Massey, if you want to do somethin' useful," she said, "send somebody out to tell Burns we found his mama. She's got a few cuts and scrapes, but she'll be all right."

Ezra looked back at the scene. Mrs. Burns moaned and stirred in Miss Saunders's arms.

Alive! Thank You, Lord!

"Thank the good Lord." Massey took off his hat and wiped his forehead with his sleeve. "Awright, you take her on inside. I'll send for Burns."

Miss Saunders snorted and shook her head. "Sure thing. Why didn't I think of that?" She turned around and continued walking toward the house. "C'mon, Delia."

Delia smiled at Ezra. She hesitated, as if she wanted to come talk to him. But instead, she obeyed Miss Saunders.

Ezra longed to learn what had happened, but two things made it easier to be patient. Mrs. Burns was alive and well. And Delia had smiled at him.

✤❖❀❖✤

Miz Burns sat on a wooden chair while Delia bathed her and dressed her in a fresh nightgown. The old lady had been through so much that Delia was surprised she had no broken bones. With her sparse gray hair brushed back from her wrinkled face, she seemed peaceful and lady-like, nothing like the wild woman Miz Kate had once described to Delia.

"You feel all better now?" Delia bent down to look directly in her eyes.

Miz Burns blinked and looked back. "Why, yes, I feel fine, dear. Thank you." Her eyes widened, and she grinned like she had a secret. She leaned toward Delia. "I got 'em, you know."

"Ma'am?" Delia felt a funny tickle on the back of her neck. Miz Kate had told her not to ask Miz Burns about the bloody butcher knife they'd found beside her on the riverbank.

"I got 'em. I got those darkies."

"Yes, ma'am." Delia wondered why Miz Kate was taking so long outside. And where was Miz May? She'd told Delia she knew how to talk to this old lady.

"I snuck up on 'em while they was asleep. Now we can all rest easy. They can't hurt us again." Miz Burns reached out to Delia. "Would you give me a hand, dear? I think I'll go to bed."

Delia helped her into the four-poster bed, which was much like Miz Suzanne's. Miz Burns let out a happy sigh as she sank a little ways into the down-filled mattress.

"Don't know why I'm so tired." She smiled as Delia covered her with the top sheet. "You may go, now, Letty. Take a few minutes to yourself before you finish your chores."

"Yes, ma'am, Miz Burns." Delia didn't tell her she'd used the wrong name.

Delia watched from the bedroom door until the woman fell asleep, then closed the door and went outside.

There she saw Miz Kate with the butcher knife talking a blue streak with the one she called Massey. Delia looked at Ezra. He looked worn out. She'd take him some water and something to eat.

Just then Mr. Burns came running, while Mr. Willard and Miz May hurried back through the tall grass in the distance behind him.

"Where's Mama?" Mr. Burns huffed out the words like he was out of breath. He looked around, then started toward the house.

Miz Kate stepped in front of him. "She's fine, Owen. Just a few scratches. Me and Delia found her down by the river. She had this." She held up the bloody knife.

Mr. Burns looked like he'd been hit. "What on earth?"

Massey scratched his chin. "Miz Kate's tryin' to tell me your mama is the one who killed that darkie." He nodded toward Jack's body over where they'd moved it out of the sun and under some pine trees. "Just don't know how I can believe that."

"Look." Miz Kate held the knife out to Mr. Burns. "Some of Jack's shirt's stuck between the handle and blade." She tilted her head toward Ezra. "Let him go. He's innocent."

Mr. Burns stood there looking from one to the other. When he finally got his wind back, he wiped his hand across his face. "I'll go ask Mama. Massey, you want to come?"

"That's my duty, Owen."

Delia didn't know if she trusted the lawman, but Mr. Burns must have, because the two men entered the house like old friends.

The barnyard buzzed with everybody talking about what happened. Delia fetched water and food for Ezra.

"Thank you." Ezra tried to smile at her, but it was more like a grimace.

"She killed him, Ezra." Delia lifted water to his lips. "She done told me she did."

He nodded. "I guessed as much, but I don't know how she could. He was a big, strong man."

"Don't I know that?" Delia shook away the awful memory of Jack on top of her.

Ezra frowned, but his eyes were filled with kindness. "Yes, I guess you do." He seemed wounded by the thought, which eased Delia's pain.

The men came out of the house, and Mr. Burns hurried over to the tree. Delia stood back while he untied Ezra.

"Ezra, I'm so sorry about this." Mr. Burns helped Ezra stand. "I can't believe it, but she did it."

Ezra blinked and rubbed his eyes. "Yes, sir. You have my sympathy."

Mr. Burns supported Ezra while he went behind the tree to relieve himself. When they returned, Ezra reached out to Delia. She quickly moved under his arm and let him lean on her while he shook out his legs. As they started to walk away, Mr. Burns came up on Ezra's other side to support him again.

"You've been with me almost four months." Mr. Burns talked in a broken way. "I respect you, and you know it. That's why I'm gonna tell you this."

Ezra stopped. The late afternoon sun beat down on them all, and Delia wanted to get Ezra away from there. Would Miz Kate still take them down to Spartanburg? Delia had a hard time not giving Mr. Burns a cross look.

"I told you about her folks bein' killed when she was just a little girl," Mr. Burns said.

Ezra nodded. "The Charles Deslonde revolt."

Charles who? Delia raised her eyebrows to question Ezra.

"I'll tell you later." He bent down to touch his forehead to hers for just a second. "At least we know she was telling the truth about someone looking in her window. She wasn't delusional after all."

Mr. Burns let out a harsh laugh. "Not about that, anyways. I guess it got too much for her. She must have been scared the killings were happening all over again. And she must have thought she was killin' one of those men who murdered her parents." Mr. Burns's voice broke. "I'm so sorry for thinkin' you did it, Ezra." He stared hard at Ezra. "Please forgive me."

"I do forgive you, Mr. Burns. You've been a good man to work for this summer, a good friend, if I may say so." Ezra gave him a kind look, one that almost made Delia mad. They could have hanged Ezra, but he was being nice about it. All she wanted to do was leave right that minute.

They reached the middle of the barnyard, where the other people still stood around talking.

"I guess I'll take the body into town and have somebody bury it in the colored cemetery." Mr. Massey and the one called Case made their plans. They decided that two of their men would ride together, and the extra horse would carry the body. Mr. Burns had covered Jack's body with an old piece of canvas, which they used to protect the saddle from the blood.

While all that was going on, Delia watched Miz Kate and Mr. Burns talking off to the side. She couldn't hear their words, but they acted like they were more than just neighbors. A happy feeling swept through Delia. Miz Kate deserved happiness.

"Hey," Miz Kate called out all of a sudden. "Did somebody put my horse in the barn or out to pasture?"

"Oh, no." Ezra spoke so soft that Delia almost didn't hear him. "What's wrong?"

Ezra pulled her away from the others. "Adam borrowed her horse to go get help." He swayed just a little bit, and Delia helped him steady himself.

"Help?"

"The Union soldiers in Spartanburg."

Delia's heart leaped. "Why, that's grand, ain't it?" She grinned real big. "Union soldiers can tell the deputy what to do, can't they?"

Ezra gave her a worried frown. "Yes, but if these people learn I was…and *am* a Union soldier, too, they'll…I don't know what they'll do."

Delia swayed with fear. "We gotta git outa here."

He nodded. "That's precisely what I'm thinking."

CHAPTER THIRTY-SIX

ℰzra fought panic. They should leave, but without the horse, they couldn't travel in Miss Saunders's wagon. Should they start walking and hope to meet the soldiers along the way? What if the deputies said they could not be out on the road this late in the day? Had it been a mistake to send Adam for help?

"Now don't tell me we've got a horse thief to deal with." Mr. Massey paced back and forth, looking at the field hands one at a time. "And don't tell me you didn't see nothin'."

"I didn't see nothin'." One of the Negro men spoke up, while the other three nodded their agreement.

"No, suh, boss." Another man shook his head vigorously. "I didn't see nothin'. I was watchin' that fellow like I was tol' to do." He pointed to Ezra and shrugged an apology in his direction.

Ezra shrugged back. He could not imagine what their lives had been like here in the South. Yet surely they could have shown him a little compassion, if only by bringing him a cup of cold water in the heat of the day or permitting him to relieve himself.

The two white men who also had guarded Ezra mumbled to each other. One of them stepped over to Massey.

"There was a colored boy who come with Miz Saunders. He took off on the horse. We figured he knew what he was doin'."

"Well, why didn't you say so in the first place?" Massey shook his head in disgust. "How 'bout that, Miz Kate?"

She walked to her wagon and looked inside. "Maybe he forgot somethin' over at my place. I was haulin' these folks down to Spartanburg so they could head north on the main highway."

"North?" Massey looked at Ezra. "Y'all headin' north?"

"Yessuh, boss." Ezra puckered away a grin. This was no time to be laughing. But he could not help but think Miss Saunders was covering for Adam, Lord, bless her. Had she figured out where the youth had gone?

"Why, boy…." Massey ambled over to Ezra. "I don't know what you think you gonna find up there. They don't have jobs for field hands. Most coloreds with any sense are working right where they was before the war and where they belong. Them Yankees came down here to destroy our way of life, and they pretty near done it. But we'll bide our time, and things'll get back to normal."

"Yessuh." Now Ezra's teeth ached from clenching his jaw. Why didn't the deputy and his men just leave before the soldiers came?

Massey stared at him for a moment and then at Miss Saunders. "You awright about your horse?"

"Adam's a good boy. He'll bring her back."

"Awright, then." Massey turned to Burns. "Now about your mama…."

Mr. Burns's shoulders slumped. "What are you gonna do?"

"Just see that sweet lady gets rested up and forgets all about this little incident."

Ezra felt Delia shudder beside him.

"They was gonna hang you," she whispered. "What they gonna do to her for killin', even if it was Jack?"

"Shh." Ezra squeezed her hand.

Mr. Burns nodded. "I'm mighty grateful, Massey."

"Just remember that when election time comes around, y'hear." Massey laughed and slapped Mr. Burns on the shoulder as if they were old friends.

Mr. Burns's smile seemed a little strained. "You can count on me rememberin' you."

Once again, the sound of horses' hooves thundered up the roadway. As everyone turned their attention to the newcomers, Ezra's heart sank. He gripped Delia's hand and led her over to the wagon, where Miss Saunders and Mr. Burns stood.

"What now?" Massey paced around as if he owned the place.

Led by Adam on Miss Saunders's horse, five blue-uniformed soldiers rode into the barnyard. Following behind Adam was an officer with fiery red hair flowing from beneath his broad-brimmed blue hat.

The moment Ezra saw Major Hutchins, he felt a wave of relief. He was the man who had saved Ezra and Miss May from the tree after the flood. An officer of his rank would not respond to a plea for help if he did not intend to see it through to the end. Despite his hopes that the major would not expose him to these men, Ezra could not hold back his wide grin.

The deputies did not smile. Once the soldiers pulled up in front of the assorted assembly, Major Hutchins looked around the group with self-assurance.

"You boys having a little trouble?" A sardonic smile played at the corner of his lips.

Bristling, Massey stepped forward. "No trouble at all, major. What brings you way out here? Colonel Rule made it clear we were to have local jurisdiction now that the 'hostilities' are over." He spoke with unbridled contempt.

Ezra felt the hairs on the back of his neck stand on end. If only he could signal Hutchins not to announce that he was one of them. But that would only draw attention Ezra did not want.

The major looked around the barnyard with the calm demeanor of a man used to being in charge. His gaze stopped in the direction of Jack's body draped across a horse.

"That the one?" He directed his question to Adam.

"Yessuh." Adam shot a glance at Miss Saunders and slid off the horse. He was about to speak to her, but she shushed him.

Like Ezra, everyone seemed on the edge of anxiety as they watched to see what would develop.

Hutchins grunted. "Well, deputy, here in your local *jurisdiction,* what do you have to say about that?" Now *his* voice was bristling with sarcasm. He raised his riding crop and pointed toward the body.

"Now, major, we got it all under control. There's no need...."

"Maybe you're a bit confused about the meaning of martial law. It means that in a matter such as this, you answer to me." Hutchins leaned out of the saddle toward Massey. "Who killed him?"

Massey stiffened; his face was creased with indignation. He looked briefly at Mr. Burns. "That darkie was scaring the daylights out of this man's mama. She took a knife to him, and rightly so."

Hutchins leaned back, blinking his disbelief. As if against his will, his attention swung to Ezra. "Is that right?"

Ezra's heart plummeted. His secret was out. Abandoning all attempts to sound southern, he drew himself up to stand at attention. "Yes, sir. That's right."

"What the devil…?" Massey glared at Hutchins. "Why're you asking *him?*" He spat out a curse and directed his glare toward Ezra. "Who are you?"

Ezra leveled a firm stare on the man. "Corporal Ezra Johns, 54th Massachusetts Negro Regiment." He would never say "sir" to this man again.

Angry words erupted from the deputy's men. Low whistles of appreciation came from the direction of the Negro workers. If Ezra was not mistaken, he heard chuckles from Mr. Burns and Miss Saunders.

Again Massey cursed. "I knew it. I knew it the first time I saw you there was something I didn't like. Why, you dirty n—"

"That's enough, deputy." Major Hutchins's tone left no room for response. He turned to Ezra. "Soldier, I'm here to escort you safely out. Are you ready to go?"

Ezra gulped. "Sir, I have some folks who also need safe passage. Could you…?"

"Hold on." Hutchins glared at Massey. "Deputy, you're finished here. Take that body and see to it. Do whatever you people do in this part of the country with the bodies of criminals."

"Why, you—" Massey stopped and swore. For a moment, he seemed about to refuse the major's order.

Deputy Case nudged him. "Let's go." He walked past Ezra and bumped his shoulder hard. "Watch out behind you, boy. You'll get yours one day." He nodded toward Jack's body.

The six men mounted their horses and rode out, taking their gruesome burden with them. Just past the house, they sent up raucous rebel yells that continued for several moments, then faded away.

"I heard that sound a little too often during the war." Major Hutchins shook his head and grinned. "Guess they forgot who won."

His men snickered and made a few rude remarks.

"That'll be enough," Hutchins barked. "We have ladies present." He nodded to Miss Saunders, Delia, and Miss May. He dismounted and came over to Ezra. "All right, now, soldier, let's see what we can figure out."

"Sir, if we could just get on the highway headed north, I can escort my friends to Boston."

"I have a better plan." The major eyed Ezra, a friendly smile on his lips. "We're getting you down to Mount Pleasant so you can sail home with your regiment."

"M-my regiment, sir?" Ezra stared at the officer. "Sir, I thought they went home last spring."

"Well, soldier, that's what you get for thinking." Hutchins chuckled. "The 54th has been all over the state helping to establish peace. Now they've all been ordered to Mount Pleasant to muster out and return to Boston."

Ezra could hardly grasp this news. "B-but, sir, won't I be charged with desertion under these circumstances?" He had been a fool for not trying harder to find his unit.

"Colonel Rule's orders still stand." Hutchins reached up to remove Ezra's knapsack from his saddle. "Your papers are safe right in here, along with your uniform jacket."

Ezra felt a wave of relief so profound, his knees almost buckled. As he clasped his knapsack to his chest, he felt Delia lean in to give him support.

"Thank you, sir."

"Now let's get this operation under way."

"How are you going to do it, major?" Mr. Burns stepped forward. "You got five people to take over two hundred miles down to the coast. How you gonna manage that?"

Major Hutchins regarded Mr. Burns for a moment, as if taking his measure. Apparently, he liked what he saw, for he grinned widely and clapped Mr. Burns on the shoulder.

"Well, sir, my pa was a farmer, just like you, and he always used to say, 'We'll figure something out.'"

✬ ✬ ✬ ✬

CHAPTER THIRTY-SEVEN

*E*zra helped the Brewsters and Delia climb into the back of Miss Saunders's weathered box wagon. While Adam found each of them a comfortable spot amidst their baggage, Ezra took his place beside Miss Saunders on the driver's bench. Major Hutchins and his men waited to escort the travelers on their journey.

Mr. Burns came to the wagon and handed a small leather wallet to Ezra. "Your pay, and it's in U.S. dollars, so you know it's good money." He gave Ezra a sly look. "I hid it during the war." He snorted with disgust. "Lord knows my Confederate cash ain't worth the paper it's printed on. This ain't much, but it's fair."

"I'm sure it is. Thank you, sir." Ezra put the wallet in his knapsack. He would not insult the man by counting its contents.

Mr. Burns looked beyond Ezra to Miss Saunders. "Marry me, Kate."

Ezra stifled a smile. Didn't they ever get tired of this game?

"You gonna take your mama down to the state asylum like you said?" she asked.

Mr. Burns bristled. "I said I'd do it, and I will."

"And she'll stay there, no matter what?" Miss Saunders eyed him as if she had doubts.

"She'll stay there no matter what."

"Then I'll marry you."

A pleased grin stretched Mr. Burns's lips wide across his face. "It's about time."

Miss Saunders made a noise that sounded like the combination of a snort and a chuckle. This lady certainly never put on airs.

"Good-bye, sir." Ezra tipped his hat to Mr. Burns and slapped the reins against the mare's haunches to begin their journey. What a strange pair of sweethearts these two people were. Before he asked Delia to marry him, he would make sure nothing stood in their way. And if she said yes, he would say much more than "It's about time."

When the wagon pulled on to the main road, Miss May began to sing one of her songs, one that told of their coming adventure. The others quickly joined in the echoing chorus. Even Miss Saunders kept time by tapping her boot against the footboard, while Ezra added the tenor line. In spite of some nagging concerns about the road ahead, he could not help joining in their gaiety.

As much as Ezra wanted to don his uniform, Major Hutchins had ordered him to keep it hidden in the knapsack until he reached Mount Pleasant. Between here and there, he was simply a former slave taking his family down to Charleston. Martial law notwithstanding, any other course would invite trouble, perhaps even death, for them all.

Delia couldn't believe how fast they got across the entire state of South Carolina. First they rode on a flatboat out of Spartanburg down the twisty Pacolet River that flowed directly into the very fast Broad River that led right into burned-out Columbia. Then they hung on to the back of a farmer's wagon from Columbia to Orangeburg. Then came the most exciting thing she'd ever done in her life—the train ride from Orangeburg to Charleston. The steam engine screeched in her ears. Its stinky smoke choked her and got her hair and clothes sooty. But even having to ride in the baggage car, she loved how fast the train had clacked down the tracks past forests of oak and pine and hickory and magnolia, swampland and plains and burned-out farms where weeds and brush tried to cover the charred ruins. The trip across the state took just over a week.

The only part she didn't like was not having any time to talk to Ezra privately, like they'd done down by the river at Miz Kate's. But he was taking care of all of them, so she let him do his job and sent him a sweet smile every chance she got. He seemed to like it, because he always smiled back.

Once in Charleston, he helped her and Miz May and Mr. Willard get set up down at the wharf where other poor travelers camped. Then he and Adam took a barge across the river to Mount Pleasant so Ezra could get his papers saying he wasn't in the army anymore. Adam said he wanted to be in the army when he got old enough, so Ezra let him tag along.

As soon as they returned, everybody'd board a ship and go to Boston. Delia's heart just about burst with excitement every time she thought about that.

What kind of ship would they ride on? One of the bucket-like boats, she saw in the harbor, with tall masts and a lot of billowy white sails? Or a steamer with smoke stacks blowing black smoke up into the sky like the train? Ezra said the steamers were faster, so Delia hoped they'd go that way even if it meant more smoke and soot all over her. She could stand anything that got them to Boston faster.

She sat with the Brewsters by a mostly burned-out building. Only one wall still stood, but it was enough to shade them from the hot afternoon sun. While the old folks slept, she watched the busy wharfs, wondering about the people there. Lots of travelers were coming and going. Horses and buggies took folks to their ships. Delia didn't see much finery on the ladies and gentlemen, probably because of the South being defeated in the war. She did see soldiers in blue uniforms walking up and down the wharf, keeping the peace. With Ezra and Adam gone, that made her feel especially safe.

A stiff wind blew in from the ocean and sent waves of waterfront smells in every direction. One minute Delia would smell the horses. The next she'd smell the choking odor of coal from the steamships. Then would come the awful smell of newly caught fish from the other direction, where fishermen sold their day's catch right by their boats. But every once in a while, a fresh sea breeze would sweep it all away and clean out Delia's lungs, filling her with new hope.

Men, both colored and white, were busy all over the place. Some were loading or unloading ships. Others were working on new wooden buildings going up in place of the ones that burned down during the war.

It must have been something to see Charleston on fire, with homes and churches and places where people worked all going up in smoke. Not that Delia wished any kind of evil on anybody. Not even Jack. Not even her old mistress. But a fire that big? Yes, that would be something to see.

The day wore on, and more people came and went. Delia's clothes stuck to her, and her head itched. Sitting here was so tiresome.

She got up and paced around for a bit. The old folks seemed to be resting just fine. The soldiers were still on duty. She decided to walk down the wharf and back again to get the stiffness out of her legs.

She hadn't gone a hundred feet before she knew she'd made a mistake.

"Hey, pretty girl, what you got for sale?" A young white man in a threadbare suit leered at her from horseback. "Come on over here, and let's talk."

Delia ducked behind a wagon and kept walking. She should go back but found herself in a swarm of people greeting a newly arrived ship. This was a better part of the waterfront. Most everybody ignored her, but some of the white folks made her feel that she had no business being there.

"Delia!" A voice shrieked her name like an echo from the past.

Delia shuddered clear down to her bare toes, and the hair on her neck stood on end. Her knees felt like they would give out on her. She turned in the direction of the hated sound.

There, not ten feet away, in a familiar, tattered black buggy sat Miz Suzanne, primly holding up her old ivory parasol to protect her pale skin from the sun. Her green cotton dress had lost much of its color, and her bonnet brim had not been properly starched. She looked like she'd gone out in the rain and her once-fine clothing had wilted and faded.

"Well, get over here, girl." Miz Suzanne's pretty face wore an ugly look, with her eyes all squinty and her skinny lips all twisted. "You ungrateful little wretch, I said come here."

Delia could not move. She could not breathe. She could hardly think.

Did she have to mind? Did she have to go to Miz Suzanne?

"If you don't get over here right now, I'll have one of those Yankee officers arrest you for stealing. That's my skirt you have on. That's my blouse." Miz Suzanne looked around like she was trying to find somebody. Somebody to arrest Delia? Her eyes quit moving, and she smirked.

Delia looked in the same direction, and what she saw nearly made her heart stop.

Massuh!

Before she could force her legs to turn and run, he caught sight of her.

"Daddy, Daddy, look who I found." All of a sudden, Miz Suzanne was as sweet as sugar. "It's our Delia. Our very own Delia." She turned to Delia. "Come on, sweet child—come sit with me and tell me all you've been doing this summer."

"Delia." Massuh came over to the buggy and smiled at her. His brown hair seemed to have a lot more gray in it, and his blue eyes were filled with kindness and maybe just a hint of tears. "How good to see you." He beckoned to her.

Delia chewed her lip and hung her head. She took a step toward him, shaking so hard she could barely keep her balance.

"My, my, girl, you sure are dirty." Miz Suzanne wrinkled her nose. "Look at that soot all over you. We always took better care of you than that. What's got into you, being so dirty that way?"

"That's enough, Suzanne." Massuh spoke with his firm voice, the one that sometimes scared Delia and sometimes made her glad. This time it made her glad. "We've missed you, Delia, the missus and I. And it broke Beulah's heart when you left. She cried for days." He shook his head, as if he hadn't meant to say that. "Have you been well?"

She nodded, venturing a look into his eyes. A memory of her unhappy talk with Alice sparked in her mind, and she gasped. This man was her father. This horrible girl, her sister.

"Delia, do get into the buggy." Miz Suzanne grinned far too big for a lady. "We're headed on home as soon as Daddy buys me some material for a new dress. Beulah was going to make it, but you sew better than she does." She picked impatiently at the buttons on one sleeve. "Why, I haven't had a new dress since...since I don't know when. And when you get it all made, I'll give you this one."

Give me that one? Right after you called me a thief?

Miz Suzanne pouted and leaned out of the buggy, pointing to her head. "Just look at my hair." Her hair was frizzy and needed a good brushing. "I haven't had anybody to do my hair since you left, you naughty little thing."

Thing?

Delia jolted back just like she'd been hit by lightning. Miz Kate never treated her this way. Miz Kate never called her a "thing." She made Delia feel like she was *somebody.*

Anger roared up in Delia like the Charleston fire. Oh, how she longed to scream out her hate at Miz Suzanne. But she wasn't sure about the law. Maybe they could arrest her for talking back to a white woman, even if the Yankees did win the war and she wasn't a slave anymore.

"Are you just going to stand there like a stupid little—"

"Enough." Massuh scowled at his daughter. His *other* daughter. "Delia, I...."

Delia did not have to listen to this. She willed her body to turn, willed her feet to move. But this time she would not run. She would *not.* She was not their slave. She did not have to do their bidding.

"Delia." The pain in Massuh's voice stopped her.

She turned to see his hand lifted toward her, not in anger, not to hit her, but asking her to come back. *My daddy. My daddy.*

He reached into his stained white jacket and drew out his battered wallet. Thumbing through the dollar bills, he drew several out. He glanced at her, then removed almost the entire contents, folded the bills, and held them out to her.

"Delia, I want you to have this." His kind eyes begged her to accept the gift.

"It's the least I can do." He inhaled a raggedy breath. "It's *all* I can do."

"No!" Miz Suzanne started to get out of the buggy. "That's for my new dress, and I'll not have you giving it to this wicked, ugly little darkie."

"Suzanne, sit down and shut up." Massuh spoke so loud that a bunch of people around them stopped and stared at the sight of a southern gentleman acting so rude.

Miz Suzanne blinked and sat down.

Massuh stepped over to Delia. "There are so many things I wish I could say to you." His voice was soft and kind. "I...I'm your—"

"Yessuh, I know." Delia did not wish to hear the words.

He nodded. "Then you'll take this." He held up the money.

Delia stared at it for a bit. What would Ezra have her do?

"Please?" Massuh's eyes were now filled with tears.

Did that mean he loved her? Delia felt her throat close, like she was about to cry, too. She reached up and took the wad of money and tucked it in her blouse. *Her* blouse.

"Thank you, Massuh."

"No. Don't call me that again." He smiled so kindly that Delia's heart ached. "I'm Mr. Young. And you have the right to carry my name, if you wish."

Tears choked her again. "You was always kind to me, Mass...Mr. Young. I'll think about carrying your name." And all those years, she'd feared that his kindness had meant something else.

He inhaled a deep breath and looked beyond her toward the ships. "Are you going someplace? Leaving the South?"

"I'm goin' to Boston with some friends."

He nodded. "Boston. Hmph. Those abolitionist troublemakers from up there started this whole thing."

"No, suh." Delia felt her courage growing. "No, suh. It was the slaveholders started this whole thing."

"Hmph," he grunted again. "We won't ever agree on that." A sparkle came to his eyes. "Delia, do one thing for me."

"Yessuh."

"Learn to read."

She gasped, but his request tickled her, so she laughed. "Read? Me?" She wouldn't tell him Ezra was already teaching her. She would not tell him about Ezra at all.

He laughed, too. "Yes. Read and write. Then write to me." He bent down like he was about to kiss her cheek.

"Daddy!" Miz Suzanne shrieked.

He pulled back and didn't kiss Delia, but he did squeeze her shoulder and stare at her kindly for a minute like he wished he *could* kiss her.

But it didn't matter. Miz Delia Young was going to Boston, and she didn't have time to mind such things.

✯ ✯ ✯ ✯

CHAPTER THIRTY-EIGHT

"*E*zra! Praise God, man. We thought you were dead." Peter Blake threw his arms around Ezra and nearly knocked the wind out of him.

Other friends crowded around proclaiming their joy over Ezra's sudden appearance at army headquarters in Mount Pleasant.

"Where were you?"

"Did you get shot?"

"Anybody help you?"

Randall Simpson hung on Ezra's neck and cried. "I didn't want to leave until we found out what happened to you. But the rebs were beating us back pretty bad, and the sergeant ordered us to retreat." He swiped his sleeve across his eyes. "God is good. God is good. I have my best friend back."

"Randall." Ezra struggled to swallow his own emotions. "Peter. Joseph. Judah." Breaking free of Randall, he shook hands and patted shoulders as he made his way through the throng of soldiers who welcomed him. "Come on, Adam."

The youth hung close to Ezra, but his dark eyes were round with admiration as he stared at the soldiers.

"Wait, Ezra." Randall followed him and gripped his arm. "You can't just walk on past me. You have to tell me what happened." He patted Ezra's shoulder, and dust flew into the air. "Just look at your uniform. It looks as if it's been wadded up and kept in a sack. And those trousers are not exactly military issue."

Ezra tugged against Randall's grasp. "I'll tell you all about it later. Right now, I have to report in. I have to make sure they don't think I deserted." Even as he said the words, his heart beat faster. Would these friends from his company vouch for his performance in that skirmish outside of Abbeville? Would they assure those in command that he had not run from battle?

"Deserted?" Peter came near. "Why, no one in his right mind would think you deserted. You were cited for courage more times than I can count."

"Thank you, Peter."

"Who's this young man?" Peter eyed Adam with a stern look.

Ezra chuckled. Peter had a way of bringing out the best in younger men. "This is Adam Monroe. We've been traveling together since last spring. Adam, this is Peter Blake."

"Mighty pleased to meet you, suh."

Peter shook his hand, and his eyes held a glint of kindness. "It's a pleasure to meet you. Were you a slave, son?"

"Yessuh."

Peter's expression softened into a smile. "You watch this man." He nodded toward Ezra. "He'll set you on the right path for your new life of freedom."

"Oh, yessuh, I plan on doin' jus' that."

Ezra tried to shrug off the compliment, but his chest swelled with pleasure. His fellow soldiers were reaffirming him just when he needed it. "Well, we have to be going." He glanced toward the three-storied Whilden mansion. The paint on the exterior was pristine white, and the grounds around it were military clean. "Is this where we muster out?"

"No. That's headquarters. We muster out over there." Peter pointed toward a one-story outbuilding across the yard.

"Some of us." Randall kept grinning at Ezra just as he used to do when they were boys and had won a baseball game with their friends. "I'm waiting until I get to Boston because it will mean another few days of pay. Old Blake here is going to take his money and run." Randall punched Peter's arm.

Peter laughed. "I'm not running anywhere. I'm going to stay here and become a schoolteacher. Think of all the former slaves who must be taught to read and write, not to mention how to do sums and manage money. In fact, I heard that Sergeant Major Lewis Douglass is planning to return here to teach as well."

"What does your family think of that?" Ezra could not imagine his own parents' anguish if he did not return home.

Peter chuckled. "You ask me that, knowing how long Father worked with Frederick Douglass to abolish slavery?"

Ezra and the others nearby laughed, too. "Looks like they succeeded," someone said.

"With a little help." Randall puffed up his chest.

The men erupted in loud, carefree laughter, revealing excitement over their imminent return to normal life. Ezra longed to stay and banter with them, but he could not feel complete joy or even peace until he spoke with his commander. He excused himself and strode toward headquarters, taking Adam with him.

They climbed the elegant staircase to the front porch, where guards stood on either side of the entrance.

"With your permission, private." Ezra addressed one soldier. "May I speak to the officer in charge?" He held up his papers, which clearly showed Colonel Rule's name.

The private stepped aside. "Yes, sir. First door on the right."

The spotless, polished wooden floor creaked under Ezra's badly worn boots. Adam padded barefoot behind him.

"Sir?" Ezra stood in the doorway of the large parlor, now a makeshift office.

Bent over the desk, a white captain wearing the insignia of the 54th Massachusetts Regiment perused papers and puffed on a pipe. Its fragrant cherry odor filled the room and gave Ezra a heady feeling, reminding him of his father's evening custom of smoking a pipe.

The captain looked up, his brown eyes boring into Ezra. "What do you want, corporal?" His glance took in Adam, who stood in the hallway.

Ezra had forgotten what it felt like to endure an officer's unyielding stare. He barely kept from gulping. "Sir, I'm Corporal Ezra Johns of B Company, and I—"

"Who're you trying to fool, mister? Corporal Johns was reported missing in action back in March. You trying to get his pay?" The captain set his pipe in a pipe stand, stood, and walked around the desk, where he glared up at Ezra again. "Well, what've you got to say for yourself?"

Ezra drew in a bracing breath. "Sir, the men in my company will vouch for me."

"Hmph." The captain snorted out his disdain. "So you'll all split the money, eh?"

A flash of anger jolted through Ezra. "No, *sir.*" The man could cast aspersions on him, but not on his friends. "This isn't about money." That wasn't entirely true. Ezra had spent almost all of the wages Mr. Burns had given him on passage across the state for him and his friends. He needed his back pay for their passage to Boston. "It's about my obligation to report in." Ezra clenched his jaw. Had he spoken too firmly? "Sir," he quickly added.

The man glared at him for another moment. "All right, then, state your case." He moved back around the desk and sat down, but he was clearly skeptical.

Encouraged nevertheless, Ezra exhaled a long sigh of relief. Behind him, he heard Adam do the same. The boy was becoming his shadow.

"Sir, last March my unit was on patrol outside of Abbeville. When I became separated from them during a skirmish, I hid out from the rebs. While I was hiding, I overheard some travelers saying the war was over. Now, we all assumed we would go home when it ended, so I headed north. A couple of weeks later, I came upon Colonel Thaddeus Rule's regiment, and I reported to him. He wrote this letter for me...sir." Ezra held it out. He had said all of that in one breath.

The captain snatched the paper and read it, eyeing Ezra every few seconds. He stood and walked to a file cabinet in the corner, where he pulled out an official document and held the letter beside it.

"Hmph. Signature looks the same." The captain returned the document to the file and moved back behind his desk. "There will have to be an inquiry when we get back to Boston. If we can verify your story, you'll be mustered out there. That's when you'll get your pay and possibly some back pay." He handed the letter to Ezra. "Now go join your unit."

Ezra's heart sank. "Yes, sir." He could not ask for money now, not after this man had accused him of being a crook.

"Dismissed." The captain gave Ezra a poor excuse for a salute and resumed his work.

"Yes, sir. Thank you, sir." Ezra saluted him and left.

In the yard again, Ezra could hardly think or breathe. What could he do now?

Lord, help me. I can't desert Delia and the Brewsters.

Right away, he knew the answer. He put his hand on Adam's shoulder. "When you asked to come with me, I almost said no. But the Lord prompted me to bring you along so you could take word back to Delia and the Brewsters. Tell them what happened and say that I can't take you to Boston."

"Then what we gonna do?"

A dead weight seemed to press against Ezra's heart, but he managed to level a firm stare into Adam's eyes. "You're going to take care of them." He reached into his pocket and pulled out his wallet. "There are only a few dollars left in there. All of you will have to work for food and fare for your passage, but there should be plenty of jobs in Charleston these days."

Even as he spoke, despair thundered in his soul. Working in the city was far more dangerous than working on a remote farm, especially for two elderly people and a beautiful young woman. Maybe Ezra would desert the army after all.

Adam gulped. "Yessuh. I can do that. Miz Delia and I will take care of the old folks."

Ezra had his doubts. Why had he reported back to the army? Why had he thought they would let him go back to his friends?

A thin ray of hope beamed into his aching breast. In spite of Ezra's misgivings, God had prompted him to bring Adam along so his friends would know what had become of him. Surely He could be trusted to take care of them.

"Say, Ezra." Peter Blake ran across the yard waving a paper. "I have them. I have my official papers. I'm no longer in the army." He clapped Ezra on the shoulder. "Now tell me what happened in there. Is there anything I can do to help you?"

Ezra blinked away the sudden mist in his eyes. Then he chuckled. Then he laughed out loud.

"Lord, why do I ever doubt You? You never fail to keep Your promise to care for Your children."

Ezra grinned at his friend. "Why, yes, Peter. Now that you mention it, there is something you can do to help."

✳ ✳ ✳ ✳

CHAPTER THIRTY-NINE

"There they are!" Delia jumped up from where she sat against the baggage. "Look, Miz May, Mr. Willard. Ezra and Adam are back." She stepped out into the fading sunlight and watched the two men come down the wharf.

Miz May blinked her eyes and rubbed them. "My, my, that don't look like—"

"That ain't Ezra." Delia looked hard to try and figure out what she was seeing. "It's Adam, awright, but that soldier ain't as tall as Ezra." And his uniform looked a lot better, but she wouldn't say that.

Mr. Willard hobbled out of the shadows, shading his eyes with his hands. "Nope, nope. Ain't Ezra. Now what do you s'pose happened to him?"

Delia's heart jumped a bit. That question scared her.

"Oh, now, settle down, old man. Nothin's happened to our Ezra." Miz May wagged a finger at her husband. Just by doing that, she showed Delia she was worried, too. Miz May never said a cross word to Mr. Willard.

The two men closed the last fifteen yards in just a few strides. Adam looked agitated, like he was fit to be tied. Delia took one look at the soldier, and her heart jumped all around inside her. *What a fine-looking man.* Right away, she could've kicked herself. She loved Ezra, and nobody was as fine looking as him.

"Ezra ain't comin', y'all." Adam beat a fist into his opposite palm. "The army got ahold of him and won't let him go."

"Adam, don't alarm these good people." The soldier tipped his army cap at Miz May, then Delia, then Mr. Willard. "Don't worry about Ezra. He's just fine."

Even as relief filled Delia's breast, warmth crept up her cheeks. She was still covered with soot, but he was treating her like a lady. Delia looked at Miz May, hoping she would say something.

"Well, praise the Lawd." Miz May grinned. "I knew it'd be awright."

"Where is he?" Mr. Willard's tone was a mite cross. "And who are you?"

The soldier smiled. "Forgive me for not introducing myself right away. I'm Peter Blake. I served with Ezra in the 54th. We grew up together in Boston, so he's an old friend." He looked at Delia. "Please call me Peter."

Delia's face got even hotter. She should've tried to wash her face, but water to wash with was scarce on the wharf.

"Peter. Like in the Bible." Miz May beamed at him. "I like that."

"Where's Ezra?" Mr. Willard's tone was softer this time.

"The army done took ahold of him," Adam repeated. His lower lip stuck out, and he furrowed his brow like he was real mad. Adam never got mad. "They say he gotta go back to Boston with his reg'ment."

Delia's heart plummeted. "But...but can they do that?" She looked up at the soldier, no longer caring about how she looked.

"I'm afraid so, miss." Peter shrugged a little. "But he said to tell you..."—he looked at the old folks and back at Delia—"...all of you, that he would see you in Boston."

"But how we gonna git there without him?" Delia heard the whine in her voice. *Oh, my, I sound just like Miz Suzanne.* She almost shuddered at the thought, but she had more important things to worry about at that minute.

"*I'm* gonna take you." Adam stuck out his chest. "Ezra tol' me jus' what to do 'bout the ship and where to go once we git to Boston."

Delia saw Peter hide a smile.

"That's right." He set his hand on Adam's shoulder. "This fine young man will escort you safely to your destination. I'm just here to help you find a place to stay until we can book your passage on a ship."

"Did…did Ezra say anythin' 'bout payin' for it?" Mr. Willard asked nervous like.

"Did he send some of his pay to hep us out with the ship?" Miz May looked back and forth from Peter to Adam. "He said dat was what we'd use to pay fo' it."

Adam cleared his throat. "Well, no ma'am, not jus' that. They wouldn't pay him till he gits back to Boston. But he sent what he had left from what Mr. Burns paid you and Mr. Willard and him. He said we was gonna have to work to earn our passage." He looked up at Peter and got a big grin on his face. "But then Corporal Blake here steps up and says he'll loan us the money. Ezra says he'll pay him back. So's now all we got to do is find a ship."

Delia felt the wad of cash against her skin, hot as a cinder fresh from the fire. All of a sudden, she felt like a liar for not telling Miz May about the money right away.

"I got money." The words popped out. Delia turned away from Adam and Peter and pulled out the wad, tucked her blouse back in her skirt, then turned back and held it up for everybody to see.

"Lawd, have mercy, chile, where'd you git that?" Miz May's eyes got as big as saucers.

Adam whistled. "Ooo-eee! How long you had that?""

"A man give it to me today." Delia hadn't felt this bad since getting in trouble on the plantation.

Peter looked worried. "Miss Delia, please assure me you didn't steal that."

She gasped. "No, suh, I never stole it. I never steal anything." She looked around at everybody. "A white man give it to me, I swear."

"But why would a white man…why would *anybody* give you money like dat?" Miz May looked worried, just like everybody else. "What'd you do dat made him give you money?"

Delia's face felt hot. "No, *ma'am*. I never did nothin' wrong." She had to tell the truth. "He was my old massuh."

She looked around again. Everybody but Peter knew what that meant, and it showed. Mr. Willard relaxed. Adam nodded, and his eyes lit up like they did when he was happy.

"Well, then, dat settles it fo' me." Miz May wrapped her arms around Delia. "I jes' know'd you was a good girl."

Delia wanted to bust out crying. She shot a quick look at Peter.

He had a big grin on his handsome face. "Well, I'd say that was poetic justice, although I also must say it's quite unlike anything I've ever heard of. Can you imagine how it would be if all the former slave owners did the same thing? Think of how much they owe you for working without pay all of your lives." He shook his head. "Of course, it's too late for that, now—the war ruined just about all of them financially. But maybe some will try to help their former slaves establish new lives."

Peter talked like Ezra did, like an educated northern man. Like Ezra, he was a good-looking man with character. Delia liked him already. She liked him a lot. But he wasn't Ezra. And her heart ached as she wondered how long it would be before she saw her Ezra again.

CHAPTER FORTY

"Colorado?" Ezra leaned against the rail of the SS *Ashland* as it steamed toward Boston "Now, Randall, why would you want to go there?"

Randall gazed out over the ocean with a faraway look in his eyes. "For one thing, Colorado Territory has always fascinated me. I believe the West is where our country's future lies. Millions of acres are just waiting to be settled. I want to stake a claim on some of that land."

Ezra studied his friend's profile. Randall had always been so practical. Did he really mean to go out west? "But you've never even worked on a farm. What would a city boy like you know about surviving in that untamed wilderness?"

Randall shrugged. "I learned to survive in the war. I can learn to survive out there." He eyed Ezra. "Why don't you go with me?"

"I?" Ezra chuckled. "That's a crazy idea if I ever heard one."

Without warning, the ship plunged into a deep trough and rose high on the next wave. The men grasped the railing as water sprayed across the deck. All around them, sailors dashed about securing barrels and lines. Once the vessel leveled, Ezra and Randall brushed water from their thick wool uniforms. It was surprising how cold it was out on the ocean in early September.

"Whoo. That was a big one." Ezra studied the northern horizon for signs of any more large waves. "You can count on one thing. I'll never be a sailor." He willed away the queasy feeling in his stomach, refusing to succumb to the seasickness that had plagued others in the regiment.

"There. You see?" Randall nudged him with his elbow. "Colorado would be perfect for a landlubber like you."

"No, I'll let you be the adventurous one. I'm going to finish college."

"That's good. So am I." Randall gripped the railing as a swell raised the ship once more. "Then what?"

Then what? Ezra let the question roll around in his mind for a moment. In the spring, he had felt certain that God wanted him to be a minister. Over the summer, as he had read his Bible to his friends each Sunday, the dream had still been alive. Yet the intensity of his anger toward Jack caused Ezra to question his suitability to be called a man of God.

Randall nudged him again. "I said 'then what?'"

Ezra nudged him back. "I'll let you know when I figure it out."

Randall turned and made his way toward the hatch that led to their quarters. "Coloraaadooo," he crooned, punctuating his song with a silly dance that was all the more comical because of the rolling deck of the ship.

Chuckling at his friend's antics, Ezra gazed back at the ocean. In the distance, billowing white cumulus clouds floated above the horizon like great snow-covered mountains. He had heard that the

Rocky Mountains stood thousands of feet higher than any range in the East. They must be a sight to behold.

What was he thinking? He had no intention of going out west. He would return home, finish college, decide on his life's work, marry, have children....

Another wave rocked the ship. That was enough for him. It was time to go below.

How would Delia, Adam, and the Brewsters fare on their voyage? Ezra prayed the ocean *and* the weather would be calmer for them. After all they had suffered in slavery, they deserved smooth sailing, both on this ocean and in their lives.

Ezra planned to enlist his aunt's help in finding Delia a job. But he would permit her to work only until he finished college. Then they would marry—if she still cared for him after meeting other eligible men. That thought saddened him.

Had Delia ever heard of Colorado?

✦╫╫)❀(╫╫✦

The *Ashland* sailed into Boston Harbor and berthed at Commercial Wharf on September 2, followed within hours by the SS *C.F. Thomas,* bringing the rest of the 54th Massachusetts Regiment.

Ezra had managed to borrow boots, trousers, and a cap to complete his uniform. With great pride, he took his place in the ranks and marched into the city.

To the amazement of the soldiers, large crowds of people, both Negro and white, lined the streets to cheer them. The Stars and Stripes hung from many buildings and lampposts and trees, while music accompanied their every step along the way. Lemonade and coffee, cakes and cookies were shoved into their hands by the welcoming throng. The regiment marched up Beacon Hill to the state house for review by Governor John Andrews, after which the vast crowds cheered their formations on Boston Common.

In the few days since he had reached the 54th's southern headquarters and sailed up the East Coast to his home city, Ezra had managed to reestablish his reputation among his fellow soldiers and with his officers. Now, here in his hometown, Ezra found no obstacles to his being mustered out of the army or receiving full back pay.

"After all," his commander said, "you were in the army the whole time. You weren't the only man to straggle in to Mount Pleasant after the war ended. We just thanked the good Lord that you survived. Too many others did not."

After the elaborate ceremonies in front of the gray-domed capitol building, Ezra bid farewell to his comrades and made his way up Beacon Hill. Weariness from the voyage and the day's activities began to set in. His knapsack seemed to weigh a hundred pounds, making his trek all the more laborious.

He had scanned the crowds for family members but could not find anyone. Father undoubtedly was at work, perhaps even providing a carriage or two for some wealthy Beacon Hill residents who had attended the festivities. Mother might be taking care of a sick neighbor, as she often did. As for Luella, she surely must be attending classes. He was proud of his sister's interest in becoming a teacher. She would be just the person to help Delia learn about life in the city. With every step, he made excuses for each of them. Yet he could not deny his disappointment that not one had come to greet him in his proudest moment.

On his way home, he passed strangers who called out greetings and little boys who stood at attention and saluted. Their welcoming reactions to his uniform restored a spring to his step and a measure of joy to his heart.

When Ezra turned on to Phillips Street, he threw off the last of his disappointment and surrendered to unbounded joy. The street had hardly changed at all. The red brick townhouses that extended up the block were just as he remembered them, with narrow, gleaming-white front porches, windowboxes filled with autumn flowers, and evidence in the street that much horse traffic had come this way.

All of his exhaustion melted away. With renewed energy, he hurried up the street, where he stood for a moment savoring the sight of his boyhood home.

"Ezra?" An elderly lady rose from the steps of the house next door to his and hobbled over to him. "Why, Ezra, is that you?" She squinted at him through gold-rimmed spectacles.

"Yes, ma'am, Mrs. Warren." Ezra bent to kiss her wrinkled cheek. "You don't look a day older than when I left." This woman had often fed him pie when he was a boy.

She began to tremble and weep. "Oh, Ezra, thank the Lord you're alive. We heard that you were dead."

Ezra gasped. "Why, no, ma'am. I'm...I'm very much alive, as you can see." Of course. The army must have written his family to say he was missing. He should have tried harder to write them a letter from the farm, no matter how difficult it would have been to post it. No wonder his family had not come to the celebration.

"Oh, mercy, mercy." Mrs. Warren glanced up at his house. "Maybe I'd better go in and tell your dear mother. She might have apoplexy if you just walk in."

He looked at the beloved front door, the brass knocker, the green shutters on the tall windows of the three-story building. With difficulty, he managed a smile instead of tears.

"Yes, that's a good idea. Thank you, ma'am."

She reached for the banister and pulled herself up the front steps. At the top, she turned around. "Now you go over beyond my porch where she can't see you."

Ezra did as she said, his heart aching with each step over the shock his mother would soon experience.

Mrs. Warren banged the brass knocker. Several moments passed before the door opened.

"Why, Mrs. Warren, do come in."

The beloved voice, rich and deep and full of graciousness, nearly drove Ezra to rush into his mother's arms. He pressed back against the building, his heart pounding. Soon enough, soon enough, he promised his bursting heart.

Within seconds, he heard her cry out. Within seconds, she ran from the house and into his arms.

"Mother! Mother!" he shouted.

"Oh, Ezra, my son! My dear, dear boy! Oh, Lord, thank You, thank You!"

Neighbors began to spill out of their houses. Men and women were returning home from a day at work. The world seemed to converge on the scene as word spread through the street that Ezra Johns had come home, alive after all. A joyful scream pierced the din, and in moments, Luella—tall, beautiful, and at last fully a woman—flung herself into his arms.

"Ezra, oh, Ezra." Luella wept and hugged him, then hugged their mother, then hugged him again. Then she put her hands on her hips. "Ezra Johns, shame on you. How dare you not write and tell us you're alive?"

Dizzy from all the attention, he could only laugh. "Same bossy big sister, I see." Describing his summer in a remote area of the South would take some time. He would save that for his family, no matter how interested the neighbors might be.

Mother laughed and wept at the same time. "Oh, dear, I don't have anything special to serve you for supper. It's too late to go down to the market."

"I'll bring your supper," a neighbor lady said. "Ezra, what's your favorite?"

"He likes lamb chops," Luella said.

"Now, wait a minute." Ezra frowned at his sister. "I might have changed my mind these past two years."

"Oh, will you listen?" Mother's laughter came more freely now. "Not home two minutes and already arguing with his sister."

The crowd laughed along with them.

"I'll bring a cake," someone said.

"I have fresh vegetables."

Others joined in, offering what was becoming nothing less than a feast. Before Ezra or his mother could stop them, they had decided to set up tables on the sidewalks and have a neighborhood celebration.

"Is that all right with you, Mother?" Ezra pulled her back into an embrace.

"Why, you haven't even taken off your pack." Her sweet face wrinkled with maternal concern. "You haven't even seen your room." She wiped away renewed tears. "I didn't change a thing."

"Thank you," he whispered. A tiny dart of fear struck his heart. "Where's Father?"

Mother looked around at the neighbors, who had begun to bring tables and food from their houses. She looked beyond them toward the street corner where Father always appeared at the end of a workday. "Since word came about your, um, your d-death, he isn't home much. He takes on more work every week. You remember the Lazarus family in Louisburg Square?"

"How could I not remember them? Timothy was one of my first friends."

She winced, then shook her head. "Your father still takes care of their horses and carriages. They are so pleased with his work that they recommend him to all their friends. He never turns anyone down, no matter what the hour." She sighed. "He'll probably be taking someone to some grand affair tonight. Humph. I should be glad that he's found solace in his work, but I miss him so much."

"Let me through." A gruff voice sounded above the cacophony of the crowd. "Get out of my way." The man muttered curses that generated clicking tongues and reproaches throughout the street.

"That's the other thing." Mother shook her head and gave a ladylike grimace.

Ezra questioned her with a look.

"He's lost all his manners."

"Ezra!" The tall, thin man who suddenly hastened toward Ezra was a cruel imitation of his father. His once-straight posture now slumped unnaturally. His hair, so black just two years before, was as white as table salt. Deep lines creased his features, and the hands that reached for Ezra were bony and gnarled.

"Look at you. Look at you." Father's voice cracked, but no tears came. Ezra had never seen him weep, even when Grandmama had died.

"Boy, what's the idea of not letting us know you're alive?"

In spite of Father's cross tone, Ezra saw pride in his eyes. "May I tell you later?"

"Very well." The old man gave a curt nod and reached out to shake his hand. "Now get yourself inside the house and get rid of that stink. It's bad enough that I bring horse smells into your mother's parlor. I'll not have you making it any worse by smelling like a sailor."

"Yes, sir." Ezra grinned. From the way his father scolded him, one would think he had been caught plucking blossoms from a neighbor's flower bed or tying his sister's braids together. But it did not matter. Ezra was home, and those he loved were here with him.

Those he loved, all except one.

CHAPTER FORTY-ONE

Delia hugged the bucket and spewed everything from her belly into it. Beside her, Miz May and Mr. Willard took turns throwing up in another bucket. In the back of Delia's mind, she hoped Adam wouldn't get sick, too. Somebody'd have to tell Ezra that they'd died of seasickness and been thrown overboard. Sure as anything, nobody on this boat cared whether they lived or died.

They'd all been excited to get on the boat in Charleston Harbor. It was a big steamship and carried lots of cargo and passengers. With Peter Blake's help, they'd found cheap passage in the cargo hold with other poor folks. But they were only allowed to stand on a back part of the deck as the boat sailed out to sea.

They hadn't been on the ocean for a half hour before the waves got big and mean and the wind blew so fierce that Delia and the Brewsters had to run downstairs to their little spot in the hold. There they clung to each other until the sickness came over them and they had to grab the slop buckets.

Why, oh, why hadn't they taken a train? Even walking clear to Boston wouldn't have killed them like this shaking boat was doing.

"Lord, hep us," somebody moaned nearby.

Delia and her friends weren't the only ones suffering. Would it ever end?

When she had nothing left to vomit, Delia rested her head against the leather satchel Miz Kate had given her. She was so weak she couldn't even help the old couple or lift her head to see how they were doing. If she lived through this, Delia would never, ever ride in a boat again.

She must've slept through the night, because the next thing she knew, she heard somebody laughing. How anybody could laugh when there was such an awful stink in the air, she didn't know. Lots of people had been throwing up and doing other smelly things.

She opened her eyes real slow. A kerosene lantern near the doorway gave the only light to the dim room. Two men played cards and smoked cigars under the light, and they were the ones who were laughing. Miz May leaned against Mr. Willard, and both of them were sound asleep. Other folks slept or talked real quiet. A mama in a patchwork dress nursed her baby and sang a little lullaby.

Paying no mind to the stink, Delia drew in a long, deep breath, and it felt good clear down to her toes. Just then, she figured it all out. The boat wasn't jumping all over the water anymore. It was just swaying real calm and peaceful like somebody rocking in a hammock on a lazy summer day.

Her stomach rumbled, but she shushed it. She wouldn't take a bite of anything until her feet were on dry, firm land.

At the end of the two-day trip, the man in charge of the boat gave leave for everybody to come upstairs and watch as the ship came into Boston Harbor. Delia helped the old folks climb the wooden steps and hang onto the railing so they could see it with her. Their big boat had to make its way to the wharfs through a crowd of other ships and boats. Above the wharfs, the city was spread out a long ways in all directions. The land had some hills going up from the water, and Delia could see church steeples and shiny roofs. She wondered which direction Ezra lived in.

"What a sight to behold." Miz May grinned. "Won't the chi'-drun be surprised to see us?"

"I hope they's still at the same place." Mr. Willard gripped his canvas bag with one hand and held the rail with the other.

The white passengers got off the boat first. Then Adam and Delia helped the old couple cross the wide board onto the wharf. One sailor called it a gangplank, but Delia wouldn't put herself out to remember that.

Both feet on firm land, she felt her heart beat faster. She'd be with Ezra just as soon as she and Adam made sure the Brewsters found their children. But the first thing she was gonna do was put on her pretty blue gingham dress. After all, she was in the city now.

"Which way you think we should go?" Miz May's eyes were lit with happiness and maybe a bit of concern.

"Can we ask somebody?" Adam asked.

They all looked around the wharf for a friendly face. Delia was checking for a black one 'cause whites wouldn't be likely to help.

A tall white man with dark suit and hat stood talking to some colored folks who'd just got off the boat, too. He smiled real big, pointed up the street, and shook hands with them like they were white people.

Delia and Adam looked at each other.

"You s'pose he's one of them Boston abolitionists?" Adam said.

"Go ask him." Delia nudged him with her elbow.

"Me? You go ask him."

Before either one could do a thing, the man caught sight of them and walked over like they were old friends.

"Good afternoon. Welcome to Boston." He reached out to shake Mr. Willard's hand, then Adam's. He took off that black bowler hat and nodded to Miz May and Delia. "I'm Jeremiah Harris. Do you need help finding your destination?"

They all stared around at each other until Mr. Willard took charge.

"Thank ya kindly, suh." He introduced everybody to Mr. Harris. "We needs hep findin' this address." He held out the old letter from his son. "Can you direct us?"

After he checked the paper, the white man gave them all a real nice smile, and his pretty blue eyes gave out a little twinkle. "Better than that, I'd be happy to take you there. It's not far from my mission."

Again everybody stared around at each other.

"A white man givin' colored that kinda hep." Miz May laughed out loud. "Thank ya, Lawd. Thank ya."

"Did you say mission?" Adam asked as they followed the man to the street. "You a rev'rend, suh?"

Mr. Harris nodded. "Yes, I am. I manage Grace Seaman's Mission. But due to the war, we've branched out in other ministries." He helped Miz May up to his one-horse buggy and took his place in the driver's seat.

The others climbed on to the rear, gripping their bags real tight. The reverend lifted the reins and gave them a little shake, and the horse started off. Her hooves made a hollow sound on the stone-covered street, and the wheels rattled and shook so much that Delia feared they'd fall off. But the reverend didn't seem worried.

Delia turned so she could see Miz May sitting there beside him. The dear old soul was wearing a big grin and staring around at all the sights of the city. My, she looked happy, as happy as Delia felt. But why would this white man help them this way?

She nudged Adam. "Ask him," she whispered.

"You ask him."

The reverend sent a grin over his shoulder. "Ask me what?"

Adam cleared his throat. "Is you an abolitionist, suh?"

Reverend Harris laughed. "I'm proud to say I was. Since the war has ended, and Congress will soon pass a law to outlaw slavery, I guess I'm just about finished with that job."

"Lawd, Lawd," Miz May crooned. "We can't thank ya enough."

"Did you hep anybody from the South escape?" Adam twisted his neck half off turning around to see the reverend.

The man's eyes got a real bright spark in them, not like he was proud, but just pleased. "Not by myself, by any means. But yes, I did."

Miz May choked out a tearful thank you, and Delia let some tears loose, too.

"Do you just go down to the dock to greet folks now?" Adam asked.

The reverend chuckled a bit. "I do try to get down there every day to hand out gospel tracts to sailors. I invite them to the mission services." He dug in his coat pocket. "I might have one left. Ah, here it is." He pulled out the paper and offered it to Miz May.

"Lawd, son, I cain't read." She gave him a long look. "Give it to Adam. He's jus' startin' to."

Adam took the slim paper and thanked the reverend.

At a nice, white clapboard house just off a main street, Reverend Harris pulled his horse to a stop. "I think this is your destination."

While Mr. Willard jumped down and hobbled over to knock on the door, the reverend helped Miz May down. In just a minute, a short, stout colored man opened the door. He wore a dark blue shirt, brown trousers held up by gleaming leather suspenders, and some fine, shiny black boots.

"May I help you?" He looked around the group. Then his eyes got round like saucers. "Pappy. Mammy." He started crying real loud and pulled them into his arms. Miz May and Mr. Willard cried and laughed at the same time.

Glad as she was for them, Delia hung back. She noticed Adam did, too.

"Aren't you going to greet your brother?" Reverend Harris wore a pleased smile. Delia decided she'd never seen such a kind face on a white man.

"He ain't our brother, suh." Adam dug at a loose rock on the stone street. "We's headed someplace else, a house on Phillips Street."

The reverend took a watch from his waistcoat and studied it. "I have just enough time to take you part way there."

Delia and Adam traded a look.

"That'd be mighty kind, suh."

With hugs and tears and promises to visit each other, they said good-bye to the Brewsters and hurried to climb onto the buggy's platform. Clear up until the reverend drove around the corner and on to the main street, Delia waved and waved at the sweet couple who had been like family to her. Then she turned around and stared at all the new sights. My, it would take some getting used to for her to like the city. But if Ezra helped her, she could do it.

"I'll leave you on lower Phillips Street," the reverend said over his shoulder. "It won't take you long from there."

"Thank ya, suh." Adam sat on one leg with other hanging off the back of the buggy. "Suh, do you mind me askin' you another question?"

"Not at all."

"I know you're a reverend and all, but you're a white man. Why do you hep colored people this way?"

The reverend glanced back at him. "Oh, I saw the old folks come off the ship and thought they looked too tired to be wandering all over a strange city." He gave Adam a wink. "Are they colored? I didn't notice."

Delia let a little giggle escape.

Adam pulled up his leg and crossed it over the other one. He seemed to get bolder by the minute. Delia didn't know whether to smack him or goad him on.

"Well, now, it's one thing to give some old folks a ride, and that's real good, but why'd you become an abolitionist and hep folks escape from the south? They said that was against the law. Folks died for that. Wasn't you scared?"

Delia felt a big dose of pride in Adam, almost like he was her brother. She'd never ask a white person a question like that.

"Hmm. Can't say I never felt fear. But I went to New Orleans back in '37, and I didn't like what I saw. Slavery is an evil institution, and we can all thank the Lord it's coming to an end." He clucked to the horse and guided her around a large wagon. "In fact, I'm going back to New Orleans in a few days to visit my daughter, Julianna. It will be good to see the changes being made through reconstruction."

Delia shook her head. What a wonder to hear of a white man talking that way. Right then, she knew she liked Reverend Jeremiah Harris. And she also knew she was going to like living in Boston.

✦ ✦ ✦ ✦

CHAPTER FORTY-TWO

"I'll visit Grandfather this afternoon." Ezra dried a plate and placed it in the kitchen cupboard. "Do you think I should visit Timothy, too?"

Mother swished another plate in the rinse water and handed it to him. "If you do, be prepared for a difference. He came home badly wounded in July of '63, and from all accounts, he was very bitter. Your Aunt Patience tells us that once he recovered he traveled quite a bit. All up north, of course. He came home just last month."

"Hm." Ezra pondered her words for a moment. Timothy had been such a jolly fellow. How unlike him to become bitter.

Right now, he wanted to tell Mother about Delia, but he could not think of how to begin. He had lain awake for some time the night before praying that Peter had been able to send his friends on their way to Boston.

Mother handed Ezra a dripping bowl. "Your father was a different man when he woke up this morning. For the first time since April, he knelt beside the bed and prayed." Her lovely dark eyes glowed. "He was sorry not to see you before he left for work, but he insisted I let you sleep in."

Ezra dried the bowl and hung the embroidered dish towel on its rack. "I'm sorry I missed him. I didn't expect to sleep so late. It was all that good food last night."

"And being at home in your own bed." Mother coughed away a little catch in her voice, dried her hands, and took off her apron.

"I wanted to go to work with him. He said last night that he needs more help."

She shook her head. "You know he won't let you. He'll find a good man. You're going back to school."

Staring out the back window for a moment, Ezra heaved out a sigh. "I could work with him until classes begin."

"But he said no." Mother brushed her hand across his cheek. "Don't worry, dear. You'll have plenty of time with him. Now, shall we go into the front parlor? The minister will be calling soon."

Ezra rolled down the sleeves of his white shirt. The cuffs did not quite reach his wrists, and the shirt barely buttoned across his chest. "Looks like I'll need some new clothes." He slipped on his old black suit jacket, which fit him just as snugly as the shirt. His trousers were a little short, but the waist was so loose he had to wear a pair of Father's suspenders. All that farm work had greatly improved his form.

In the parlor, Mother led him to the front window, where she inspected his clothing in the sunlight. She picked off lint and tugged at the sleeves and trouser legs, *tsk-ing* and *hmm-ing* her concern. "Oh, I do want you to look nice when the minister calls."

Ezra chuckled. "Surely no one expects a soldier to have his civilian wardrobe in order so soon after returning."

She gave him a sidelong look. "Well, not ordinarily, but...."

Something in her look warned him. "Mother, what's going on?"

"Why, nothing." With a dismissive wave of her hand, she walked toward the parlor door. "I'm going to frost the cake. You'll answer the door, won't you?"

"Yes, ma'am." Ezra watched her leave. She was up to something, but he would let it be a surprise.

A quick look around the room showed no visible changes since he had left more than two years earlier. Starched white doilies still protected the arms and headrests of the brown-velvet overstuffed chairs. The carved wood on the couch had been polished to a shine. The coffee table held a pair of small Limoges figurines—a milkmaid dressed in blue carrying two full buckets and a gentleman farmer wearing a brown suit.

Ezra and Luella had often made up stories about the two, sometimes arguing over whether or not they were sweethearts. Only by closest scrutiny could anyone see the fine line around the milkmaid's white neck. Ezra's antics as a ten-year-old had resulted in the poor girl's losing her head. Mother had taken it to a jeweler who glued it back on. In spite of the value of the little treasure, she had forbidden Father to whip Ezra, stating that boyish energy was not a character flaw to be beaten out of a child.

The bookcase behind the couch held numerous familiar volumes. Ezra reached for Milton's *Paradise Lost*. Perhaps he should read this one first. Or perhaps *Paradise Regained*. Or something by Shakespeare. For a moment, he felt overwhelmed by the choices.

Ah, to read great literature again! To enjoy the opera or a museum—and all the culture of the city. Never worrying about the enemy shooting him. Never again experiencing near starvation because he had run out of rations in enemy territory.

The sound of the brass knocker on the front door echoed through the entry hall. The minister!

"Ah, yes." Ezra replaced the book on the shelf and walked across the room. The best of all the activities he could now resume? Attending the church where he had grown up learning of God's great love for mankind. As he opened the door, he knew without a doubt that the minister would help him sort out his questions about entering the ministry.

"Ezra." The short, stocky minister exuded a sense of dignity in his well-cut black suit.

Behind him stood two ladies whom Ezra knew well.

"Reverend Wentworth, Mrs. Wentworth, Rebecca, do come in." Ezra gave a little bow to each as they entered the foyer.

The minister shook Ezra's hand heartily. "Young man, you have been resurrected. We praise God for His deliverance." Ezra heard traces of the man's beloved, booming preacher voice, now modulated to suit his surroundings.

"Thank you, sir." Ezra turned to Mrs. Wentworth, took her offered hand, and bowed over it. "Mrs. Wentworth, you are a vision of loveliness." Indeed, the slender lady looked as elegant as ever in her fashionable, bustled gray dress.

"Dear Ezra." She lifted a handkerchief to her eyes. "I promised myself I wouldn't cry, but I can't help it. Praise the Lord for His goodness." She squeezed his hand affectionately.

"Come in, come in." He waved them toward the parlor and included Rebecca in the invitation with a smile. "Oh, little Rebecca, when did you grow into such a lovely young lady, a worthy copy of your mother? The last time I saw you, you were chasing butterflies on Boston Common."

"Isn't that just like you, Ezra?" Rebecca's pleasant laughter was the epitome of refinement. Her pretty blue dress had been cut to fit and suited her exquisite figure very well. "Always teasing. But I will permit it just for today since you have come home such a hero." Her eyes also filled with tears, and she quickly dabbed them away.

Once seated in the parlor, each with a plate of Mother's delicious lemon cake, the old friends chatted about the weather and baseball and the price of cotton goods now that the war had ended. Reverend Wentworth commented on God's goodness in the growth of his church, and Ezra promised it would grow by one more on the coming Sunday.

While they talked, Ezra's attention turned more than once to the lovely Rebecca. Her black hair had been elegantly arranged, with pretty ringlets hanging to one side and a small, blue silk hat placed at her crown. She had removed her white lace gloves to eat her cake, and her long, graceful fingers reminded Ezra that she played the piano very well. Her flawless complexion matched the color of her coffee, with just the right amount of cream.

As if she sensed his stare, she turned from speaking to Mother. "Ezra, have you heard that Charles Dickens has written a new serial? It's entitled *Our Mutual Friend.* I've been saving the episodes as they arrive from England. The last one is due in November. If you would like to read them, I'll gladly lend them to you."

"Dickens?" Was it possible she still remembered his passionate discussion about *Great Expectations?* "That would be excellent. Thank you, Rebecca." So often during the war Ezra had longed for stimulating conversation about a good book in the company of educated friends.

Mother tilted her head and gave Ezra a knowing smile. In that moment, he understood her. During his college days, she had stood between him and any young miss who might show interest in him. Now she appeared to be promoting the lovely Miss Wentworth. He looked back at Rebecca and gave her a crooked grin, as he used to when they were much younger.

Instead of a playful wrinkling of her nose, as *she* used to do, she lowered her eyelashes and smiled in a demure fashion.

Ezra wondered if everyone in the room heard him gulp.

A loud rap-rap on the front door drew their attention.

"Now, who could that be?" Mother waved at Ezra to remain in his chair. "I'll get it."

She went to the door, and soon they could hear her refined voice echo with gentle tones. "You must have the wrong address, my dears. The charity house is three blocks over."

"Don't Ezra Johns live here?"

Adam!

Ezra rose quickly and dashed to the door.

There on the front stoop stood Adam, with Delia standing a few steps below.

"I done it, Ezra. I done got ever'body here, jus' like you tol' me to." Adam beamed with pride.

"Good job, Adam." Ezra clapped him on the shoulder and drew him into the house. Then he turned to Delia.

Her face was filled with apprehension, much as it had been the day he met her in the musty old barn in South Carolina. *Stricken,* he thought, stricken with fear. And just as when he had met her, something popped in his chest, like the first time he had fired a rifle. How he longed to pull her into his arms and soothe away her fears.

"Ezra, do you know this…this young lady?" Mother's voice bore a hint of concern.

Ezra reached out to Delia. Her eyes wide, she stared at his hand. He thrust it closer to her. Why did she hesitate to take it? She stared at his face. Slowly, she reached back and let him draw her up the last two steps and into the foyer.

"Mother, may I present Miss Delia?"

CHAPTER FORTY-THREE

*D*elia could hardly make her feet move up those steps. Her legs ached, and even as tough as her feet were, the cobblestone streets had bruised them. The higher she and Adam climbed up Beacon Hill, the lower her heart had sunk. And now that she was in Ezra's house, she wished more than ever that she was back on the farm with Miz Kate. Ezra never said he lived in such a fine brick house, narrow and tall and in a long row of others just like it.

"Miss Delia?"

The pretty colored lady Ezra had called Mother looked surprised. It seemed he hadn't told her Delia and Adam were coming. Delia could feel her heart pounding in her throat. This house and this lady were too elegant for the likes of her. Even Ezra didn't look the same, all cleaned up and in his fine black suit and white shirt.

"Yes, ma'am." Ezra still held Delia's hand while he talked, but it didn't make her feel any better. "And this is Adam. I haven't had a chance to tell you about my friends. We had some grand adventures together this summer. Didn't we, Adam? Delia?"

Ezra looked a little uneasy, like he wasn't sure what to say next.

"We sure did, Ezra." Adam looked a bit uneasy, too.

"My, my." The lady glanced toward a wide door, and Delia thought she saw her nose twitch just a bit. "Well, then, do come in. We're having a visit with the minister and his family." She led them into the next room, a pretty parlor almost as nice as the drawing rooms at the plantation, even if it was smaller.

Three colored folks stood up to greet them.

"Why, what have we here?" The short man in the handsome suit came over. He had some white in his curly black hair, but he didn't look as old as Mr. Willard. Delia liked the sound of his deep, strong voice.

The two ladies were very pretty, especially the young one. Her fancy blue dress was the prettiest thing Delia had ever seen on a colored girl. Right then, Delia figured out that her own blue dress wasn't pretty at all. And it was dirty and wrinkled, too. Shame crept up and made her cheeks burn. She didn't know how Adam felt, but Delia knew for sure she didn't belong here.

A sweet, welcoming smile rested on Missus Johns's face as she introduced Delia and Adam to the minister and his wife and daughter.

"Welcome to Boston, Miss Delia, Adam." The minister gave Delia a little bow and shook hands with Adam. The ladies said their hellos in a nice way.

Missus Johns told Ezra to fetch a couple of chairs, told everybody where to sit, and then looked at Delia and Adam, who were sitting by the brick fireplace. "May I offer you some cake?"

"Yessum." Adam put a hand on his belly. "That'd be mighty nice."

"And you, Delia?"

Missus Johns spoke kindly, but Delia couldn't do more than nod even though she was hungry. As Missus Johns left the room, Delia wondered if she should offer to help. She looked at Ezra, but he was talking to the minister.

"Why, that's interesting." The minister gave Ezra a long look, then looked at Delia and Adam. "Ezra just told me that you young folks are former slaves."

"Yessuh." Adam nodded. "We gots Ezra to thank for us bein' free, him and all the other soldiers who come down south and fought the war." He fidgeted in his chair, something Delia tried not to do.

"Delia, what do you think of Boston?" Miz Wentworth sat there like a white girl, like Miz Suzanne, like she was used to visiting in people's parlors.

Delia's throat closed. She couldn't think of a word to say. She tried to tuck her bare feet under her dress, but her aching legs hurt when she pressed them against the wooden chair.

"Now, Rebecca," Missus Wentworth said, "these young people have just arrived. I'm sure they haven't had a chance to form opinions about our city."

She gave Delia such a nice smile that Delia had to look away.

Missus Johns returned and served cake and coffee. Delia managed to say a proper "thank you, ma'am," echoed by Adam. While they ate, the others talked about Boston and church and what Ezra planned to do. The cake tasted good, but after just a few minutes, its sweetness made her belly ache because she hadn't eaten since throwing up on the ship. She drank her coffee as quiet as she could, but it didn't help the ache—not the ache in her belly or the ache in her heart. It was a long way to come to figure out real quick she should've stayed in South Carolina.

"We must be going." The minister stood up. "The Pruitts have a new baby, and we must call on them today." He put a hand out to his missus. "Mrs. Wentworth."

Everybody got up except Adam until Delia nudged his arm, and then he got to his feet.

Missus Wentworth came over and stood in front of Delia.

"My dear child, many former slaves came to Boston before Emancipation. Some traveled on to Canada or other places. Some stayed here, even though they constantly lived in fear of the slave-catchers who could return them to bondage. Unlike those dear souls, you will never have to be afraid." She leaned forward to kiss Delia's cheek. "We will help you find your place," she whispered in her ear.

A shiver went down Delia's side, and she swallowed back the tears. "Thank you, ma'am." She whispered, too. When she looked over at Ezra, she saw his eyes shining.

Miz Rebecca came over by her mama. "Delia, I know we'll be good friends. If you ever need anything, please ask me."

"Yessum." Delia bit her lip. "Yes, ma'am."

"You must call me Rebecca."

Delia didn't know what to say. Looking at Miz Rebecca was like looking at one of Miz Suzanne's kinder friends. Quality folks—except she was colored.

Ezra and his mama walked the Wentworths out the door, leaving Adam and Delia to finish their cake.

"Whoo-eeee." Adam gave out one of his soft whistles. "Never dreamed I'd ever set foot in such a fine house. You think they'll let us sleep in the back shed? 'Cause it's sure as anything we're too dirty to sleep inside."

"Maybe they don't even have a back shed." Delia tiptoed over to the front window. Ezra was standing on the sidewalk laughing at something Miz Rebecca had said, and Miz Rebecca had her hand on Ezra's arm. Delia jumped back from the window because she didn't want to be caught watching them.

"Maybe not. But I know one thing." Adam lifted up a small glass figure of a white girl from the coffee table. He brought it up close to his eyes and touched a little line on the neck.

"You better put that down." Delia glanced toward the door.

"As I was sayin', I know Ezra wouldn'ta had us come here if he didn't want us to be here." He set the figure down and stared at Delia. "He's gonna keep his promise and find us jobs. You can count on it."

Delia nodded. She knew Ezra would do what he said. Only trouble was, there was only just one job she wanted. And she figured Miz Rebecca already had that one spoken for.

⇥╫╟╳❀╳╢╫⇤

"Mother, I deeply regret not having a chance to tell you we had guests coming. After the neighbors finally went home last night, we were all too exhausted for further conversation." Ezra watched the Wentworths walk up the hill toward their street. Their visit and their graciousness to Delia and Adam encouraged him. "Actually, I didn't expect them to arrive so soon."

"We cannot discuss this on the sidewalk." Mother started up the front steps. "And we cannot leave our new guests any longer. I just wish I'd had time to prepare. They'll both need clothes and shoes and, goodness, I wonder when they had their last decent meal." She paused at the door. "Would they be offended if I offered them a bath?"

Ezra reached around her and opened the door. "You haven't changed a bit, have you? Always taking care of people in need."

"Shh." She put a finger to her lips. "Watch what you say. I've already made the mistake of thinking they were beggars."

In the parlor, Delia and Adam sat stiffly in the wooden chairs. When Ezra and Mother entered, Adam jumped up, and Delia slowly stood.

"Miz Johns," Adam said, "you got some work I can do?"

"Me, too." Delia stared at Mother as if avoiding Ezra's gaze.

"Oh, nonsense." Mother began to pick up the cake plates and coffee service. "You're our guests. We're happy to have you here."

In spite of her words, Delia hurried to gather the china and silver and place them on the tray Mother carried.

"Thank you, dear." Mother moved toward the door. "Now you young people just sit down and visit while I clean up these dishes."

"Can't I help?" Delia sounded worried.

Mother graciously refused, leaving Delia with a forlorn expression on her face.

Ezra longed to pull her into his arms and console her. But the familiarity that had been acceptable on the farm, no matter how innocent, had no place in polite society. And as much as his own thoughts displeased him, he wondered how the Wentworths had managed to be so gracious, considering the way Delia smelled—just like his fellow soldiers who had become seasick.

"Did you have a rough voyage?" He could think of nothing else to say.

Delia nodded and stared down at the floor, but he could see a soft blush appear on her fair cheeks. This was the girl he had met last April—shy, ashamed, fearful. Had all this summer's progress been lost?

He would try another tactic. "Where did you get that new dress?"

To his shock, Delia covered her face in her hands and burst into tears.

✯ ✯ ✯ ✯

hat on earth?" Missus Johns sat down beside her and touched her shoulder. "Delia, what's the matter?"

Delia felt so ashamed that she couldn't look up, but she did make herself quit crying.

"Ezra, what happened?" his mother asked.

"Um, I, uh, I don't know." He sounded like he was choking, but Delia could not look up to see for sure. "I just asked her where she got her new dress."

Missus Johns didn't say anything for a minute, then she sighed in a ladylike way. "Oh, Ezra, how could you?"

"How could I?" Now he sounded to Delia like his feelings were hurt. "How could I *what?*"

Missus Johns was quiet for another minute, so Delia wiped her face on her sleeve and gave her a sidelong look. How could this nice lady tolerate sitting by her?

"Come, Delia." Missus Johns took her hand and stood up. "Ezra, you see to Adam about that matter we discussed. I'm going to take care of Delia. Come along, dear."

From the way she talked, Delia could tell Missus Johns wasn't mad at her, but she just about dragged Delia into the hall and out to the kitchen.

"Dear child, you have come a long way, and I know you're hot and tired. Would you like to take a bath?"

A bath? How good that sounded. "Yes, ma'am. Is this your bath night?"

Missus Johns blinked. "Why, no. But you don't have to wait until then."

Ezra's mother drew water from the indoor pump and started heating it in a big pot on the stove. With Delia's help, she pulled a copper bathtub out of the closet into the corner of the room and set up a folding screen around it. When everything was ready, Delia slipped off her dress and well-worn underpinnings. Then she stepped into the deliciously scalding bath. As the aches eased out of her legs and her heart, she had to pinch herself to make sure she wasn't dreaming.

For the first time in her life, she was in bathwater that nobody had already used.

"I think this dress could use a good washing." Missus Johns stood on the other side of the screen. "Our laundry woman comes on Wednesday."

Delia chewed her lip for a minute. Her skirt and blouse didn't smell any better; they were the clothes she threw up on. But she'd rather die than put that blue dress on again. "Yes, ma'am. Thank you, ma'am."

"I'll get something from Luella's wardrobe for you to wear. Luella is Ezra's sister."

Delia gulped back a sob. Missus Johns was being so good to her, even better than Miz Kate, lending Delia her own daughter's dress. "Thank you, ma'am. That'd be real nice."

She scrubbed deep and hard to get all of the dirt out of her hide—her skin and feet and fingernails and hair. When she finished, the water was so cloudy with dirt and soap, she couldn't see the bottom of the tub. But once she stepped out onto the clean kitchen floor, dried with a fuzzy white cotton towel, and wrapped herself in Miz Luella's dressing gown, she felt cleaner than she ever had in her life. Not just clean on the outside, but clean on the inside, like she'd finally scrubbed away her slave life and was ready to start a new one. And that felt good.

Pretty soon Ezra's sister came home, and she turned out to be just as nice as Missus Johns.

"Let me comb out your hair." Luella sat Delia in front of a dressing table in her upstairs bedroom. "Then we'll find something for you to wear."

While Luella combed and arranged Delia's thick, wet hair up on top of her head, Delia studied Luella in the mirror. Her skin was a deep, rich brown, just a bit darker than Ezra's, lots darker than Delia's, and smooth and pretty. The steady look in Luella's eyes showed she felt like she was as good as anybody. Her ready smile showed she liked Delia.

"There." Luella stood back and stared at Delia's hair. "When it's all dry, we'll finish. Now let's find some clothes." She walked over to the tall wardrobe in the corner.

Her strong but friendly voice encouraged Delia.

"I ain't never knowed any Yankee colored folks before I met Ezra. Are y'all real society folks?"

Luella laughed. "I suppose it must look that way, but we're not. Not many Negroes in Boston are a part of the upper crust. We hope that will change soon. Several Negro men are planning to run for the state legislature next year. And more Negroes like my father are establishing successful businesses." She took a yellow dress from a hook in the wardrobe and gave it a shake. "Let's try this one."

Delia gasped. The pretty dress had puffy sleeves and all sorts of ruffles. She'd never worn anything so nice.

Luella helped Delia slip the dress over her head and buttoned the back buttons. She tied the broad satin sash at Delia's waist and stood her in front of the wardrobe mirror.

"There." Luella adjusted the shoulders and fluffed the sleeves, then stood back and looked at the dress like she'd looked at Delia's hair. "It's a little large for you, but it will do until we can get you more clothes."

Delia could hardly believe how she looked. The warm yellow seemed to make her skin shine. She turned to Luella.

"Miz Luella, I ain't never knowed such nice folks. Y'all are bein' so good to me."

Luella gave her another pretty smile. "It's our privilege, Delia. God wants us to help one another, especially our Negro sisters and brothers who come north. Our community helped many escaped slaves over the years, and now that slavery is abolished, we must help former slaves find a way to support themselves."

"I heard colored folks can get jobs working for white folks." Delia looked back in the mirror and smoothed the front of her skirt. "You s'pose I could get a job like that?"

Luella came up behind her and gave her shoulders a friendly squeeze that sent a warm feeling through Delia's heart. She already missed Miz May's hugs.

"Well, first of all, we need to work on the way you talk."

Delia felt heat creeping up her face. She'd become lazy about this lately. "Yes, ma'am. I s'pose so." But she wouldn't let shame stop her. "Will you tell me the right way to say things?"

Luella raised her eyebrows, and she seemed glad to be asked. "I certainly will."

She took Delia's hand and led her back to sit on the dressing table chair. Then she sat on the bed.

"The first words I want you to change are 'colored folks.'" She lifted her head just a bit, not prideful but in a way that showed she thought she was as good as anybody. "We are members of the *Negro* race. God made us as we are, so we can be proud of that."

Delia gave her a doubtful look. "I hear'd a white preacher say we're the sons of Ham, the wicked son of Noah. He said the Bible says we're the slave race and s'posed to belong to white folks."

Luella reached out and took Delia's face in both her hands. "Well, what you *heard* was wrong. We may have descended from Ham, but the Bible also says that when Jesus came, He made us all the same in His sight. In the book of Romans, we are told that He is rich unto *all* who call upon Him. In the book of Acts, there is a story about an important, wealthy Ethiopian—a man from Africa—who became a Christian after the apostle Philip explained the book of Isaiah to him."

Delia stared at her, wishing she could feel good about herself that way. Luella sounded like Ezra, believing that God loved them just like He loved white folks. But then, they'd never been slaves. Maybe God made Delia and her mama slaves because they deserved it. If Delia could be really good, stopped telling lies, and learned to speak proper, could He love her the way He loved Ezra?

Delia and Luella went down to the kitchen to help Missus Johns fix supper. Delia peeled potatoes and carrots while Luella shelled peas. Watching the mother and daughter talk and seeing how much they loved each other made Delia long for her own mama with a fierce ache, but she didn't let herself cry.

"Now if you girls will set the table, I'll make the gravy." Missus Johns lifted the pot roast from the oven, sending waves of mouth-watering smells throughout the kitchen. "Mr. Johns will be home soon, and I'd like for us to sit down to supper as soon as he washes up."

In the dining room, Luella took plates and silverware from the china cabinet. "Do you know how to set the table?" She frowned and bit her lip. "I'm sorry, Delia. I didn't mean to be rude."

Delia shook her head. "Ain't no rudeness in it. You don't know what work I done." She took a plate and some silverware and made a perfect setting. "I worked in the massuh's house as a lady's maid for Miz Suzanne, and I helped Beulah in the kitchen. At mealtime, I always stood behind where Miz Suzanne sat and made sure she had everything she needed." She counted the plates Luella had taken from the cabinet. "Y'all having company tonight?"

Luella giggled like a little child, and her black eyes twinkled. "Silly girl, you're the company, you and Adam."

"Me and Adam?" Delia could hardly grasp the thought of eating supper at the dining room table with the family.

"No, my dear. Say 'Adam and I.'"

Delia drew back. All these months since she'd met Ezra, she'd heard him talk proper, yet he never once told her she was talking wrong. She should've worked harder to copy him.

"Is…are Adam and I…"—it sounded so strange coming from her own lips—"are we eating with y'all?"

Luella laughed again. "Of course you are. You're our guests." She finished their task by putting a freshly ironed linen napkin at each place and a small bouquet of flowers at the center of the table.

All Delia could do was stare at the pretty arrangement. To think she'd soon be sitting here with the family. All summer, she'd never thought about manners when she and Ezra and all their friends had eaten together on the grass under the oak tree at Miz Kate's place. Then on the road, they mostly had to use their fingers and eat out of tin plates. Would she embarrass herself? Would she embarrass Ezra?

More memories came to mind, memories of standing behind Miz Suzanne all those years. Miz Suzanne might have been mean, but she knew her social manners, and Delia'd watched that all her life. She would sit at this pretty table and pretend to be her spoiled white sister. Only Delia'd act nice as could be. After all, she was their guest.

Chapter Forty-Five

☆ ☆ ☆ ☆

"How was I supposed to know?" Ezra whispered to Mother in the kitchen pantry. "Delia and I have been…friends since last April." More than friends, but he could not tell Mother yet. "I've never seen her in that dress."

"Hand me that jar of pickles." Mother pointed to the upper shelf far above her reach. "Let this be a lesson to you. If you see two ladies dressed in the same color, be very careful of what you say, especially when one dress is old and the other one is new. Didn't you notice little Delia's horrified expression when she was introduced to Rebecca?"

Groaning, Ezra plucked the jar from the top shelf, feeling in a bit of a pickle himself. He had been delighted to see Delia but a little flustered about her early arrival, so much so that he had not noticed *her* chagrin. He thought she was simply feeling shy. He had much to learn about women.

"She told Luella that someone named Miss Kate had given it to her. It's very old, but obviously she tried to make it look nice, poor child." Mother opened the jar and sniffed, then took out a thinly sliced pickle and ate it. "Um, just perfect." She handed him the jar. "Please put these in the pickle dish. It's on the kitchen counter."

They moved out into the larger room where empty bowls waited to be filled with steaming food from the stove. Ezra found the cut-glass dish and forked out the jar's contents. His mouth began to water, so he popped a slice into his mouth.

Mother slapped his hand. "Didn't I teach you any manners? Wait until dinner."

Her chuckle warmed his heart. It was good to be home.

"Of course, Rebecca was a vision of loveliness." Mother spooned potatoes into a bowl. "As always." She eyed him as if she expected a response.

"Yes. As always." The sudden tightness of Ezra's collar reminded him that he must purchase some new clothes soon.

Continuing with her work, Mother smiled, apparently satisfied with his answer.

Father came home from work shortly before seven. The spring in his step and the exuberance on his face clearly displayed that his faith and joy had been restored by Ezra's homecoming. The return of his former manners became evident in the way he welcomed Adam and Delia before dinner. Carving the roast at the head of the table, Father teased Ezra and Luella, praised Mother's appearance and cooking, and made appropriate remarks to their guests. This was the gracious man Ezra remembered.

"Miss Delia, Adam," Father said, "you are welcome to stay in my home until you have established yourselves here in Boston. We will do all that we can to help you do that."

Seated beside Adam, Ezra felt a measure of satisfaction. The young man had not objected to his trip to the local bathhouse and had been delighted when the barber found a few whiskers on his upper lip.

"Thank you, suh." Adam's confidence seemed to grow as Ezra watched. "I'll find a job right away. Can't wait to earn wages for my work. Miz Kate was gonna pay us, but she couldn't manage afore we left."

"What would you like to do?" Father sat down after serving everyone.

"I'd do most anythin' honest, suh," Adam said. "But I guess there ain't much plantin' and plowin' in the city."

Everyone laughed except Delia. Ezra tried to question her with a look, but she kept her attention on Adam.

"Do you know how to work with horses?" Father glanced at Ezra and back at Adam.

"Well, suh, I ain't scared of 'em. I helped Miz Kate hitch up her wagon, and I rode her horse once." Adam gave Ezra a questioning look.

Ezra frowned and gave his head a little shake. He was not ready to tell his family that he had almost been hanged.

"Then that settles it." Father tapped the table with his fist. "You'll work for me at my stable."

"Me, suh?" Adam grinned broadly.

"Yes, you, my boy." Father straightened in his chair, clearly pleased with himself. "I'll train you myself. You can even sleep in the room above the stable. I need someone trustworthy to stay there at night."

Adam sat up straighter, too. "Thank you, suh. I'll do my best." He turned to Delia. "Did you notice these fine clothes Ezra got for me?"

Ezra wanted to nudge Adam to be quiet, but it was too late.

Delia nodded and gave Adam a nice smile. She still would not look at Ezra.

"Ezra took me down the street to Mr. Hayden's house," Adam continued. "He gots a used clothes business and lots of clothes there for folks just comin' to town and needin' somethin' to wear." Adam leaned over his plate, his eyes wide. "You ever heard of Mr. Lewis Hayden?"

"Not that I recollect." Her voice barely rose above a whisper.

"Why, he's the man who kept escaped slaves in his house till they could go north to Canada. Mr. Hayden kept dynamite under his front door stoop. When the slave-catchers come to his door and tol' him to bring 'em out, he tol' 'em he'd blow 'em all to kingdom come afore he'd let one slave go back south. Ain't that somethin'?"

"Is that so?" Now Delia looked at Ezra, her eyes wide and her lips parted in disbelief.

The innocence of her expression stirred Ezra. "Yes, that's so."

"Indeed it is." Father chuckled. "We were proud of Lewis's work, but we lived in fear that he would have to make good his threat and our own house would collapse around us."

"Long before the 54th regiment was recruited," Ezra said, "it was Lewis Hayden's example that made me want to join the fight."

"Mr. Hayden did that for folks like us?" Delia looked around the table, her eyes shining. "To set us free?"

"Miss Delia." Father set his silverware across his plate and wiped his lips with his napkin. "Many, many people worked to end slavery. Many of them suffered great loss. And many brave people died trying to reach freedom." He moved his empty plate a few inches away and took a sip of coffee from his china cup.

"God never meant for any of us to be slaves. With every man or woman held in cruel bondage, with every child sold away from his mother, with every lash of the whip across the back of someone who had tried to flee his bonds..."—Father's voice reverberated throughout the room—"...I believe God wept just as surely as I wept when I thought my only son had died."

For several moments, no one spoke. Delia dabbed at her tears. Mother and Luella sat quietly. Ezra did not dare to trust his voice.

"Kinda makes a man beholden, don't it?" Adam's eyes shone. "Makes me want to work hard and make somethin' of myself." He sniffed and brushed his jacket sleeve under his nose.

Ezra forbade himself to cringe. Adam had much to learn, and he could not learn it all at once. But there was one thing Ezra would encourage. Willing away his overflowing emotions, he cleared his throat. "Adam, Miss Delia, do you remember your reading and writing competition back on the farm?"

"Yessuh." Adam grinned.

Delia nodded, but her frown worried Ezra.

"Tomorrow," he said. "Tomorrow we'll start reading lessons again. What do you think about that?"

"Whoo-eee." Adam fidgeted in his chair. "Can't hardly wait. I'll be readin' quicker than Miss Delia can learn all her letters." He shot a smug look at Delia.

While everyone else laughed at his boyish banter, a flicker of annoyance crossed her face. She set her mouth in a firm line and wrinkled her nose at Adam.

That small show of spirit eased Ezra's concern. Delia was going to be all right, after all.

Delia lay on the soft feather bed beside Luella, listening to her quiet breaths.

It had been a long, hard day, but she couldn't sleep. Through it all, she'd come to realize a few things. She remembered the time down by the Pacolet River when Ezra said he wanted her to meet his parents. Then she remembered how he hugged her something fierce after Jack beat up on her.

Delia hugged her feather pillow close at that memory, wishing it could be Ezra. But that long-ago hug didn't mean he loved her. Why, he'd never even said he loved her.

Like all these Boston folks, he was just a good man who didn't want his kind to be slaves anymore. He wanted to bring her here so she could have a better life than the one she would have waiting on Miz Kate on her rundown farm. No, Ezra didn't love her. After all, he had a nice society girl, a preacher's daughter, who liked him. Her heart ached to think of it, but there was nothing she could do. It would take a lot of work, but she would try to think about other things. She decided to think about what they'd talked about at supper.

It pleased her to hear that Mr. Johns had strong feelings about the wickedness of slavery. And he was sure God felt the same way. "With every lash of the whip across the back of someone—"

Across Mama's back, not because she'd tried to run away, but because Massuh took a liking to her, and Missus hated her for it.

Deep inside Delia's heart, understanding suddenly welled up like a flood. She closed her eyes and brought forth a stream of scalding tears to think of the wonder of it all. When Mama was beat to death, Delia wasn't the only one who wept.

God wept, too.

CHAPTER FORTY-SIX

With the taste of toast and strawberry jam still delighting her mouth and excitement filling her heart, Delia hurried up the street beside Luella. An hour before dawn, gaslights lit their way to Smith's Court, while the cool September breeze blew through Delia's thin brown cotton dress. She'd wanted to wear the pretty yellow one, but Luella had insisted it was too bright for a serving girl. If Luella was going to find her a job, Delia was more than ready to take her advice.

"I'll leave you with Aunt Patience." Luella pointed toward a white wood-frame house that looked a bit nicer than the others around it. "She'll find just the right job for you. I have to hurry over to Louisburg Square and prepare breakfast for a white family."

Luella knocked on the door and then entered, taking Delia with her. "Good morning, Aunt Patience," she called down the center hallway. "We're here."

The small, tidy house smelled of flowers and baking bread. Pocket doors opened into a parlor on their right, and a single hinged door was closed on their left.

A round, dark woman of medium height came from the back room drying her hands on a tea towel. "Good morning, Luella." Her strong voice rang through the narrow hall, sending a shiver down Delia's back. "Whom do we have here?" She peered sternly at Delia over narrow, gold-rimmed glasses perched on the end of her broad nose.

"This is Delia, the girl I told you about." Luella didn't seem the least bit scared, but Delia was. "We've been working for a few days on proper speech, so I think she's ready."

"Hmph. I'll be the judge of that." The woman raised her eyebrows and stared at her niece. "You don't even seem to recall how to introduce people."

Delia cringed, but Luella laughed.

"Auntie, this is Delia Young. Delia, this is my aunt, your new boss, Mrs. Patience Hancock. Auntie, Delia has been a wonderful help around the house, and I know you'll find a place for her."

"Well, young lady, if you don't hurry over to the Lazarus house and fix breakfast, she might just have your job." Missus Hancock put her hands on her hips and glared at Luella.

Luella looked at the little pin watch on her bodice. "Oh, yes, I'd better hurry." She started toward the front door.

"Don't forget the flowers." Missus Hancock waved her hand toward the parlor. "You know how Mrs. Lazarus likes her roses on the breakfast table."

"Yes, ma'am." Luella ducked into the parlor and brought out a pretty little bouquet of white roses. She gave Delia a quick kiss on the cheek. "Don't worry. You'll be fine."

When Luella shut the door on her way out, Delia wanted to chase after her or at least run back to the Johns' house. But she made herself turn to Missus Hancock and give her a polite smile.

"I'm much obliged to you for givin' me a chance to work, Missus Hancock." Delia wondered if she should curtsy, but feared her knees would buckle from fright.

Missus Hancock still had her hands on her hips. "I thought Luella said you could speak properly."

Delia willed away the tears that threatened to ruin everything. "I'm sorry, ma'am. If you just tell me what I said wrong, I'll say it right next time."

Missus Hancock tilted her head just a bit, like she appreciated what Delia said. "Well, then, first you must not say 'mizus' with that lazy *z* sound. Say 'Mrs.' with a crisp *s* but not a hiss."

Delia blinked. Should she try it? "Mrs.?"

Mrs. Hancock seemed to pucker her lips a bit, like she might laugh. "Hmph. Not bad. Now come with me to the kitchen. I have bread baking, and my delivery boys will be here soon."

The kitchen sparkled, reminding Delia of how clean Beulah had kept her kitchen at the plantation and how Delia had tried to clean up Miz Kate's kitchen. Except here there were two large woodstoves with roaring fires and bubbling pots on top. A slender, light brown, middle-aged woman kneaded bread dough on a heavy table across from the stoves.

"Leah, this is Delia." Mrs. Hancock checked a pot on the stove. "She's our new girl. Delia, this is Leah. She's been with me for almost twenty years."

Leah gave Delia a friendly smile. "Nice to meet you."

"How do, Miz Leah."

Mrs. Hancock stared at Delia and cleared her throat, just like Beulah used to do.

"I mean, *Miss* Leah." A sudden feeling of sadness swept over Delia. How could she be missing Beulah? Was it because Mrs. Hancock was a Yankee version of the old woman who had been forced to raise her?

She didn't have time to figure it out, because Mrs. Hancock thrust an apron in her hands.

"We'll see how you do here before we send you out to cook for one of our ladies."

When the women finished making bread and sent the loaves off with delivery boys, they started on the pies, cakes, and cookies.

At midmorning, Mrs. Hancock washed flour from her hands and put on a hat and cape. "I'll be back soon. You two may have some of the beans and ham that's in the ice box for your dinner. After you eat, Leah, show Delia how we prepare the desserts for delivery."

Leah hadn't said much that morning. She and Delia had been too busy to do much more than take orders from Mrs. Hancock. Now the two sat at a small kitchen table to eat.

"Delia, I'd like to hear about what brought you to Boston." Leah's voice had a hint of the South in it, and her amber eyes glowed with kindness. "But only what you want to tell me."

"I don't mind tellin' you. Telling you." Delia would learn Yankee talk if it killed her. "I was a slave. I just come...came North with some other folks." She frowned. "Is it awright...all right to say 'folks'?"

Leah nodded. "Yes, that's all right, but 'people' sounds a little more educated." She leaned across the little table and patted Delia's hand. "I was a slave, too. I came north on the Underground Railroad when I was fifteen, way back in '46. It took me a long time to learn proper speech."

Delia gazed at her with deep respect. "I wish I'd been that brave." She played with the last bites on her plate. "I guess that's why you sound a bit southern."

"I don't suppose one ever loses it completely." Leah stood and gathered her dishes. "You'll do well. I can already see that Patience likes you."

"She does?"

Leah just laughed. "Oh, yes. She would have sent you home if she didn't like you. I know she seems gruff, but that's her way of weeding out girls who don't plan to work hard." She poured hot water into a dishpan and added soap. "If you can endure her sternness, you'll earn her respect."

While Delia dried the dishes, she considered the idea—and more than that. Mrs. Hancock's severity meant she was pushing her workers to do their best. Maybe all those years, Beulah's sternness was just her way of pushing Delia to do her best.

Massuh…Mr. Young—Delia would never call him Daddy—he said Beulah cried for days after Delia left.

Funny how memories crept up and bit a person. Funny how one memory came together with another to tell a story.

After they had buried Mama's body in the slave cemetery on the property, Beulah had gone out there and cried like a baby more than once. But she never shed a tear in the house.

Had the old woman loved Mama? Had she loved Delia, in spite of her gruffness? But if Beulah loved her, why had she told her not to run away? Why had she said nobody would want Delia?

Because she didn't want Delia to leave.

Because she loved Delia.

And, Lord help her, Delia had loved the old woman in return.

She began to shake, unable to stop the hot tears that were burning her cheeks. She could hardly breathe and barely had time to set down the plate she was drying before she collapsed in Leah's wet arms.

"Child, what is it?" Leah held her tight like she'd never let go. "Is it something you want to talk about?"

Delia shook her head. "No, ma'am. No, ma'am."

Leah led her to a chair, knelt before her, and held her hands. "Shh. There, there." Tears covered Leah's face, too. "Did you just recall something about your slave life?"

Delia nodded and sniffed, trying to stop the tears.

"I understand," Leah said. "After all these years, I still remember things that break my heart. But it's gonna be all right, child. When something comes to mind, just go ahead and cry all you want to." She brushed her hand over Delia's cheek. "Then take it to the Lord in prayer, and He'll comfort you and help you sort it out."

Delia nodded. "Yessum." The pain in her heart slowly eased, and she could breathe again. Miz May...*Miss* May would say the Lord had sent Leah just when she needed someone to understand her. Delia's lips twitched. "Yes, *ma'am*."

Leah smiled. "If you don' tell on me for talkin' Southern, I won't tell on you."

They wiped their eyes and returned to work with Delia feeling like a boulder had been lifted from her chest. In its place was a warm, peaceful feeling, an assurance that no matter what happened, everything would be all right. She loved Beulah. She missed her. She forgave her. And when she learned to write, she would write to tell her so.

In the early afternoon, Luella returned, followed shortly by Mrs. Hancock.

"Auntie, Mrs. Lazarus needs someone to arrange her hair today." Luella nibbled on a ginger cookie. "Do we know anyone who can do white ladies' hair?"

Mrs. Hancock took a ledger book from a side drawer. "I think I may have someone here." She thumbed through the pages, clicking her tongue and shaking her head.

"Missus, uh, Mrs. Hancock, I do ladies' hair." Delia held her breath, hoping she had not spoken out of turn.

Mrs. Hancock stared at her for a moment. "Are you certain? You're not just saying that, are you? Mrs. Lazarus is my best client. I can't afford to lose her favor."

"Now, Auntie, you know Mrs. Lazarus would never think ill of you."

Mrs. Hancock wrinkled her forehead. "That's true, but I never want to let her down."

"I can do it, ma'am." Delia's pulse raced. She was so tired of cooking. But getting to arrange hair would be a dream come true. "I did the ladies' hair on the plantation, and all their friends said I did it better than anybody."

Mrs. Hancock gave Delia one of her stern looks, like she was taking her measure. Finally, she relaxed.

"All right. Luella, take Delia over there. We'll give her a chance."

Once again, Delia hastened along beside Luella as they wended their way through the neighborhood streets. As before, excitement filled her heart, but this time she knew what to do.

"Lord, help me do a good job so Mrs. Hancock will be proud of me."

CHAPTER FORTY-SEVEN

"And so Mrs. Lazarus wrote a note to Auntie and told her she was so pleased that she wanted Delia to do her hair three times a week." Luella sat at the dinner table across from Ezra, beaming as if she had received the compliment herself. Beside her, Delia stared down at her plate with a soft pink blush coloring her cheeks.

"I'm very proud of you, Delia." Ezra hurried to say something before his parents commented. In the four days since they had come home, he and Delia had barely exchanged two dozen words. In fact, she seemed to avoid him. Was she still upset about the blue dress? That did not seem like his Delia.

"Yes, dear Delia," Mother said. "I just knew you would find your place here in Boston."

"*I* just knew Patience would help her." Father's voice overflowed with joviality. "Miss Delia, if you impressed my sister, that's quite an accomplishment in itself."

While his parents and sister laughed, Ezra tried to get Delia's attention. But she seemed overly interested in her supper, at least in moving it around her plate. Perhaps this evening, he could take her out for a walk so they could be alone. With Adam now living above the stable, he was no longer around to shadow Ezra's every move.

After supper, the ladies shoved him out of the kitchen, refusing his offer to help with the dishes. Father sat in his chair in the parlor, reading the newspaper by the kerosene lamp and smoking his pipe. From childhood, Ezra had learned not to disturb Father for at least an hour after supper.

Seated outside on the front stoop, he stared down Phillips Street toward Boston Harbor. The city was growing so quickly that he wondered if buildings would soon block the view. Ezra wished it were earlier in the evening so he could take Delia down to Boston Common and show her one of the places where American freedom had its beginnings.

"Ezra!" Randall Simpson strode up the street just as the lamp-lighter came along to illuminate the streetlamps with his torch.

"Randall, good to see you." Ezra spoke the truth, but a small dart of disappointment crossed his thoughts. This unexpected visit might fill the evening, leaving no time for a walk with Delia. Nevertheless, he stood and reached out to his friend. "What brings you here tonight?"

"Say, now, can't a fellow visit a friend now that the army no longer owns our time?" Randall shook his hand, and they both sat on the concrete steps.

"Uh-oh." Ezra chuckled. "I recognize that tone. You're selling something. What is it?"

"Who, me?" Randall gave him a wounded look, but a grin played at the corner of his lips.

"Still thinking about Colorado?" Ezra had often thought about it, but it was too soon to ask his parents' advice when he hadn't even told them of his feelings for Delia.

"I haven't stopped." Randall grew serious. "In truth, I've been working on my plans. I'll finish my law degree next spring. Then I'll practice law for as long as it takes to save money to move out there. It seems a certainty that Colorado will be a state in the next decade or so, but the territory doesn't have its identity set in stone." He bit his lip. "I don't know about you, but I'm tired of being considered only good enough to work for whites. If we go out to Colorado, we can help build Negro communities."

"Whoa, slow down. 'We'?" Ezra's plans had not progressed that far.

"Of course, 'we.'"

"Ezra," Father called out the front window. "Do you have company? Bring them inside for coffee."

Ezra cringed. Had Father heard their conversation?

Inside, Father welcomed Randall and inquired about his family. He questioned him briefly about the war and made a few comments about articles he had just read in the newspaper. He made no mention of Ezra's conversation with Randall.

Soon Mother, Luella, and Delia joined them, and the men quickly stood to greet the ladies. Mother and Luella welcomed Randall as an old friend. Then all eyes turned to Delia.

"Miss Delia," Father said, "may I present Mr. Randall Simpson? He was one of Ezra's fellow soldiers during the war. Randall, this is Miss Delia Young, formerly of South Carolina."

Randall stepped over, lifted Delia's hand, and placed a kiss on her fingertips. "Miss Young, I am honored."

Even in the dim lantern light, Ezra could see the blush on her cheeks. An unreasonable heat burned in his chest at Randall's gesture.

But why? He should be pleased to see her honored by his friends. She surely had suffered enough abuse in her short life.

"How do you do, Mr. Simpson?"

Delia's proper response both pleased and perplexed Ezra. He had expected Luella to teach her good manners, but he had not expected her to learn so quickly.

"Why, very fine indeed, dear lady." Randall seemed reluctant to release her hand until Ezra, Father, and Mother all cleared their throats in unison. Luella merely laughed and then announced that she would serve the coffee.

Mother managed to seat Delia between herself and Randall. Seated opposite that arrangement, Ezra noticed the pleased expression on Randall's face, and the burn in his own chest grew hotter. For the briefest moment, he wanted to punch his friend in the nose. Or at least throw him out of the house.

Didn't Randall realize that Delia was...was what? Perhaps, in spite of all she and Ezra had been through together, her heart had not settled on him, as his had on her. From the way she was laughing at Randall's foolish banter, Ezra could see she liked his friend. The urge to eject Randall from the premises intensified.

Jack's sneering face flashed across Ezra's memory. He must never again give in to the kind of rage he had felt toward that unscrupulous man. But what could he do with these jealous impulses?

"And so there we were." Randall waved his arm expansively as he leaned toward Delia. "Surrounded by Johnny Reb and down on powder and shot. Then just when the sergeant sent ol' Ezra here for ammunition, the rebs made their move. We had a fierce skirmish that lasted for several hours and scattered our unit all over the countryside. After it was over, we just assumed he'd been killed until he came walking up to Union headquarters last week." Randall sent an affectionate glance in Ezra's direction. "You can imagine how we rejoiced to see him still alive."

Mother dabbed her eyes with a handkerchief. "Thank you for telling us all these stories, Randall. Ezra would never tell us about his own courage the way you have."

"That's true. He wouldn't." Father's eyes shone.

Ezra shrugged, feeling more foolish than complimented. Instead of paying attention to the conversation, he had let jealousy cloud his mind. *Lord, forgive me.* This temper must be subdued.

"Mr. and Mrs. Johns, thank you for your hospitality." Randall placed his cup and saucer on the coffee table. "I must be going, or my mother will send my little brother out to fetch me." His voice was filled with good humor. "She hasn't wanted to let me out of her sight since I came home."

Mother glanced across the room at Ezra. "I know exactly how she feels."

Ezra accompanied his friend out into the night. "Say, what do you think of getting some men together for a baseball game?"

"I've already been working on that." Randall nodded. "Some of the men from the regiment are eager to play."

"That's grand. Maybe we could play against a team of other Boston veterans." Ezra wondered if Corporal Ballinger had returned home yet.

Randall sent him a skeptical look, which was intensified in the wavering light of the street lamps. "You mean white veterans? That will never happen."

"But we made our mark in the war. We earned respect. Didn't you pay any attention to the cheering crowds the other day? We're heroes. With a little work on everyone's part—"

"Listen," Randall said, "I attended a recruitment meeting two days ago. I saw some of the old gang there, and it was the white boys who told me that Negroes weren't wanted." The shadows on Randall's face deepened.

"I can't believe it." Ezra shook his head. "We were friends before the war."

"That was when we were boys playing in the street. Now that they're clearing fields and forming official teams, they don't want to compete with us." Randall emitted a humorless chuckle. "I guess when people come out to watch the games, they don't want anyone to see that we can play as well as they do."

"Or better." Ezra pictured his boyhood friends, and disappointment filled him. "What about Smith?"

Again, Randall chuckled. "One of the worst."

"McDill?"

"You know the Irish. They've always competed against us, even though we were here first."

Ezra hesitated. "Don't tell me that Timothy was one of them."

Randall shook his head. "He wasn't there. Didn't you hear about his war injuries? He'll never play baseball again."

A sudden desire to see his old friend swept through Ezra. "If he could play, he would never agree with the others."

Randall clapped him on the shoulder. "You just keep thinking that way, my friend. You trust a white man, and you'll be disappointed."

Late into the night, Ezra did think about it. Timothy's family had risked everything to help slaves escape. Could the boy who insisted that Ezra walk beside him on the streets of pre-war Boston become a man who would refuse his friendship now?

CHAPTER FORTY-EIGHT

*S*tanding before the dressing table in Mrs. Lazarus's bedroom, Delia twisted a thick strand of auburn hair above her customer's right ear, secured it with an ivory comb, and looked in the mirror to be sure both sides matched. The lady's light perfume smelled nice and made fixing her hair a pure pleasure. "Do you like that, ma'am?"

Mrs. Lazarus turned her head to one side and then the other. "Yes, Delia, it's lovely." Her green eyes caught Delia's gaze in the mirror, and she smiled. "I have several friends who are looking forward to your coiffing their hair. You'll soon be a very busy girl."

Delia curtsied. "Thank you, ma'am." She combed loose hair from the lady's hairbrush and tucked it into a little cotton bag. "Would you like me to collect your hair and make you a pin cushion?"

"Why, yes. What a splendid idea." Mrs. Lazarus reached for her coin purse. "Now, how much do I owe you?"

Delia fussed with the brush and comb a bit more. "Um, well...."

"How about this?" Mrs. Lazarus handed her two silver coins. "This is the same amount I gave you the other day, but I wondered if it was enough."

Taking the money, Delia forced a smile. "I'm sure it is, ma'am."

"If it's not...." The lady frowned and dug into her purse again.

"Oh, no, ma'am." Delia's face grew hot. "I'm sure it's enough. It's just that I don't know how to count money."

"Ah, I see." Mrs. Lazarus put another coin in her hand. "Well, then, we must make certain that you learn. Let's go over here." She stood, took Delia's hand, and led her to two chairs with a small table between them. "Sit down, dear. Now, put those three coins on the table."

Delia did as she was told.

"Do you know how to count and do sums?"

"Yes, ma'am." Delia nodded. Beulah had made sure she learned how to count so she could keep track of the chickens and kitchen supplies in case somebody tried to steal them.

"Very good. This will be easy for you. Our monetary system is based on the dollar. One dollar is one hundred cents." Mrs. Lazarus pointed to the first coins she had given Delia. "These two coins are quarters, meaning that they are one quarter of a dollar. They are worth twenty-five cents apiece, and together they add up to fifty cents, or a half-dollar. This one..."—she pointed to the third coin—"...is a dime. It's worth ten cents. Altogether, you have sixty cents."

"My, my, that seems like a lot." Delia stared at the money. She would have to work on all these numbers.

Mrs. Lazarus laughed in her soft, ladylike way. "Not really. But when you put it with what I gave you the other day and what you'll be earning from the other ladies, it will soon add up to a tidy sum. Just be sure you tell everyone that your hairdressing services cost sixty cents. If you do anything more than a simple arrangement, add another twenty-five cents to total eighty-five cents."

"Oh, my," Delia said again. "Thank you, Mrs. Lazarus." Would she be able to remember all those numbers?

The lady smiled at her as if they shared a secret. "Will you buy something, or will you save it?"

Delia gave her a shy smile back. "I'd like a new dress."

"Of course." Mrs. Lazarus nodded. Then she raised her eyebrows. "Hm. Wait right here." She left the room and soon came back carrying a bright blue bombazine dress, like one of Miss Suzanne's. Mrs. Lazarus held it up to Delia's shoulders. "Why, I think it will be a very good fit."

"You gonna give me this dress?" Delia hugged it to herself. "It don't look like it's ever been worn." She knew she had used the wrong words, but she was too excited to fix them. With puffy sleeves and two rows of dark blue ribbon around the skirt, the dress was just right for wearing in Boston. The skirt even had pockets.

"Yes, indeed." Mrs. Lazarus's pretty eyes sparkled.

"Can I pay you, ma'am?"

"Oh, no, dear." Mrs. Lazarus shook her head. "I will be pleased that someone I know can make use of it. I had it made for one of my daughters, but she suddenly decided to grow four inches up and several inches around."

Delia could hardly keep from laughing out loud. Her own dress. One that no one had ever worn. Maybe now she could buy some white cotton and make a new chemise.

"Thank you, Mrs. Lazarus."

They wrapped the silk and wool dress in clean tissue paper and tied it with brown twine. Delia couldn't wait to show it to Mrs. Johns and Luella and tell them that she had something brand new to wear to church the next day. She wondered if Ezra would notice it.

Halfway home, she started laughing. This blue dress was a far sight better than the last one he'd seen her in. And she wouldn't feel a bit shy wearing it next to Miss Wentworth's blue gown anyday.

✦ ═ ❈ ═ ✦

Ezra looked around the elegant front parlor of the Lazarus home. Little had changed since his last visit three years earlier. Autumn sunshine filtered through gauzy curtains, brightening the room.

Timothy sat in a straight wooden chair with his ebony cane resting on the floor beside him. "When I learned that you had joined the 54th regiment, I couldn't have been prouder. You men secured your place in history, by all the accounts I've heard."

Looking at his well-dressed friend, Ezra could see only a little evidence of the terrible war wounds he had received in the 1863 rebel attack on the USS *Monongahela*. A pale, jagged scar ran down his deeply-tanned right cheek; it looked as if he had been slashed with a saber. Above the scar, a swath of white streaked through his jet-black hair. Timothy had always carried himself well, and despite his losses, he still looked every inch the aristocrat in his new black suit.

"I don't think the Union navy has anything to be ashamed of." Ezra spoke in a light tone to keep his emotions subdued. Timothy had lost so much, while Ezra had come through the entire war unscathed.

"You managed to blockade the South and render their navy almost completely ineffective."

Timothy shrugged and tilted his head in a humble gesture. "Ah, well, I didn't have much to do with that. By the time I arrived in New Orleans, Farragut had it all under control." He chuckled but then grew serious. "On my first trip up the Mississippi, the only action I saw was getting my first ship shot out from under me. On my second trip...." He waved his left hand down the length of his body and clenched his jaw. "But we won, Ezra." His voice grew soft with intensity. "We won the war. There's no more slavery, and the United States is one nation again. Now you and I can walk down the street together without public censure, proud of our friendship." With difficulty, he tapped his wounded right hand on his injured knee and gave Ezra a crooked, boyish grin. "However, I might have to wait awhile before I can join you for a game of baseball such as we played in the old days."

Ezra stared out the window to compose himself. Randall had been wrong about this white man. The war may have shattered his body, but his soul had not changed. When Ezra was able to speak, he mirrored Timothy's shrug.

"It won't be the same without you."

"Ha." Timothy's black eyes snapped. "Don't use me as an excuse not to get back in the game. I expect to hear great things about your playing in the new leagues."

"But surely you've heard." Ezra sat up on the edge of his chair. "They won't let Negroes play."

Timothy frowned. "What? I can't believe it." He let out a long, low whistle. "After all the work we did to change things."

"Maybe we'll just have to work harder." Ezra wondered if his friend had the strength for any more battles.

Timothy punched his uninjured left fist into his crooked right hand. "Maybe we will."

Even as he appreciated that show of spirit, Ezra glanced at the large clock on the mantelpiece. "Well, I promised Mother I would come home by six, and I still need to stop by my grandfather's house. Guess I'd better go."

"Tell the old gentleman hello for me." Timothy bent to pick up his cane and started to stand.

"No, no. Sit still." Ezra waved him down.

"Never mind that. I'm stronger than I look." Timothy slowly rose to his feet and hobbled across the room with the help of his cane.

When they reached the front hallway, Ezra turned toward the back door, but Timothy grasped his arm. For a moment, Ezra thought his friend might be falling. Instead, Timothy gave him a pained look.

"The front door, Ezra. Next time—and every time after that, you come in the front door of this house. Do you understand?"

Ezra smiled and reached out for the doorknob. "Yes, Timothy, I understand."

$\mathscr{S}$eated between Ezra and Luella in the African Meeting House, Delia smoothed the skirt of her dress once more. She still had a hard time believing this dress was her very own. Touching the soft, shiny fabric was pure pleasure. She glanced around the room at the other people who were gathering for the church service, and contentment filled her heart. In this pretty gown, she was fit to be there, just the same as anybody. Of course, it would be nice to have a hat, gloves, and shoes that weren't borrowed, but those things would come soon enough. Right now it felt good to be sitting on the bench in the congregation instead of standing in the balcony, as the slaves at the plantation always had to do.

That morning when Delia had come downstairs at the Johns' house, Ezra's eyes had just about popped. He had told her how nice she looked and how she ought to wear blue all the time. As shy as that made her feel, she had managed to say a proper thank you. Then the family had walked together to the red brick church.

Luella had told her that many abolition meetings had taken place in the building before the war broke out. Delia still felt surprised to see white folks...white *people*...seated right there on the benches beside Negroes in this large, clean, white-walled room.

What didn't surprise her was seeing Miss Rebecca Wentworth come in and sit down on the other side of Ezra. She wore a dark green dress with a tight fitting bodice, a cinched waist, and far too many crinolines puffing out the skirt. How many nice dresses did this girl have?

"Miss Delia, I'm so pleased that you came to hear Father preach today." Miss Wentworth bent across Ezra as if she owned him. "How pretty you look."

"Thank you, Miss Rebecca." Delia tried to smile, but her heart seemed to drop to her stomach. On the way to church, Ezra had offered Delia his arm. It made her feel special, even though Luella held his other arm as they followed Mr. and Mrs. Johns. But now she could see he had just been showing good manners. His welcoming smile to Miss Wentworth told Delia all she needed to know about that.

The church service began with singing and a man talking and even some kind laughter when a little boy got up and said a Bible verse. Just about everybody had a Bible, and when they turned the pages, a soft fluttering sound filled the room. Delia looked across the aisle at a nice-looking white lady with a boy about Adam's age. They joined in the singing with everybody else, even on a song that reminded Delia of the ones Miz May...*Miss* May always made up.

At the front of the room stood a raised platform where Reverend Wentworth and two other men sat in fine oak chairs. Pretty paintings of handsome Negro men were hung on the walls. Delia wondered who they were. She could smell perfume on some of the ladies, including

Miss Wentworth. A vanilla scent floated back from the lady seated in front of them. Delia thought that made a nice perfume.

"Finally, brethren, stand fast!"

Delia jumped at the sound of Reverend Wentworth's voice booming out into the room. How long had he been standing up there preaching?

Ezra patted her arm, and Miss Wentworth leaned across him again to give Delia another nice smile. She just felt worse. What if someone asked her about the sermon, as Beulah used to do?

"'Stand fast therefore in the liberty wherewith Christ hath made us free.'" Reverend Wentworth paced back and forth across the platform. "'And be not entangled again with the yoke of bondage.' Many of us..."—he waved his arm to take in the whole room—"...were enslaved to man. *All* of us were enslaved to sin. Just as you would never return to the old master of your body, do not return to the old master of your soul. If you will hear the voice of God today, if you will believe He sent His Son to die for your sins, then you are accepted in the Beloved, who is none other than Jesus Christ. And He makes you a beloved child of God. You are freed from your old life. And 'if the Son therefore shall make you free, ye shall be free indeed.'"

That was the same Bible verse Ezra had read back at Miss Kate's one Sunday afternoon. A deep shiver ran down Delia's back, as if somebody had poured cold water on her. But it felt good, not bad. *Accepted by God.* Accepted in the Beloved, Jesus Christ. The good feeling flowed right into Delia's heart and turned warm and sweet.

Ungrateful!

Lazy!

Worthless!

God will punish you!

Plantation voices screamed in her head.

No! she screamed back. *I am free! I will not be in bondage to those voices again. I am accepted by God. Accepted in Jesus Christ.* Just like Miss Wentworth. Just like everybody in this room, even the ones whose clothes were ragged and smelly.

"Lord, forgive me for doubting You." Delia's eyes misted, not from sorrow, but from joy.

"And if you have prayed that prayer with me," Reverend Wentworth said, "go forth this day and ask God what He would have you do, for servitude to your heavenly Father is not burdensome. It is not bondage. It is the ultimate freedom."

Delia almost jumped again. She must learn to pay attention in church. But it wasn't as if her mind had been wandering this time. At last her heart felt settled with God. She wasn't mad at Him anymore for Mama's death or for her own lonely childhood. More than that, she felt a deep love for Him. Oh, how she wished she could show Him her gratitude. Reverend Wentworth had said to ask God what to do, so she would.

"Lord, what do You want me to do?"

Before she could finish her prayer, one word came to mind.

Ezra.

Ezra?

As the church service ended, Delia looked over to see him talking with Miss Wentworth, and her heart sank again. Was God telling her to forget about Ezra, as she had already been trying to do?

"Mother." Ezra looked beyond Delia toward his parents. "Rebecca has invited me to dinner. Will that spoil your plans?" He lowered his chin, raised one eyebrow, and twisted his lips to one side as if he was trying to say something more than his words.

"Not at all, son." Mrs. Johns gave him a big smile. "You go along and enjoy yourself."

All the way home with Luella and Mr. and Mrs. Johns, Delia wondered why God had spoken Ezra's name to her that way.

Or maybe God hadn't spoken to her at all.

⁘✻⁘

"Mrs. Wentworth, that salmon was delicious." Ezra sat across from Rebecca in his hosts' well-appointed dining room. "If the recipe isn't a secret, would you give it to Mother? I don't believe she's ever prepared salmon this way, and she always welcomes new ideas."

The minister's wife glanced at her daughter. "Why, didn't Rebecca tell you? She prepared this fine dinner for you...for us." She arched her eyebrows and tilted her head toward Rebecca as if inviting him to redirect his praise.

"Well, then." Ezra turned to Rebecca, his every nerve on guard. "My compliments on this fine dinner, Rebecca." He looked at Reverend Wentworth. "And my compliments on a fine sermon, sir. When I heard that you were to address the topic of grace, I knew your words would truly be inspired." Where were his manners? He had not given Rebecca a chance to respond.

The minister was kind enough to ignore Ezra's rudeness. "Yes, I have observed these many years that former slaves sometimes have difficulty grasping the idea that they do not have to work for their salvation.

As I watched your little friend Delia from the podium, I believe she found a measure of peace in today's message. When I said—"

"Now, Father," Rebecca said with a laugh, "I hear you warming up for another sermon. But I invited Ezra over to discuss…that topic I told you about."

"Oh, my, yes." Mrs. Wentworth stood up and began stacking plates. "Charles, will you please help me clear the table? These young people need some time to themselves."

"Indeed?" Reverend Wentworth blustered for a moment until his wife cleared her throat and glared at him. "Ah, oh, yes, of course."

"Come along, Ezra." Rebecca stood and reached out her hand. "I want to give you those back issues of the Dickens story so you can catch up with our book club."

Ezra tugged at his new shirt collar, which had suddenly become tight. He permitted Rebecca to draw him into the parlor, where she sat beside him on the couch. Not one English periodical lay in sight.

"I do love Sunday afternoons." Rebecca retrieved a lace fan from the side table and began to fan herself, although the day was pleasantly cool. "They're always so restful, don't you think?"

Ezra glanced about the room, still trying to locate the Dickens' chapters.

"In fact," she continued, "perhaps we should go out for a walk."

Lord, help. All he could think about was Sunday afternoon walks with Delia in South Carolina.

"My, you're so quiet, Ezra. Are you ill?" She set down her fan and touched his forehead. "Hm. No fever. However, you do look a little unsettled." A smile crept over her lips. "Now, why do you suppose that is?"

Ezra slowly exhaled. Going into battle against his enemies had been easier than having this conversation. He did not wish to inflict any wounds on his lifelong friend.

"May I confide in you?" He hoped this was not the wrong approach.

Rebecca sat back, surprised. "Of course. I've always kept my friends' secrets."

He nodded. "I know you have. One day you'll make a very fine pastor's wife."

"Oh, Ezra." She gave him a radiant smile.

He had said the wrong thing. He must hasten to amend it, must throw everything on the table.

"My secret is that I'm considering plans to go out west."

She gasped. "What?" She gripped her fan and began to wave it in front of her face with vigor. "What are you talking about?"

"My plans are not complete, but I've been talking with others who want to travel west after they've completed their education. We have a great opportunity to form Negro communities where—"

"Out west?" Her full, beautiful lips formed a grim line. "Why would anyone want to go out west? Why, there are heathen savages living out there. It's a wilderness."

Certainty settled in Ezra's chest. "Isn't that exactly why Christians, especially pastors, should go there?"

Rebecca put down her fan and stared at him for several seconds. Her eyebrows dipped into a frown, and she stared at her hands. He could see her inhale quick, shallow breaths, as Luella often did when she was upset and had her corset on. Terrible devices! He hoped Delia would never wear one.

Rebecca slowly looked up to meet his gaze. Her eyes were moist but not overflowing. She gave him a trembling smile.

"I don't suppose that an…an old friend could dissuade you from this course?"

"If the Lord directs me to do something, should I be dissuaded by even the kindest of friends?"

She shook her head. "No. Never." She grasped his hand. "Above all else, obey the Lord." She reopened her fan and began moving it gently, almost as if unaware of what she had done. Then she snapped it shut. "I shall keep your secret. Now, where are those Dickens installments?" She rose and crossed to a bookshelf. "Here they are. Ah, Ezra, Dickens has done it again. Wait until you meet this enchanting host of characters."

For another half hour, Ezra glanced over the newsprint chapters and discussed them with feigned interest. He did wish to read this story. Further, Rebecca was making a great effort to be brave. But as they talked, a thin fiber of unease threaded through the back of his mind. What if Delia did not want to go west?

As he walked home, he could not think of how to pray. Should he wait to make his final decision until after he proposed to Delia? Then, if she refused to accompany him to Colorado, he would know the move was not God's will. Yet, sitting in the Wentworth parlor, he had felt certain he must migrate west. Did that mean he must solidify his decision now, then ask if she wanted to accompany him, and *then* propose to her if she proved willing to face the wilderness with him?

His head swimming, he bounded up the front steps of his home. Of one thing he was certain. He would not lay out a fleece before the Lord but instead would wait upon His direction.

CHAPTER FIFTY

"I don't want to give him up." Delia paced Luella's bedroom and whispered to herself. "He cared for me on the farm. I know he did." Miss Kate had told her not to waste time the way she had, to go with Ezra and marry him. Was it too late for that now?

Would Luella think she was crazy for talking to herself this way? But the Johns family had gone Sunday afternoon visiting, so there was no danger of her being heard.

Delia sat at the dressing table and chewed her thumbnail. How she longed to talk to Miss May and Mr. Willard. They would know if she had a chance to win Ezra away from the preacher's daughter. But after six days in Boston, she was afraid she couldn't find her way back to their son's house.

She looked into the large round mirror. Beulah had always told her no one would want her, that she might as well accept it. But somehow now, with Luella doing her hair, she felt almost pretty. She'd have to learn how to work with her coarse hair. All those years on the plantation, she'd been forced to wear a bandanna. Now she was free to look as good as she could.

But that wouldn't do any good if Ezra liked—or *loved*—Miss Wentworth. Maybe he'd even gone over to the preacher's house to propose to her this very day.

Delia slumped down in her chair. She might as well take off her pretty blue dress and put on something old. She might even put on that awful blue calico. Once the laundry woman washed it in bluing and ironed it the other day, the color improved a bit. But Delia still hated it for being a country dress. Even then, after she'd looked at her new dress in the mirror one last time, she changed into the calico.

"Mother." Ezra's voice echoed up the staircase. "Father? Anyone home?"

Delia thought her heart had stopped that very second. Ezra was home. Had he brought Miss Wentworth? Were they engaged?

She breathed in and out for courage, then got up and went to the hallway and looked over the banister.

"What you yelling 'bout down there?" Irritation pecked at her heart. Why had she changed out of her pretty dress into this old thing?

"Delia." A big smile bloomed across Ezra's handsome face. "Hello."

She couldn't keep from smiling back. "Hello."

"Anybody else home?"

"No."

"Hm." He looked toward the front door and then toward the kitchen. "Well, I suppose to be proper, since we're not chaperoned, we should wait in the parlor until someone else comes home."

Delia snorted, then wished she hadn't. She'd bet Miss Wentworth never snorted. "We never had a chaperone down by the Pacolet River."

"Delia." He pouted and frowned like his feelings were hurt. "Miss May and Mr. Willard always kept watch over us. We never did anything improper."

"I'm glad you mentioned that." Delia walked down the stairs and headed toward the parlor. "Can we go see them?" she said over her shoulder. How she missed Miss May's songs and hugs and Mr. Willard's funny, duck-quack laugh. Then she wondered if Ezra could see the mended rips in the back of her dress as he followed her down the hall.

"That would be grand. I've missed them, and I want Mother and Father to meet them."

Delia sat on her favorite brown brocade chair and smoothed the lace doily on the arm. "How about Luella? They got a real fine-looking son who's not too old for her."

Sitting down on the couch, Ezra crinkled his face into a grimace, but he laughed. "Are you playing matchmaker?"

"I s'pose." No, that wasn't the way to say it. "I suppose. Did you have a nice dinner at the preacher's house?"

Now he grinned at her. "I'm glad you mentioned that."

Was he taunting her by copying what she had said a minute ago? "Why?"

"Because Rebecca and I had a nice discussion. I think the Lord is showing me His plans for my future."

Delia's heart sank. He'd already proposed. She swallowed hard but refused to cry.

He picked up the little white figurine from the coffee table. "Did I ever tell you that I broke this when I was a boy?"

She shook her head.

"Well, I did, and it broke Mother's heart." He put it back down again. "I promised myself right then that I would never break another lady's heart."

Delia wouldn't tell him that he'd already broken that promise—and her heart.

He studied his fingernails, half humming to himself, half glancing her way every few seconds.

Heat crept up Delia's face. She'd bet he hadn't sat there humming in Miss Wentworth's parlor. Well, Delia didn't have to sit still for that, either. She might be out of place sitting here in this fancy chair in this fancy parlor in an old dress nobody in the world would ever want. But she was doing good work for white ladies and making her own money, and one day would have clothes she bought herself. And if Ezra didn't love her, God still said He loved *and* accepted her, and that was even more important.

"Ezra Johns, you know you've got to make up your mind, don't you?"

His eyes widened in surprise. "Y-yes. How did you know?"

"It's plain as puddin', that's how. You have to choose right now between Rebecca Wentworth and me. What do you think of that?" She started to shake, but whether from anger or fear of his answer, she wasn't sure.

He started chuckling. "Oh, Delia, I never had to decide about that." He came to kneel by her chair. "Dear one, don't you know that I love you?" He brushed his thumb across her cheek, and for the first time, she realized she was crying. He *loved* her. He loved *her*.

"You never said it before."

"I never had a chance."

She gulped back her tears and tried to laugh, but all that came out was a little sob.

He pulled her head to his shoulder. "Shh. Don't cry." He moved back and caught her gaze. "Marry me instead."

She hiccoughed out another few sobs as joy spread through her chest. "Awright. All right. I will." Oh, how she hoped he would kiss her. Just one kiss before the family came home.

But then he frowned. "I didn't do that right."

She gave out a shaky little laugh. "I didn't mind how you did it."

He shook his head and ran his hand across his forehead. "No, I mean I have to tell you something else. Delia, I believe the Lord wants me to go out west, maybe to Colorado, maybe someplace else, to build a Negro community. I should have told you that before I proposed."

Delia stared into his eyes, and a bit of sadness settled in her heart. She hadn't been in Boston long, but she liked the city. She liked doing ladies' hair. She liked the church, even if Miss Wentworth was there. But she liked—and loved—Ezra a whole heap more.

"Will we go soon?"

"Will we—? Do you mean you'll go with me?" Ezra looked like Frederick when Miss Kate gave him the puppy.

"Well, I sure ain't gonna let that Miz Wentworth take my place."

He shook his head real hard. "Oh, no, she will never take your place, my dear, dear Delia." He took her face in his hands and stared at her.

"Well, go on. You can kiss me now, Ezra Johns."

And so he did.

ecember 1865

"Read it again, Ezra." Delia snuggled next to him as they sat against pillows at the head of the bed.

"All right." Ezra unfolded the two-page letter. *"Dear Ezra and Delia—"*

"No, honey, don't start there." Delia flipped over the envelope. "Read this."

Ezra chuckled. "Ah, I see what your game is." He took the envelope, held it up high, and read in a deep, grand voice. *"Mr. and Mrs. Ezra Johns, 123 Phillips Street, Boston, Massachusetts."*

"Oh, yes, that's what I like to hear. Mr. and Mrs. Ezra Johns." She stretched up and kissed his cheek. "Mrs. Ezra Johns. I can't hardly believe it's true."

A little shadow crossed his eyes, but he smiled. "I like to hear it, too, my sweet wife." He gave her a gentle kiss and let his lips linger.

Delia moved back. "I didn't say it right, did I?"

"Well...."

"It's awright…all right, honey. I want to talk right, so you have to tell me when I make mistakes."

He brushed his hand across her cheek and gazed into her eyes. "If you want me to, then I will." Looking down at the letter, he smoothed out its folds. "Do you want to read it?"

A little thrill swept through Delia. "I'll try." She'd already heard Ezra read it, so it shouldn't be too hard. She took the pages and read, stopping frequently to figure out the words or ask help from her husband.

"Dear Ezra and Delia, We were real glad to hear from you all and hear you are married. We figured that would not take long. Miss Kate misses you, Delia. If you change your mind about going out West, you can come back down here, and we will make a place for you both.

"We are also happy to learn of how well dear old May and Willard are doing. Please tell them hello for us.

"Alice and Leviticus's baby girl is fat and healthy. They named her Delia May. Are you surprised?

"You will be glad to know that after all these years Miss Saunders agreed to be my bride. We were wed the Sunday after Thanksgiving. We visit Ma at the asylum once a month, and she is not doing too poorly. She will probably outlive us all."

"Whew. All this reading wears me out," Delia said. "I'll read the rest to you later."

"You did a fine job, Delia." His eyes sparkled with pride.

Delia noticed a little something more in his look. She set the letter on the bedside table and snuggled back into his arms. "You may kiss me, Ezra Johns."

He obliged with a quick peck.

"Is that all I get?" Delia tried out a little pout just for fun.

"Hold on, now, honey. I needed to ask you something."

"All right. Ask me."

"We've been invited to a reception and—"

"A reception?" Delia sat up and squealed with delight. "When? What should I wear? Do I have time to make a new dress?" Imagine getting all dressed up and going to a party, just like Miss Suzanne used to do.

"Now, wait a minute. There's more. Do you remember Timothy Lazarus, who came to our wedding? He's getting married in a couple of weeks. I know you still feel shy around white people, so if you don't want to go—"

Delia gasped. "You mean we been invited to Missus Lazarus's boy's weddin' reception?" She shook her head impatiently. "I'm gonna say that right. Do you mean we've been invited to Mrs. Lazarus's son's wedding reception?"

Ezra laughed out loud and took her face in his hands. "Yes, my darling bride. And we can attend the wedding, too, if you'd like to."

She studied his tender expression, so filled with pride in her. That look could carry her through anything, even being surrounded by white folks.

"Oh, Ezra, I do want to go. I'll be scared, but if you're with me, everything will turn out all right."

"That's my girl." He drew her into his arms and kissed her again.

Delia nestled close to her handsome husband, and a warm, joyful feeling surged through her heart. Whoever could believe that just last spring, she'd been a slave? Now she was a married woman safe in the arms of the man the Lord had sent into her life, once she'd gathered enough courage to run away from her cruel young mistress. And because of brave men like Ezra and all the other soldiers who fought for the North, no one could ever put her in bondage again.

Miss May would say "praise the Lord" about all that.

And that's just what Delia did.

A bit of history:

Before the Fifty-fourth Massachusetts Negro Regiment was formed, black men were not permitted to serve in the Union army. After Abraham Lincoln signed the Emancipation Proclamation in January 1863, Frederick Douglass and other abolitionists at last convinced the President that well-educated northern blacks should and must be permitted to join the fight to free southern slaves. The heroism of the various Negro regiments is legendary, as shown in the 1989 film *Glory.* But there is more to the story. Once these men were trained and sent to fight, they received far worse treatment by southern troops. None were taken as prisoners after a battle, as white Union soldiers usually were, but rather, they were brutally slaughtered, their bodies were desecrated, and those who became separated from their units were never heard from again. Nevertheless, northern black men lined up to prove themselves qualified to fight.

1. The entire fabric of the southern way of life was destroyed by the Civil War. In the tenuous social climate of the South immediately after the war ended, Union soldiers enforced martial law while southern men desperately tried to regain control of their own destiny. How did former soldiers turned lawmen, Massey and Case, try to be fair to Ezra even as they intimidated him to keep him from getting "uppity." Considering the pre-Civil War southern social structure, was the behavior of these men and other southerners understandable? How might they have responded differently?

2. Ezra has grown up a free person in Boston, where he received his education alongside white students. How does this affect his self-concept compared to the former slaves' attitudes about themselves? Why does Ezra doubt his calling to become a minister? How does he change through the course of the story? What/who causes those changes?

3. Delia has been a mistreated slave all her life. She has never had a chance to develop her own personality, so she copies what she has seen in others. Are her feelings of low self-esteem understandable? How does she grow and change throughout the

story? What does she learn through working for Miz Kate? How does she grow to maturity in other ways?

4. Delia frequently remembers Beulah, who became a sort of surrogate mother when Delia's mother died. Yet the old woman also seemed to mistreat Delia. Do you agree with Delia's eventual reasoning, that Beulah had tried to keep her from running away because she loved her? Why or why not?

5. What does Jack represent in this story? If he had not been murdered, what might the future have held for him if he did not change his attitude and tactics?

6. Many people in the pre-Civil War South did not own slaves or believe in slavery. Owen Burns and Kate Saunders represent this segment of the population. Each is an enigma, eschewing slavery and working on their small farms. Although they obviously have been in love since childhood, why didn't they initially get married? What will the future hold for them now that Mama has been placed in an asylum and they are married?

7. A caste system frequently existed among house slaves and field hands. Beulah had taught Delia that she was better than field slaves. Alice resented Delia because of her supposedly easier life in the "big house." How did these women resolve their differences? How did Miss May and Mr. Willard change Delia's opinion about field slaves? In what other ways did they affect her life?

8. At the end of the Civil War, approximately two million former slaves needed to decide what to do with their lives, while northern free blacks no longer needed to fear being kidnapped and sold "down the river" into the South. What will the future hold for Ezra and each of the seven former slaves in our story who traveled together? For Leviticus, Alice, and their children? For Adam, staying in Boston in a service job? For Miss May and Mr. Willard? For Ezra and Delia if they go West? What will the future hold for any children they may have after they marry? At that time in history (trying not to think with today's knowledge and sensibilities), where would you have chosen to build your life if you were an African-American? How does history validate or prove unfortunate the various choices these people made?

9. Delia's white father, Mr. Young, seemed fond of Delia. While Delia was growing up, why couldn't he simply stop his white daughter's cruel treatment of Delia? When they met again on the Charleston wharf, why do you think he gave money to Delia? He clearly blamed the North, Boston abolitionists in particular, for the war and destruction. How did Delia respond? Was this a step of growth for her? What would you have done?

10. Delia had great pride in owning Miz Kate's old, redesigned calico dress until she saw the fine clothing of northern black women. Once the old dress was washed and the color brightened, she again felt comfortable wearing it. How might this symbolize Delia's transitions in life? When Ezra proposed, do you think it would have made a difference in Delia's feelings about herself if she had still worn her new dress instead of her old one?

11. It has been said that the Union won the Civil War on the battle-field, but the South won the war of ideology. Many hate groups still exist in the United States, especially in the South. Is our country still suffering the effects of the Civil War? If so, what do you think it will take to change that? What can Christians of all races do to help bring about change? Do African-Americans and other minorities where you live have the same rights as white Americans? Why or why not?

12. Unlike today, in the mid-1800s American society as a whole had a high consciousness of God's movement in the affairs of mankind. In the South, slave owners believed that God ordained slavery, with even some slaves accepting this belief as a part of their Christian faith. In the North, abolitionists believed slavery was a crime against God and humanity, even going so far as to be willing to kill slave owners to free slaves. How can two utterly opposing ideas both come from the same Bible-based faith?

13. The Civil War nearly destroyed the United States as a nation, yet gradually through other historic events (World War I, among others), we once again became united and grew into a great nation. What issues divide us today? What can Christians do? What can you do?

An Interview with
Author Louise M. Gouge

1) **When did you first realize that you wanted to be a writer? Was there anything in your childhood that influenced you to become a writer?**

Like most children, I always had my own imaginary little world. Then, when I was ten years old, Mary Martin appeared on black and white television playing Peter Pan. If you'll forgive the pun, that's when my fantasies really took flight because it was such a happy tale. I wanted to make up stories like that, too. I loved to write in school, often turning ordinary term papers into fiction that incorporated my research. There was always a story simmering in my imagination. But my children were all in school when I finally began to write seriously.

2) **Although you have written several novels, what inspired you to specifically write a historical trilogy of the post-Civil War era?**

The Civil War was such an important turning point in United States history because it defined what we would become as a nation. In this series, I wanted to explore why Reconstruction failed and why we still suffer the consequences of that failure. As with my school term papers, I show my historical perspective and research best through fiction.

3) **Knowing that you have several writing awards to your credit, please share with us which novelists and other writers have influenced your writing and in what ways?**

Charlotte Brontë was my first strong influence. In my opinion, her *Jane Eyre* is not only a perfect romance novel but also an eloquent social and spiritual commentary. DiAnn Mills is a prolific and talented author whose "expect an adventure" style has shown me how to use just the right amount of research rather than doing an "information dump" on my readers. Francine Rivers has one of the most powerful spiritual voices in today's Christian fiction. Every one of her novels deeply moves me and brings me closer to God. I hope to emulate these three authors so that God's message can be clear, deep, and exciting in my stories.

4) **Why did you write *Then Came Hope* rather than some other story?**

In this trilogy, I wanted to tell the stories of three very different men who returned home after fighting in the Civil War. The first man is a southern naval officer. The second one is Ezra Johns, an educated Negro man from Boston who volunteered to fight in the first black Union regiment, the Fifty-Fourth Massachusetts Negro Regiment. The third story will be about a northern white man. Each had his own reasons for fighting in the war.

In Ezra's case, he had a great deal to prove because the prevailing view of the day was that Negro men would not make good soldiers or good fighters.

Ezra and his real-life counterparts put an end to such uninformed speculation. If not for their courageous service all over the South, the Union might not have been preserved. It is my goal to honor their remarkable legacy.

5) **Your characters are distinctive, multifaceted, and even endearing at times. What inspired the development of the plot and characters in your story? Are they based upon themes and people you already know?**

Addressing the question of themes: because I was a child in the Civil Rights era, I've always wondered why things did not turn out better for this nation after the Civil War and why the Civil Rights movement was even necessary. I have come to understand that national identities are formed through the choices that individual people make. In this country, the generation after the Civil War failed to take up the torch and "fix" the racial divide, failed to bring African-Americans fully into American society, so that all of us could work together to build the greatest nation this world has ever known. We are still suffering because of that. We had a chance to become a beacon to a world where tribal and ethnic identities often wreak havoc and destruction. But we failed. By placing my characters in the post-Civil War, I show that many Americans had great hope for a better world, and there is still a chance we can overcome that failure.

With that in mind, I created a cast of characters for *Then Came Hope* that included a variety of southern former slaves and one northern freeman. Their interactions with white people and with other blacks, along with their ultimate decisions about where to begin their futures in freedom, propel this story forward through a hostile South and a not-so-perfect North.

6) **You have a way of taking the reader right into your literary landscape—in this case the post Civil War era. How much research did you use to set the mood and ambiance of your story?**

Once upon a time, before television, radio, and movies, people enjoyed novels that were filled with great historical and scenic details. They would sit around the hearth listening to the family patriarch reading a great novel such as *Moby Dick* or *A Tale of Two Cities,* from which they learned about a world they did not know. Today, we know all that stuff just by watching the Discovery or History channels. In today's novels, we readers want an author to throw in just a few details of setting and history to give us the picture. Then tell us all about the people: their struggles, their hopes, their triumphs, and tragedies. That's what we're concerned with because that's what touches the core of our unchanging humanity. So I go to the heart of the human issues involved in my story and intersperse the history around it.

7) **How would you describe your writing style—not your literary style—but the actual writing itself? What kind of techniques do you use?**

I park myself in front of my computer and start putting words on the page. Sometimes I delete, and sometimes I save. But all of this comes after first imagining my characters, my basic plot line, and my themes, and then researching the novel's time period extensively. Actually, the research continues as I write and all through the editing process.

8) **Many novelists say ending the novel is the most difficult part of writing. Why do you think that is and how do you know when you have reached the end of your story?**

I think this is all about feelings. If I've solved all the problems and my characters look forward to happily-ever-after, how do I end with a nice little punch line? I want my readers to feel satisfied, so once those two problems are solved, I usually put in a sweet little kiss to seal the romance. Or, in one case, I had my hero and heroine merely reaching out to hold hands. It just felt right.

9) **There's obviously more to a novel than just an entertaining read. What do you want readers to take away from *Then Came Hope*?**

I believe God speaks to every believer's heart about His truth. My prayer is that my readers will listen to God rather than to their all-too-human "conscience" or to whatever is popular or expedient in their time or their social group. I pray that they will be Christ's representative in their sphere of influence, however large or small that may be. And I pray that they will look beyond race, politics, and religion to see the humanity of every person they meet. If I have created characters who live by these ideals, perhaps my readers will gain the courage to "go forth and do likewise."

10) **We've talked about the novelists who have most influenced you as a writer, so now let us make the question a little more personal. Who is the one person most influential in your life today?**

At the risk of sounding predictable or corny, I would say that my husband of forty-two years is the most influential person in my life. He has worked very hard to make it possible for me to write. He comes home every day and asks to read what I've written, which means he holds me accountable. And he cooks! Not only when I have a deadline, but most of the time. What a guy! He *sets me free* to indulge in my art and fulfill my soul's desires.

11) **In conclusion, tell us something personal about Louise Gouge that most people may not know?**

Shortly before I met my dear hubby, I was a single girl in Denver, Colorado. This was 1964, the year of the Beatles' first U. S. tour. I had a friend who worked security at the Beatles' concert at Red Rocks amphitheater, and he took me backstage because he knew I was not a screamer. I stood within five feet of the Fab Four. But "Imagine" this: I now stand hand-in-hand with the Fab ONE, my Savior, Jesus Christ, and that's really "Something."

LOUISE M. GOUGE earned her BA in English/Creative Writing at the University of Central Florida in Orlando and her Master of Liberal Studies degree at Rollins College in Winter Park, Florida. Her novel, *Ahab's Bride,* Book One of Ahab's Legacy (2004), was her master's thesis at Rollins College. *Hannah Rose,* Book Two of Ahab's Legacy, was released in 2005, and *Son of Perdition,* Book Three of Ahab's Legacy, was released in February 2006. *Then Came Faith* is the first in a historical fiction trilogy featuring the post-Civil War era.

To her credit, Louise is the recipient of several writing awards, including the Inspirational Readers' Choice Award for Historical Fiction, the Road to Romance Reviewers' Choice Award, placing second with the prestigious American Christian Fiction Writers' Book of the Year, placed first in the esteemed Inspirational Readers' Choice Award, and garnering a rare four-star review from Romantic Times Bookclub Magazine.

While writing Christian fiction is her primary occupation and labor of love, Louise is also an adjunct professor of English and Humanities at Valencia Community College in Kissimmee, Florida. Having received her advanced education in middle age, she tries to inspire her younger students to complete their own education early. For her older students, Louise hopes that her experiences prove that it is never too late for them to work toward their dreams. (Her first novel was published after she turned fifty!) In the classroom, she attempts to live out her Christian faith both in words and in action.

Louise has been married to David Gouge for forty-two years. They have four grown children and five grandchildren.

Her favorite Bible verse is "He shall choose our inheritance for us" (Psalm 47:4), a testimony to her belief that God has chosen a path for each believer. To seek that path and to trust His wisdom is to find the greatest happiness in life.

0-97851-372-X

Following the Civil War, Juliana, a beautiful, young abolitionist, seeks to help the South heal and repent of its past, when she meets a former Confederate naval officer, Andre, who swears never to forgive the North for the devastation to his family. The question is whether these two strong-willed individuals will be able to swallow their pride and discover a common path to rebuilding the city—and their own lives.

A story about the North and South, a man and a woman, courage and resilience in the face of fierce opposition, and the triumphant dignity of the human spirit.

0-98751-371-1

Luke Hatcher is the pride of Magnolia Springs, Louisiana. The perfect kid, he's the star of the high school baseball team and is on his way to LSU after graduation on a full scholarship—destined for the big leagues. Little did he know that a simple dare from his high school sweetheart, would change his whole life.

A riveting novel that celebrates the God who gives second chances. If you've ever looked back on your life, feeling you threw away a golden moment, you will walk away from this passionate story cheering and with a renewed outlook on your own life.

Additional copies of this book and other titles by
Emerald Pointe Books are available from your local bookstore.

If you have enjoyed this book, or if it has impacted your life,
we would like to hear from you:

Please contact us at:

Emerald Pointe Books
Attention: Editorial Department
P.O. Box 35327
Tulsa, OK 74153

Emerald Pointe Books